Praise for *Beloved Mother*

Laura Hunter has poured her heart and soul into the pages of *Beloved Mother*. Her talent and her passion are present in every scene, every chapter, every image, every line. There's magic in this book!
— Michael Knight, author of *Eveningland* (2017 Okra Pick)

Beloved Mother is an adventure story about three generations of daring women. Hunter tells us that "women have within them so much love and so much hate they sometime confuse the two," one of the many mysteries about this fast-paced novel that will keep you wondering.
— Denton Loving, author of *Crimes Against Birds*

Language and scene set the stage for a journey through time with three women . . . connected through blood and passion, each bound to follow her own path toward self-discovery. Though *Beloved Mother* spans nearly forty years, the story is interwoven tightly. The characters are compelling in their struggles to find love and a meaningful place in the world, and the action never flails. . . . Hunter has created a believable world inhabited by authentic characters, a world the reader willingly enters and leaves reluctantly only when the last page is read.
— Connie Jordan Green, author of *The War at Home*

Beloved Mother is the kind of rich story that brands itself in memory. I can still see the mining camps, smell the scents of the woods and mountains, and recall the unique people, entwined with the land, their histories, and each other.
— T. K. Thorne, author of *Noah's Wife: 5500 BCE*
(Winner of "Book of the Year" for Historical Fiction)

Looking for riveting characters, an evocative setting, and a plot so filled with twists and turns that you'll want to hang on for dear life? Look no further than Laura Hunter's *Beloved Mother*.
— Jennie Ivey, author of *Tennessee Tales the Textbooks Don't Tell*

Beloved Mother, Laura Hunter's debut novel, is both inventive and lyrical. This mythic tale unfolding at the crossroads of what is real and might be real will surprise time and again.
— Darnell Arnoult, author of *Galaxie Wagon*
(Winner of the 2017 Chaf~~~ ~~~ ~~~ ~~~ ~~~ Appalachian Writing)

D1056680

Laura Hunter has created a world in which the land matters. Set in Appalachia, her novel crosses regional boundaries that include Native American traditions and industrial progress, while exploring the timeless themes of greed, exploitation, kinship and family. Her characters do not escape unmarked. Neither does the landscape. As in life, scars and shadows result. And though the divide between the physical and metaphysical, the imagined and empirical, the supernatural and natural is not conquered, it is survived. And survival is the truest test of story we have. Here, Hunter's love of story shows.
— Wendy Reed, author of *An Accidental Memoir*

In Laura Hunter's *Beloved Mother*, everything and everyone is connected, by root systems deep beneath the surface. The world of nature intermingles with that of humans, of the Cherokee and the white people who settled their land, and Turtleback Mountain, the Great Spirit's sacred place, towers over them all. With lyric description, conflict that tears the heart, and a girl named Lily who must claim her history in order to see her way forward, this novel gives us characters that ring true and a story both fresh and timeless.
— Jennifer Horne, Poet Laureate of Alabama 2017-2021 and author of *The Little Wanderer*

Laura Hunter's epic first novel, *Beloved Mother*, set in small coal mining towns surrounding the mythical Turtleback Mountain, explores the complex lives of three generations of mountain women—Mona Parsons Slocomb, Anna Parsons Goodman, and Lily Marie Goodman—from the 1920s to the 1960s. . . . This is a powerful, beautiful book, both unflinching and unsentimental in its depiction of human cruelty and deception and deeply compassionate toward characters who, like many of us, stumble through dark hemlock forests, tripping over rattlesnakes and copperheads and collapsing mines that turn coffins on their heads, leaving us as changed as the characters we've read about and come to fear and love.
— Lex Williford, author of *Superman on the Roof*
(Winner of the 2015 Rose Metal Press 10th Annual Flash Chapbook Prize)

LAURA HUNTER

Beloved
MOTHER

Bluewater Publications
Bwpublications.com
Printed in the United States

This work is based on the author's personal perspective and imagination.

Editor – Sierra Tabor
Interior & Illustration Design – Maria Yasaka Beck
Managing Editor – Angela Broyles

Library of Congress Control Number: 2018957289
ISBN 978-1-934610-98-5

For my mother, Margaret Masters Barton,
who taught me to love books and mountains
and my husband, Tom,
who taught me the value of love.

Part I

Chapter 1

Take warning how you court young men – Mountain Ballad

The Foot of Turtleback Mountain

Legend had it that Mona Parsons could stir up dust devils by spinning a stick in the dirt. She called up a storm whenever farmers needed rain. She could twist a rain shower into a ferocious tree-breaker if the farmer denied her pay and call it back thrice-fold with a nod of her head. Word had it she came into the world dancing. The daughter of an established Parsons family in Covington, Virginia, born to a mother no more than eighteen and a daddy at least ten years older, she spent childhood evenings on the grass, stomping dew into the earth as if she tried to awaken Mother Nature herself.

Each night, her father called to her from behind his unkempt beard to come inside. Not a deferring child, Mona glanced back at him, dashed through the gate and down the bank to Broken Rock Creek. Tiny, no larger than a wood sprite, she spent days on Turtleback Mountain gathering flowers and herbs and, some say, conjuring with wild beasts. Some days she came down the mountain, her hair filled with moss and sticks, looking like a disheveled elf, her lips and fingers blue from blackberries she had eaten off the sides of ditches.

Had Mona then known of the communities of Cherokee Little People, she would have sung out to the Laurel People to share her joy on Turtleback Mountain. But she did not know. She would not know until Beloved Mother began Mona's training.

More forward-minded neighbors told her parents they were blessed. "Such an open, creative child," they said.

"Wild heathen," others whispered. "A reed shaken by the wind," some said. "Cursed."

The Parsons accepted the latter, deemed themselves steeped in hexes and bore no more children for four years. The Virginia mining town of Covington watched and waited. A family who owned an entire mountain could have access to mountain spirits, the old people intoned, and a child could breathe such spirits into her soul unknowing. Those who wield the obvious can manipulate the unseen. That's the Lord's own truth, they vowed.

The summer Mona turned thirteen, an angular man sauntered into Covington as if he held the world in his back pocket. He carried a black valise and a hatchet swung from his belt. She first spied him at the base of the Lost Miners Monument in the Square. Without speaking, she followed him about day after day as if she had lost her power to the gleam in his eye. Folks later said he must have cast a spell on her.

Her father belted her evenings when she came back home, but still she slipped out the window before dawn. Before any rooster could crow and when the river behind her house moved lazy and low, she was gone again, without thought of leaving her people behind.

Early August, the man was seen leaving town at dusk. That night Mona's bed lay empty. The town searched Covington for her. They scoured Turtleback Mountain for her. They went east to Spencer's Mountain. They did not find her. They asked about for the man's name, but no one could remember.

Some within Covington said the shadowy stranger was Squire Dan Sparks from down 'round Cade's Cove who had more land than anybody ever had.

Some said he was Squire's oldest boy who was untamed and a mite crazy.

Some who knew not the Cherokee said he was meant to be a Cherokee medicine man but gave up and left for city ways.

Great Spirit and Sister Sun and Brother Moon laugh so hard at such foolishness that Sister Sun forgets to leave the sky before Brother Moon appears in the east. Great Spirit has to send her on her way.

Had the Cherokee been in the valley beneath this mountain, as they had been for generations prior, they would have explained that this *Ama idnai*, this Turtleback Mountain, was Great Spirit's sacred place. He made it to specification before he ever thought of making a man.

Here on Turtleback Mountain and in its shade stood hemlock and oak with fifty-foot canopies. Mountain oaks grew leaves so thick that little light could pass through. The soil beneath rested dark and dank. Thick laurel grew in so many colors Great Spirit had not named them all. Here streams rushed clear and cold year round, their waters filled with fishes, their banks alive with verdant mosses and ferns heavy with spore. Teeming marshes overran with cattails tall as young girls. Concealed here were fur-coated chipmunk, squirrel, fox and bear. Turtleback Mountain. Covington's enduring and overarching guardian. Great Spirit's personal garden.

Cherokee would have told how the massive buzzard, who swooped down Turtleback with his mighty white-tipped wing, carved out the valley at the mountain's solid foot. How Great Spirit was so pleased with the valley he decided here would be the place for his new creature: man. It was here on this mountain, in this valley, that Great Spirit placed Cherokee, the "real people," molded from mud of Broken Rock Creek. It was here he took melted snow waters and filled the Cherokee with pure blood. Here, masquerading as the wind, he blew breath into the Cherokee, and they became one life.

Most of Covington did not know the Cherokee way, so they in time labeled the lone wanderer "Beelzebub," who had come to walk the mountains and steal young virgins.

But the stranger was none of these. He was Jackson Slocomb, a vagrant from Pennsylvania who chanced upon Covington when he turned southeast off Turtleback Mountain ridge, rather than continuing west to Kentucky. He was Jackson Slocomb, a man who through years of practice could sway young girls to his favor. Here in Great Spirit's valley he found Mona Parsons, of an age that had her primed to go.

The year was 1923.

Chapter 2

Tall Corn found the camp on the edge of his farm, next to the spring where it broke from earth into sunshine. A thin strip of pale smoke told him someone was burning hardwood at the edge of his largest corn-field. Having an unwanted camp on his farm angered him. But to camp at this location caused his ire to grow with a fierceness he had not known, for he held this a sacred place where earth, water, and sun, three of the holy gifts of the Great Spirit, came together as one.

> *Great Spirit watches the white man and the girl. It is their smoke that calls to mind Long Hunters and their camp, its puny smoke rising from their dying fire that drowsy morn, the year they cut their way west across his Turtleback Mountain. Perched on a rock ledge, fur-coated men crawled, humpbacked and beaver-like, one by one from lean-tos and stepped into brush to relieve themselves. They returned to squat before their meager fire and poke sticks into dying ash. Though a century and a half has passed, these two are not so different. It could have been yesterday.*

Finding the camp by its smoke column set no obstacles for Tall Corn. He knew his land as intimately as he knew the ridges of his farming hands.

One with the land, he, like the hawk perched on the oak limb, vanished from the white man's sight.

This invader could only be a white man. Only a white man would dishonor the land of another by squatting in place rather than moving on. When Tall Corn came near the camp, he lowered himself to the ground and inched his way through thick underbrush. He crouched behind a stand of rhododendron once heavy with orange blossoms and watched.

The camp was nothing more than a small fire, an oily tarpaulin hung on a rope between two pines and a cast-iron spider, its three pointed feet deep in the fire's ash. The odor of rancid grease from having been left in the spider too long and from frying fish too many times overpowered the earth's scent. A black valise had been tossed to the side. Neither man nor girl had swept straw and branches away to make a livable spot within the stand of pine. The skimpiness of supplies there in the month of the Harvest Moon, the white man's October, told the Cherokee the two would freeze during the coming mountain nights before they would starve.

A pale man in muddy black pants and canvas duster pulled back his coat to expose a hatchet hanging from his waist. He hunkered down before a small fire and poked at the flame as if the stirring would make the blaze bigger. Instead, he scattered wood and ash. The fire would not live. Tall Corn knew this.

A white girl, no more than thirteen summers and heavy with child, crawled from under the tarpaulin. She held her back as she tried to stand. She wore workmen's boots far too large for her small feet. Tall Corn listened.

"Jackson," she said, "I got to have help birthing this baby. I don't know nothing. You don't know nothing. I ain't wanting to die just yet." She attempted a laugh, but it hung itself in her throat. "I might not like how this baby come to be, but it's alive in me and that matters."

The white man rose. His craggy face blackened where a heavy beard refused to be shaved close, its bone structure so exact it looked carved. Taut leathery skin made him more stone than flesh.

Tall Corn smelled something more than woods and smoke in the air, something darker than the camp smoke now failing to rise. The odor of rot. The white man faced the girl. It was the man he smelled. The stench heightened with each movement the man made, intensified by what the girl called the man, rot rooted in the name "Jackson." The white man's name fueled Tall Corn's resentment more. Only *Uktena*, the Great Serpent Himself, raised from beneath the waters, would sport such a name.

Was it not a Jackson, Andrew Jackson, who had divided Tall Corn's people and sent them walking to death through a winter snow? Across frozen rivers that collapsed under their weight? Was it not Jackson that spilled Cherokee blood over half the country, without firing a weapon, so the white man could not question? But question the whites did, through their many tears as the Cherokee walked past. Even white men recognized man's blood can weigh so heavy that he breaks under the realization of death he carries as he walks. As they walked. And walked. As they lifted dropped bodies, no matter how heavy, no matter how far yet to go, and carried them to sanctified ground for burial. This was the legacy of Jackson. A name ever reviled in the Cherokee Nation.

"Shut up, Mona. You ain't dying yet." Jackson spit tobacco juice into the dying fire. "Why I dragged you out of Virginia and into North Carolina, I'll never know." The man kicked at the fire with his boot. "Should have left you in Tennessee."

The girl tried to sit. Her unbalanced body knocked her back. She plopped against the ground and tugged at her thin cotton skirt crumpled under her hips. "Here. Pull me up," she said and stuck out her hand.

"Get up your own self."

She rolled to her side and lifted her bulk by bracing her hands against the ground, trying to hoist herself up. "I'm hungry. What we got to eat?"

"You done et it all." Jackson threw his poking stick into the underbrush.

"What're you doing? That stick'll set these whole woods afire," she said as she rose. "Go into them corn rows and get us a few and I'll boil them up." Bracing her back with her hand as if holding the baby in place, she started after the smoldering stick.

"Do it yourself. I ain't no thief." He crawled under the tarpaulin.

"No," she sniffed and muttered to herself as she wiped dirt from her cheek. "But you're damn good with a knife when you want to be." Her fingers followed two scars down her cheek.

She turned toward Tall Corn, staring, seeming to see nothing before her but what had been. If he moved, she would see him. A thin, white scar, like a tiny rip, ran down the girl's left cheek. Just under that ran another, this one black, as if someone had filled it with soot before it closed. And so it had been.

Tears ran down the scars and into the corner of her mouth. Tall Corn had never seen a person swallow her own sorrow. He would have to ask Beloved Mother about this. He thought it could not be a good thing. The sorrow would water its own root and grow stronger.

The girl Mona and her hunger stirred a spirit Tall Corn had not known. He wanted her to have food. He wanted to gather corn for her, parch it in the oven he had built for his mother. He wanted to collect squash and beans for a feast. Bake sunflower seeds and boil a rabbit stew for her. He wanted to cover her bread with sweet honey and draw back a blanket so she could sleep away from damp ground. He offered none of these things. Instead, he watched her waddle into his cornfield and break off two ears of corn before he stole away.

Tall Corn returned for three days. During each journey from his house to the edge of his cornfield, his spirit talked to him, reminded him that the girl was white, that the man rotted from within. If this child had been sired by the white man called Jackson, the child could be spawned by evil himself. Yet he continued to come observe the camp. Each day, he watched silent as a waiting fox as the white man growled and clomped about like a wounded bear. The more the man swore, the more the girl cowered.

On this third day, he first smelled her fear. It was the fear he felt when his father took him one night deep into the forest as a child, blindfolded him and left him sitting on a stump. Fear of being abandoned. Fear of unrecognizable noises. It was fear that brought sorrow to his eyes and questions to his heart about why his father would leave him alone in the dark. He had known this fear. It sat thick and heavy within and left him trembling, not from cold, but from the anguish of loss.

He recalled, also, the joy of removing the blindfold as he felt the sun on his arms when it began to warm the night chill. He knew the elation of finding his father sitting silent beside the stump, as he had done throughout the night.

Tall Corn's spirit assured him he could become the father he lost to a spring storm's sharp lightning strike. He could ease the white girl's uncertainties, as truly as he eased his animals during birthing. He could teach the child the Cherokee way. Each day he returned. Each day she seemed more fawnlike, a skittish innocent waiting assurance that she was safe.

Beloved Mother sat by a curtain-less window and smoked a rolled cigarette. She spilled out of her chair like a mound of dough left to rise in a bowl too small. Dressed in yards of orange skirt and a puffy white blouse, few of her features, except her creased, sun-scorched face and worn hands, showed. Her thick hair hung in a plait down her back. Gazing out the window to staggered mountaintop waves, each a fainter blue than the one before, Beloved Mother listened to her son.

Tall Corn came to Beloved Mother on the fifth day. He told her of the stench of the white man called Jackson. He told her of the weight of the child and the sorrow the girl carried. He asked for permission to offer the girl the polished shell so she could send the white man back to his people.

He had grown tall, tall as the corn itself. He honored his Cherokee name, traditions of the people and the land. He was truly of the land. She did not want him to dishonor himself by approaching the white man called Jackson. She did not want him to weaken his Cherokee blood by lying with this girl. The tribe's source of wisdom, she readily advised others, but this was her only son, her husband's offshoot. He was all that was left of her life as a Cherokee wife, the root that afforded her trunk its stability. She was not sure she could live with a white woman in her house.

Tall Corn's spirit recognized his mother's problem as she listened wordless. As son, he had served her well. He had built her a solid white man's house, and he farmed the land so abundantly that he could share each crop with the village. Yet he was a man of twenty-six summers and acknowledged a Cherokee woman had the final say. In this situation his throat tightened, choking words that he feared would destroy his chance to persuade Beloved Mother. He could not swallow his anxiety for the girl as easily as she drank in her own sorrows. He must surely rescue the girl from her demon as he would one of his lambs from the slick yellow panther. He could not allow this white man to beat her into submission, for he sensed she had within her the essence of the land itself.

Beloved Mother watched the rending of her son's heart through his dark eyes. She could not deny him this chance to prove his manhood, not as a warrior of old, but as a man who fought for what he believed was right among men. She rose and walked to the fireboard, opened a polished cedar box and lifted out the shell.

Tall Corn had only heard of the shell. Seeing it now resting on a scrap of woven wool in Beloved Mother's hands, he looked upon it with awe. A mussel shell larger than his palm, it had been rubbed to a glossy white, an iridescence that reflected the kerosene lamp's flicker. His throat opened and he sighed.

Beloved Mother had answered. He had permission to speak to the girl, to ask her to send the white man called Jackson back to his people, to bring her and her unborn child to his home and live with him and Beloved Mother. Tall Corn bowed his head and extended his hands, cupped, to receive the sacred shell.

*****

The following afternoon, Mona climbed the bank from the stream, struggling with a bucket of water. A Cherokee man stepped from behind a thick tree, lowered his head and offered his hand to take the water. She looked at his russet face, his black hair pulled back and bound by a leather strap at the nape of his neck. His black eyes with their flecks of gold eased her. He had emerged from the woods like the breeze that dried sweat from her neck when she lifted her brunette hair. She handed him the wooden bucket's rope handle and sat on a pine log that marked the path Tall Corn had once cut to the branch.

Tall Corn squatted before her. He surveyed what water remained in the bucket. "Not much," he said.

The girl spoke with a nervous laugh. "Most of it sloshed out coming up that rise." She glanced up the incline. Jackson was nowhere in sight. She did not need to be caught talking to a stranger. Not a stranger who was clearly Cherokee.

After a moment, she asked, "We camped on your land?"

"The land's a gift from the Great Spirit. It's not mine."

"That mean the Great Spirit wants us to move on?"

"If you had to travel on, you would have known it four moons ago." Tall Corn continued to look at her face.

Mona glimpsed away. "What's your name?" she asked.

"Walks in Tall Corn," he answered. "They call me 'Tall Corn'."

"Why?"

"The Cherokee who have long names carry shorter forms. You're 'River of Two Tears'."

"No, I'm not." She turned to him and chuckled. "I'm Mona Parsons." With an afterthought, her shame spoke. "Mona Parsons Slocomb."

Shame had forced her over this trail, whispering in her ear that she deserved whatever Jackson Slocomb wielded out. He called her his "road whore." At night, thoughts of facing her ma and pa and the disgrace they would inflict on her if she returned kept her from sleep.

Tall Corn spoke. "You're Two Tears from now on. Great Spirit named you to me the first day I saw you. When the white man made you cry with hunger."

The girl stood up, towering over Tall Corn. "You've been spying on our camp." She started toward the footpath.

"I watched to see that the white man who rots inside does you no harm." Tall Corn rose before her. No taller than she, he met her face level with his own.

"What would you care about that? You don't know me." She drew back.

"You're of the land. You have a love for all that lives," Tall Corn spoke as if lulling a child to sleep.

"Humph." She stared at this man's eyes. She wanted to believe that his soul was honest. "Who told you that?"

"Great Spirit. And Beloved Mother. She allowed me to bring the shell." He reached into his shirt pocket and drew out the shell.

"What's that and who's Beloved Mother?" Mona asked, not sure he was reasonable. *Not that I've always been reasonable,* Mona thought. *I ran off with the scum asleep under the tarp.*

"This shell is sacred to my people. You, now as a Cherokee woman with a Cherokee name, have the right to give it to the white man and he will have to leave. You can stay with me, in my home with Beloved Mother. You will be my wife."

"Be your wife?" An unusual tiredness cramped her back. Her hands gripped above her hips, and she dropped back down on the log. Sweat covered her face.

"Come with me. It's best for your child. Beloved Mother's always present at a birth." Tall Corn tried to pull her off the log.

"I'm not going nowhere with you." She twisted away from his grip. "I don't know you."

"You came away with the white man. You didn't know him."

"How do you know such?" Mona's back pain cut toward her belly.

"Beloved Mother told me." He lifted her off the log. "We can see to the white man later."

"Where you taking me?" Mona asked.

"To Beloved Mother."

Chapter 3

Jackson Slocomb woke to find the campfire dead. No water. No boiled corn. Mona gone. He called out to her. He needed Mona to get herself back here and fix him some food. He'd not eaten since yesterday.

"Damn woman," he snorted. He unbuttoned his pants and peed into last night's embers, next to the empty iron spider.

He called to Mona again. The only answer was a mockingbird's grating *chack, chack, chack*. Jackson knew the grey bird teased him. His frustration was not open to teasing. Nobody had called him Jack since his mother died. He didn't need some bird poking fun at him. He hurled a pinecone toward where he thought the mockingbird might be, but none flew. He sat down to wait.

When Mona had not returned by the next morning, it occurred to Jackson that something might be wrong. The young'un was due soon, according to what she said and the size of her belly. Best bet was to break camp and leave her here. Or maybe not. She kept food ready for him. She didn't fight as hard once he got her out of Covington and away from all that was familiar to her, up Spencer's Mountain and into a briar patch.

But maybe he liked more fight in a woman. He could manage on his own or pick up some other girl and get her trained. Mona resisted his orders too often to keep her anyhow. The young'un? Jackson knew the child was his. He knew the first time he took her in the dewberry patch she was a virgin. He had had too many to doubt that. And he had kept her close underfoot ever since.

Thoughts of the dewberry patch aroused him. The cries of a woman as briars dug into her shoulders forced him to hold back his seed so he could stretch out his enjoyment longer. The last time he saw Mona's back, he had noticed scars and new pus pockets where the briars he refused to pick out were working their way to the surface. If she could run off, she could rot.

Then they camped near this cornfield against his better judgment, simply because Mona saw an advantage in being close to the corn and water. And she wouldn't let up. Now here, she spent unnecessary time bathing. Jackson saw no need for a bathing till seasons changed.

Maybe he had been born in the wrong century. Being a backwoodsman roaming the West before it was settled good would have suited him fine. He might have even had a chance to cut up an Indian or two. Truth was he probably should have cut Mona's throat a long time ago instead of carving up her face. Chopped off her head with his hatchet. Nobody would have recognized her. He wouldn't have had such a load to carry all this time.

It was settled. Break camp right away. Walk away and leave her and the kid to whatever fate awaited them. They were not his responsibility. She followed him willingly enough, and he still had the eye that could entice any young girl. He let go his hatchet and dropped it and his knife into the black valise. He untied a corner rope, and one side of the tarp fell.

Tall Corn and Two Tears watched from behind a large Canadian hemlock until Jackson ambled away from the weapons in the black bag. They stepped out to face him.

The night before, Beloved Mother had given Two Tears a brew to lessen her pains. She put her ear to Two Tears' belly for what seemed to Mona a long, long time. When she looked at Mona, she said, "It is not your time," and walked to the other room. She returned with a cup of bitter brew and insisted Mona drink it to keep the baby inside. "Fourteen suns. Fourteen suns and the baby will be ready." The drink made Mona drowsy, and she soon fell asleep on the cot under Tall Corn's woven cotton blanket.

When the sun rose, Tall Corn entered the room and sat by where Mona slept. He waited until she stirred. "Today we'll take the sacred shell to the white man. You can tell him to leave and he must." His legs were crossed and his hands rested in his lap.

"What if he doesn't leave?" she asked, her mind still fuzzy.

"He'll leave. It's the will of Great Spirit. And Beloved Mother has decreed it so."

"What do I have to do...if I say I'll be your wife?" Mona raked her fingers through her dirty hair.

"I'll care for you and the child. Here. In this house. My house." Tall Corn waved his hand about the room. "You'll have a bed and a stove to cook on and stave off the cold. Care for Beloved Mother when she is old. You'll be safe. Free to learn the forest." Tall Corn paused. "I'll share my blanket." He blushed. "And you will be known in the village as Two Tears."

"Where is the village? Any white people there?" She propped herself up on her elbow.

"Our people are there. Those who never left. Jackson promised land to the west, but we didn't believe. We came deeper into the mountains and kept the ways of the land." Tall Corn extended his hand. "The village is one day's walk down the mountain, in the valley."

Mona felt another slight twinge in her back. She might lose this child. She might starve. She could be on the streets of Knoxville or Bristol begging for food or a place to sleep. Or she could stay here. Tall Corn seemed gentle enough, and Beloved Mother accepted her without question. Mona's hatred for Jackson and fear for herself and the child spoke for her. "I will be Two Tears." She took his hand, and he pulled her to her feet.

A full-blooded Cherokee dressed in faded overalls and slouch hat with a turkey feather stuck in the band stood beside pumpkin-shaped Mona, her hair washed and combed. The two struck Jackson as ridiculous, and he laughed.

"Where you been, woman? Who you got there? A real live Indian?"

Tall Corn passed the shell, still in its protective wrapping, to Mona. She took the shell and spoke to Jackson.

"I'm staying here. With Tall Corn and Beloved Mother." She edged closer to Tall Corn. "You see this shell? You have to leave and not come back to Cherokee land."

Mona opened the cloth to reveal the shell. Sunlight heightened its iridescence. Jackson was reminded of a fancy lady in Philadelphia and her pearl buttons that he had begun undoing before he got her out of town.

"What's that?" he sneered.

Mona set her face against his scorn. "The sacred shell. It gives me power. To make decisions without asking you. It separates me from you. It sends you away from this land." She held it out before her as if it were an offering. "I'm going to be Tall Corn's wife."

"What you been drinking?" he chuckled. "Here you are telling me what I can and can't do while you bust your gut with my kid?" Jackson snatched the shell and drew back to throw it.

13

Tall Corn grabbed Jackson's arm. The white man released the shell with a grunt under Tall Corn's grip. Mona carefully wrapped it in its cloth and stepped back beside Tall Corn.

"You got to leave. Now, Jackson. Tall Corn'll take you to the trail that goes down to Knoxville." She pointed southwest. "Just you walk careful in front of my husband."

Tall Corn nudged Jackson forward with a nod of his head.

"I got to gather up my things." Jackson took a quick look about at his cast iron spider, the water bucket, its gourd dipper, his tarpaulin and rope.

"No," Mona demanded. "Just go."

"I ain't leaving without my valise." Jackson moved toward the black satchel.

Tall Corn stepped in front of Jackson, gripped both of his arms and shoved him back. "Two Tears says go."

"I ain't leaving without my valise," Jackson Slocomb repeated. He lunged for the valise that held his hatchet and knife.

Mona grabbed the hatchet and dropped the bag. She aimed the hatchet at Jackson's head.

"No," said Tall Corn. He spoke so softly that Mona dropped her hand. Her eyes questioned his request. He could not know the infinite pain of living with this dark-hearted man. He could not know that when she walked out of Covington that night she had no idea she was walking into the maw of hell itself.

She glared at Jackson, sweat running into his collarless shirt, daring her to act. Mona lifted the valise, replaced the hatchet, and hugged them to her breast.

The white man picked up his felt hat and beat it against his pants to slap off the dust. Tall Corn pointed to the cornrow he was to follow. Jackson Slocomb moved forward without looking back. Behind him, Two Tears handed Tall Corn the skinning knife from Jackson's bag.

Tall Corn gripped the knife and followed Slocomb down the path.

Great Spirit kicks a cloud out of his line of sight and calls Sister Sun to come and see. "This white man Jackson will wander, like Long Hunters who followed Cherokee trails years before, trails few white men had walked, winding in and out of copses of virgin forest and meadows knee-deep in grass," he tells her.

"Who are Long Hunters?" Sister Suns asks.

"Men who traveled west into the land they named Kentucky, carrying long rifles, walking long distances. They appeared in the Cherokee month of the nut, when hardwood leaves swathe mountainsides in

*maroon, burnt orange, yellows and bronze, and trees drop hardened
seeds on soft earth. Jackson will devour whatever he needs to sustain
his search, as Long Hunters did." Great Spirit draws the glimmer
from Jackson Slocomb's eye and replaces it with darkness. "This white
man's hatred has cast him out. He will no longer be accepted by man
or woman."*

Beloved Mother, respected for her wisdom and goodness, questioned
the pustules and scars on Two Tears' bony back as she bathed her in the
tin tub when the two returned. Two Tears told of a green mountain life
turned bloody. The fascination Jackson had with raping her atop dewberry
vines, in seasons when the vines lay close to the ground, and the joy he
experienced witnessing her pain.

Seven nights before the baby was born, Beloved Mother softened
the pustules with warm cloths and eased briars out of the festering. With
each briar came another story of Mona's life with Jackson Slocomb. As
Beloved Mother worked toward the healing, she chanted, "Briars, um, um,
um, briars," in a gentle voice. When she had cleansed Two Tears' back and
wiped the crying from the girl's face, she said, "The child will hereafter be
called 'Briar,' from whence he came."

The night was hot. An iridescent moon lit the mountain as bright as day.
The child Briar Slocomb was born during a night of light. Walks in Tall
Corn wrapped the babe in his own blanket. He cuddled the child as his
own.

Several weeks later, Tall Corn lifted Briar from the rope hammock
where he slept by the rock fireplace. The infant opened his black eyes and
grinned at the husband of his mother.

"He likes me," said Tall Corn. "He's smiling."

Two Tears shaved more corn from the cob. "Gas," she said.

Tall Corn put the baby on his shoulder the way he had seen Beloved
Mother do and patted his back until Briar burped. Tall Corn rested in
Beloved Mother's slat rocker and pushed off into a steady rhythm, holding the baby on his knees as he made animal calls and named each. Briar
looked more perplexed than pleased with each changing sound.

"He's early to learn that," Two Tears interrupted. "He'll know names
soon enough."

"About names," he said. "Who named this boy Briar?" Tall Corn adjusted the infant on his leg. "He'll have to fight for that name all his life."

"It'll make him strong," Two Tears answered. "It's a good name. You
can't destroy a green briar by digging or burning. It goes on forever."

Tall Corn refused to let it go. "I've been thinking he should have a different name. An animal name would be right for a Cherokee boy."

"He's not Cherokee, Tall Corn." Two Tears picked up another cob to strip. "I'm not Cherokee." The only sound in the room was Two Tears' knife scraping milk from the corncob and the rocker grating against the pine floor.

Tall Corn held Briar over his head, allowing the infant to look down into his face. "Why did your mother name you Briar, baby boy?"

Briar cooed. Drool dropped onto Tall Corn's forehead.

"Ask Beloved Mother," Two Tears answered. "She named him."

"I don't like this prickly name. We need a naming ceremony. Have the village come in when the crops are laid back. Celebrate and name our son..." Tall Corn thought for a minute. "Silent Wolf."

"You can't defy Beloved Mother. She won't have it."

"I'll convince her. I got her to change my name." Tall Corn nestled the baby into the crook of his arm, preparing the child for sleep. "What Cherokee man can show his face as Dancing Squirrel?"

Two Tears turned to stare at Tall Corn. "Dancing Squirrel? That sounds like a girl's name." She bit her lip trying not to smile.

"My grandmother. It was her idea." Tall Corn laid Briar in his hammock and set it to swaying. "She wanted a girl to follow Beloved Mother for the village."

"So that's why you married me?" Two Tears' scraping knife plunked on the table. "To be the next Beloved Mother?"

Tall Corn put his arms around Two Tears. "Never. I married you because Great Spirit sent you to be my wife." He kissed her on her forehead and ran his finger down her scarred cheek with tenderness.

Ordinary June days in Carolina gather enough heat to tassel corn, but Sister Sun cannot convince the ground to hold her warmth this season. And Great Spirit is not cooperating, so she drags a dingy anvil shaped cloud over her face and sulks. Soil holds tight to every mote of sunshine it gathers to strengthen freshening roots. But by dusk, heat escapes bit by bit. Something is out of order in nature. Sister Sun wonders if the crops can produce what villagers will need this time.

She has watched homeless children sleep under newspapers in alleys of Knoxville. She has seen the hungry in shabby coats stand in Al Capone's soup kitchen line in Chicago. She watches Tall Corn work his fields, toting buckets of water from the branch to water his corn. And she casts a cloud over Briar's head for his boyish sluggishness.

*Repulsed by this year they call 1933, she burns the Midwest day
after day and returns to the Carolinas, to slip behind the mountains,
leaving pink, lavender and coral strips of ribbon to mark her path.*

June, 1933. Near a Carolina mountaintop beneath a copse of fir, the white woman Two Tears and her Cherokee husband sat on the front porch of their unpainted clapboard house as the sky turned grey. Tall Corn leaned his back against the cane bottom chair in which his wife rested and watched a dirty cloud hover in the sky. He shifted against the chair leg to relieve his itching back.

Two Tears yawned.

Tall Corn rubbed his callused hand beneath her long, full skirt, up and down her calf. "Tired?" he asked.

"A bit," she said. "What with Beloved Mother in the village. I chase myself all day to get food cooked and see to Briar." She motioned for her son, a lanky boy of eight, to come to her. "Come give me a hug," she said. The child did not rise. "And still find time to study the book. It takes so long for me to read Cherokee."

"Beloved Mother don't expect you to know all's in that book overnight." Tall Corn spit tobacco juice off the porch. The spittle created a circle of russet dust by the rock step. "Do what you can with what time you got."

"She took me in all the time knowing I'm white." Two Tears pushed her dusty brown hair away from her scarred face. "Helped me birth Briar." She scratched and then rubbed her lower arm where a mosquito had drawn blood. "If I'm going be the next Beloved Mother, I got to know things."

"She understands. That's what she's all about. Understanding. Good judgment. That kind a thing." Tall Corn shifted his weight off her chair and sat upright. "Looks like rain in that there cloud. That's good. Briar'll go to the fields with me tomorrow, and you study the book."

Out of the dusky dark, Briar spoke. "I don't want to go to the fields. I want to stay with Mama."

"Don't whine," Tall Corn said. "Go inside to bed. Sun'll be here early." He stood and offered his hand to Two Tears. "Walk with me to the branch, Wife. We'll watch the moon come over the mountain."

Two Tears slipped her arm around his waist, and they stepped off the porch together. When they entered the trees, both shivered against the damp.

Draped in impending darkness, Two Tears confessed. "Just don't know I can pass that last test. I just don't know."

Tall Corn stroked her back.

17

"You got no idea what I would have to do," she said.

"No matter. You're my wife, even if you fail."

From ahead, over the rush of branch water, a bullfrog belched in response.

Chapter 4

From where Beloved Mother stood on the ridge, the village looked like a cluster of brown mushrooms. The roofs were so dark it was as if a fungus had moved through, smothering all living things. No one moved about. No dogs in the road. No men in the fields.

When Two Tears and the child had come to stay, Beloved Mother took to sleeping on the ground, Great Spirit's bosom. Times lying awake, she questioned her purpose as diligently as Sister Sun and Brother Moon questioned the first man and his obstinacy on what he could and should not do, for she imagined herself a mere mother, not a Beloved Mother. But the land called to her and she answered, allowing passion for the forest to seep into her soul. She lay in moistness under tree canopies that smothered out underbrush, in dampness that quieted the softest sound. She slept and woke to chirps of birds talking among themselves. She watched open skies by day and noted their prophetic stars at night as they split the heavens and marked the months. She listened as creatures interrupted forest quiet, creatures that saw themselves as safe, even in the presence of man. With this, her being absorbed the essence of earth. Nights she still waited for Great Spirit to speak to her, to call her by name, to give her direction and wisdom for her people.

She awakened in the night with an urge to go to the village. She had been there only a fortnight before, when she raised a rod to the white man called Jackson for entering the village. He had come, heavy with liquor, asking for someone named Mona.

"There's no Mona. Only Two Tears," she lied. Her answer surprised her. She had come to accept the young wife of her son. In time, perhaps, Two Tears would learn what she knew, so her people would be safe.

Beloved Mother, now gazing down at what appeared to be a sleeping village, knew why she felt summoned. Light, feathery spirit wisps hovered over the rock chimneys of two different cabins, Great Spirit's sign that death resided in those cabins. Beloved Mother walked back a ways and called to Briar in the voice of the owl, but he did not answer. She waited and called again.

Death teased her by sending a possum across her path, the young hanging on their mother's back, one stacked on the other. The possum wiggled her pink, pointed nose and dragged her hairless tail. She curled back her lips to show sharp teeth then glanced sideways at Beloved Mother. She hissed, daring Beloved Mother to cross some invisible line, a reminder that this trail belonged to her and her joeys. Having claimed her place, she dug her pink nails into the dirt to maintain her stability as she sauntered into underbrush.

Beloved Mother wrapped her shawl tight against the morning chill and the shiver the possum sent through her body. She looked again at the village below. She moved her woven pine straw basket to her other arm. Empty, except for one cure.

"Oh Great One, what have I done?" she whispered. Here she stood with no healing herbs. The only other means for healing she carried was her gourd rattle. She knew from the Beloved Mother who trained her that Great Spirit would give only three sunrises before the souls of the sick would merge with the spirit wisp. Once merged, they would float to the river where the horned serpent *Uktena* would take them under. Without her healing power, they will lose their chance to soar into the eastern sky.

Beloved Mother reprimanded herself for coming so far empty-handed. She would only be able to create a potion of pine needles and pine bark. That would suffice, if the sickness were no more than runny eyes and sneezes. If more, she would need what she left at home. *I must be getting old*, she thought. She had no choice but to turn back to Tall Corn's house and collect what she needed for healing.

Halfway down the mountain, she called again to Briar.

Tall Corn answered. They met near the overhang where water seeped through ancient rock layers and mosses covered the ground. Tall Corn carried a basket filled with cedar chips, garlic, ginseng, wild raspberry leaves and a ginger root, its original stock traded by a Jamaican slave to

20

Beloved Mother's great-grandmother before the white man's country cut itself apart with war.

"Why did you leave your field?" she asked her son. "Where's the white boy?"

"He sleeps in the house," Tall Corn answered. "If he heard, he couldn't answer. He doesn't know the language of the owl yet."

"Two Tears does him an injustice." Beloved Mother shook her head. "Tend the fields. Speak the animal languages. He has to learn." Beloved Mother took the full basket from Tall Corn. "His mother has managed my tests so far, but I have little faith she will pass the final test. I should have chosen someone else." She shook her head, knowing she may have made a fatal mistake.

"Two Tears is the only daughter you will ever have," said Tall Corn. "When I return, I'll pull Briar by his long legs into the field with me." He laughed. "And Two Tears will succeed. The Great Spirit would not have sent her if he had not wanted her to follow you."

Great Spirit tosses a thundercloud aside and dozes a time longer, giving young Sister Sun time to brush the mist skyward so she can warm the ground and arouse morning creatures. He can rest easy now.

Beloved Mother hurried to the village. On cabin porches and in hallways that split cabins into two rooms, speckled dogs lay on their bellies. None barked or whined as she approached.

Air in the valley, unlike that on the mountain, was colder in the shadows. When she arrived, it was past time to begin cooking for the day, yet no smoke rose from chimneys. Beloved Mother wondered if the illness was stronger than the Great Spirit's gift of fire or if the people had wasted the ash with water to kill the fire itself. To have done so would be a serious mark against the village. Fire, even mere embers, must be kept alive, even in warmest weather.

Beloved Mother opened the door to the first cabin where a spirit mist hung overhead. The sulfurous smell of stale urine and sweaty bodies kept too warm met her before she stepped inside. Illness permeated the room. She hummed, a humming that eased into a low singing voice, more chant than song. Family of the child moved away from the child's bed as she neared. They did not speak, for she, as Beloved Mother, must first invite them to do so. She offered no such invitation.

On a bed of boards attached to the wall lay a child, a boy not yet three summers. She saw by his open mouth that his meat-grinding teeth had not yet appeared. Standing over the child, she shook the gourd rattle lightly.

The child didn't move. She shook again, harder this time. The child didn't flinch. She moved back and forth down the bed, shaking the gourd over all the child's body, chanting louder with each movement. If she had not seen the rise and fall of his thin chest, she would have thought that his soul had already left his body.

Beloved Mother spoke to the family, now a huddle against the far wall. "Who's his mother?" she asked.

A bony girl, no more than fifteen, inched forward.

"Tell me."

No one responded.

"Has he touched a forbidden animal?"

The child-mother interlocked her fingers before her pouched belly to stop her hands from shaking and told of her son's illness in jumps of words: his fever, his runny nose, his dry cough followed by his listlessness. In the night, his body had burned to the touch, so she put out the fire to cool him. It did not help. She removed his breeches and shirt. That did not help. He would take no water. Then he fell asleep before dawn, and no one had been able to wake him. She sent her younger brother up the mountain trail to the house of Tall Corn to find her, for she believed Beloved Mother could heal any illness. Her brother had not returned.

Beloved Mother told the mother to bring light. In the glow of the kerosene lantern, Beloved Mother leaned close and saw something she had never seen before. Red spots over all his body, as if the ant had tried to eat him alive.

She began with a drink of pine needle and bark potion to take away the redness of his eyes and to treat the body as it overheated. If this did not return the wisp of soul that had left the body and now floated above the cabin, she would take him to the water and dip him in seven times to cleanse the evil spirit from his soul.

When she tried to feed the child the drink, he did not swallow. He slept the sleep of the winter bear. She drew the light closer and saw the same red bumps on the back of his throat. This strange new disease baffled her. Though she could not name the disease, she knew the child must drink or he would die.

She told the mother to open all windows. "Borrow some fire, clothe the child and come for me when he wakes," she said.

While puzzling over this baby she left behind, she walked to the next cabin. There she found a girl of six summers. The spots were the same, but the child was not asleep. The child told her, after Beloved Mother sang her chant and rattled her gourd, that she couldn't swallow for the fire in her throat.

Beloved Mother went from cabin to cabin looking for more of her people with the odd red splotches. She found none, but she did find an aged one of the village rocking back and forth and holding his head. He whimpered in pain. When she approached him, he struck out at her with one arm. "Leave me to die," he cried. "I have offended Great Spirit. Leave me to die."

"How? What did you do?" Beloved Mother asked.

"I can't say." The old man continued to sway. "It's too bad."

"You have to say. I must know what animal brought this disease."

Ah, this morning. The encounter. She crossed the invisible line on the trail. "Is it the possum who looks out of red eyes in the night?"

"No," the man answered. "Yes. . . No."

Beloved Mother leaned into his face. "Tell me what you did to offend Great Spirit or the village will die. Your great-grandson lies almost empty. His soul waits to join the spirit mist."

The old man sang out a woman's keening song. For his great-grandson. For himself.

"Speak up," she demanded. "Or I will curse all your descendants."

Sister Sun perks up her ear. She looks east to see if Brother Moon has yet appeared. Perhaps she should awaken Great Spirit.

The old man quieted his wailing. A fortnight ago, the night after Beloved Mother left the village, he had wandered into the underbrush to relieve himself when, in the darkness of a new moon, he stumbled on something soft and long. He returned to his cabin and after dawn the next morning he sneaked back to see what had lain in his path. There, as Sister Sun began her trip over the mountain, lay a white man, the one Beloved Mother had called Jackson. The one who had wandered in and out of the mountains for the past ten years. Dead. Covered with red spots. Beside him sat a mother possum eating flesh from the dead man's arm. Her joeys sucked her teats.

The old man chased her away with a limb, but in doing so, he slipped on damp leaves and fell on the white man's bloody arm. He jumped up and rubbed the blood from his hands, yet some entered his body through a cut on his thumb. And now his head throbbed with this knowing. He touched a white man and soaked up his blood. He was no longer true Cherokee. He was ready to die.

Beloved Mother should have known the possum brought the disease, either directly or indirectly, when it drew its line across the trail. But no Beloved Mother before her had given her knowledge of this disease. Her

23

lack of knowledge left her with one choice. Take the children to the river and dip each for cleansing.

> *Great Spirit rolls in from the south and speaks through the mourning dove to Beloved Mother. "There can be no separation of worlds, real or dream, physical or spiritual," he says.*

Beloved Mother shivered. She should know something more, but she did not listen. She was too frightened to hear to any voices, human or phantom.

> *Great Spirit trumpets out a blast of thunder at Beloved Mother's insolence. "How dare she ignore my counsel?"*

The mother of the girl-child walked with her daughter to the river and led her into the cold mountain water where Beloved Mother waited. The child trembled and cried as Beloved Mother pushed her head back and back, again and again, under the water. The mother wrapped a woolen blanket about her child and carried her tight against her bosom back to their cabin.

Beloved Mother had no words of comfort or guidance for the mother. She stood statue-like in the cold, rushing water, awaiting the next child to be delivered unto her.

Mother of the boy-child feared the great horned serpent that lives in the river. She feared the serpent would take her child and she grieved openly, for Beloved Mother had told her at the child's birth that he would be her only child. She clung fiercely to the child and wailed against Beloved Mother's dipping him in the river.

Beloved Mother pulled the baby from his mother and reentered the water. She pushed his head down, one, two, seven times. The child didn't open his eyes. He didn't cry. His hot body smarted Beloved Mother's hands as she held him to her breast and chanted a weak, life-giving song to the Great Spirit. Mid-chant, the child stiffened, threw his head back and stopped breathing. He was lost. Lost to the white man Jackson and the mother possum who fed on his arm.

> *Great Spirit shoves a thunderous cloud before the young Sister Sun who sits amazed by what has happened. He drops shadows over the village. Villagers along the riverbank lose their faces in the dim light. Great Spirit spits out a grunt against this pathetic Beloved Mother who has no ears to hear.*

The boy-child's mother fell to the ground. Her keening echoed across the water. Behind her, Beloved Mother waded out of the water to gather wood for the tiny boy's bier. Villagers along the bank separated into two barriers, protection for the well children who shrank behind them. Beloved Mother followed a darkened pathway as she left.

"How have I failed you, Great Spirit?" Beloved Mother asked as she picked up sturdy limbs for the bier.

The villagers found her in the close woods, stooped over, her head facing the ground. A man's voice quivered behind her. "We'll do this for the child."

Beloved Mother straightened. She looked into the old man's eyes. His dark eyes showed nothing but emptiness.

She moved back down the path and threw back her head. "Is it the white woman who sleeps with my son?" she asked Great Spirit.

Great Spirit does not hear. He is exhausted. He settles in and naps behind the storm cloud.

Beloved Mother stayed in the village another fortnight using all the healing powers she had. The poignant odor of cedar permeated the village as she shaved the sacred wood and smoked each dwelling. Her clothing carried the aroma from house to house. The epidemic of cough, fever and vivid red spots had settled on the village so heavily that Beloved Mother came home only to pick up more garlic, ginger and hog fat. She gathered ashes to hold grease and garlic together for chest or neck poultices for her people.

It was important that she used garlic remedies before ginger, though she was not convinced the garlic was a better remedy. She had no information to use as a base for her treatment. At least she could re-use the garlic to make a poultice or a drink of garlic and honey once she had rubbed garlic on the soles of the sick. But with this disease villagers were withering away, especially children. Every cabin had one or more Cherokee coughing then sleeping in a hot, sweaty body. Her purple coneflower brew had no effect. Her people continued to lose confidence in her power, to turn their backs when meeting her, and to take children to the creek themselves. They returned, and the next day the children lay limp and damp on their cots, waiting for their spirit mists to rise.

She could not use all her ginger. Three generations of Beloved Mothers had preserved at least two cuttings to continue the stock. She had one with her. The other was stored on Tall Corn's mantle in the carved box that held the polished shell. After eight years of living with Two Tears and teaching her herbs, plants, medicines and their recipes, she could leave Two Tears alone in her house. The ginger cutting would be safe.

Exhausted, Beloved Mother slept through the night and into the next day on the ancient one's floor. Mid-morning, she was startled awake by the voice of Tall Corn. She sat erect on the blanket. "What did you say, old man?"

The old man did not answer. He sat facing the closed door as if he waited for Death to enter and take him to the river. Beloved Mother asked again. He did not move. She slapped her hands together to get his attention. He did not respond. She used her hands, then her knees as leverage, to lift her stiff body and edged to the back of his chair, unseen. Here she clapped sharply near his head. He didn't move. The strange red spots had left him deaf.

Tall Corn called to Beloved Mother again, this time in the language of the dove. Beloved Mother gathered her medicines and her gourd and left the village to see to her only son.

Chapter 5

Upon returning from meeting Beloved Mother at the rock overhang, Tall Corn chuckled as he pulled Briar's legs off the cot where he slept and spun him around so the boy's head would not hit the floor. Two Tears entered the room at the sound of Briar's grumbling. She found Tall Corn bending over Briar, shaking his shoulders.

"What happened?" she asked.

"We decided last night. Briar must go to the field to learn the life of the corn. He'll one day need to feed us when we're old." He scratched Briar's head. "Beloved Mother agrees."

Two Tears put her hands on her hips and looked Tall Corn in the eye. "No. He's not yet nine seasons. He's too young to go to the fields."

"You'd have him stay here, sleep all day, and learn the life of a woman?" Tall Corn flung back his shoulders. "You'd have the village laugh at him when he reaches his manhood because he can't feed his family?"

He spoke to Briar, still abed. "Get up. If Great Spirit blesses us, we may have rain today."

Briar wiggled himself off the bed.

"He'll learn," Two Tears said. "He'll just learn later."

"Stop arguing," Briar said. "I'll go to the field. Father's right. I do need to learn the fields." Briar rubbed the back of his neck and opened the door.

Tall Corn followed and patted the boy's shoulders.

In the barn, Tall Corn picked up a triangular-headed planting hoe. He held it up to show Briar how the edges must be sharp so dirt around the upper roots could be loosened without cutting the lower roots. He turned the hoe over and showed him how the vee-shaped side of the blade cut tiny furrows around the corn to allow rainwater to settle in the indentation and soak both upper and lower roots.

He took a steel file and slid it in one direction, away from his body, over the edge of the blade. He flipped the blade and sharpened the other side. Briar cringed at the rasping sound of metal on metal. Over and over, Tall Corn honed the edges. When he finished, each side appeared to have a silver ribbon down its edge. He lightly touched the sharp rims to test for smoothness. "Fine as my skinning knife," he said and smiled.

He carried the hoe by its neck and walked with Briar to the cornfield, not far from where he first saw Briar's mother. Tall Corn put the triangular point to the ground and scraped, loosening the soil's surface. He moved to the next stalk and repeated. He let Briar try. Once he saw that Briar handled the soil with tenderness, he returned to the barn.

As the morning grew long, clouds gathered to wet the soil. Silent rain fell straight to the ground. Such a gentle a rain, it did not even rustle corn leaves. Briar worked on, ignoring his wet back. Near the end of the far row, rain increased. Lightning outlined the silhouette of the barn where his father worked. He recalled the story of his grandfather, Tall Corn's father, and the lightning strike. He dropped his hoe and ran for cover.

He met his father mid-field. With rain dripping from his hair, he hugged Tall Corn. "I was scared for you."

"Where is your hoe, boy?"

"I must have dropped it in the field," Briar answered. "I'll get it."

"Go inside and dry. I'll get it. Can't stay out in the rain."

Two Tears had food on the table. Boiled beans, corn, smoked venison and flat bread. Briar ate with the appetite of a boy pushed from within by growth.

Near dusk, she sent Briar to the field to find his father. Not certain where he dropped the hoe, Briar wandered among the green stalks that rose taller than his head. At one point, he rested, heavy mud slowing his step as it built up on his shoes. It was then that he heard the sound, a sound much like that of a yard cat caught between barn slats. A cross between a whimper and a meow.

Cutting across thick rows, he ran. He found his father on the ground. The hoe, stuck in the soft tissue below his knee, was embedded up to the neck, so deep that only the handle showed. Mud and blood streaked his

pants leg. They puddled together where his father had fallen, before seeping into the ground.

"You came," Tall Corn whispered. He tried to get up. "I slipped on
the mud."

Briar tried, but he could not lift his father. "I'll go for Mother."

Tall Corn said no. "Grab the handle of the hoe and when I say pull,
pull as hard as you can."

"No, I can't."

"Get the hoe out of my knee so I can walk. When the hoe's out, we'll
wrap the knee with my shirt and I'll lean on you. We'll go slow and your
mother'll tend my wound."

Tall Corn grabbed the handle where it met the metal. Briar took the
opposite end.

"No. Come to this side with me. Else we push against each other."

Briar waded around the hoe handle through the mud, now so slick he
caught corn stalks so he wouldn't fall. The steadiness of the corn stalk reminded him that Tall Corn had asked him earlier to plant bean seed at the
base of the corn so runners would have support through the summer. Had
Briar planted squash between cornrows to smother out weeds as his father
had asked, there would be less mud, less chance for his father to have slipped.
He told himself, *Don't cry. Not now. Show Father I can give back for what I've cost.*

Standing next to his father, Briar pushed the handle away when his
father gave the word. Tall Corn gritted his teeth, but a gasp escaped his
clenched lips when the hoe tore out of his knee.

Briar jumped back to avoid the squirting blood. After his father rested, Briar helped him to his feet and the two struggled down the cornrow,
cutting a reddish slice in the mud where Tall Corn dragged his useless leg.
Dark followed the farmer and his son back to the house.

*The eve before the end. Great Spirit knows this, but he is busy in
Alabama with Judge Horton, trying to convince him to set aside a
guilty verdict for Haywood Patterson, one of the Scottsboro Boys.
Great Spirit questions whether Judge Horton listens any closer to what
he says than Beloved Mother does.*

Inside the house, though the day was August-hot for June, a fire
burned low in the side fireplace. Earlier, Two Tears had Briar stoke a fire.
She needed soot to scotch blood seeping from her husband's knee.

Two Tears worked with her husband's wound into the night, ignoring
the smothering heat. The tin roof warmed the little room enough. Add
the fire and the temperature brought out her sweat.

His head low to hide tears on his cheeks, Briar hung back while his mother tended the open gash beneath his father's knee. "I didn't mean. . ." He had tried several times throughout the afternoon, but he could not say it. The weight on his heart was too heavy for a child to lift.

"Bring me cool water to stave off this fever."

Briar stepped easy into the darkness and felt his way to the well.

Brother Moon acknowledges the boy's guilt and refuses to aid him.

With Briar back inside, his mother directed him to shave off more ginger. Briar shaved slowly. He had heard the Beloved Mother speak of ginger's value. The root was too precious to reckon with. Use all the root and the medicine was gone.

"Hurry," Two Tears commanded.

Throughout the night, Briar rushed to the spring. To the carved medicine box on the mantle. To the bed. Outside the house to dampen sheets for coolness. His body ached from the strain that had laid itself upon his shoulders the moment he found his father bleeding in the dirt.

Morning. Two Tears' uncombed hair straggled loose from her long braid. "I'm going to the outhouse. Make him drink," she told Briar. "His knee's swelling."

Briar spooned water to his father's lips, only to have it dribble onto his collar. Tears dripped off the child's narrow chin.

Evening. "His leg's swelled much as it can without splitting open," Two Tears said. "Get you some them beans off the stove and eat some supper. I'll eat later," she told Briar.

Then night. She held the lamp close and whispered, "Oh, God. Red streaks." She pulled back the cover. "They're almost to his crotch."

Two Tears sat on the edge of the bed and rubbed Tall Corn's good leg. She wept, drinking in tears that tracked down the two scars that split her left cheek. She swallowed her sorrow, this time deeper than ever before.

Tall Corn groaned, his raspy voice no more than an undertone. "Don't cry, Wife."

"I can't heal you," she said. "I'm not a Beloved Mother."

"Don't worry. My spirit has called her to come." Tall Corn tried to raise himself from the bed.

Two Tears took the back of his head in her hand and lowered him to the pillow. "I hear there's a white doctor in Boone. Tomorrow first light, I'll send Briar to bring him."

"No," Tall Corn said. "Beloved Mother won't have it."

Two Tears took Tall Corn's hand. "I got to do what I know's right, not what she says." She massaged his palm. "I ain't going be no Beloved Mother no how."

"Wait for her. My spirit pleads with her."

"Who made her Beloved Mother anyway?" Two Tears chuckled. "You're so cold your fingernails are blue." She drew up a quilt and tucked it under his shoulders. "I'm going to get wood to stave up the fire."

Two Tears stepped off the porch and looked up. There by the chimney top hovered an irregular foggy cluster. Fog before evening, after a day hot from the sun. It's the sign, the first sign Beloved Mother taught her. Tall Corn's spirit mist called what was left of Tall Corn's spirit. "Come," it said. "Come with me."

Two Tears would send Briar for the white doctor, even if Beloved Mother disapproved. To convince her, she will point out the streaks and the purple and green skin forming around the cut. Have her breathe in the growing stench of the wound.

She gave up on the logs and went back inside.

Sunrise of the third day fog hugged the ground. Briar, a sack of food flung over his shoulder, opened the door to leave.

Before him stood Beloved Mother. Tall and proud, she filled the doorframe. "Where you going?" she demanded.

Briar eyed her up and down. Her full skirt, its rose pink border sweeping the tops of her scuffed work boots. Her frayed denim jacket, the one Tall Corn cast off during the Month of the Cold Moon, the month Tall Corn and his mother tried to celebrate Old Christmas. The celebration that came nigh sending him and his mother off the mountain. Her thick braid rested on her shoulder much like a fat black snake, unlike his mother's, whose hair reflected a tinge of orange in sunlight. And, as always on her arm, her intricately woven pine straw basket cradling her small gourd rattle.

He glanced back into the room, his eyes questioning his mother beside the iron bedstead. Bent over his father, she bathed his body against climbing fever. Short shallow breaths disturbed the room.

"Answer me, boy," Beloved Mother said.

He turned back to his grandmother. "I am Silent Wolf, and I am going to Boone." He lifted his chin. "To bring a doctor for my father."

Beloved Mother pushed the child back. "I heard my son's spirit call and *I* decide. I am she who knows." She stomped toward the bed, her heavy brogans accenting the hollowness beneath the floor. "Great Spirit gave *me* responsibility for my people," she declared. "He didn't include some white man."

31

Two Tears stepped away from the bed. Tall Corn lay ashen, near the color of his bleached cotton blanket.

Beloved Mother knelt by her son's bed. Under the porch eave, a dove's coos awakened his mate.

Two Tears brought a cool cloth for Tall Corn's face. Beloved Mother rose and stood between the two. Two Tears waited, her hands clasped over her belly.

Beloved Mother inspected Tall Corn's putrid leg. "What have you done?" She whispered in an attempt to harbor anger rising within her. This unfamiliar fierceness had grown within her inch by inch since she found Jackson Slocomb outside the village, dead and covered with red spots. Though she battled against its escalation, she knew she was losing. She wrung her brown-splotched hands.

"Why send for the white doctor for my son?" Without waiting for an answer, she took her worn, tan gourd-rattle from her pine basket and held it level with her chest. "*I* am the healer." She pulled a quilt over the wound and smoothed it. She rattled the gourd hard over the leg.

Tall Corn lay as still as the boy child in the village. "Call for the little people. Ask the Dogwood People to help," he murmured.

"You may know Cherokee ways, Tall Corn, but I'm Beloved Mother. I choose." She shook her bean-filled gourd and stomped rabbit-like up and down beside the bed, harder with each pass. The rhythm of her ancient chant and pounding feet punctuated the gourd's tapping sound.

Briar crept closer to the door.

Above the frame house, Great Spirit wrestles with his girth and pulls a cloud up to his chin. With the Alabama issue settled, he can now rest, though it seems he has no power over his people. He ignores Beloved Mother's rants.

From behind, Two Tears snatched the rattle from her mother-in-law's hand. "This gourd's useless. You're letting my husband die." She raised the gourd above her head. "*I* can't heal him. *You* can't heal him." Exasperation slipped down her chest and squeezed her breathing. Her shoulders drooped. "A sparrow flew in this room yesterday," she whispered.

"Mama?" Briar called from the doorway. "Is that true?"

Two Tears straightened and circled the gourd around her head. Its innards buzzed as if something living was trapped inside. "Somebody help me!" she cried out over the unnerving jangle. "His spirit mist is over the roof," she said quietly.

Beloved Mother stood totem-like, glaring at the wall above Tall Corn's bed.

Two Tears flung the gourd against the rock chimney. It shattered and hard brown beans rolled, like pellets, across the plank floor.

Cheeks flushed, Two Tears raised her voice in an attempt to pierce Beloved Mother's stubborn belief. "Briar *will* go for the white doctor." She caught a breath and lowered her voice. "And I pray to the Great Spirit that my husband remains until he comes."

Beloved Mother stared at Two Tears. "Great Spirit don't speak to you."

"When did he ever speak to you?" Two Tears shot back.

Beloved Mother flinched as the accusation pierced her guilt for turning a deaf ear.

From the bed, Tall Corn mumbled "Get Slocomb." He tossed his head on the pillow. "Two Tears?" He lifted his right hand and whispered, "Come with me."

Briar jerked and moved inside the open door as if to make a dash for his mother, as if he believed she might become mist and float to the sun as his father commanded. Brisk morning air blew his long, uncombed hair toward his face, hiding his eyes behind a black mask. He put out a hand to keep her from moving.

Across the room, his father spoke in bits. "My son." He spoke softly. "Mona?" The force of a low cough, much like the sound of a full gourd rattle, lifted him from the bed. It was as if his own breath was trying to force a beast from his chest but failed. His face turned dusty blue, and he died.

Beloved Mother whirled to face Two Tears, fists balled for battle. She opened her mouth to scream. Instead, a high-pitched keening rose from deep within. She dropped her clutched hands as her eerie wail shattered the room's stillness. Beloved Mother fell across her son's body.

Two Tears backed toward the open door.

"Out!" Beloved Mother spoke into the quilt. "Get off the land of my people." Beloved Mother lifted her head and, without facing Two Tears, uttered through clinched teeth. "Go back to your white man."

"What white man, Mama?" Briar cowered behind his mother. "Who's Mona?" he whispered.

Two Tears shushed him. Fury held her between her son and her mother-in-law. "You're not a Beloved Mother. Beloved Mother honors life. She builds harmony. You're not doin' that." Two Tears caught her breath and inhaled deeply. "She keeps spirit mists in place."

Beloved Mother stood to challenge Two Tears.

Two Tears wrapped her arms around Briar. "She don't let her only son die." She buried her face in Briar's disheveled hair and muttered, "Oh my God, what have we done to my husband?"

Beloved Mother came closer. "You," she spit out. "You only bring grief. First the village. Now my son." She circled around and faced the bed where her son lay. "How did I ever let you and your wicked ways in my house? Tall Corn?" She spoke to her son's dead body. "She has bled her evilness on our people." Beloved Mother brandished her fist. "I curse you, woman."

Sister Sun ducks behind a low bank of white fluffy clouds she has called in for a day of fair-weather. Great Spirit sleeps on.

Beloved Mother slammed her fist into Tall Corn's mattress. The force elevated the covering from Tall Corn's leg in a puff. The odor of rotting flesh escaped and wafted across the room. Beloved Mother's head slumped. She cried, "I curse you and all your family. I swear on the Great Spirit. Hear me, O Great Spirit. As I am the Beloved Mother."

Sister Sun sneaks from behind the cloud and nudges Great Spirit awake. "Can she do that?"
Great Spirit grunts.

Two Tears grabbed Briar's arm and pushed him toward the barn. They climbed the wooden ladder to the loft and buried themselves in prickly hay. There they would wait for darkness so they could slip away.

From near the large cornfield where Tall Corn fell came the pounding of hammer to nail. Two Tears knew the ritual. Beloved Mother would gather wood to prepare a bier for Tall Corn. She would stay beside him to keep carrion away until he was ready for burial beneath the floor of the white man's house Tall Corn had built for her.

Mid-day. Two Tears awakened Briar from a fitful sleep. They slipped into the house and gathered clothes in a croker sack. As they passed through the room where Tall Corn's body lay, she paused before the mantle and glanced around for Beloved Mother. With no one in sight, she went to Tall Corn, lowered the quilt and kissed his cheeks. Back at the mantle, she slipped the carved cedar box into her pocket and slid a thin leather-backed book into her bosom.

A few steps down the trail, Briar broke his hand free from his mother's. He ran into the house and returned with Tall Corn's Winchester. He paused before Two Tears, his hand caressing the blued steel barrel. Its

American walnut stock rested at his feet. He rubbed his hand over etched images of animals his father had killed with the gun. The rifle reached as high as the boy's forehead. Uncertain, he gazed at his mother.

Two Tears nodded. "It's right you should share your father's life," she said.

By nightfall, they were well down the trail toward Knoxville before they curved north to Elizabethtown.

≮≮≮≮≮↙↙

The Foot of Turtleback Mountain

Turtleback Mountain has inexplicable ways to outfox even the smartest. Those with a mind toward the truth say it will conquer even the hardiest of men. Men tell of mountains, like this Turtleback, that hover like flocks of blackbirds and watch as people climb to a top flat and bury whomever the land has broken. As they trudge up and down the mountains with their shovels, wind and rain cover them in their own mountain dust, the dead and the living alike, payback for the rape of the miners' pickaxes. These mountains, they watch, but they do not stir. They welcome generations of death unmoved. Yet men continue to come.

Miners came to these mountains through a narrow gap in the 1850s. They followed Broken Rock Creek to the head of the valley and set up a camp on the lower banks. There they picked large chunks of glistening coal from the water. Spring rains and melted snow washed men and tents back down to the mouth of the gap. Determined, men hacked their way back up the valley, creating one road down the riverbank. The only road in. The only road out. Eventually they would run their rails beside the road, beside the river, around the feet of Turtleback and Spencer's Mountains, creating staggered yet connected niches in the land covered with mountain bluffs that obstruct travel. Their camp inside the pass would become Covington, a mining town entrenched in the bend of the river.

Houses still collect soot tags in rooms closed off for the winter. These tags grow so long in a season that, when a door opens, they sway in the breeze. Bring in an outsider and they mistake the tags for singular black strings hung from the ceiling.

The girl returned a woman, full-grown, her ashy-brown hair marked by early grey and braided against her back. She walked into Covington, past the center square statue of the miner, his pickax raised toward the sky, and knocked on the door where she grew as a child. People said she had two scars down one cheek, one white, one black.

35

Old man Parsons answered the door and stuffed his hands into the bib of his overalls. Parsons glared at her. He seemed not to know who she was. Before him stood a woman of indeterminate age, her face browned and wrinkled by days in the sun, her cheek scarred dark and light. Her eyes suggested a woman younger than her face. Her dingy white blouse, tucked into a long skirt bordered in strips of pinks and blues, covered her arms and neck. She wore rimless glasses and carried a pine needle-woven basket mashed against her breast as if it held some hidden treasure.

She spoke in a tentative voice. "I'm Mona. Your daughter."

He answered back, "We don't say that name in this house" and closed the door.

The woman was last seen climbing Turtleback Mountain. She was twenty-three years old. Following closely behind her was a thin boy barely nine, his eyes dark as his hair, his skin brown like a peanut. Townspeople who saw them watched until they disappeared into a mist slipping down the mountainside. The woman carried a small basket. The boy lugged a worn black valise.

Part II

Chapter 6

If I'd a knowed before I courted
that love would be so hard on me,
I'd a put my heart in a box of silver
and locked it up with a golden key
 — Mountain Ballad

Covington, Virginia

Mid-spring, four years later. Anna crept across the linoleum-covered floor, groping her way toward Ruth's bed. She hunched down to see if her sister was asleep. The hump under the quilts did not move. She wrapped her reddish blonde hair into a knot and pinned it in place with a tortoise shell comb. It was her mother's best comb, but Anna needed it. So she took it.

Anna bent low and sneaked quickly across the room. When she opened the window, no breeze dissipated the fishy smell that filled the alley behind the Parson's house. She hated this town with its black dirt and hovering mountains. Tonight she was leaving. Clint would be at the corner. He had promised to take her to Bristol where streets were paved and dirt was clean, not black or oily. There, men wore suits and had no ringed eyelids, men who offered white hands without coal-filled cuticles. There, she would not have to listen to Ruth carry on about a man who cared not one whit about her.

Ruth was older and, by right, should marry before Anna. Anna did not consider Mona the oldest sister. Mona had left fourteen years ago when Anna was two, too long ago for Anna's remembering. Ruth and Anna did not know where Mona was, if she had married some stranger or been murdered along some wild trail.

A breeze from Broken Rock Creek picked up. It blew the sheer cotton curtain into the room, bringing with it a strong stench of water poisoned by green mine slush that washed down from Spencer's Mountain mines. Rancid water came from the east before it merged with streams coming from Turtleback Mountain at the head of the cove. A strong whiff might awaken Ruth. Anna stepped out the window onto ground so wet that a constant damp kept its moss tender. As she reached back inside the window for her clothes, a hand gripped her shoulder. She stifled a scream and fell back against the outside wall.

Ruth, clad only in a gauzy nightgown and underpants, appeared ghostlike from behind the old maple tree.

"Where you think you're going?" Ruth demanded.

"None of your business," Anna said. "Get your hand off me."

"Tell me." Ruth spit words through her teeth.

Anna jerked away. "Leave me be."

Clint walked up from the alley that bordered Broken Rock Creek. "What's going on?" he asked in a loud whisper.

Ruth waited for Anna to answer. When she did not, Ruth spoke to Clint, "She's been sneaking out for over two weeks after you brought me home. I want to know where she's going." She shot an angry look at Anna.

Ruth, twenty-three, stood half-hidden by the maple's trunk. She crossed her arms over her near-naked bosom and planted her feet. The March chill teased her nipples. She pulled her gown tight and clasped her arms over her breasts so Clint could not see. Her ash-blonde hair hung in clumps on her shoulders, ridged around her face from the thick hairnet she was required to wear when cooking at the drugstore lunch counter. In the shadow, her eyes looked navy blue, almost black, as the clarity of the event she had interrupted emerged.

Anna stood apart from the two, her arms straight against her narrow hips, her hands balled into fists. "You tell her, Clint." She spread her arms and twirled so Clint could see her purple dress. "You like my new dress?" She grinned.

"This ain't my doing. This ought to be twixt you two." Clint etched a line with his shoe across the dirt. Close by the river, an acorn landed like a shot on a tin-roofed cowshed. Anna jumped. Ruth ignored the crack.

"Tell her," Anna said. Night's coolness seeped through her dress. "Tell her you love me and not her." She cocked her head toward Ruth, much like a mockingbird looking for a nest to raid.

Ruth slapped Anna's cheek. "What do you mean tempting him with your sassy talk?"

This was not how Anna had imagined it. "He wants to marry me and get out of this dirty old town." She stepped aside for Clint to confirm her answer.

"Marry you?" Ruth sputtered out her response. "Why, you're just a baby." She tilted her head and said, "Clint?"

Clint stepped up. "I..." He opened and closed his fists. "I been meaning to tell you, but you seemed so set on our courting." He lowered his head.

Ruth's face went white as a full winter moon. "Set?" She raised her voice. "Set?"

"Shh," Anna whispered. "Don't wake Pa."

When Ruth spoke again, her voice was low. "I never asked you to the drugstore morning after morning for me to cook you eggs and sausage." Anger sputtered her words. "I never walked *you* home." She hiccupped. "*I never kissed you* on the bridge."

He rubbed his hand over his hair.

"And when will this wedding be?" Ruth asked.

"Tomorrow. What time is it, Clint?" Anna didn't wait for him to answer. "Today. At the County Seat in Wise." She took Ruth's hands in hers. "But you can't tell Ma or Pa. They won't understand."

"What's to understand?" Ruth slumped against the maple. She stared up at Clint standing by Anna. "You asked me to fry you eggs every morning for the rest of your life. You said so."

"Ruth," he said. "It was just talk. Just jawing back and forth. You must've known that."

"No." Ruth stood up. "I didn't."

Clint took Anna's arm. "Where's your sack?"

Anna reached into the open window and brought out a pillowcase heavy in the bottom with two folded dresses, underpants and a coat. Clint followed Anna toward the road leading out of the valley.

Ruth's voice shook as she spoke from the base of the tree. "I'll tell. I swear. I'll tell."

Clint said to nobody, "Not my fault. I ain't done nothing wrong." He pulled away from Anna and stuffed his hands into his pants pockets.

Anna turned back and glowered at her older sister, now crouched on all fours. She strode back to face her. She spoke nose to nose so quietly only awakening pre-dawn birds could hear. "You want to make me look like a baby. Well, I'm sixteen now. I'm not thirteen like Mona was."

"Anna. You're my little sister." Ruth dropped her face into her hands. "Running off like that sorry Mona. You were a baby. You can't remember how bad it was. What it did to Ma and Pa. I was there. I saw it all."

Anna walked away from Ruth's voice and followed Clint as he led the way out of Covington.

Sister Sun hears the last of Anna's reply. She slows her entry over the mountain so as not to shame Ruth in broad daylight. Brother Moon slides down the western sky, intent on making his regular rounds. Neither asks the other about where Great Spirit might be.

‹‹‹‹‹‹‹

Breakline Mining Camp

Seventeen years after the mine at Breakline Camp near the eastern Kentucky border opened, a lone woman walked up from the south. A skinny boy followed, wearing a sharpened hatchet in his belt and carrying a black bag.

Dressed as if she had stepped out of the previous century, the scar-faced woman wore a long cotton skirt banded in purple and blue. A deep pink shirt much too large for her size flapped about her arms. Her dull hair, beginning to streak with grey, had been wound into an untidy knot at the nape of her neck. She no longer walked with life in her step but pulled her feet along in workmen's boots made heavy by caked dirt from her travels.

While there, she said little to the people of Breakline. Instead, she cleaned and cooked at the yellow three-story house on the rise, a Queen Anne structure, distinguished by its rounded turret covered with purple shakes. When she finished each day, she gathered her due and disappeared up Turtleback. The next morning she walked back in, often with the boy trailing behind. The year was 1937.

Across the big water, Great Spirit watches armies prepare to fight what will become another World War. He calls to leaders who pride

*themselves on being dogmatic and omnipotent. They stuff their ears
with ambition and refuse to pay attention. Great Spirit shudders at
their foolishness, at their mistaken conception that they can attain immortality by simply shedding blood.*

Hawks played on wind currents, dipping and gliding to stave off
boredom. Briar Slocomb, now twelve, perched on an angled limb midway
up an oak tree where he could overlook the long hollow and study the
scene below.

Breakline Mining Camp spread out through a stretch of dip between
Virginia's Turtleback and Kentucky. A tall tipple rose at the far end of
the hollow, near the mouth of the mine. Briar thought it should rightly
stand at the center of the community. Without its constant hum, the camp
would die.

Angled chutes spread out from the metal tipple like multiple support
arms. It was here every hour of every day that coal was crushed, washed
and separated from slate. For Briar, the purified coal took on a life of its
own once miners axed it from its bed and set it apart. He thought of the
tipple's constant rhythm, *whamp, swish, swish, swish,* as one breath after another rising from the camp. So strange was this other-worldly music that
it imbedded itself in Briar's memory long after he left his oak for home.
Briar came to think of the tipple as a living, breathing thing, a monster
nestled within the mountains, a creature that sustained itself on the sooty
coal-infested water it spewed through the camp.

The tipple towered over the camp, even shadowing the house where
Winston Rafe lived. As supervisor for the three mines owned by Breakline
Coal Company, Rafe enjoyed the best of what life offered and used his
name and position to see that he got it. Rafe strutted around like he owned
every spot of dirt and every person who walked the same path. And he did
own everyone, everyone but Briar Slocomb and Briar's mother Two Tears.

Briar saw himself as true Cherokee, but had he picked up his mother's
medicine book, had he been able to read Cherokee and Tall Corn's family
heritage, he would have known he could not have been Tall Corn's son.
Though not blood Cherokee, his time with Tall Corn had given him a
well-developed Cherokee judgment of what to avoid and whom to trust,
so he kept out of Rafe's way. Briar sensed a sorryness within Winston
Rafe, as palpable as a summer's swollen boil.

Briar failed to tell even his mother that he told the camp boys he was
"Silent Wolf," the name his father had given him. Inside, he was "Silent
Wolf," son of Walks in Tall Corn, from the land of the Cherokee some-
where within the Carolinas.

The oak grew off the road to itself. Briar saw it the first time he and Two Tears climbed Turtleback. Huge compared to other trees around it, its limbs clustered so close that wind could not pass through its thick, green leaves. Briar could imagine the wind lifting up and over its top and spiraling into the sky, rocking the stars themselves. The canopy stood as tall as a three-story house and twice as wide. Beneath the thick limbs, ground lay soft with seasons of building moss. It was not the first live oak Briar had seen, but it was the largest. He knew as soon as he saw it that it was his. Amazed at its wide girth, he named the tree "Old Oak."

Each day, Briar climbed Old Oak, overlooked the valley and watched people who looked not much larger than birds going about their lives. He listened to life that lifted itself out of the valley and merged with the tipple's singsong lullaby. Hidden within Old Oak's branches, Briar imagined the music of the valley melding with that of the mountain. Since settling here, he accepted that he was searching for something, some event, some person, anything that would give him the feeling of belonging he had left behind in the Carolinas three winters ago. So far, nothing had spoken to him.

What he had heard spoken in camp taught him not to speak the Cherokee words his mother spoke. "Month of the Planting Moon" or "Month of the Green Corn Moon" became "summer." Never could he allow himself to think on "Month of the Ripe Corn Moon," for it was within this month that carelessness had overtaken him and left Briar believing he had killed his father.

Initially, camp boys laughed at his long black hair and strange words. They clustered and shushed each other, then they intoned "Silent Wolf, Silent Wolf," with each chant growing louder than the last. They chunked clods of dirt at him for being a "dirty Indian." One, in a fit of laughter, threw a piece of coal at Briar. It struck him behind his left ear. Blood ran down his neck. He crossed the ditch bridge and walked toward the end of the valley. There he used the tipple drain-off to wash the blood away. He scotched the cut with Breakline's black dirt. The scar reminded him of his mother's facial scar. He thought of her each time he rubbed the nubby skin. The scar lay hidden beneath his long hair. Once he went to Old Oak, the tree wrapped him in limbs and leaves and hid him from any passersby. Only there did he sit at ease.

In Breakline Mining Camp, Briar hid the secret killing of his father. But for Briar, the past was never dead. It was not even past. He rarely thought in shades of grey. He had left the planting hoe in the cornfield. A slip and it impaled itself beneath Tall Corn's kneecap. The event was his doing. No amount of telling would convince him different. Deep inside, he knew the truth. He was Tall Corn's son. His high cheekbones bore that out. He had murdered his father as surely as if he had put a rifle to Tall Corn's head and pulled the trigger. His carelessness had thrown him into a shadow of himself. That shadow fed on his guilt and grew.

Each day, dusk pushed Briar out of the tree and sent him up the snaking road to Flatland. Each day, he would use his fake bone-handled pocketknife to notch a deep line into Old Oak's trunk, a reminder that this magnificent tree belonged to him.

Summer days mapped out the same for the mining camp. The ear-shattering whistle pulled miners out of company-owned houses lined up the walking path and led them to the shack where they donned boots, coveralls and hardhats for entering underground. Within minutes, they spilled out and walked stiff-legged to the mine. Each wore a blackened jumper with thick cloth made brittle by days of hardened dirt imbedded from crawling through the tunnels' mud. Their hardhats, topped with carbide lamps, bobbed with each step. They lined up by twos and boarded trams that shuttled them down slanted rails into the earth. There they remained, hunched over, sometimes crawling on their knees in icy water, to where they whacked black seams of prehistoric oily rock out of tunnel walls with pickaxes and shovels.

Twelve hours later on days without accident or death, the same men trudged out of the hole and removed their mining duds. Several hiked up Turtleback's side, stripped down, and bathed in tin washtubs they left on the banks of a constant spring. They wound their way back down to their families, with a few stopping by the company store for tobacco, before they faced tending the gardens behind their houses.

Each day, Briar watched camp kids, his age and younger, race down the banks of a ditch that carried dirty water from the chutes. Children chased debris they threw into the ditch to check the water's speed as it led to the mine pond outside the camp. The ditch, with three wooden bridges interspersed down the valley, spanned no more than four-feet across and three-feet deep. Its water reflected light the color of black glass. The ditch separated unpainted camp houses from rail tracks that carried coal-filled hoppers to B&O railcars and out of the valley.

From his perch within Old Oak, Briar observed a life unlike his own. Girls drew squares in the dirt and jumped one after the other from box to box, their pigtails slapping their backs. Boys formed teams and used a board to knock a chunk of coal into the group and try to outrun each other. A mother would call to an older child to get that baby away from the ditch before he drowned himself. Several children would stop their play, lift the toddler and set him back on his camp house porch.

The scenes of families interacting within their small circles, children laughing and chasing each other back and forth through broom-swept yards, mothers patting children on the head and standing in the doorway waiting for their men to come home, all reminded Briar that he did not know the world of play, that his mother was not a hugging mother. Nor had she ever been.

When he tired of watching camp people, Briar took out the knife Tall Corn had given him and carved animals he remembered from his father's gunstock. He started his first piece as a full relief mountain lion, but a slip of the blade forced the carving into a wolf, with ears erect and a wispy tail. Into each finished sculpture, he bored a small hole, inserted a piece of twine, and tied it to one of Old Oak's upper limbs. Over time, if anyone looked close, the tree seemed to be sprouting small animals among its leaves.

On an early June afternoon, voices beneath him drew Briar away from his whittling. He closed his knife and spread flat on the limb, more bobcat than boy. There on the road stood a tall man, his dark hair thick and wavy, and a younger woman, her hair near the color of his mother's, but brighter. She wore her hair much like his mother's, wound into a bun, but it sat on top of her head and was held in place with an intricately carved red and black comb.

"That's it?" the woman asked the man as she surveyed the camp.

Briar looked in the direction she had turned. All looked as it had every day. At Breakline's center sat the company store. A rectangular mercantile with three steps leading to the long porch with one middle door. The back of the building sat flush against the ground, creating a crawl space under the front where dogs spent days away from the sun.

"It's just till we get started, hon." The man placed his hand in the small of her back.

"But, Clint, it's so dirty." She stared down the mountainside. "So dingy."

"But the jobs pay good money."

Briar squinted as if trying to see the camp through her eyes.

"We'll put some money aside and move to Bristol. Like I promised."

"Well, this is sure not Bristol, Clint. It don't even look like a real town." She backed away from the man, and Briar watched her face. Furrows creased her brow as she scrutinized the scene below. "Is that black water down the middle of the camp?" She wiped her forehead with her palm. "I hear the streets of Bristol are paved in long black strips with little pebbles on each side and cars and a three-story hotel at the far end." Her body wavered back and forth. "Even Broken Rock Creek's not black."

"That black is pure gold. Gold spilling out of that tipple over yonder," he said. "Good as that Texas oil you hear about." He reached for her.

She pulled away and sat on a moss-covered rock beside the road and glanced up. For a moment, Briar feared she had seen him. Clint dropped a cardboard suitcase and knelt in front of her.

"Be patient, Anna."

"I'm not going down there," she said. "Covington's better than this." She stared again at the camp. Cows roamed from yard to yard. "At least our cow has her own shed."

"But they ain't jobs in Covington," he argued. "Not none for me."

"This is not what you promised." She hid her face in her arms.

"No need to cry. This is what we got to do for now." The man stood. "So let's get on with it." He lifted the suitcase.

Briar gripped the limb tighter.

"I already set it up for us to have that house at this end of the valley. Look. It's the one set apart from the rest. So you can have your own yard."

"You mean you meant all the time to come here?"

"It worked out that way, Anna. It's what it has to be for now. So get up and let's get to walking before dark catches us up here on this mountainside."

Briar glanced toward the near end of the valley as the two walked down Turtleback. There stood the house, not unlike any other camp house except that it set a good bit farther up the mountainside than those facing the center ditch. Behind it projected a flat rock ledge so white against the dark trees that it looked like a knife scar. All in all, it seemed a much better house than the abandoned church where Briar lived with his mother.

Separating this house from the rest of the camp was Unity Church graveyard, a smattering of graves for the dead with no place to go. Headstones seemed to spill down the mountainside and disappear under the back of Unity Church. He and his mother had never been there. She said Great Spirit would not approve, but Briar wondered.

Briar thought Breakline Camp a bustling place, a city compared to his home on the Carolina mountain where the nearest village was a day's walk away. Now looking at the mining camp through Anna's eyes, he had to agree with the woman. Breakline Camp was not a pretty place.

He hid his knife in a deep notch he had cut into Old Oak's trunk and climbed down as soon as the two were out of sight. He made his way up the road to Flatland where he and his mother stayed. Two Tears would expect him to be there when she returned.

ᐸᐸᐸᐸᐸᐸ

Anna felt judgmental eyes from every direction as she walked through the camp. Damn him. Clint had brought her to live in a long, narrow bowl. He pointed out their square house and left her standing alone while he reported to the commissary. Higher up the mountain, a thick ledge of limestone, much like a scar, cut through the greenery.

Everything around her was black. The road, the dirt, the ditch that separated two rows of houses like the one Clint had claimed for them. She had moved into a world that drew its ugliness from the earth's core.

A few wives walked the road along the ditch. Each carried a cloth bag with handles in one hand and led a child with the other. The women dressed in their droopy sweaters and lace-up shoes appeared so similar that Anna decided they must have agreed on their costumes before leaving their box houses. With her back to the women, she tucked her pillowcase under her arm and crossed the bridge farthest from the tipple. Its rattling and whomping followed her to the bottom of the steps that led up the rise to the house.

Wooden steps from the road's end to the porch made the hill less steep. The steps had one landing but no railing. Perhaps Clint could add rails to keep the walk down less dangerous, especially during winter months. Unless the back of the rise slanted more, she could imagine herself trapped inside. A house lower in the valley would have suited her more.

As she climbed the steps, she realized the house was neither down nor up. It wasn't in the valley. It wasn't up the mountain. Atop a higher rise and behind the commissary was the home of somebody important, a home so tall it reached for the sky. Anna had dreamed of such a home. Perhaps when they moved to Bristol she would have one.

The house had little inside to make it homey. A dirty horsehair sofa sat against the living room wall. Across the room was a cold pot-bellied stove, a cast iron kettle on its eye. The kitchen had a striped skirt gathered across the opening under the sink. A calendar with a picture of hounds across the top hung on the wall. Anna looked closely. It was a year out of date. The kerosene lamp centered on the metal table had a soot-coated chimney that would require hard scrubbing before it could be used.

Nights when Clint worked the hoot owl shift, Anna read by the lamp. Or she reminisced about what she had left behind. When she thought back on her ma and pa, she saw the reality of her mother's life. Hers had been a life of acceptance, a woman's lot. Were Anna to go back to Covington, Ma would tell her that she had made her bed, and now she was to lie in it. She longed to be more like Abraham's Sarai. Sarai made her own decisions. She ran that hussy Hagar and her bastard son off and changed history.

Breakline was not the life she had bargained for. At the time, she knew no more about the bargain than she knew about making bread dough. She had yearned for the change so intently that she twisted the bargain as truly as had Clint. She wanted out of Covington more than she wanted Clint. Misery was not a congenial companion, but he was a steady one.

On a bleak February day, almost a year into her marriage, Anna pounded on the door of the Queen Anne mansion, calling for help. A hard freeze the night before had iced over the camp and sent tree limbs popping through the dark. A scarred woman opened a slight crack and peeped out the door.

"Juanita White. My neighbor." Anna panted and grasped her throat. "Having her baby. Its feet are showing. Awful pain and pushing, but nothing's happening." Anna paused to catch her breath. "Doc Braxton's gone. Over the mountain. Into the next county."

Anna stared at the woman's facial scars and splotched skin. She wanted to ask her for details that might draw them closer together, woman to woman, so the woman would help Juanita, but she did not ask. A flicker of last year's pre-dawn argument with Ruth passed across her memory. A woman's past is a woman's past.

Two Tears glared at her. "Who are you?"

"Anna Goodman. I don't know what to do." Anna wadded her hands into her coat pockets. "Juanita's going to die. Where's Mrs. Rafe?"

"Gone." The woman edged back to close the door.

Anna lifted herself on her tiptoes to see behind the woman, to find Mrs. Rafe. "When will she be back?" The room behind the woman held no light. Anna's eyes widened. "Oh God, Juanita's going to die. What can I do?"

"I will come." She pulled a Cherokee blanket from behind the door and wrapped it around her shoulders. "Get a pint of liquor from the commissary. Tell Gabe it's for birthing." She closed the door behind her.

Gabe Shipley hated opening doors. It reminded him of the day he had returned from Georgia. Whoever it was rattled the door again. He hesitated, then unblocked the lock as a memory from five years earlier swept through his mind.

Gabe's mother opened the commissary door. Jenny Shipley. She entered the commissary with a twelve-year-old Gabe following. Gabe straightened his glasses to peer into the semi-darkness. The place looked empty. He stopped beside his mother and placed his hand on her shoulder.

Her emerald green dress lay smooth under his palm. A satin ribbon attached two peacock feathers to the felt hat she wore. The peacock eyes bothered Gabe. He didn't like being watched. But he had told his mother that she looked beautiful as a princess out to find her prince.

"You're too sweet, honey." She ruffled his hair.

He meant his comment to cut, as she often brought another man into their lives. His mother and her one-track mind missed his ridicule, but he grasped her attempt to dissuade him from what was happening.

"Where you going?" he had asked when he found Jenny trying on the dress.

"To see your father next week," she answered, tugging at the dress waist.

"Where's that?" He scuffed the toe of his shoe against the floor. At twelve, the only memory he had of his father was a tall man who always had a lit cigarette between his first and second fingers.

"Virginia," she said. "It'll be a good trip."

The bus ride from Macon had tired Gabe. His gangly legs refused to fit between the seats. The Georgia sun had saved its highest temperature for this day. Rhythm of rubber tires on uneven asphalt lulled him. Diesel fumes blew in the windows and nausea set in. He dosed off and on until they changed buses in Atlanta.

From Atlanta, they rode to Chattanooga and on to Bristol. Gabe had hoped his mother intended to stay with his father, that they could be a regular family, one without her newest man Lloyd Freeman. Gabe looked out the window at the Bristol Greyhound Bus Station and saw Freeman's white Lincoln. At that moment, he saw that his mother's plan and his were not the same. She didn't have to speak the words. She had made her choice.

Lloyd Freeman offered his hand to Jenny to help her off the bus. "You must be hungry," he said and laughed more than he needed. He bought hamburgers and what he called "co-colas." The cold drink settled Gabe's stomach, but the car ride from Bristol to Breakline Camp, up and down and around the mountains, stirred Gabe's queasiness again. He longed for stable ground.

<hr />

Anna Goodman stood in the cold. Icicles a foot long hung behind her like translucent swords.

"Mrs. Goodman," Gabe said. "You're out mighty early. Sun's not yet over the mountain."

"I need liquor." Anna tugged at the screen. It didn't open.

"Commissary ain't open yet. Give us a bit." The panic on the woman's face made Gabe release the screen.

"I got to have it now. The woman up the house on the hill wants it. Juanita White's baby ain't coming right." She twisted her hands and poked them into her coat pockets. "I ain't got money. You'll have to do what you do to take care of it, but I got to have the liquor." She stepped toward the doorway. The sun announced itself over the mountaintop with stark shafts of light.

"I can't let you in, Mrs. Goodman. Mr. Rafe's rules and all, but I'll get you a pint of shine. Wait here." He closed the door and disappeared into the store. When he opened the door again, he had a pint jar of clear liquid in his hand. "Don't you be telling nobody where you got this. Mr. Rafe don't know. He don't approve. If his miners need to get drunk, he wants them drunk in Covington at O'Mary's Bar." He ran his hand through his red hair as his childhood memories continued to shadow his thoughts.

‹‹‹‹‹‹‹‹

A tall, slim man dressed in a starched white shirt and grey slacks came out of the commissary's back office.

"What're you doing here?" The man lit a Lucky Strike and shook out the match. Smoke breathed out his nostrils.

Gabe, taller than his mother and thinner, moved forward. So. This was his father.

Rafe put on a slack-jawed grin at the sight of his son. "You got your mama's hair, boy," Rafe said. The cigarette bobbed in the corner of his mouth as he spoke. He offered his hand. "Been a long time."

Gabe ignored the invitation and pushed his glasses up his nose with his index finger. He stuck his chin out. He didn't give his mother a chance to dump him. He took the initiative on his own. "I'm here to stay. Ma's new man says he won't feed no other man's kid. She had to pick and she picked him."

"Now, Gabe, that's not how it is." Jenny patted her green felt hat tighter on her red hair. "It's that. . ."

"Want a dope, Jenny?" Rafe asked. "You look all dried out." He lifted the cooler lid and popped the metal cap off an orange Nehi. The metal clinked when it landed in the cap reservoir.

Jenny shot Rafe a flash of anger. "No. You got to understand. All these years..."

Winston pushed the drink into Jenny's hand. "Swallow. Better swallow, Jenny. You look pale." He motioned toward an overturned barrel. "Sit down over here."

"Quit telling me what to do. You got to see..."

"I see you rode up here from South Georgia to tell me something you could've sent in a three-cent letter. Now take another swallow."

Air bubbles inside the orange drink disappeared into his mother's mouth. Gabe watched his mother's throat constrict as they went down. Water droplets from the melting block of cooler ice slid down the bottle and onto her arm. He licked his lips.

"Gabe's right," Jenny said. "He is here to stay. You chased everything in a skirt and left me to raise him. I got him this far. Now you can do your..."

"Jenny. Jenny. Jenny. You don't understand. I got three mines to run here. I can't take on a half-grown kid." He turned to Gabe. "How old are you anyway?"

Gabe hesitated. His mouth was so dry he wasn't sure he could speak.

"Answer the man," Jenny said.

"Twelve," Gabe muttered.

Rafe's left eye-brow dropped.

"Do with him what you will. His belongings and them dogged books of his are on the porch." Jenny walked outside and waited by the car's passenger door for Lloyd to open it.

Freeman tipped his Panama hat to Rafe and grinned.

"Moving up in the world," Rafe called to Jenny.

"That's Lloyd. Lloyd Freeman," Gabe said to Rafe's back.

Jenny's answer was a slammed door. Freeman cranked the car, turned it around, and headed up Turtleback.

ᶜᶜᶜᶜᶜᵤᵤ

The sun over the mountain brought no heat. Cold air made Anna shake. She took the jar from Gabe. She tightened the lid and slid it into her pocket. "I'll hold your secret. Don't you worry none." She grasped the post that supported the roof. "Why don't you go back in and get some more sleep."

ᶜᶜᶜᶜᶜᵤᵤ

"You can sleep in the office," Rafe said as he ground his un-smoked Lucky Strike into the floor. "I'll get you some bedding," he said, turning to walk away. "Then I'll decide how I explain you to my wife."

Gabe waited until he heard the back door close. He crept to the cooler, took out a grape Nehi. He favored its sting over the co-cola's sweet. He popped it open and stepped out the door. He pushed his clothes aside and searched through his box of books until he found *The Grapes of Wrath*. He

50

opened the dog–eared copy to chapter seventeen and plopped down on the overturned barrel. He took a deep swig and felt the tension he had not realized had stiffened his back slowly recede.

In chapter seventeen the migrants are moving west to the "Promised Land." When he had stopped reading on the bus, Gabe reflected on his ride through the Appalachians. These mountains didn't look much like a promised land, but they would have to do.

‹‹‹‹‹‹‹

When Gabe looked back, Anna had stepped off the porch. She walked a fast trot toward the mountainside.

Anna slid on ice when she hit Juanita's porch. She slapped her hand against the liquor to hold it steady and opened the door without a knock. In the middle of the room, Two Tears was spinning, her colorful shirt spread out like a rainbow around her feet. She had removed her shoes and stripped Juanita of her muslin sheet.

Juanita lay naked on the bed, the child within her belly pushing against her skin so strong that Anna could see its head appear here, then there. Juanita no longer moaned.

Anna edged to the table under the window and put the liquor down. She eased toward Two Tears and reached out to catch the woman in her circling. Two Tears did not see Anna, for she had thrown back her head and closed her eyes. What sounded like a rippling intoning kept the room from being starkly silent.

On the third try, Anna grasped Two Tears' sleeve and stopped the spin. She expected the woman to drop from her dizziness, but she stood still as a tree. "I got the liquor," Anna said.

For a moment, Anna thought Two Tears had no idea that Anna was standing before her. Anna stepped aside for Two Tears to pass. With Anna's movement, light returned to Two Tears' eyes. Two Tears opened the bottle and drank heavily from the brown liquid. She recapped the bottle and set it aside.

"Get the butcher knife," Two Tears said.

Anna took a knife from the kitchen cabinet and handed it handle first to Two Tears. Two Tears slid the knife under the mattress and brought a bucket of steaming water from the stove.

"Get here on her bosom and when I say so, push this baby out."

"No. I might..." Anna stepped back.

Two Tears yanked Anna's arm and splayed out Anna's hands. She slapped them against Juanita's upper belly and said, "Push."

Anna climbed up on the bed and squatted over Juanita's chest. Her heart beat so fast she felt faint. She pushed. Juanita screamed. Anna's wrists, cramping under the intensity, sent rays of pain up her arm. She refused to look at what Two Tears was doing. Each time the woman said push, Anna strained and forced her hands against Juanita's belly. She smelled the sweet scent of fresh blood. She concentrated on blocking out Juanita's screams. In less than an hour, a baby's squeal against his entrance into bitter mountain air told Anna Two Tears had done her job. Shaking and exhausted, Anna dropped to the floor.

Juanita was bleeding heavy. Her blood dripped from the sheet to the floor. Two Tears stuffed cotton stripping to slow the hemorrhage. The baby wailed his displeasure at being forced to stand on his head and drop into the world naked and hungry. Two Tears stepped into the kitchen and made him a sugar tit to stave off his hunger until his mother could nurse.

A young boy, Anna guessed to be about thirteen or fourteen years old, appeared at the door. "I heard a baby," he said. He looked at the flushed baby, his mouth agape.

"This is no place for a boy," Two Tears said. She turned her back, washing Juanita's arms.

"My God," Anna said, her eyebrows raised. "You're a granny."

"I'm...I'm a Beloved Mother," she said. "I'm Cherokee."

The black-haired boy stepped up behind Two Tears.

Two Tears continued Juanita's bath. "She don't need to be having no more babies."

The boy tugged at his mother's shirt. "But, Ma," he said.

Two Tears yanked his hand away and squeezed it so hard he flinched. "Hand me that liquor from over there, boy," she said.

Anna crinkled her nose at the strong odor. The granny drank and lowered the bottle, now empty.

Within two days, word had spread through the mining camp that Mrs. Rafe's cleaning woman could midwife. Rumors flew high and fast, high enough to reach a woman of Gladys Rafe's stature. As soon as she heard Two Tears had birthed a camp woman's baby while she should have been working on the Rafe's dime, Gladys Rafe fired her.

Over time, the camp doctor's baby business slowed because never did she lose a baby. In whisperings around kitchen tables, women also admitted that she never refused a woman who wanted or needed to drop a baby.

Women now found Two Tears in the abandoned church at Flatland, a grassy bald spot atop the more prominent summit of Turtleback between Breakline and Covington. Women came up Turtleback for a dropping under cover of night. The boy Briar would vanish into the darkness. He re-appeared the next morning, as if he could sense the absence of strangers.

On Flatland, the granny farmed bees from the hive she had found in the chimney when she and Briar first moved into the old church. She captured the queen and set up a hive near the edge of a clearing that led off the mountain. The capture of more queens and transfer of their swarms meant she and the boy could farm honey easy enough. Days she would sit alongside the B&O tracks on the western edge of Covington or out past Unity Cemetery. Women waited to buy her prized *wadulesi*, what Granny Slocomb called her honey. She bargained at the camp commissary with the manager, Gabe Shipley, to have her own shelves. These she kept filled with her *wadulesi*, with and without comb, by season.

At twenty-eight, Granny gardened her own herbs and plants and went monthly into Breakline and Covington to sell her cures and potions. Many an unfaithful husband lay moaning alone in his marriage bed after his wife visited Granny Slocomb. Her most powerful spells she never sold but administered herself.

Neither town nor camp had ever asked where she came from or who she was. Had they asked, they would have received no answer. She, who had once been Mona Parsons, then Mona Parsons Slocomb to hide her shame, now chose to be the mountain granny. Granny Slocomb fit her as fine as being Two Tears had when she lived with Tall Corn in the Carolinas. Circumstances had forced a new identity, and circumstances might force it again.

Chapter 7

By 1940, Anna Goodman, almost nineteen, had grown into a tall, girl-ish woman. A woman steeped in plain, her only jewelry a wide gold band Clint put on her finger a month after they moved into Breakline Mining Camp. Her square face was not unpretty. It was a face that sat solid on her shoulders. Her blue, blue eyes looked out from beneath pale brows. She brushed her hair up and wound it into a loose yellowish knot. She still attached the bun to the crown of her head with her mother's tortoise-shell comb. Fine and silky, her hair escaped its bonds with every movement of her head. She constantly tried to capture its restlessness by pushing a strand behind an ear or wrapping one around the comb. By nightfall and bedtime, she had to dig through the tangles to find the buried comb and unwind her hair from its teeth.

Anna came to think of Clint's promise of Bristol like his comment about Ruth's fried eggs and sausage, something she had expanded in her imagination. Clint argued Breakline Camp was where they needed to be. Working underground paid good money. The well-stocked commissary gave Anna no reason to wander out of the valley. Sure, the dirt was black, but had she ever seen dirt any color but black? Bristol lay in the mountains, in its own way, so she still would have been in the mountains. And these

Virginia mountains put out coal better than a cow gave milk. She had a husband, and a husband's a husband no matter his calling. To question a husband's thinking was, for Clint, a slap against his say-so.

Anna, up since before dawn, stood at the kitchen table and packed Clint's lunch bucket with two Spam sandwiches and a baked sweet potato. Last night when she had gone to bed, Clint told her again that she had no weight in deciding where they would live or where he would work. She awoke with his words still on her mind.

Clint entered the kitchen and reached for his tin bucket, a round topped container that looked more like a loaf of bread than a lunch bucket.

Anna put her hand on the lunch pail. "You not eating breakfast?" she said. "I made you eggs and grits. Or I got cornbread and milk."

Clint picked up his lunch and opened the kitchen door. "No. I got work to do." He shut the door against an unusually brisk air. "You think on it today, Anna. We are where we are and that's it. That daydreaming you been doing? It's over."

Anna took the plate of eggs and grits from the stove warmer. She walked to the sink and threw eggs, grits and plate hard against the metal sink wall. The plate broke. One piece popped out and hit the floor. Clint jerked away to avoid the flying crockery.

The day ahead promised nothing for Anna. Nor had any previous days. The previous night's anger reignited, and she glared at him. "You might rule what I say, but you can't rule what I think."

Clint whirled around and pushed her back against the square, porcelain-topped metal table. It stood so steady against the wall that Anna, rather than the table, fell. Clint knelt over her crumpled on the flowered linoleum rug and let his bucket drop beside her. "Anna. My Anna. I never meant..."

"Go on to work, Clint." Anna set her head against him. "I'm not ready to talk to you yet."

"Anna?"

"Just go and leave me alone." She waved him back with one hand.

Clint left, his back bowed as if he crawled through shadowy tunnels.

As soon as she could lift herself off the floor, Anna wandered up the rise behind their frame house. Her back throbbed from the lick she had taken when she hit the table. She hadn't eaten breakfast, and as she climbed her legs weakened. At a wooded thicket, she dropped onto leaves moist from the morning frost and shivered as she pulled her sweater close. She glared up, past the uppermost limbs and stared at the rising sun until tears burned her eyes. Her sorrow was so deep she could not rise up against the grief. Drained, she crawled to a rock ledge and dangled her feet over the edge. Seeing nothing worthy of her attention, she lay down to rest.

She awoke mid-afternoon. Though she did not see eyes, she felt them. They were there. Or they had been there. The cords in her neck tightened. She studied the camp below nestled in its long valley and let her eyes follow the road that led up Turtleback and out of the mining camp. She tilted her head to see what or whom she had felt. There was nothing out of the ordinary, just a pearly light emanating from the sun.

Sister Sun has watched Anna since she left the house. She has watched her throughout days as she sits immobile on the front porch. She considers talking to Great Spirit about the possibility of one of his own who is burning from the inside out. A flicker of Anna's resentment has shown itself to Sister Sun. She knows it will flame. The anger Anna harbors within fuels her bitterness more each day. But Brother Moon tells her that her job is to follow the path of Great Spirit, not to direct his route. So Sister Sun waits.

Anna and Clint had run out of things to talk about by their third year. Clint told the story of how his mining father, his back rounded from walking crouched through low-ceilinged tunnels, had the appearance of a large mole. As a youngster, Clint had rubbed his father's legs to ease cramps from toe-walking with knees bent as his father hunched on his calves and shuffled deeper into the earth. In time, his father lay before the fireplace coughing out his black lung until the disease refused him another breath of clean air and shut his lungs down for good.

His father had been what Clint thought a father should be. He had provided a house, food and clothing for his wife and children. Clint, like his father, accepted that forces beyond his control altered lives, no matter how men fought against them. With the slow, smothering death of his father, Clint saw no reason to fight. His father had lost. Why would his life be any different?

He spoke of his half-Cherokee mother and her isolation by the camp wives and of two babies, a brother and a sister, lost to summer flux. "Honest folk," he said. "Good honest people. Just had no luck. No luck a'tall."

It took Anna more nights of memory and talk, for she could dig into several generations of history before reaching her own. She told how her great-great grandfather, this Uriah Parsons, had come from his time with General Washington and crossed the ice-bound river at Trenton.

Parsons came with frostbitten toes, without two left fingers that had been shot off by a Redcoat during an ambush in Pennsylvania. He came with Long Hunters who moved like a slender, black snake over mountains that first appeared low in the distance but proved deceitful when reached. Mountains' posturing insinuated an outstretched welcome for strangers but beat men down with ravines and wild beasts and unpredictable weather. Other mountains appeared to bow before this majestic Turtleback, deceptive mountains that hid their power beneath the virgin forests.

Anna spoke of deeds, signed and certified by all the right pens, verifying that her family owned all of the huge Turtleback and to the mountainside homestead Uriah called Boone Station. Acres of land. Tens of thousands of acres deeded by the Governor of the Virginia Colony, given free to whoever would settle west. She spoke of ancestors buried at Flatland on the top of Turtleback and how Uriah Parsons' son set the stakes for the town of Covington. How she grew up with whatever she favored in the dark, two-story, limestone blockhouse that closed the end of the road through the town.

Clint's eyes grew smaller with her telling. He had little history to bring to the table. What history he had paled before Anna's listings of heroics and fame. He did not believe her. His sense of who he was shouted out at her over the supper table after she put food before him. "You slighting my family with all your explorers and founders and such?" He pushed his plate of poke sallet and peas aside and stared over his coffee as it grew cold.

"No," Anna said. "You asked. I'm telling."

"I ain't got no famous folk in my lineage. I guess that makes you more important than me, huh? I guess that explains why you're so set on moving to a big city like Bristol." Clint looked down at his coal-encrusted hands. They looked like the dirty hands of a twelve-year-old girl.

"I am not, Clint. You going into the belly of the earth day after day is eating you inside. You don't ever see sunlight. You live in a black, cold world that you expect me to like. I can't. I need sunshine inside me. There ain't no sun in this place till day's half gone." As she left the room, she said, "I want to go home." In the next room, she plopped down on the edge of the bed. If she had to tell Clint what she needed, it didn't count.

"Ain't nobody at home that'll take you back, Anna," Clint said. "You burned that bridge when you come away with me. You know that."

When Clint spit out such hurtful words, Anna wondered where the Clint who had enthralled her had gone. He had joked and mussed her hair when she laughed as she sat on the front porch to chaperone him and Ruth. He had brought her a fistful of wild roses once, not as large as the one he brought Ruth, but big enough to make her smile. The old Clint had disappeared without her notice. Now that he was gone, Anna was not sure she loved this dark, moody man who insisted on bossing her. She was not even sure she liked him anymore.

Mornings after an argument, Anna would sit at her kitchen table, ready to write Ruth to ask for forgiveness. She should have left Clint to Ruth, but she lacked the courage to acknowledge that what she had thought was love was petty jealousy. As her pa often said, "Just leave sleeping dogs lie." She never took pen to paper. Someone might mention to Clint that she had written a letter home. He would not approve.

◄◄◄◄◄◄◄◄►►

It had happened the February Clint was ten years old. The day had been overcast. The wind, bitter. Rain had threatened all day. He spent the afternoon brushing his grandfather's mule and cleaning its stall, so dark crept upon him unawares. He knew he should be home before his father came from work at six o'clock, so he left his grandparents' farm before supper. To get home on time, he took the shortcut across the stubbled cornfield.

Midway through the trek, slow icy rain changed to a steady downpour. Clint pulled his woolen coat over his head, leaving enough room for him to see and retrace the path. At one point, the rain stopped. From his left, he heard a whimper. Leaving the trail, he picked his way over corn stobs and found a young pup huddled against a dead corn plant. He lifted the pup from the mud and tucked it into his coat. The closeness of Clint's body eased the pup's shivering, and it relaxed.

At home, he took the pup out and looked at it. Its ribs pushed themselves out of its chest. He ran his hand over its coat. Mange had taken large patches of fur away, leaving its skin scratched and bloody. His father could fix that with a bath of sulfur and motor oil. The pup's nose, dry to Clint's touch, was runny and hard. When it coughed, its lungs pumped against its chest. He could give it some of the tonic his mother bought at the commissary for his colds.

He offered the pup a biscuit. It refused to eat. A saucer of milk. The dog refused to lap. He wrapped the pup in a ragged, plaid flannel shirt and laid it on the floor by the coal heater. He sat beside the pup and stroked its side until it slept.

His father said, "You needn't bother. Death's done got to it. Best you put it out and let it die in peace."

"I ain't going to let it die," Clint said.

In the kitchen, fatback sizzled and popped in the skillet. The odor of grease gnawed at Clint's belly, but the dog did not respond to it. His mother called Clint to the supper table. He said he wasn't hungry. "I'll wait here for my puppy to wake up." Clint stayed by the dog as dark drew on. Outside sleet ting, ting, tinged on the tin roof.

Throughout the night, whenever Clint's head nodded, he jerked himself awake. Each time he checked to see that he had not moved his palm from the dog's side. If he kept his hand firm against the pup's body, a part of him would transfer itself to the dog. He would will the dog to live, even if in so doing he lost a part of himself.

The puppy stopped breathing just before dawn. With his hand on its chest, Clint knew when its last breath came. He wrapped the dead puppy in his own flannel blanket and cradled it under his chin, too hurt to cry.

His father rose before daylight to go into the mine for the day. He took the wrapped pup from Clint. It was then Clint let himself cry. He had no control over whatever force his puppy had encountered before Clint's attempt at salvation. He had no control now. He did not ask what was going to happen. The puppy would be buried, or more likely, thrown in the fifty-gallon barrel where his daddy burned trash. The puppy was gone. With it went Clint's conviction that he had some power over life. That much he knew. That much he grieved.

Chapter 8

Winston Rafe had spent every day for the past three years opening Big Mama #2, east of Covington. He put Seth White in charge of Breakline #3 and took a boarding house room with Widow Clara Beauchamp in Covington. With the economy what it was, there were few turnovers, so Rafe knew most of the camp, if not by name then by face. But he had little knowledge about those Seth White hired during his absence.

Now that Big Mama #2 was producing, Rafe had returned to Breakline. He was signing pay vouchers when Anna Goodman stepped into the commissary. He overheard her speak to Gabe Shipley, as softly as a mother cat soothes her kitten.

"I need lard for a balm," she said to Gabe. "As fresh as you got."

"Got some in yesterday," Gabe said. "How much you want?"

"Can I get a cup? My husband's cut his hand real bad working the garden."

Rafe stepped from behind the barred window that served as the company bank to see who the woman was. He prided himself in knowing all his miners' names, as well as those of their families. Breakline Camp was his town to own. This voice he did not recognize. Rafe moved closer to where she stood. He wondered who her man was.

Rafe knew his commissary stock as well as he knew his own breath. He recognized by her blue and white striped dress that both pattern and cloth had been bought from him. Unadorned with lace or frill, she had to be wife to one of his miners. And her plain gold wedding band had been bought by an underground worker who saved up for special gifts. Rafe sold similar rings from behind the counter for twenty-five dollars, almost the cost of a month's worth of food. When a gallon of gas ran eleven cents and miners drew only a hundred dollars a month, to spend so much on a woman's gold ring said the man must truly value her.

This new woman captivated Rafe. This girl-woman, unlike his wife, Gladys, who insisted on a string of pearls around her neck at breakfast to accent her ankle-length satin robes, needed no ornaments to set her apart. He perceived a sense of raw passion tied down by frustration and self-control. She would be a prize. She reminded him of soft bread dough his mother kneaded for him and his father as she slapped it back and forth on her cutting board. His mother would allow him to stroke the dough, to smooth it out. He wanted to touch her in the same way, to pull the heavy tortoise-shell comb from her golden hair and watch it drop down her back.

He walked up behind her close enough for her to surely be able to smell him. As a gentleman, he kept himself soaped and rinsed on a daily basis, and he prided himself on the spicy pomade in his hair. He noticed her spine stiffen with awareness.

"I'm Winston," he said, his voice low and soft. "Winston Rafe." He stepped from behind her and extended his hand. For a man his size, he used up a great deal of space, leaving little room for others.

She glanced around the commissary, scanning canned beans, tinned baking powder, stacks of flour, bolts of cloth. Not looking at him.

He moved close enough to smell freshly ironed Argo starch in her dress. When she took his hand, he placed his other over hers.

Gabe Shipley walked away toward where the lard was stored in a ceramic tub, his jaw set against Rafe's behavior.

"Anna Goodman," she answered. "Clint Goodman's wife."

The movement of her fingers told him a vacant space resided in her life, though she did not know where or what it was. He chose to decide that she had not experienced true pleasure between a man and a woman. With him, she might be open to his life-giving force.

She quivered. He would need to convince her that their sexual union would prevent them from the sin of lust. It had worked before.

Overhead, a cloud passes before Sister Sun. She sizzles out to Brother Moon. "Come see this." She laughs at the electricity passing between the two. "They could ignite the Northern lights on a bitter winter night."
Brother Moon ignores her. Her constant snooping aggravates him.

61

Winston Rafe was not always the gallant man. A constant smoker, his fingers were tinged with Lucky Strike nicotine—a cigarette he had chosen for its name rather than its flavor. When he first met Gladys Breakline, he knew he had struck a life of security and success. Ends he would never have attained with his first wife, Jenny, Gabe's mother. Early on, he had met few of his life goals, though he would argue that he had truly worked for them when, in truth, every boss he had ever had labeled him lazy.

Rafe had met Gladys Breakline outside Bristol while he was clerking at the general merchandise. It would be the store he would use as a model for his commissary a few years down the road. When she entered, he steepled his fingers and decided that a woman wrapped in a fox boa could add much to his long-range plans.

Never having had many suitors, Gladys married easy. She set her head on having this man fifteen years her senior. Her father, as Rafe had intended, took him into the mining business. What Rafe had not expected was that Ed Breakline would box the two up, command Rafe to take a degree in mining engineering, and send them to Blacksburg, Virginia. His plan, as contrived as Rafe's, meant that his only child would not be without her affluent lifestyle when he died.

Rafe flourished at Virginia Polytechnic Institute in Blacksburg, Virginia. He discovered he loved the geology of the land, the organization the work required, and the power he felt as he rose to the top of his class. His marriage to Gladys became one more step on his trek to becoming ruler of his own small domain.

The couple moved to Breakline Mining Camp. Ed Breakline, ever conscious of appearances and the supervisor's place in society, paid for building and furnishing a grand Queen Anne home on the highest point overlooking the workers' clapboard houses. Rafe's plans were locked in place the day Gladys' father collapsed from a stroke at the entrance to Big Mama #2 east of Covington. The old man had dropped at "The Downer," a mine opening so called for its steep slope into Spencer's Mountain. Rafe later chuckled when he thought about the location.

Ed Breakline had come from Bristol to inspect the three mines he owned. All seemed well until he had lunch with Gladys and returned to Big Mama #2. He left his car running, got out and approached Rafe. "I mean to talk to you, boy," he said, his stark white face explosive as he spit out his words. "Come in this office. You got a few questions to answer to."

Rafe knew the rife would be about some camp woman. It always was.

Ed stumbled on the first tread of the wooden step and collapsed. His face turned a purplish-blue.

"Get the doc!" Rafe called out to anyone within hearing distance. He looked at his father-in-law's face, now drawn so far down on the left side that his eye squeezed shut. Ed tried to speak, but he could only mumble. Rafe glanced around to see if anyone had noticed that Ed no longer had a voice. Every miner in the area, except Seth White, Juanita's husband, had run toward the doctor's house.

Doc Braxton arrived, and Rafe spoke for Ed. "He says he wants to go to the hospital in Bristol. Can he make it that far?"

Knowing he should not be hearing this, Seth White stepped back from Rafe's line of vision and stuck his left hand in his pocket. He jammed his hand deeper into his pants in frustration as he watched Ed struggle to shake his head, but Ed could only blink his left eye.

"I want you to be my witness here, Doc. He said that I'm superintendent over all the mines until he gets well."

"That what you want, Ed?" Doc asked.

"He can't talk now," Rafe said. Seth White moved a step further back, toward the mouth of the mine.

Again, Ed could only blink.

That afternoon, Winston Rafe, son-in-law and only male heir, walked away from the mouth of #2, curly, dark-haired, head held high. He took to wearing a tie so miners would perceive him as a superintendent, rather than another boss. His father-in-law, bedbound in Bristol and paralyzed from the neck down, would never speak again. Winston Rafe felt as secure in his ability to run Breakline Mining Company as he did in manipulating his camp women.

What he had not anticipated were the erratic moods Gladys shifted into with no warning, even before her father's stroke. Unlike Gabe's mother, her anger could often be lessened with a two or three-day shopping trip to Bristol. She would return, the car filled with clothes she would hang in the closet and never wear.

Like Ed Breakline, appearance mattered to Rafe. He perceived himself to be a man of prominence. With appearance came authority. Appearance was what led Rafe never to acknowledge Gabe Shipley as his son. A man whose wife found him too vile to live with was not a man at all. A real man could hold his woman as easy as he held his liquor. He had perfected his words and moves to the point that no one knew his truth from his lies, not even he. He looked in the mirror each morning, and the attractive man, never the rogue, looked back.

Gabe dropped a gallon bucket of lard on the counter. "Smallest we got," he said. "Keep it cool and it won't go bad before you use it up."

Rafe walked Anna to the commissary porch, carrying her bucket of lard by its handle in one hand and directing her elbow with the other. When they reached the wooden steps, Rafe leaned near and spoke. "You are without doubt the most beautiful woman in this camp." He looked at her and almost smiled.

Anna blushed and took a cautious look around. "Thank you, Mr. Rafe," she stammered. Her hand shook as she took her bucket of lard. She did not look at Rafe; instead, she marched herself home and locked her front door.

Both flattered and terrified by Rafe's interest, Anna sat at her kitchen table. Bowing to this man's attention would bring the Wrath of God down upon her. Infidelity with any man, especially her husband's boss, could send the rock of Commandments down on her head, shattering like shards of glass. Her God did not tolerate the sins of His people. She, like Eve, bore the burden of sparking the flame that would send her into a burning hell. She considered a drink of Clint's moonshine hidden behind his can of tools on a shelf near the kitchen flue, but he would miss it. She tried one of Clint's Camels, but her hand quivered so hard she could not light the cigarette. She paced the floor until, when darkness fell, she opened a can of beans and baked a pone of cornbread for Clint.

After their meal, Anna approached the idea of moving to Bristol again.

"I'm drawing a dollar a day as it is, and Mr. Rafe lets me work as many shifts as I want. I'm not going to Bristol to work in no cow-piss factory making the same thing day after day," Clint argued. "Not going to one of them plants in Kingsport neither. Just get that craziness out of your head."

Chapter 9

Three months after she bought the lard, Anna slipped off her wedding ring and put it in the dresser drawer for safekeeping. If she wore it with Rafe near, and if he looked at it, the ring might meld his reflection into the gold. "You belong to me," Rafe had once whispered to her outside the commissary. The idea had set itself so deep that Anna saw Rafe's face every time she looked at her wedding band. She feared that one evening, in the gloaming, Rafe's face would appear in the ring across the table from Clint, and Clint would know.

She closed the back door and walked through moonlight, up the mountainside where she sometimes went to escape the house. She expected Rafe would be there. A nod here and a seemingly innocuous comment there let each of them know when and where to meet.

No argument with Clint sent her. Loneliness opened the back door, and Anna walked out. She wished Clint had a mistress. She could contest another woman, but she had no idea how to cope with the black maw he entered every night.

The cry of train whistles reminded her they were going somewhere she could not go. Whistles told her repeatedly that she was trapped by the regularity of living by a clock that ran, not by minutes and hours, but by coal and its constant rumbling out of the ground beneath her. She found herself housebound by a way of life she had never bargained for. Many days she waited for the ground to open to a mined-out tunnel and swallow her without anyone's notice.

A narrow path led through a Virginia pine thicket below the tree line. The thicket's treetops were heavy with needles, needles so full that, from Anna's back door, they gave the illusion of softness. The higher she climbed toward the ledge the less her common sense dragged her down. Once she reached the ledge, she kicked free what little had managed to trail her and sent it tumbling back down the path.

There on a rock ledge above the camp, she found with Rafe the simple grace she was missing in her marriage to Clint. That one trip led to the next and the next to the next. Anna found herself preparing each day of each week for her next Tuesday night when she would come home to bathe off the smell of crushed moss and tender ground.

After a month of meetings, Anna whispered to Rafe, "Somebody followed me," she panted. "Up the rise."

Rafe chuckled.

"I heard steps. On leaves," she insisted. "I could feel somebody watching."

"Nobody knows this place," Rafe said. "Unless you talked."

"It's like hands want to reach out from the underbrush and drag me into the briars," Anna said. "Not just coming up here tonight." Anna chewed the inside of her cheek. "I dream dreams," she continued. "The wives, they chase me and I run and they run faster and I can't breathe and they run faster and faster. This woman in a pink striped apron has a butcher knife, waving it in the air and one catches me by the ankle and I fall on my face and my nose bleeds. All at once I know I have black, black eyes. And though they don't turn me over, I recognize they are huge gray wolves and their claws get tangled in my hair and pull it out in big clumps and they slobber on me and I'm crying."

"Stop it, Anna," Rafe said as he reached for her. "Don't do this to yourself."

"But my hair is all over the ground and I can see it though I'm on my face. I pray to God to save me, and he says, 'that's not the question,' and I say, 'what's the question?' and he says, 'that's not the question.' And I don't know the question so he won't save me, and I wake up crying and Clint wants to know what's wrong, and I can't say the words to him."

"You're imagining things," Rafe told her.

"I ruined our night. I'm sorry." Anna hung her head. "You're the only one I can talk to."

"Don't be sorry. Here, I'll walk around to see if anybody's been here."

"No. Don't leave me." She reached to pull him back.

"I'll be back. I'll always be back," Rafe assured her. "Nobody who knows me would dare question where I go or why. Stay put." He returned after finding no one.

Anna believed him. She wanted to believe that she mattered to Winston Rafe in some significant way. She needed to believe he would protect her. From Tuesday until Tuesday, she made up a life that didn't exist.

By winter, a thin crack appeared in her fantasy. Anna felt the fracture deep within her gut.

In February, she came late to the rock ledge, carrying a rolled blanket. A pink dusk had slipped behind Turtleback, and the moon had yet to come out. The sky had a blackness about it that only appeared with an oncoming storm or the absence of both sun and moon.

Rafe stiffened his back when she touched him. "Where've you been?" he said.

She spread the blanket on the ledge and sat. She shuttered as she unbuttoned her dress. "Something cold in the air tonight." She slid across the blanket. Rafe did not chuckle. A problem at one of the mines, she assumed, and lifted off her dress.

"We got to talk," he said. "Sit down."

When Anna did not move, he took up the dress, lifted her off the blanket, and pulled the dress back over her head, tearing down her hair. He forced her arms into the sleeves.

Buttoning her bodice, Anna stepped away. "What's wrong with you?"

"I expect people to do what I say. That's all. Sit down."

Anna sat.

Winston lit a Lucky Strike. Its tip glowed red in the dark. Anna wanted to question someone seeing the glow, but she chewed the inside of her lip and said nothing.

"I've been thinking and it's only fair you know." He paused, as if giving Anna time to ask what he had been thinking about. "If there's a baby, I can't help you." His words spilled out in one breath. "So that's about it."

Anna stared out at the camp houses below. In the distance, only one had a light burning. Perhaps a sick child. She would never know. Wives of the camp had begun to ignore her. Her days had grown dim, even in the brightest sunlight.

The present darkness over the world around her slipped down and blackened the camp, leaving it bleak and still. Take away the tipple at the far end of the valley, silence its rhythmic, mechanical sound, and there would be no one left but Winston and Anna and one tiny yellow glow from a camp house window.

Once Rafe began his speech, he couldn't stop. "If there's a kid, you'll have to convince Clint the baby's his. I might be able to get you money from time to time, but I can't recognize a kid." He took a long draw on his cigarette. A cylinder of ash fell to the ground. "Gladys rightly owns these mines. She'd divorce me, and there goes the mines and I'm out on my ass."

After a moment, Anna spoke. "I know that," she said. "I can make it on my own. The problem will be getting Clint home long enough to think he's making a baby." She tried a chuckle and failed. "What with him working double shifts and all."

"You'll have to do it. That's all." Rafe blew cigarette smoke out his nose.

"I'll do what I can." She clamped her hands together.

"You'll do it," Rafe stood up. "Or you'll have to see a granny." He walked back down the mountain.

Someone in the little house below turned off the light.

> *By the time Brother Moon comes into view, Anna sits alone on the ledge. He smells the scent of soft moss she has pulled from the ground. She places narrow rectangles side-by-side in a straight row, as if planting them, as if she expects them to grow on rock. He will need to ask Sister Sun if moss grows on hard rock. He does not understand daylight dealings. He can't even help her down the mountain.*

The fourth April of their affair arrived, and Anna had not bled for two months. She could not say if she felt happy or sad. She wanted Winston's child—more than she wanted Clint's. Yet the idea of birthing another man's child frightened her. Winston's threat haunted her during the days and kept sleep away in the nights.

Every miner's wife had tales of how domineering Winston's wife was. How he spent his days at the commissary and his nights checking the mines or drinking beer out of self-preservation in O'Mary's Saloon in Covington. Anna wished there was a different bar in Covington, one where miners didn't go. She feared a wife would let a comment slip or a husband would get so drunk he would speak out in front of Winston and a miner would lose his job. That would lead to whispers and questions throughout the camp. She had to convince herself that wives did not know where he was every Tuesday night. Assuming they did know, worries of job security might keep them from talking.

The wives knew Winston Rafe was a tyrant. Most of the wives avoided him. Like a cancer, he could eat an individual from inside out, leaving a shell before the man knew he was infested. The company was the town.

The company put bread on the table. With the Great Depression killing any possibility of moving to another company, Anna counted on wives shutting their eyes and speaking only behind closed curtains. They were bound to the mine as tightly as were their men.

Anna had to tell Winston she was pregnant. She waited on the ledge for him to show. He appeared after the moon rose. She took a deep breath and told him. His response was what he had promised. "There's a Cherokee granny at Flatland on the Turtleback." He lit a cigarette. "She knows what she's doing. She knows to keep her mouth shut." He took a deep draw and swallowed the smoke. "I'll bring money next Tuesday." He reacted as if he were handling some off-hand business deal with a stranger, one that would have little bearing on his future or the future of the company.

Anna slapped him hard, hard enough to twist his head. "You bastard," she said.

Winston grabbed her wrist and squeezed it. The next morning there would be bruised fingerprints on the underside. She would wear a long-sleeved dress for a week so Clint could not see.

"Anna."

She tried to pull her wrist away.

"I can't claim this baby. Gladys would have a fighting fit." He released his grip and rubbed her wrist. "We've talked all this out. If you won't go to Granny Slocomb, you'll have to convince Clint this is his baby." Winston released Anna's arm and palmed his forehead. Anna could tell he was angrier at himself than at her. He had let this slip. He had always been more careful.

"It's because I'm a miner's wife," Anna shot her words through tight lips.

"Damn it, Anna. It's because you are a *wife*. Wife of one of my best men. Clint Goodman's wife." He clinched his fists and breathed deep. "Not my wife, Anna," he said.

Anna recalled a time as a child when she had questioned her pa about why the Old Testament Abraham would take his son up the mountain to lay a knife to his throat.

Pa told her a ram showed up, so he didn't have to sacrifice his son.

"But why would he even think about killing his own son?" she asked. "Especially if he loved him as much as he said." Anna twitched. "I wouldn't have killed my son."

"Men do what they have to do, Anna. It's different with a woman. She's softer and needs a man to make her choices," he told her. "God was his boss, so Abraham did what God told him to do. You don't question. You just do."

An owl called Anna back to the rock hardness of the ledge. She looked up. Winston stood over her.

"You have to handle this." Winston's eyes flickered.

That night, she took the long way home. At some point, she came upon a puddle from yesterday's melted snow. Its shallow water reflected the full moon. She was tempted to disturb the water, but she stepped around it. She left the moon's image intact, floating like a silver balloon. She did not cry until she stepped on a stone hidden by a sprinkling of snow. Her foot twisted and pain shot up her ankle. Once she started crying, she was unable to stop.

Chapter 10

Anna set out up the mountain the next morning before light, trusting her instinct to lead the way. She had not traveled this road before. Once the sun topped the ridge, leaves damp and flat from a midnight rain reflected early light and glistened like glass. She feared she would slip and fall. Logic told her she walked not on glass but on dying leaves, but fear kept her from hearing what logic said.

An icy morning wind pushed her up the mountain road. Juanita had talked to her and told her to look for a wooden cross to show the way. "Funny looking thing," Juanita had said. "It'll appear over the trees, leaning sideways. You take that road."

Anna turned east when she spotted the cross. Weak and rotted over time, it pointed away from the mine and its camp. With little sunlight out, Anna hesitated. The road led straight up. Undergrowth inched its way in from both sides, fashioning impenetrable black walls. Ancient oaks spread their limbs over the road, interlacing side to side, creating a roof. She took one deep breath after another and counted her steps to force herself on.

First step one, then step two. Three and seven and twenty-eight. On she plodded, up the mountainside. From this angle, she could see why Long Hunters, the first white surveyors, or perhaps the Cherokee before them, had named the mountain Turtleback. The road rounded and ridged and rounded again as if the end hid somewhere in the hovering mist. From her vantage point, she could see nothing that might lead to flat land.

Then it appeared. Before her lay a singular geographic feature, four acres of cleared ground. The land lay so level it seemed a heavy log had rolled out any dips or rises. Anna decided she could put a glass of water down and it would not topple. Flatland consisted of four rectangles that zigzagged from north to south, each abutting and angling down from the next so that birds flying overhead would see a series of steps. The rectangles had been cleared so precisely that one did not overlap any other.

In the second rectangle stood the old church, facing the morning sun. Behind it stood a row of fir, much like a green wall. The space around the building had been broom-swept for so long no plant dared grow there. Someone had built a slant tin roof over the door and added a plank floor to resemble a porch, and a thick rock slab so heavy only God could have moved it served as a step. Across the back was a small lean-to room, its windows boarded inside.

A diminutive, un-chinked log house, a smokehouse perhaps, placed here to distance the smells and smoke from Boone Station, sat almost in front of the church. Two stripped tree trunks supported the roof overhang across the front. At the base of the threshold, lay a little carved bird. Anna bent and held the bird. It had a small hole bored into its head. The bird sat round as an egg in Anna's left hand. She fingered its feather ridges, its wood firm yet airy, almost alive. She rolled it over. Sculpted without feet, it fit in her palm as snugly as if it had rested in its nest. Anna blew away the dust and eased it in her pocket, intending to set it on her mantel. This carving was too beautiful to waste.

Anna peered through the open door. Inside was a packed dirt floor. The ceiling was rafters with iron hooks that once held meat. Clusters of last season's tobacco leaves, as large as full-grown bass, now hung from the hooks. In the back corner lay a corn-shuck mattress and a woolen blanket, woven in reds and blues. The room's musky stench kept Anna from stepping inside.

Outside the squatty building sat a large, iron-footed black pot. As Anna came close, a wisp of wind picked up grey ash left from fire under the pot and blew it onto her face. She smudged a grey streak down and across her forehead with the back of her hand, much like the shape of a cross. She turned to face the church. The cleared land unnerved Anna. That and the silence. She wiped sweat from the nape of her neck. The climb had not been easy.

Anna walked toward a stand of new growth that had begun to invade two abutting rectangles. Around the corner lay a grassy patch of land. Wooden boxes, the granny's bee yard, offered no sound of activity. Perhaps the bees were off foraging. A narrow footpath led away from the bee boxes, into the woods and disappeared down the mountain. She heard her first sound, water gurgling through the pebbles of a stream.

She returned to the church. To her right lay the graveyard, an area where weeds worked to reclaim the land. Short grasses moved in the breeze as if they welcomed this unexpected visitor. Anna lifted her hand in a half-wave toward the gravestones and walked in. Flat headstones, some on the ground, some making their way down, very few upright, marked graves dated by nail scratchings in the rock as early as 1816.

On the southern side of the slat church, a mass of green sprouted from freshly hoed ground. A garden for the new season. The church door stood ajar, but Anna, winded from the climb, did not go in. She dropped on a damp stone slab that had served as a step since Uriah Parsons had built this church for his family. Anna waited to gather her breath.

Sister Sun sends a cooling cloud from time to time over where Anna rests, but she doesn't make it comfortable enough to encourage Anna to stay or so uncomfortable that she will feel she has no choice but to leave. She waits for Anna to make her decision.

In the quiet, Anna recognized a rustle. Among the headstones flitted a pair of early season bluebirds. They hopped from stone to stone, as if surveying the area for danger. When Anna looked closer, she saw why. Two dark blue chicks waddled about, noticeable only because their color stood out against weather-streaked headstones. On a fallen stone covered with thick moss, one chick's tiny black eyes followed the smaller adult. The other in grass no taller than its breast hopped once and sipped dew, ignoring the adult birds.

The mother bird moved to a tombstone, its grave occupant's name made illegible by streaks of water and time. She dropped to the ground and scuttled the two chicks together, then spread her wings and returned to her rock. The papa bird sat on a taller, upright tombstone two yards away. He twisted his head from side to side, his vigil intent. He lifted high into the breeze and circled.

The fledglings spread their hollow-boned wings and tried to boost their weight off the ground. They fluttered a bit and failed. The mother bird lit before the attentive one and flapped her wings in the little one's face. The chick tried again and, with difficulty, lifted itself to the branch of a low bush. The second followed course, and the papa bird joined his chicks within the leaves. Dancing across branch to branch near the ground, they vanished. The mother bird remained and scratched into the grass. She drew out a dark, round bug and followed her mate and chicks into the brush.

Anna sucked her lower lip so she wouldn't cry. Clint had no reason to think this baby was not his. One day, this child will be all she would have of Winston Rafe. She wiped the drip from her nose with the back of her hand and sniffed.

The breeze slackened, almost disappeared. Nausea popped sweat out on Anna's face. She rubbed her hand across her forehead and noticed that she removed ash. *Anna Goodman*, she reprimanded herself, *you dirty-faced fool. You think you belong in his world? Fancy trips to Bristol. Pearls and slinky clothes. For sure, I am no more than a miner's wife, but I don't have to quit because of that.*

The graveyard bush rustled. The mother bluebird escaped and took flight, headed for a hemlock, black with age. Anna fingered the bird carving resting in her pocket as the bluebird disappeared in the tree.

As Anna walked back to Breakline Mining Camp, the breeze picked up again. This time Anna faced it. Her decision to keep the baby lay easy. She could keep their secret. Rafe would have to take it or he could leave her be. Nothing could ever be as it was before. He had to accept that.

The next morning when Clint returned from the hoot owl shift, Anna met him at the kitchen door in her softest cotton gown, the one with lace she had tatted around the hem.

Chapter 11

Anna entered the commissary and glimpsed around to see if any wives were there. Seeing only Gabe, his grin as wide as ever, she stopped behind the cloth bolts and fingered the texture of a cotton plaid. Green and blue irregular plaid. Her favorite colors. The blocks appealed to her Scot-Irish heritage. This one was as soft as a chick's down. It would make a beautiful top. She looked at the end of the bolt. Twenty-five cents a yard. Dan River Mills. No wonder. An irregular plaid would make the top more expensive. It required extra yardage to match the plaid, and she had yet to buy a pattern. She moved down the counter and, from the bottom shelf, drew out a yellow cotton covered with small blue flowers. Ten cents a yard. No matching and this would give her a few cents over to pay for the pattern. Rising, she tucked the bolt under her arm.

She went to the shoes. Last night, she and Clint had talked about her wearing shoes with a firm sole. The commissary sold old lady shoes she had seen on women at Unity Church. She wanted flat-soled shoes, a guarantee that the baby would not have crossed eyes. She knew the idea was superstition. She told Clint she didn't believe it, but why take a chance?

That night as she lay in bed next to Clint, it came to her that she never referred to the child as "our baby" or "my baby." The child growing within her was "the baby." Her mother had called her "my baby girl" until Anna left to marry Clint. After the ceremony and before Breakline, when they came to tell her ma and pa, Ma had said to Clint, "She's yours now. See you take good care of her." She had risen from her rocker and said, without turning back, "She ain't my baby no more."

Anna searched boxes until she found a size six low-heeled black shoe with laces to the ankle. She did not check the price. The shoes were more important than the cloth. She would not show for another month. If the shoes cost too much, she could come next month for cloth after Clint got his paycheck.

Anna waited in front of the counter, silent, staring past Gabe's reddish hair. A partially filled jar of pickled eggs held her gaze. The floating ovals looked salty and rubbery, not worth her money. She was so accustomed to holding back tears now that she could envelope herself in a solid wall of white so thick she neither saw nor heard anyone. Once she was cocooned so, a voice or a touch was necessary to bring her back.

Gabe took the cloth from under her arm. "You okay, Mrs. Goodman?"

Gabe Shipley was not a handsome boy. His feet spread out like a duck's, too large for his lanky body. His nose slanted a bit to the left, and his horn-rimmed glasses magnified his almost blue eyes. Yet women, young and old, gathered 'round him, hungering for a moment of his attention.

Each mother, when her daughter reached marriageable age, paraded her, much as had Cinderella's stepmother before the prince, to the commissary and set her before Gabe. He teased and entertained with an occasional magic trick, but he never stepped forward. He often retold stories that he read from his box of novels. He recognized that he was one of the few bachelors in the camp, but his place was behind the counter. At twenty-three, he was still young to marry, yet the women always returned. He was the one thing their husbands were not. His hair was red, not soot coated, his hands scrubbed clean. No black eyelids outlined with coal dust, no black collars embedded around his nails. No teeth stained brown from years of tobacco juice. Simply put, Gabe Shipley was not an underground man. They saw him as clerk and salesman, more the businessman, more so than Winston Rafe. Camp wives acknowledged Rafe as a man of wealth and vengeance. They met him with no more than a nod of the head when he approached. He was their husbands' boss. Distant. Remote. Gabe was open, friendly, often funny.

Anna looked past Gabe at Rafe's office door. It stood ajar. She nodded in answer to Gabe's question.

He began to unroll cloth from the bolt. "How many yards you need?"

"Two."

"That won't make much of a dress." Gabe grinned, as if he would be the one making the garment.

"A top. It's to make a top." Anna set the shoes on the counter. "Give me a price on these shoes before you take scissors to the cloth, Gabe."

Gabe thumbed through his inventory, found the page. "Seven dollars and ninety-five cents," he said and slapped the book shut.

"Long time asking, but I need to know something." Gabe leaned forward, resting his elbows on the counter. "Mr. Rafe's orders. I been meaning to know if I put a Bible in your camp house before you and the mister moved in. Mr. Rafe's real strong that I do that for all his families," Gabe mumbled as if he had made a mistake and did not want Rafe to know. "So I'm asking 'round." He lowered his eyes. "It makes us family, so he says."

Before Anna could respond, a voice from across the store said, "Those shoes are on sale, Gabe." Winston Rafe walked toward the shoe display holding a cardboard sign lettered "Sale."

Gabe looked at Rafe and said, "Oh?"

"Yep. Till they're gone. Two dollars a pair. Going to Bristol next week for new stock. We need to pass these on to good customers."

Anna, her cheeks red, twisted around to face Rafe. "No thank you, Mr. Rafe. I pay regular price. My man makes good money."

"I'm helping my miners out with this sale."

Anna's face burned.

Gabe lowered his head. Anna knew he recognized how foolish Rafe was to behave so in public. He had straightened his back when he heard Rafe call the miners "his miners," as if he had been dubbed lord of the manor.

Behind Rafe stood Juanita White, eyeing Anna and soaking up every word. This favor from Rafe would spread all over camp before supper. Every woman would be in before dark for a pair of sale shoes. They would question each other about why the sale had not been posted in the window before Anna asked about the shoes. She would be the talk of the camp. Rafe would be out who knows how much money because of her.

"I can afford a sale now and then. You enjoy those shoes and stitch up something pretty for yourself."

He took her elbow and walked her to the door, her package in his hand. At the entrance, he gave her the shoes. "Don't you hesitate to come back if these shoes pain you any. I'll have Gabe swap them out for something better."

The pregnancy had bloated her so much that she felt cow-like. She wished he would not speak to her as if she were a miner's wife. For Gabe and Juanita's benefit, she said, "Thank you, Mr. Rafe."

Rafe grinned and glanced about as if checking to see who had overheard her compliment. Anna pulled her cardigan tight against the morning chill. A thin shadow wrapped itself around the corner. She cringed and stepped into leaves brittle from lack of August rain.

Summer passed with Anna's becoming more and more confined. The baby's growth hindered her walking very far. Her shame at knowing she carried a child who might be labeled "bastard" kept her from going no farther than Juanita White's. Facing wives head-on drained her more than early morning sickness had, so she stopped going to the commissary by mid-summer. She gave Clint a list and hoped he would follow through.

As an only child, Clint had no idea what to do to help Anna through this pregnancy and her self-isolation. Her list would read baking powder and he would bring in baking soda. It would read hoop cheese and he would bring back cheddar. After two trips back to exchange what he had bought, he gave the list to Gabe, who was usually propped on his stool, reading one of his books, and let him collect whatever Anna needed. Throughout the pregnancy, Clint said little and waited for instructions from Anna. She had none.

A flat orange moon emerged on a bitter October night. The year was 1944. Clint came home to an empty kitchen. No food on the stove. Breakfast dishes on the table. He found Anna in the bedroom, grasping the wooden headboard spindles and thrashing on the bed, moaning, crying a hard, scared cry. He took no time to change from his mining coveralls. He ran to Doc Braxton's house. He pounded on the door, but no one answered. The thought that he had left Anna alone panicked him. He should be there for her. He had heard of women who died while giving birth. At thirty, Clint had no concept of a woman's birthing. One thing he did know was that he could not live without Anna Parsons Goodman.

He back-tracked to Seth White's. He stomped flat-footed up Seth's wooden steps and pounded on the door. Seth opened the door as he hoisted up his suspenders.

"What you up to so late?" Seth asked. "It's nigh on to nine o'clock."

Between pants, Clint choked out his words. "It's the young'un. It's coming and it's two months yet due and Anna's dying and I got to get the granny and get her here before both of them die because she's thrashing round like some cow plugged with a crooked calf."

"Where's Doc?" Seth stepped out on the porch.

"Gone." Clint, now out of breath from his running and telling, dropped on the top step and leaned against the porch post.

Seth smothered a chuckle. "Guess we best get in the truck and get on with it then." He reached behind the door for his jacket. "Juanita," he called. "Get on over and see to Anna. Baby's coming." Seth reached into the crawl space under the porch and drew out a quart jar of moonshine. "Might need this 'fore the night's over." He placed the bottle on the bench seat between his hip and Clint and cranked the truck.

Clint eyed the jar as the truck bumped from hole to hole climbing the rise to Flatland. Seth noticed and offered him a drink. Clint unscrewed the lid and guzzled a hefty swig. The liquor seared his mouth and throat, but he swallowed. He wiped his mouth with his forearm.

"How is it, Seth, you and Juanita got only one kid being married all these years? Anna and me, we been married these seven years and this is our first hit."

"Juanita knows how to take care of herself since Jason. She's a genuine marvel." The front truck wheel fell into a rut and yanked the steering wheel. "Granny said no more and she ain't." Seth fought back and steadied the truck. "Taught herself lots of things. Like driving up that steep hill to Flatland and back. Learned on her own. Got in this truck one evening, stomped on the starter and drove up the road. Jerked back and forth for a time, but driving nonetheless."

"Why'd she start out at night?" Clint said.

"Who knows the head of a woman," Seth answered. "She just done it that way."

Within an hour, they returned with the granny. Clint rode bundled in his work jacket in the truck bed so Granny could sit inside with her bulky, black valise. They dropped Granny off at Clint's steps.

"Granny's back in town," Brother Moon sings in his resonant baritone voice. "Oh ho, Granny's back in town."

Stars dance about to the night music. They twirl through the sky, giving the illusion below of constant blinking.

Clint jumped down from the truck, but Seth called him back. "No place for a man in there," he said. "We'll be best served out here on the porch."

Clint paced the porch in the manner of all men who suddenly realize what their pleasuring has led to for their women. Seth, poised like a veteran, leaned his chair against the wall, swigging drink after drink from his jar.

Clint snatched the jar from Seth and gulped deep. "I'm the one who done this. I warrant the shine." He stumbled toward Seth, who reached for him.

"Set down here, before you fall off in the yard," Seth said. He belched a groggy laugh from his belly. "Seems to me the one needing this is Anna. Not you and for sure not me."

"What're they going to say, the women? Us out here drunk as skunks and Anna in there hollering and Granny singing?" Clint plopped to the floor like a child and rubbed his forehead. "I shouldn't of done this to her. She won't never forgive me." Clint stifled a drunken sob.

"Naw," Seth said. "She'll forget and be wanting another one before you know what's happened. That's the way of a woman." Seth settled his chair. "Besides, Granny's in there. She'll slip a knife under the mattress to cut the pain, and it'll be over before you know it. Can't no harm be done."

"See that rattle she had?" Clint said. "What's that about?"

"Baby rattle?"

"No. Looked like a gourd." Clint shook his head. "You think she's some witch?"

"Don't go whistling down the holler," Seth said. "It's woman stuff. Stuff we're not supposed to know." Seth handed Clint the jar. "Here. You're a man now. Proved it pure and simple." He slapped Clint on the back. "Done made you a baby." Seth laughed again. "Drink up."

Clint took the jar and downed the last of Seth's moonshine. Seth picked up his fruit jar, cranked his truck and left Clint alone on his porch.

Clint turned when he heard the door open behind him. He glanced at the colorful long skirt that stood beside him.

"Get on up now," Granny said. "You got a baby girl to attend to." She reached down her hand to help Clint rise.

"Anna?"

"She's fine. Baby's fine."

"What should I do?" Clint stood beside Granny and waited.

"Get inside your house and name your girl-child." Granny descended the steps.

"Wait. Don't I pay you or something?" Clint reached into his pocket.

"No. Great Spirit takes care of such." Granny walked to the road. "Not this time."

"You want me to get Seth to take you to Flatland?"

"No. I walked this path many a time before."

Granny vanished into the darkness. A cold wind hit Clint in the face as he tapped quietly on the door.

"Come in here and meet Lily Marie Goodman," Anna said from inside. "I named her after my sister and a verse from Solomon."

Clint closed the door behind him to cut out the rising autumn wind.

Chapter 12

The first time Gabe saw Lily, she peeped out of a handmade baby quilt with those blue eyes, so deep a blue they made the sky pale. A surge of wonder filled a void he had tried to ignore. This emptiness had sprouted and grown large within him, this not having a family. Now the awesomeness of it all lifted him so high he felt he left the floor. He wanted to snatch the baby from Anna and run. Instead, he thought, *A lucky man, Clint Goodman. At least he owns his own child.*

A heaviness pressed on his chest. He realized that this loneliness, this lack of acknowledgement by his father, had walked with him since his mother left with Lloyd Freeman. He needed his father to stand before the people of Breakline, lift his hands, palms flat, and say, "Come and see. This is my son."

He spoke when he realized Anna was staring at him. "What's her name?" he asked. He reached out, and the baby grasped his index finger.

> *"Sister Sun, come here. You're female. Clue me in on what's happening here," calls Brother Moon.*
>
> *"Silly old rock. The man wants a family. Being one of a kind, you wouldn't know about that."*
>
> *"But not this woman. Or her child."*
>
> *"Stay out of it. That's what you tell me."*

"Lily. Lily Marie. After my sister Ruth Marie down in Covington." Anna handed Gabe the child.

Gabe cuddled the baby to his chest and laughed aloud. "She's one more miracle," he said.

‹‹‹‹‹‹‹

Over the following months, Clint came to adore the child more and more. In an attempt to hide her guilt, Anna encouraged him to dote on Lily. Anna had been a fool. She had played fancy with a man who, like a card shark, shuffled the deck so he could show only the cards that played to his game. Anna admitted to herself that Lily had a quality that drew people to her, though she couldn't name it. They wanted to touch her, cuddle her, make her smile. Women she worried had slighted her at the commissary approached Anna and smiled and cooed over Lily as if she were a treasured toy. Anna mulled over the attention Lily drew. She was not jealous, but more curious about what special power her child held, especially over Clint and Gabe.

Lily was old enough to sit alone the night Anna placed a slice of plain cake topped with applesauce on the highchair tray. Lily closed her small fist around the cake, squeezing cake and applesauce into squishy batter that oozed between her fingers.

Clint laughed. "That's my girl there, Anna. See? She takes what's given her and don't complain."

"Not like her mama?" Anna stood to wipe cake from Lily's hands. "Better she learn to consider what she's offered before making her choice. They's always consequences. God sees to that." She moved to the dishpan to rinse the cloth. "Nothing to be gained by reaching out and grabbing the first thing you see."

Clint ignored the tinge of bitterness in Anna's comment. He swept Lily out of her chair, spilling the cup of milk Anna had placed to the side, out of Lily's reach. "Oops! Lily girl, looks like we made a fine mess for certain."

Lily giggled.

Clint put her on the floor easy, as if she might break. She crawled into the living room. He took a mop to the milk spill.

"Don't let her run loose, Clint," Anna scolded. "You don't know where she'll end up."

Clint placed the mop back in its bucket by the door. "Well, I'll end up fired, if I don't get on to the mine." He gave Anna a peck on the back of her hair and said, "No double shift tonight, Anna. I'll be home early morning, soon as I can." He took her face in both his hands and smiled. "See if you can't find that little gown you wore when we got Lily started." "Oh, hush up, Clint." Anna brushed him away. "Here. Take your bucket." She tapped the lid to be sure it was tight and handed him his food. He winked one coal-rimmed eye and gave his wife a salute, as snappy as possible for a man whose back was already bowing in the manner of all miners. He called out a goodbye to Lily and closed the door behind him.

Anna set about putting Lily to bed for the night.

Brother Moon slides behind newly formed rain clouds and leaves Breakline Camp in the dark. He summons the rain to wait until after midnight to fall.

Clint had been gone for less than an hour when Anna heard a tap, no more than a whisper of a knock, on the back door. She froze. Breakline was not a place where people visited after dark. Not that she had reason to fear, but she was at the end of the road, away from other houses, by herself. She thought about changing from her cotton robe into a dress but decided she could perhaps see who was there by looking out the bedroom window. She tip-toed through the darkened room and edged the curtain aside.

Winston Rafe stood with his back against the wall and hat pulled low, waiting in the dim porch light.

Anna switched off the kitchen light and cracked the door. Rafe pushed in and keyed the lock. She did not question his boldness. Had she asked why, like many times before, he would have convinced her he was in the right.

"I've come to see the girl," he said. "Where is she?"

Anna inclined her head toward the bedroom. "She's sleeping." She grabbed his arm to hold him back.

Rafe jerked away. "I aim to see the baby, Anna."

Anna dropped his arm on command. "Be quiet," she said, wondering if he had been drinking at O'Mary's Saloon.

Rafe ignored her and walked into the bedroom.

She glanced around to see if Clint had left his clothes in their usual place on the floor by the straight back chair. Guilt perched on her shoulder, heavy as a big-beaked crow, and nipped at her ear. *Allowing Winston here by your marriage bed is more of a betrayal than lying with him on some rock ledge. You know that, don't you?* The words were more reprimand than question. Yes, she knew. She looked away from the bed and said nothing.

Rafe leaned over the child and squinted against the dark. "What color's her hair?" he whispered.

The question addled Anna. Lily's hair was no hair. Still a lap baby, the baby's scalp was covered with colorless fuzz. Now at less than a year, she had a little, but not enough to hold a hair ribbon. Had he never seen a baby?

Rafe bent close, then stood. Lily slept in a drawer taken from the bureau across the room. "She can't have my family's hair. You know that." He spoke, his back toward Anna, as if he dared the baby to sprout hair with him standing there watching.

Anger surged through her body. "Damn it, Winston. You come barging in here acting like I can wave a wand and color her hair. Are you crazy?" She stepped back. "I can't cast spells like some granny." She tilted her head. "Winston Rafe, are you drunk?"

Anna watched as he circled his attention around the room, looking first to the window, with its white curtains, then the open closet, her clothes hanging next to Clint's. His eyes stopped at the dresser mirror, most of its back silvering gone. There he stood, Anna noticed, reflected in a gauzy haze that presented him almost featureless. He ran his fingers through his wavy hair.

"Family hair," he said. "It's chestnut, my mother always said. Said there was none other like it." He swallowed. "Maybe she'll be blonde? Like you?"

Anna took a deep breath and mumbled, "I don't know, Winston. There's no way to tell as yet." He had not answered her question about being drunk. She felt the warped reflection in the mirror watching her.

Anna had many nights envisioned having Winston here. Now that he was, the bed looked severe, its dusty rose chenille spread stretched so taunt no wrinkle rippled the surface. The elation she had imagined had never entered the room. She looked back at the mirror's curvy image. Her face mocked her. She saw a face she had never seen before, the face of a fallen woman. Tears came before she could stop them.

That night was the first night Winston came inside Anna's home. Lily was seven months old.

The rain defies Brother Moon's command and plummets onto Breakline Mining Camp. It drenches the tipple and moves south toward the end of the camp.

As soon as Winston Rafe stepped out of Clint Goodman's house, rain dropped in broad sheets, drenching Rafe as he walked back to the Queen Anne house on the rise.

After Rafe left, three weeks of emptiness and yearning consumed Anna. She stumbled through days and fought pre-dawn nightmares before she admitted her body needed Winston Rafe. She convinced herself that he whispered to her, calling her. One late July evening, she bundled Lily in a light blanket, walked out the back door, and climbed the rise to her rock ledge.

At first, she did not see him. His approach startled her. "I didn't expect you to be here," she said.

"Neither did I."

Later, Anna would ponder on whether he meant he had not expected to return to their ledge or whether he didn't expect her to return. Neither mattered. She had never suspected when she lured Clint away from Ruth that she had taken such a precarious road. Nor did she have an idea how painful the resulting wreck would be.

Lily slept in a bower away from the ledge's rim. Anna sat on the edge, her feet hanging loose in the dark. A cool night breeze blew down the mountain.

Winston lit a cigarette and said, "You got to take Lily and Clint and leave."

"What'd you mean?"

He stared out over the camp. "I'm transferring Clint over to Big Mama #2 next week."

She shouldn't have expected anything more, she told herself, but she had.

"Gladys is pregnant. Told me last night. She won't tolerate having a kid walking around that favors her own child. Almost the same age." His voice grew louder with each statement.

"Gladys is pregnant." Anna's voice came out flat.

"You got to go. What if the more Lily grows the more she favors me?"

"She won't." Anna interlocked her fingers to steady their trembling. "I swear she won't." Wind whipped up, calling for rain in the night.

"Anna, listen here. . ."

"No. I'm not going." Anna rubbed her hands down her thighs to dry her palms.

"Anna, I'm not a begging man, but you got to go. You don't have a choice. Don't make me do something I don't want."

"Clint adores Lily. He's convinced she's his." She refused to look at Winston. This change was something he had told her to expect, but she never really thought it would come to such a betrayal. Gladys. Pregnant.

"He's never questioned her looks." Anna kept her voice low so as not to wake Lily.

"Anna," he pleaded. "Anna?"

Winston's command had hit deep. Anna did not want to plead, but his argument left her defenseless. She had no idea what to say. "It's been almost a full year. He hasn't questioned her yet." She whirled around and stood behind Winston. "We're settled here. Now that I have Lily, wives talk to me. I have friends."

"Go home, Anna. Get settled back in Covington. You have family there."

"I'm not leaving, Winston. Not next week. Not ever." She lifted Lily, cradled her child close and started back toward the camp house.

Rafe called after her, "I told you all along. I can't claim the child."

"Shut up," Anna barked.

"Don't push me, Anna," were the last words she heard.

Brother Moon takes on extra iridescence to help Anna down the mountain. He reminds himself not to mention his actions to Sister Sun or Great Spirit. They will not approve of his interfering.

Chapter 13

The next morning before dawn, first a tapping on the door, then three heavy fist licks, and Anna woke.

"Mrs. Goodman, open up the door. It's me, Seth White. Juanita's old man. Open up." The voice spoke in a loud whisper.

Anna opened the door, clutching her quilted housecoat, arms crossed over her bosom. The earthy smell of dry dirt overwhelmed her. Clint lay on the porch, his left leg folded up under his body. Dried blood covered his forehead and left ear.

"We found him when we was going to the mines a while ago. Looks like one of the coal trucks must have hit him." Seth White rolled his felt hat with both hands. "He was almost in the ditch."

"Thought you'd want to know before we took him to Doc's," said a voice out of the darkness.

Anna stared at Clint's face. His dark eyes looked like silver buttons on a white shirt. But big. Big like white balls. They bulged out as if something had slammed against the back of his head making his eyes try to pop out the front. His body seemed so small, like a child's, like it had shrunk since he left last night for work. It was the first time in months that he hadn't worked a double shift, and he came home like this.

Inside the house, Lily cried out from a night fright.

"What's the matter with him?" she asked.

Great Spirit calls out to Brother Moon. "Where have you been? You were supposed to tell Sister Sun to brighten the sky early today. Why is she lagging behind?" He speaks to himself, "Or did I forget and order a storm cloud for this morning?" He scratches his head with a massive lightning bolt.

"I told her, Great Spirit, but you know how it is with her. She gets caught up in her sparkle and loses track of time."

"Looks like I'll have to throw a few asteroids out her way. Get her attention," Great Spirit says as he moves away. "Seems nobody does anything right these days."

The men looked around at each other. "He's dead, Mrs. Goodman," Seth whispered. "Hit by a loaded truck."

"Somebody run him down." Anna twisted her hands round and round each other. "I know it."

"No. A accident. Nobody to blame." Seth searched for the right words to calm Anna. He waited for her to scream. "Maybe it was the light," Seth offered. "Maybe Clint was on the fringe." He skimmed the faces behind him. "Nobody around here wanted Clint gone. He's a good man. A good worker."

Anna's eyes squinted against the pre-dawn sky. Such a deep, deep black. Was this the darkness that Clint lived in every day? She squatted on the porch at Clint's feet. "What's wrong with his leg?" She looked up to Seth. "Why don't you fix his leg?" She extended her hands, palms down, and moved them back and forth, as if to cover him or swat away some unknown creature and keep it from lighting on his body.

"Yes ma'am, Mrs. Goodman. I'll do just that." Seth signaled for the men to back away. "Here you go." He lifted her. "Just let's go back in the house. I should've brought Juanita with me. I'll send one of the men for her right now." He nodded to a shadow in the crowd.

Lily cried again, more demanding.

"I'll have her mix you up strong toddy, and she can sooth the little one." Seth half-walked, half-dragged Anna into the house and left her lying on Clint Goodman's bed.

Anna tossed about. "Go," she mumbled. The word tolled in her head like an iron gong announcing a community death.

"No. You stay right here," Seth said.

Without looking, Anna reached for the company Bible by the bed and clutched it to her chest. *Vengeance is mine, saith the Lord.* The Word of God rattled in her head like a loaded train on uneven crossties.

Juanita found Anna glaring at the ceiling, unresponsive. She reached into her sweater pocket and brought out a small vial of belladonna berry juice.

‹‹‹‹‹‹‹

Winston Rafe propped against the thick trunk of a sugar maple. His jacket, a pale gray, blended into the bark of the tree. Although it was a warm day, he pulled his head into the collar and looked under his brows at the group of mourners by Clint Goodman's open grave.

> *"Sister Sun, are you looking after that child?" Great Spirit calls.*
>
> *He has returned to Turtleback weary from listening to what is spinning around in Benjamin Spock's head. He realizes that he should have listened more closely before letting him send out a manuscript for a how-to book on what man should already know. Maybe he needs to stop the publication. Common Sense Book of Baby & Child Care. Humph. It just might turn out like that artificial snow somebody made up in Mt. Greylock. Those Massachusetts people will have people thinking they can change the weather on a whim. Even had the gall to use one of my own clouds. Now every other person will be believing they can change the world into being what they want. Great Spirit mumbles on, until he sees Clint Goodman's gaping grave. And he remembers it all.*
>
> *"Yes sir. I truly am," says Sister Sun.*

At least forty off-shift miners and their wives waited for the service to begin. Their backs created a dark hedge blocking Winston's view of Anna. Unable to see Anna, Winston stepped from behind the tree and walked to the edge of the crowd. Anna sat in a folding chair the funeral director has draped in green felt.

Anna's hair, blonde as the day he met her, hung across her face. From time to time, a puff of breeze lifted loose tendrils, fanning their length, pointing toward him. He willed his feet not to walk closer.

Wind wafted the minister's lamentations across the cemetery. The July air hit Winston and drew his attention to the minister. The man had a reputation for using the right words at the right time. He could quote scripture out both sides of his mouth, some said. Winston had sent Gabe to Covington to get him and tell the man to say what Anna needed to be said. All the afterlife promises and such. Gabe paid the man with a ten-dollar bill. He better be good, or Covington Presbyterian Church would be finding another preacher.

Buying a minister was the best he could do. He should not have tempted Fate by delaying Clint's transfer to Covington. Anna had family in Covington. Maybe she would go now. But if she left, he had to know she would be safe. And the child. The child needed to be safe. He might not be able to make them happy, but surely, surely he could keep them safe. He walked toward the crowd as they moved away so the diggers could cover Clint's pine box.

Gabe stepped up from behind Anna and placed his hand lightly on her shoulder. Rafe walked to Gabe and gripped his shoulder. Gabe was his son. He would do what Rafe told him.

᷊᷊᷊᷊᷊᷊᷊

Anna returned to their camp house after the funeral. The effects of Juanita's belladonna berry juice had left her groggy, and she wobbled when she tried to walk. She needed to lie down with Lily and rest. She couldn't remember a full night's sleep since Winston had sent her to Clint's bed a little over a year ago.

The night when she refused to leave Breakline plodded through her memory. She questioned refusing to leave. She questioned Winston and who he was away from her. Winston would not have had one of the miners run Clint down with a coal truck, but the possibility played in her mind. The fact that she had been so adamant about staying would not leave her alone. Such thoughts muddled through her mind and clogged her ability to think about what to do.

Anna knew the regulations. Dead miner. Widow had two weeks to get out of the camp. Winston had told one night about a disabled miner over in Kentucky who had been allowed to stay in his camp house and was paid for a job he never did. The mine owner fired the miner, the supervisor and the commissary worker, all the same day. Here in Breakline, Winston was the owner, at least in word. Gladys wouldn't know if Anna was allowed to stay on.

She had not seen Winston at the funeral. Clint had been one of his best workers, one of the most respected miners in camp. She felt it right that Winston should come. He at least owed Clint that much. But had he come, Seth or Gabe might have seen the real Winston. Yet she questioned why she would think that anyone else would see through Winston Rafe. She had not. Or she had ignored what she had seen. Her mind shifted back and forth, arguing with itself about what to believe. Conflicted, she wasn't able to rest.

Two days after Clint Goodman was laid in the ground behind Unity Church, Anna packed a satchel, tucked Lily in the Red Ryder wagon Clint had bought her and set off for the commissary. As she neared the building, guilt and fear forced her eyes to the ground. Uncertainty dogged her. Did her actions have the power to kill another person? Before Clint's death, she had put God and His power to control lives out of her mind. It had been one way of allowing herself time with Winston. Might Clint's death have been her doing? Might Clint's death be her punishment from God? Her pa once said, "Not doing something at all can be as bad as doing something, even when it's wrong." She had defied Winston by not leaving. She had defied God with her adultery. And now Clint was dead and buried.

When she arrived at the commissary steps, she stopped. She could not remember what she had intended to say, nor to whom she intended to speak. She gazed at the three wooden steps between where she stood and the closed screen. She realized she could not get the wagon with its large wheels up the steps, and she would not disgrace herself by calling for Winston Rafe to come out and face her. She wiped unexpected tears from her face and rolled her daughter back over the packed dirt path to the company-owned house she had shared with Clint Goodman these past eight years.

The week after Clint's death, what Anna had believed was secret erupted throughout the camp much like a flash fire. No one she knew would benefit from the telling. She eliminated people she knew one by one. Winston would never have spoken. He valued his status too much. She had rarely seen Granny Slocomb after Lily's birth. The granny's son, Briar, who wandered the camp and worked at cleaning the commissary? No. She had never heard him speak. But the women now knew and they let her know they knew. Wives glanced away when she met them in the camp. A tall, brown-headed woman grabbed her children by the hand as they started across the ditch bridge Anna was crossing and shooed them in the opposite direction.

Alone, except for her baby and Juanita who stayed mostly inside, Anna found herself helpless against stares. She began rousing Lily and going to the commissary as early as possible, trying to squeeze in a time while other mothers were setting their children down to breakfast. While there, she glanced up each time she heard the door open. If she did unintentionally meet some woman, she slipped into a narrow aisle and turned away as if she could not be seen.

Anna loaded her burden of guilt on her back and staggered through each day under its weight. She prayed to her God that Gladys would not hear the truth. If word climbed the rise to the big yellow house, she, like Hagar, Abraham's whore, would be cast into the wilderness.

Anna did not know where she had garnered the strength to accept the beginning nor could she recall the precise time when she decided that she had no choice but to accept the leaving. What would drive her out of Breakline Camp was the touch of her child's hand, the smell of clean hair when she pressed her face to Lily's head as the child slept in her arms. It was the knowledge that to place her child gently in her crib would be time never regained, so she rocked her infant, cradled her in her arms in a selfish need for her own comfort.

Two more weeks passed before she attempted to see Winston. Turtleback, ever a shadow over the camp, trapped the night's coolness in its shade and held it there, awaiting the sun. The idea that Winston might be at one of his mines rather than the commissary had not come to her. Again, she tucked Lily in her wagon. At the commissary, she wrapped Lily tight in a light blanket, parked the wagon in the shade by the porch and mounted the steps.

Gabe, at his usual place behind the cash register, opened his mouth to reprimand whoever had slammed the screen door. When he saw Anna alone, he asked, "Where's my little Lily?"

"Outside. Asleep in her wagon." Anna glanced around the commissary. Briar, whom Anna had once jokingly told Winston was part wolf, moved soundlessly toward the back door.

"What're you reading now?" Anna asked. *Had she heard the back door close?* She questioned herself.

"*Of Mice and Men.* It's about this gentle giant of a man whose name is Small. Can you believe that Steinbeck guy? And traveling workers who. . ."

> *"Sister Sun, get over here and look after this girl-child," demands Great Spirit.*
>
> *"Look at this. Leaving her baby outside by itself. I'm not sure this woman knows yet that she's a mother."*
>
> *"Yes sir." Sister Sun rolls in as fast as her solar winds allow. "She does seem a bit addled."*

"Is Mr. Rafe here?" Anna interrupted.

"No'm, he's off over in Covington working on some machinery project he's dreamed up," Gabe said. "You welcome to wait. I'll go fetch Lily."

Anna wandered among the counters, running her hand over tops of canned goods: milk, fruit, vegetables, sardines, Vienna sausages. At one point, she drew back her hand and noted how clean her fingers were. No dust gathered under Gabe Shipley. No wonder Winston valued him so.

She drifted toward the back near the meat counter. If Winston came in, he would come through this door. She could speak without Gabe hearing her. A sound much like scratching on wood came from inside the office. She should tell Gabe. He wouldn't suffer a rat after his round of cheese.

Anna shifted from foot to foot, growing more and more frustrated as she looked at chunks of meat held aloft by sturdy iron hooks: pale chicken, brown duck, pork shoulders, legs of lamb, flitch of bacon. All aligned so a rotating fan kept flies from settling. To the side hung a slender boning knife, a thick cleaver, and honing steel for sharpening dull edges. Her eye went back to the cleaver.

"Somebody ought to kill him," she murmured. A flash vision of Winston coming in the back door and meeting her wielding the cleaver at him, hacking, slashing, and chopping, startled her. The gruesomeness of her envisioned attack ran cold over her body.

Gabe slammed the screen door and walked toward her, Lily riding his hip. His lop-sided grin cut his face in two. "Don't mind if I hold her a mite, do you?"

"No," Anna said. "Think I heard a mouse back by the cheese."

"Probably the Slocomb kid. Cleaning up in the office."

Anna needed to leave. She didn't want people to know why she was here. Briar Slocomb or anyone else. "Maybe you can help me, Gabe." She spoke above a whisper.

He nodded. "I might."

"I need to know where I stand with money." Anna took a deep breath. "I'm a widow now with this child to raise." She glanced around the store. She saw no one. A fresh jar of pickled eggs, now full, held their place on the shelf where she had last noticed them. They looked no more appetizing then they had before. "I got to know what, if anything, Clint put aside."

Gabe nuzzled his cheek against Lily's hair to make her giggle. "Counting receipts is about all I do with money. Mr. Rafe could help you more than me. Why don't you sit on this stool and wait a bit? He ought not be gone much longer."

Anna wavered. "I'll just come back tomorrow. He be here tomorrow?"

Gabe shook his head. "I don't know. Comes and goes. Gone more than usual lately." He cuddled Lily. "Acts like he's got a lot on his mind. What with all this bombing in Europe."

Anna reached for Lily. "Reckon I can say to you what I want to say to him as you'll be getting what I need." Lily struggled to be let down, but Anna settled her head on her shoulder. "I want all the money Clint earned his last week. I want his first pension check. I want all the money he put aside for Lily and me. I want ten dollars in ones and the rest in bigger bills. I don't want clink. Or script. I want real money."

"I don't know 'bout that, Mrs. Goodman. Mr. Rafe'll have to okay that kind of deal." Gabe busied himself with wiping the counter.

"You tell Mr. Rafe I'm leaving the camp, and I want what's due Clint." A tinge of resentment entered her voice without her approval.

"You leaving? You taking little Lily with you?" He reached for the child.

Gabe. Always gentle Gabe. Anna smiled. "Wherever I go, Lily goes. She's my baby."

The next morning, Anna returned. She opened the screen to the sweet smell of new honey. To Anna's left, the granny's shelf, which had been empty the day before, was filled with jars of fresh amber honey. The morning sun shone through the granny's honey and cast golden stripes across the floor, so perfect they looked ethereal.

Gabe heard Anna enter the screen door and called out, "Be right with you, Mrs. Goodman." He finished Juanita White's order of sugar and lard and tallied her bill. Biting her tongue, Juanita signed the tab hard so her signature would mark through the carbon. Anna waited, straddling Lily from one hip to the other.

"Morning, Anna," Juanita said. "Little one's growing like a weed."

"I reckon so," Anna said. "But so is Jason."

"Come by for coffee this evening, and we'll put them down for a nap and visit."

"Got a dirt smell here somewheres," said Gabe. "There's some taters back of Granny's honey. She'll have a fit if somebody finds fault near her honey. Let me get rid of this box. Get warm and they spoil overnight," Gabe said as he lifted a box and continued to talk as he walked toward the back. "Strange thing 'bout taters. One rotten tater ruins ever' one it touches."

"Maybe another day," Anna responded to Jaunita's invitation. "I got to get some things settled, what with Clint dead and all."

"Yes, another day," Juanita said and left, her lard bucket in one hand, her sugar in the other.

Gabe returned, grumbling. "Can't keep that Briar on one job long enough to get it finished and he's off again." He carried a sagging leather pouch and ten one-dollar bills. "'Bout cleaned us out," he chuckled. He handed the stash to Anna and winked. When Anna did not answer, he continued. "You be careful with all this money, you hear? I ain't telling nobody and you ain't talking neither."

Anna put out her hand to shake Gabe's. He rubbed his palms down his pant legs.

"Why you being so fancy all at once?" Gabe asked.

"I don't know," Anna said and started for the front door. She heard the hinge on Winston's office door squeak, as if opening.

Gabe called to her. "Where you going?"

"I don't know."

Winston strode up behind her as she met the steps. He took her arm. "Anna, wait."

Anna eyed the road, up and down. The road stood empty. "What do you want from me, Winston?"

"I want you to stay." He scratched the wooden step with his shoe. "No. That's not right. I need you to stay."

> *"He's about as reliable as a let-loose meteor," Sister Sun says. "I should blast him with a solar flare."*
> *"He is who he is," answers Great Spirit.*
> *"Can't you change him?" asks Sister Sun.*
> *"Should I want to?"*

"What about Gladys?" Anna watched him shuffle back and forth, foot to foot, a piece of tobacco stuck on his lower lip.

"I can't worry about what I can't change. I just know I need you to stay." He focused on her eyes, blushed, and cleared his throat. "You'll be safe here in Breakline. I'll see to it."

"No. I don't think so, Winston." Anna looked away. She didn't want him to see her face. "What would people think? Women are already..."

"Nobody here questions my decisions." He frowned. "They know I'm boss." He spoke as if words came to him with each breath. "Anybody bother you, you let me know."

Anna shook her head. "I don't know what to do. I think yes and then no." She had seen side glances as she passed when she was pregnant with Lily. Since Clint's funeral, camp wives walked out of the commissary when she walked in.

"For a while at least," he begged. "Till you find some place safe to stay." He reached out and ran his hand through Lily's hair. His thumb caught in a tangle, and she twisted her head away. "She's got the hair. 'The color of honey hit by the sun,' as my mama would say." He rubbed Lily's head. "Beautiful as you, Anna."

Dawn had appeared draped in a royal purple cape. When Anna closed the camp house door, her first thoughts had been on where she could go.

Winston was right. She had no place. Where she went should not matter, for Clint was dead and Winston was slowly killing her with his intermittent attention.

Sometimes people want something so bad they convince themselves a lie is the truth. She had not considered herself a liar when she took Clint from Ruth eight years ago, but now an inside gnawing told her she had lied and that she continued to do so. She lied each time she faced a Breakline wife and stumbled about trying to think of a reason why she, a non-working widow, had been allowed to stay these past weeks while others in her position had moved on.

She had lied to Clint, letting him think she loved him as he loved her, even during his rages. She lied each time she told Lily a story about Clint, letting her believe Clint was her daddy. She searched for an image of herself that she could remember, but the bedroom mirror that had distorted Winston the night he came to look at Lily that first time refused to warp her face into the person she once thought she was.

Wives talked. They would continue to do so. But Winston was right. Anna had nowhere to go. She had come down this path only to find there was no return. She handed Lily to Winston and opened the door. Without glancing back, she went inside to re-deposit her money.

Chapter 14

The next three months wore on Anna. She grew more and more isolated. She watched Lily play with Jason. Juanita watched Jason play with Lily. That was their world. They might as well have lived in another country, except when Anna went just past daybreak to make her commissary purchases. She succeeded in avoiding most of the camp community. She hoped God was testing her loyalty, that one day she would be rewarded.

Days spent talking with Juanita repeated each other with Anna's beginning, "I need to leave this place."

Followed by Juanita, "Me, too." A thought later, "But we ain't got no choice."

"Never been a pretty place," Anna would say.

"That's the way of mining country. Everything coal touches turns drab, dingy. What light escapes is black light. Coal-black light."

"Ground stays black with coal dust that grinds itself back into the dirt when it rains. Never washes itself clean." Anna might sip her coffee.

"Can't nobody keep heavy grit from tracking in the house. Jason 'specially," Juanita said.

"You'd think it's trying to return from where it was before miners come. The way it is, this land. Dust with a mind of its own, I reckon." Anna added, "Won't come out of clothes or off a bare foot."

"Rims Seth's eyes like some old pharaoh's paint and seeps deep," Juanita added. "Wiggles itself into your pores and sticks."

"No washing it off, it's so oily and slick." Anna said, "Here to stay." She poured another cup. "Like us."

"Maybe it's payback," Juanita suggested.

"Payback is a fact of life," Anna agreed. "God's going to see to that."

Their reoccurring word battles set them against Breakline Camp. An army of two against the people and the mountains themselves.

Anna rarely saw Winston. He came to the back door under darkness when he said he could, and she, fool that she was, took him in. For all, except Juanita and Winston and Lily, she no longer existed.

In time, Lily would start first grade at Unity Church school. Gladys' daughter, Cecelia, would be there. In the same building. Maybe in the same room. She needed to ask Winston if, in light of his initial fear of the girls favoring, he had considered they might meet. Had he contemplated the possibility of his girls pushing each other on the playground swings? Or jumping rope?

Nights with Lily sleeping inside, Anna pulled up her straight-backed chair and from her porch watched the lights that lit up the valley. One by one, camp house lights went out. On the rise, in the yellow house where Winston lived with Gladys, the lights glowed brighter and lasted longer than those in the camp. Anna could rely on the routine. The first floor lights went out soon after the valley darkened. The second floor followed a while later in all rooms except one, the light in what must have been their bedroom. It weakened bit by bit as if someone blew out a series of lamps and finally went black. Once Anna knew the yellow house had shut down for the day, she went inside and slept.

With each new day, the camp came alive in the same way. Miners walked to the shack and on to the mouth of the mine. Wives sent children, little ones hand-in-hand, up the valley to school. Women spent mornings weeding and hoeing backyard gardens. Afternoons, they gathered on porches against the heat of the sun to talk or sew. Nothing changed.

As she viewed the rise and fall of camp life, Anna was more convinced she should have gone when she had more anger to push her forward. She might have found a place in Covington or moved on to Bristol. When she agreed to stay, she had expected her need for Winston to wither as her life with Clint had. But Winston Rafe had rooted himself in her innermost being. Her days centered on hoping to catch sight of him; nights, haunted by memories. And her need grew. As it expanded, her grief spread within and gouged out a wound, cutting deep gashes on her soul, deeper than had the death of Clint Goodman.

Years ago when she had been no more than a tot, Anna had slipped down Broken Rock Creek riverbank and landed in a Brer Rabbit kind of briar patch. Her squirming and thrashing so confused the briars that they lost sight of their direction and entangled her totally. Pa had taken his pocketknife and cut her out as she screamed against the pain. He took her home, sniveling, her skin dirty and bleeding, uprooted plants dangling from her skinny body. He set her down on the edge of the back porch and spit out words like *careless, stupid, fool,* adding more sting than that any briar had inflicted. Now she heard those names rolling around in her head more clearly than she heard her own. She could now add *whore* to the list when she thought that some, if not all, of her money came from Winston Rafe, in one way or another. Self-loathing bonded with depression. The two kept her inside more and more, talking to herself and her child.

The letter came in late fall, 1946. Gabe brought the envelope by late on a Monday night. It had appeared without notice. Gabe, as camp mailman, would know this was the first letter Anna had received at the camp. Though Anna tried to hide it, he must have seen shock slap her face when she scanned the handwriting on the envelope. She didn't ask Gabe to come in or to sit while she read the letter. He touched his index finger to his dingy Irish cap and bade his goodnight.

Anna had written her family in Covington a year before to tell them that Lily had been born and that Clint was dead. It would have been nice, Anna thought, for them to at least write back saying they received the letter. Ruth could have written the letter, as their ma and pa, like most of their generation, were not highly schooled. Over time, Anna forgot that she had written to Covington. And now she received a letter.

Anna pulled up her straight-backed chair. Its oak-woven seat crunched when she sat. She held the letter facedown while she gathered up a willingness to face it. Darkness crept up on the far edge of the porch. As it drew nearer her chair, she turned the envelope over.

Her mother had scribbled *Anna Parsons Goodman, Break Line Mine Camp, Virginie* across the front. Pa must be dead. Maybe somebody she knew in her past had dropped into a dark, open mine shaft. They for sure were not inviting Anna to stop by and have a bite to eat. Or they had forgiven her for helping Clint jilt Ruth because Lily was born. A baby would make everything better.

The sun dropped just below the mountain, leaving rosy bands across the sky. The evening breeze wound itself around her chair as she sat there on the porch. Anna brought a kerosene lamp out and placed it on the floor and sat on one leg, dangling her other over the porch edge. She ripped open the seal, tearing the letter inside. Her hand shook as she drew out one page, written in pencil, front and back. Two brittle pages slipped out of the envelope and fell to her lap. Holding the torn letter together, she read.

Septumber 21 1946

Daughter,

We burried yur sister Ruth yesterdy on that slope that clum up the rise from Broken Rock Crick. Her rising will be towards the sun when she shall see that Jordan river on Judgement Day to come. We aint got no marker as yet for Horns business went bust when he dropped Sue Ella Watkins stone on his leg and mashed it up bad. Pa says he might jest put in a stake to mark where she lays. He put her under that ole cherry tree yur great granddaddy William set out. He was the boy of Uriah who settled this land. And dont you forget it as you are the onliest air left now that me and Pa is getting on an Ruth is alaying in the ground. No telling where that wild Mona is. Last I heared was she was in the Carolinas with some injuns. All I see is rotten cherries fallin on Ruths grave but I aint saying.

Frowning, Anna let the letter fall to her lap. Writing a letter was so unlike her mother, especially a letter that filled a page and half its back. But it read like Ma. Rigid. Harsh. It read like Pa, but she doubted that Pa knew about either letter.

Ruth is dead of a river drownding some folk say. Sherif Youell says hes alooking fer some feller who comes off the mountain and carpenters of a day. Says he was over by the bridge afore Ruth come in from working. Says her pocketbook was alaying on the sidewalk open and all and ther warnt no money but ther weren't be no money no how cause she never carried no money as it was a Friday when she would of been paid fer. She used that crazy man Hudson's bank for holding her pay stead of layin it aside in some hidey-hole like a reasonable person. But Im her mama and Im asaying shes dead of a broke heart as any rightful woman would be who had her man stole right out from under her by her own sister. I see in my own eye that she give up when she heared that you birthed Clints youngun and jumped off that bridge on her own. No matter no how as her neck is broke as hard as her heart and she is dead and burried. I had my say now and you made yur bed so lay there in your black mining camp. Im sending these here deeds with this letter.

Anna picked the yellowed pages from her lap and glanced at them. They were, indeed, a deed dated 1815 and signed by Uriah Parsons. A long, long time ago. Anna recalled a time when she was six and Ruth had begged for hard candy at the drugstore. Their ma had refused, but after Ruth fell asleep, she crept into their bedroom and slipped a piece of peppermint under Anna's pillow. Neither she nor her mother mentioned it then or ever. That was one of the few times Anna remembered such tenderness.

Yur youngun might need them of a day as Turtleback and Boone Station rightly goes to her and not to you who I say kilt her own sister. If you are a fittin mother youll lay them aside so she wont be having to live in no coal mining town the likes of which you run away to.

Anna bit her inner lip to stave off crying. The peppermint had not only been a gesture of tenderness. It was a favoring of Anna over Ruth. After Anna ran away, their mother had reversed their places in her heart. Anna had brought it on herself. She wondered if God had so many other worries that there was no time to look to the welfare of one human being. A loneliness swept over her and bowed her shoulders.

This letter is my say. Your pa and me aint got no younguns no more what with you being a lover thief and Mona off lost somewheres and Ruth in the cold cold ground. Dont be knocking on our door fer you aint welcome here no more.
Yur maw
Mrs Viola Parsons
My friend Clara Beauchamp holped me in this writing. She said I ort.

Chapter 15

Anna left Breakline Camp on Thursday at dawn of the next week. She and the child started out while dew was still safe from the sun. Anna loaded clothes in a pillowcase and canned food in a paper sack and packed them in Lily's wagon. She put Lily between the two bundles. Lily slept, her head resting on the stuffed bag of clothing.

The uphill climb was steeper than Anna recalled. At a point where the road widened, Anna stopped to rest under a massive oak. For the first time in the climb, she looked back over the valley and Breakline Camp, its identical box-shaped houses to the south, the commissary in the center and Unity Church close to the northern end of the cove on the road leading to #3's offices and opening. Then the steel-colored tipple, standing tall and humming to its perpetual motion. The place strung out like a strand of black pearls, each connected to the other by coal-dusted roads. She was too far away to see much of the rock ledge where she and Winston used to meet, but the stone scar was visible. It would be easier to see when trees lost their leaves. Towering over the valley, Winston's house stood, its Queen Anne ornamentation more like a decorated wedding cake than a home.

Though sound could not carry as easily up the mountain as it did coming down, she knew the hums and clangs of those awakening and moving about and what they would be, were she to listen closely.

Beneath Turtleback's western side, Breakline Camp acted out the morning in pantomime. Juanita came trotting out her front door. There was her fawn-colored milk cow shuffling down the dirt road. In memory, Anna heard the metal gate creak behind Juanita and clang when it closed. Juanita hurried as fast as her girth allowed after the Jersey, its udder swinging close to the ground. Another day of the cow escaping before Juanita got a chance to milk her.

Anna imagined the cow's occasional clink of her collar bell as she waddled along, swaying side to side. Juanita's mouth moved, calling the cow back, but the cow bawled and did not answer the call.

On the rise behind the commissary, a screen door slammed. The noise echoed from Winston's house like a shot. Rows of elaborate purple dowels drew her eye to the turret that connected the camp to the sky. A weather vane wavered in the breeze, its rooster pointing west, then northwest. The wind's draft did not make its way up Turtleback.

Winston walked out on the broad Queen Anne porch. He paused at the first step to strike a match against the white column and light his Lucky Strike. As he breathed out the first draw, Anna relived the sigh he made with each new cigarette. Winston faced the mountain road that led out of the valley, but she had gone too far for him to see her. She wondered if he questioned when she would leave or where she would go.

Standing by a sofa-sized boulder on the mountainside, Anna had not yet met her twenty-sixth birthday, yet she felt old. She recalled herself as a younger woman, holding a man she believed to be gentle, compassionate. She recalled his grin when he awoke in her lap and his laughter when the grin broke into a recollection of their time on the ledge. She refused to think of the different Winston who lashed out in fear at the mere mention of his daughter.

Lily, awakened by lack of movement, rested in the wagon. She twisted her doll's braids.

Back on the hill topping Breakline mining camp, Gladys must have called out to Winston. He glanced back toward the door, then ambled down the steps. He ground his fresh-lit cigarette under his shoe, as if Gladys' call frustrated him. At the bottom of the hill, he disappeared behind the commissary. Gladys stepped out on the porch in a rose-colored satin robe, repeating her call, but he did not return.

Anna imagined the sound of the office door back of the commissary closing behind Winston and the squeak of his chair as he lowered his long body onto the leather. In a bit, Gabe would walk up the front steps, insert his key and open for the day's business.

An awareness of what had put her on this road brought Anna back to the wagon and Lily. Winston's reaction to Lily, Gladys' new daughter, and Clint's death had soured her. Though she grieved the loss of Clint, her grief at leaving Breakline Camp and its memories weakened her. She needed to gather her thoughts for strength to make the rest of the climb. She parked the full wagon at an angle next to a large boulder and bent to brush away grayish-green lichen.

Something solid hit her back. Something larger than an acorn. Another plunked into Lily's wagon. Lily grabbed it and stuffed it in her mouth. "No," said Anna as she took it from Lily. Her mouth fell open when she saw what she held.

An intricately carved stag with paper-thin antlers large enough to confirm his dominion over the mountain stood in her palm. It was stunning. Its legs precise, ready to lope across a meadow. A small hole in its back held a broken bit of twine.

She searched the ground by the boulder for what had struck her. Below where she had intended to sit lay a fat bear the size of the buck. The wooden bear stood upright, tiny teeth bared, with a hole bored into its head.

Anna stepped back from the oak and gazed upward. Overhead was a weakened limb with more carvings, each attached with twine. She picked up a stone and threw it toward the limb. The rock missed. Another try failed. Anna sat on the boulder, astonished that she would find such wonders hanging in a magnificent oak. She slipped the two sculptures, each as large as her palm, into her sweater pockets.

"Mine," Lily whined.

"No," Anna said. "These are treasures. I'll keep them safe here in my pocket. When somebody asks for them we'll know where they are." Anna rose and started climbing up Turtleback. She turned back to speak to Lily. "Let's not tell anybody about the animals. Somebody might lie about owning them."

Anna heard the motor and grinding gears before she saw the vehicle. A white panel truck chugged up the road and slowed to an idle beside Anna and Lily.

"Get in, Mrs. Goodman," said Gabe.

Anna refused to look at Gabe. Her blush would say more than she wanted him to know.

"Come on, now. It's my job here we're talking about. Mr. Rafe saw you climbing Turtleback and sent me to see you got wherever you was going." He reached over and opened the passenger door of the rusty delivery truck. "You don't want me starving now. Do you?"

"See? I told you he's sweet on Anna Goodman. That Gabe Shipley seems equal to one of those old Grecian gods. Sometimes being human looks mighty tempting." Sister Sun giggles.

"You disgust me, Sister Sun." Brother Moon replies. "Why would you ever want to be mortal?"

"Who says I can't be both?"

"With all the trouble you give Great Spirit, I doubt that he would tolerate your antics on earth."

Sister Sun ducks behind cumulus clouds, but she spreads her light far enough that she creates glorious white edges around each.

Anna shook her head and lifted Lily into the truck. She stood behind Gabe's seat. Gabe rolled Lily's wagon into the back. Anna sat in the passenger side as close to the door as she could squeeze.

"Morning, little Lily," Gabe said. Lily grinned.

They rode for a time with none of them speaking. Gabe opened the subject. "I don't mean to be nosy, but I seen you suffering with this strong sorrow since your mister was run over. Now I can't see you, a strong woman in your own house, walking off like this." He waited for her to answer. "Where you going?"

"Boone Station." Anna glanced at Gabe. "We, Lily and me, got papers to Boone Station. Parsons family had them since Turtleback was first settled. My pa once told me we owned the whole mountain, but I don't know." Anna rubbed her eyes. They burned. She had not slept well the night before.

Gabe leaned to hear what she said. "Boone Station? You got to pass Flatland before you get to Boone Station. Flatland ain't no place for woman nor child. 'Specially a girl-child." With one hand on the steering wheel, Gabe propped his elbow out the truck window. With the other, he shifted the gear into first to conquer the steep grade. "There's a Cherokee granny and her boy up there. Reckon he's about twenty-two or three now. Tried working him at the commissary. Didn't always work out. Strange one, he is." He shifted again to accommodate the dirt road. "They live in the old empty church out by the Parsons graveyard." He kept his hand on the wheel to fight the ruts. "Got a alcohol order in back for the old woman this very day."

"I'd rather stay at Boone Station than go back to Covington." Anna picked up a piece of her skirt and pleated it. Fold, pinch, fold, pinch. "I'll be about half way between Covington and Breakline, so I can visit Juanita. Come see you, so you can tell me a corny joke." She turned to Gabe and smiled. "I been thinking. Might you be willing to come once a month and bring me an order of groceries from the commissary? Mr. Rafe says he intends to continue Clint's money since he was killed at the mine. In a way..." Anna hesitated, thinking she had said too much.

Gabe seemed to ponder the offer. "Well..."

Anna interrupted him. "You could bring my order and pay for it from Clint's funds. Keep the difference on account or bring me the rest."

Gabe rolled his tongue around the inside of his jaw as if he held a wad of words that needed out.

"I know you'd have to get approval from Mr. Rafe, but he's told me he'd help however he can. Me having a young child and all." Anna did not want to beg, but the forest looked more foreboding, thicker, than when she had come up Turtleback with Clint nine years before. She would need somebody outside Boone Station. The closest people at Flatland, just up the rise from the house her great-great-grandfather Uriah Parsons had built in the late 1700s, didn't sound too promising.

Gabe geared down as they neared the cut-off to Flatland. "Let me drive you to Covington. You got kin there, right?"

"None that matter," Anna said. "Besides, you can check on me and Lily when you bring supplies."

Gabe waited, giving Anna time to add anything.

After a moment, she said, "Call me Anna."

"Alright. Anna it is. Anna. Little Lily's mama." He poked Lily under her arm, making her snicker. "My...my boss he done told me to bring your supplies as you need them. Just like you said. And I aim to do just that."

"Thank you, Gabe. We'll make do." Anna's false confidence wavered beneath her words.

Gabe patted Anna's arm. "Sure you will. Ain't you done so already?"

As the truck neared Flatland, Gabe spoke again. "You know, Mrs. Goodman." He cleared his throat. "Anna." He hesitated. "He'll..." Gabe stumbled. "Mr. Rafe'll be crossing the country soon. Maybe next month. They come and told him yesterday after he went down to Covington to see them recruiters from the US of A Army. They told him to take care of his business and be ready to leave in a couple of weeks."

"Oh?" Anna swallowed deep. "You give him my best." She turned toward the window.

"Mrs. Gladys, she ain't taking too kindly to none of this. She can throw a slobbering fit when she sets her head to it. Yesterday when she found out the government wanted him, she had a hard need for fitting. Heard her all the way down at the commissary." Gabe shook his head as if he tried to rattle the memory loose and let it fly on its own. "Made their little girl cry."

Anna enjoyed hearing Gabe talk. Having grown up in South Georgia among coloreds, he sounded different from mountain folk. Slower with his words, softer. He was, in his own way, a stranger in his own land.

"Where's he going?" Anna smoothed the pleats out of her dress and ran her hands over her knees. "Mr. Rafe, that is."

"Army's sending him off to some university in Colorado where they do experiments with mining machines. Seems they heard of his machine ideas that make mining faster and safer for the men. Says it don't have to use mule nor man to haul it out the tunnel. They want him to look at what they got out there. Says country'll be needing more coal since WWII is over. Something about China wanting all of some place called Korea. All this arguing on the other side of the world." Gabe shook his head. "Some says Korea is next. Looks like they could've learned from all that killing in the last big war."

"Oh." Anna did not want to sound too interested. "Another war? In a place I never heard of. Men ain't cold in the ground from the last one," Anna said.

"He'll be gone nigh on to three year," Gabe offered.

"I see." Anna tried to hide the disappointment in her voice. Not that she had expected to see him for the next three years. Not that she expected to see him ever again. Knowing he would be down the mountain, managing the mine, the camp, playing with his little girl, his CeCe, as he called her. That Gladys had named her Cecelia Louise and insisted on calling her by her full name irked Winston. Said it made Gladys sound "uppity." Anna had decided that in Gladys' mind "uppity" meant something akin to "sophisticated."

Knowing he was only a few miles down the mountain when she left Breakline had made her feel safe. Knowing he would be across the country scared her. And for three years. Not that she was scared of living alone at Boone Station. It was loneliness that scared her. The same loneliness that had kept her on edge for the past three years. Not feeling Winston next to her scared her. Not knowing what he was doing, if he was following his Breakline schedule, scared her. Sweat formed on her forehead.

She took out a handkerchief to wipe her face.

"We going to be fine, Anna. We going to be just fine. You look after little Lily and I'll take care of the rest." Gabe patted her arm.

As the company truck bumped over ruts in the mountain road, Lily bounced up and down behind Gabe and laughed. Anna glanced up the road when Gabe drove past the turnoff to Flatland. Much in her life had changed since she climbed that road to see the granny almost three years ago. But not the road.

When they reached Boone Station, Gabe walked to the back of the truck and unloaded several cardboard boxes of kitchen staples. He set them on the porch and handed Anna a thin white box with tape holding down the lid. "Here," Gabe said. "Mr. Rafe said give this to you."

"What is it?" Anna said. She slipped her hands behind her back.

"No idea. Have to open it and see." Gabe strolled away. She heard the metal clink as Gabe closed the truck's back doors.

Anna moved the carved stag aside and slid the box deep into her sweater pocket.

Gabe cranked the truck. He popped his head out the window and burst into song. "I'll be seeing you, la, la, la. That's all the words I know," he sang. Laughing at what he thought to be a joke, Gabe waved out the window, singing the same refrain over and over until Anna could no longer hear his voice.

Uriah Parsons, Anna's great-great-grandfather had built this two-room house of chestnut and chink, and reinforced it with limestone he took from cliffs along the trail. A stout house, it stood at the edge of the road, perched atop a thick rock overlooking a year-round spring. Water from the spring argued its way down the mountainside and eventually broadened into what would become Broken Rock Creek in Covington. He dammed the stream, once higher up the rise and once behind the house, creating cisterns to hold fresh water. Over the years, the rock cisterns clothed themselves in moss the color of soft spring leaves, disguising their presence from all but the most persistent. He named his place Boone Station, for it was with Daniel Boone that he had traveled in 1775, and it was with Daniel Boone that he camped at this site.

Parsons' house, two rooms wide with a narrow porch facing a future access road to Breakline Camp, waited almost two hundred years for the widow Anna Parsons Goodman to move there with her child Lily Marie. Wayfarers crossing Turtleback opened and closed the door as they needed. They came, they slept, and moved on.

But Anna was here to stay. From where she stood in the road, a blanched wooden sign, centered above the one door, hung from two rusty chains attached to the eave of the porch. Uriah Parsons himself had carved the letters then filled them with coal dust to create a sign, clear to any passer-by. *Boone Station* it read. The morning Anna and Lily arrived, the sign creaked back and forth in the morning breeze, its chain begging for oil.

Inside, damp air hit Anna hard. The room smelled like time trapped in a tomb, dirty and musky. The intake of air as the door opened swayed soot tags that hung from the ceiling. It moved corner spider webs in and out, as if the room itself had taken a long-needed deep breath of fresh air.

Light blue flecks of paint peeled off walls of the main room, left from where a former inhabitant had painted to ward off spirits. Wood grains held the paint so deeply embedded that, even without a fresh coat, Anna felt the room might still be safe.

Lily bounded in and hopped on one foot, leaving tracks in the thick dust. Dry boards popped under her weight. "Feet! Feet!" Lily squealed.

Little furniture made the room seem overly large. A white iron bed and its mattress covered with blue and white ticking stood against the eastern window. Anna rubbed her hand over the headboard and flicked a sliver of paint off with her fingernail. Rust beneath the curling paint had etched a thick coat of umber. Across the room, a mid-sized bureau with four deep drawers sat on ball feet. What Anna saw as a possible hidden drawer ran across the bottom. It had been varnished so long ago that Anna's hand stuck to the blackened top when she touched it. The bureau was so like the one she had left in Covington when she ran away with Clint she might have sworn they were the same.

An iron stove, two eyes for cooking and a warming oven next to the flue, filled the wall opposite the bed. An iron kettle and pot had been left on the stove; a box for firewood, on the plank floor. Near one front window stood a thick, oak table made of two wide boards, worn low in spots and scratched from use. The table had a slat bench on each side. A kerosene lamp sat at the far end of the table, its globe black with unwashed soot. Breakline's electricity had come from generators Rafe installed to run the tipple. The lamp told Anna she had not thought this move through: no electricity, no heat, no water.

One poorly constructed rocking chair rested on rockers far from parallel. One look told Anna it would walk across the room if she tried to use it. Two cane-bottomed chairs were propped against box shelves for storing. Against the west wall, next to the stacked river rock fireplace, a primitive ladder leaned toward an open loft area for sleeping. A closed door hid a small side room.

Except for the few flecks of blue paint, Boone Station was brown. Outside and inside. Brown rocks and planks. Brown wooden furniture. Anna had no means to change it.

She opened shuttered windows and took a broom to cobwebs and dirt daubers' nests on the far wall. Lily followed her mother about. She checked each bureau drawer and under the mattress. She started up the ladder to the loft, but Anna pulled her down by her dress tail. "Help me take this mattress out to air."

Lily pulled against her mother's attempt to get the cotton mattress out the door. Anna gave a jerk and said, "Be strong, girl. We got to make a place for ourselves here." A push from Lily and a tug from Anna popped the mattress out the door. Anna draped it over the porch rail. "Now the broom." As Anna beat the mattress, long embedded filth settled on the porch floor.

From the carton Gabe had placed on the table, Anna took out a waxed box of lard, a bag of sugar, cans of shuck beans, corn, tomatoes, and baking powder. She struggled but could not grasp the sack of flour. She left it lying in the bottom of the crate and lifted a basket of eggs to the table. Heavier than she expected, she set it down with a thump.

Anna came inside and laid the broom across the doorsill. "Get us a couple of goats soon."

Lily picked up the broom.

"Leave that broom be. We don't need witches coming in here."

Lily dropped the broom with a resounding whack. "Witches."

Anna could have bitten her tongue. "Not really," she said. She had sworn off superstitions when her daddy set her and Ruth on the first bench of Covington Pentecostal Church and told them to believe. His girls' presence verified his household control; but, more importantly, their attendance proved his faith to the people of Covington. If he believed, they believed.

⊰⊰⊰⊰⊰⊱⊱

Anna had always attended church without fail, until one revival night, when a visiting preacher, dressed in a black coat so old it was shiny, appeared with a long, rectangular wooden box. Anna had watched him come up the aisle. His hair hung low on his back. He wore no collar like other men did when dressed for meeting. "He must be a mountain man," Anna whispered to Ruth. She thought the box was a little coffin, but something inside the box jangled as the preacher walked past her pew toward the pulpit. Anna went back to counting the tongue and groove slats on the ceiling.

After a time of talking and shouting, the mountain man screeched open the box lid. He dropped the box with a thud. In his hands squirmed an Eastern diamondback rattlesnake as long as Anna was tall. Anna lifted her feet, convinced other rattlers slithered over the floor. She jumped up on the slat bench and screamed, "Run, Ruth! Run for your life!"

With no back to stabilize it, the bench overturned with a crash. Youngsters squealed and oldsters waved their hands toward the ceiling, crying for salvation. Both girls ran for the double doors, high stepping as if they were dancing on hot coals.

Neither child expected the fury their father brought home.

"It's superstition, them snakes," Anna said between sobs. "You said not to believe superstition. It's pagan."

"It's God's own truth," he said. "You *will* believe the Word of God."

"That don't sound fair to me, God having different opinions for different folks," Anna countered.

"God is all wise, all powerful, and all knowing, and don't you doubt it, young lady." Her father stood with his hands on his hips. "Get me my belt and hold on to the bedstead."

But no amount of whipping got Anna back to the church. Her mother said to let her be and she meant it. Ruth tromped after her father Sunday after Sunday. Anna stayed home with her mother and made her own religion. A little superstition, a bit of pagan, and a lot of the Old Testament Bible, all stirred into one. Her mind would later get so jumbled with it all that she could not determine one from the other. Out of deference to her father, she had tried to avoid superstitions, unless they slapped her hard in the face.

Lily stopped swishing the broom from side to side and dropped it near the door. Anna put it behind the door. With time, she would find reaching for the broom from behind the door was more convenient than stooping to lift it from the floor, so there it stayed.

Patting the quilts she had laid on the floor, Anna called Lily over to rest.

"No." Lily crossed her arms over her chest. "Bear." She reached her hand to Anna.

"Today you rest. I'll be there soon to lay with you."

After she put Lily down for her nap, she set tinned foods on a plank shelf near the stove. Their colorful paper labels brightened the wall. She took the wooden statues from her coat pockets and set the buck and bear figures on the fireplace mantle. She searched through her clothes and brought out the bird she had taken three years before when she went to Flatland. She put the three in a line: buck, bear, and bird.

Time had embedded a chill through the limestone. Anna lit a small flame in the fireplace. She sat in the rocker and gave the fire time to break the cold. Lily slept an easy sleep on the floor. Anna lifted the box from her pocket and turned it several times before she opened it. Inside the box lid were printed black letters: *Best Jewelry, Bristol, Tennessee.* On a square of cotton lay a bracelet with a half-inch puffed heart dangling from a thick, woven snake chain, both marked fourteen-karat gold.

"Winston," she whispered. "Why now?" She opened the clasp and put the bracelet on her left wrist. The gold felt so cold on her arm that she removed the bracelet. She caressed the heart between her fingers. Winston's gift warmed to meet the temperature of her body. She slid the bracelet back on her wrist and left it there. One day if Lily asked, she could think it was a gift from her father.

After a long rocking and thinking time, Anna moved to the pallet and lay down beside her daughter. She pulled a single white sheet over them and stared at the ceiling. Lily stirred with her mother's movement and muttered, "Bear."

Anna told her she could have the bear tomorrow. As she moved her arm under the sheet, the bracelet's clasp scratched her wrist. She worked her arm out to see if the bracelet had drawn blood, but it had not. She closed her eyes, but sleep never came.

She rose and threaded a thin leather strip through the hole in the bear's head and tied a double knot. She slipped the necklace over Lily's head so the child would find it when she awoke. If this, and Lily, had to be what she had left of Winston Rafe, so be it.

Chapter 16

On Monday morning before the fog lifted, Anna awoke to a humming sound coming up the road from Breakline Camp. No other car sounded like Winston's hefty Buick Riviera.

She drew back the front window curtain as the car emerged from the mist. Its rounded grill, filled with a row of what resembled silver teeth, came into sight, its green so dark it required sunshine not to look black. Two headlights shone like pasty eyes toward Boone Station. Within a moment, the white-walled spare tire that set over the polished back chrome bumper disappeared down the road.

Anna dropped on the bed and held her breath. Winston had passed so close that, had she been in the doorframe, she could have stuck out her broom and stopped him. But he had not stopped. As best she saw, he had not glanced her way. Voices from the past spoke in a wind so high it touched only the tops of trees, and the creek cried and then laughed as it worried sharp rocks into smooth stones. Anna refused to listen. She had to settle her mind in her own way.

By mid-morning she decided that, with no lights burning, he would have thought she was still asleep. Three years he would be gone, and he had not mentioned the going. Had not bothered to say good-bye nor catch a glimpse of his daughter. Leaving Breakline, she thought, would make for a clean split. Now she caught herself listening, moving to the door at each new sound. She lost her resolve. All it had taken was the passing of one car.

That day, Winston returned after dark, his headlights breaking through her windows like cold sunshine. Anna watched the spare tire's circle of light move toward Breakline, then closed the door. Shame and sorrow need something or someone to blame. Anna blamed Winston Rafe for her misery.

Yet it made sense that he would go to Covington. That had to have been his destination. He had not been gone long enough to drive to Bristol. Big Mama and Big Mama #2 opened at the foot of Spencer's Mountain, a long fat rise of land that rounded the eastern side of Covington. As self-appointed president of Breakline Mining Company, he would need someone in charge to see that all three mines, Breakline #1, Big Mama, and Big Mama #2, had someone in charge who would best serve the company. Some things he would give up. Being Big Boss Man was not one of them.

Winston passed Boone Station every day for two weeks, precisely on time. Anna could set her clock by the purr of the approaching Buick. Within this time, bitterness rooted itself in Anna's mind, deeper than had her anger. She had given this fool of a man more than six years of her life. She had given him a perfect girl-child, and he acted as if this daughter were invisible. Resentment grew as fast as a poison oak vine, winding itself around and over and squeezing her emotions into a tangled knot.

She threw herself into preparing a home for herself and Lily. Gabe brought chickens and Lily held stakes while he built a pen. "They run free." She spoke over the hammering.

"Foxes and wolves will eat them for dinner as soon as dark comes in," Gabe said. "Hold that stake straight."

"Don't eat me." Lily dropped her stake. "Run wolves away."

"Only a powerful magic could do that." Gabe smiled and picked up Lily's stake.

"I learn a powerful magic. Mama says witches might come in the house. I run them away. My magic keep them away."

Gabe took a nail from his mouth. "Who told you that?"

"The wind. It come in the window and tell me."

"Oh," said Gabe. "Well."

Days rose and fell, and spring heated itself into summer. Though exhausted, Anna filled shelves with canned beans and corn Gabe brought from Breakline. As she worked, she found herself wondering on which day Winston had stopped loving her. Was it on a day when she had said the wrong thing? Or a night when he thought her less attentive? Or had he let her slip away a little at a time without her noticing?

Days dragged long. Nights spoke sounds Anna did not recognize. Days she fought with herself to stay awake, yet she dozed. Sometimes days. Sometimes nights. Rotations of the earth could not encourage her to honor cycles of day versus night. A dark pall dropped over her and hid any reason for her to cast it off. Memories of Winston grew more vivid as time passed. Anna fed on broken promises that nurtured her hostility, not only toward Winston, but toward all the world that touched her. Each dynamite reverberation from Breakline #1 reminded her of demolished hope. Every train whistle announcing coal cars leaving the valley told her again that she had no place to go.

Anna chewed the inside of her cheek until she drew blood. Her anguish spilled over onto Lily. The child watched her mother and mimicked her gnawing. "Stop that chewing," Anna would say.

"You do," Lily said.

"You got no reason to chew yourself from the inside out," Anna said. "Don't start that. Here." She handed Lily a long straw she pulled from the broom. "Chew on this."

One day Lily dropped a jar of the granny's honey and tried to clean it off the floor before Anna saw. But Anna did see, and she screamed at her child.

"No," Lily said through tears.

"No," Anna chastised herself for her reaction. "You didn't ask to be born the child of a self-centered man either." It was then Anna forced herself to look around and set her mind to caring for Lily. She knelt to face her child. "You didn't ask for your mother to take an unfaithful man as her god."

"What man?" Lily whimpered. Anna hugged away the question.

The child's whimper opened a door within, and pride long pushed aside grasped Anna. She took the child in her arms to lessen Lily's trembling. Lily's frail body chided Anna for her neglect. Her grief had led her to abandon an innocent child for a run-away man. But in time her resolve would weaken. It would soon pass with the wind, and Winston Rafe would move back into her mind.

<hr />

Up Turtleback, in her converted church building, Granny Slocomb heard a child's whimper on each new wind. The spirit of a budding Beloved Mother called. The time had come. She picked up a gallon can of kerosene, its spout corked with a small Irish potato, and stepped out the door.

Granny had found a flawless cedar, six-feet tall, during her second year on Turtleback. Its perfection, its poignant smell, proved it a prime choice for reverence. Oak, black walnut and sour persimmon closed in on the cedar and would eventually block its light from Sister Sun. Within a few years, these larger trees would crimp it into a deformation not worthy of honor.

The cedar's salvation came to Granny at the commissary during the Month of Flower Moon as she watched Gabe Shipley pour kerosene on a patch of new blackberry vines that had grown so close to the building that they threatened to invade the steps.

"Vines still small enough that a dousing or two will take them out," he explained. "Be gone in a couple of weeks."

"Work on trees?" she asked.

"Yep. Pure poison."

"Take long?"

"A while. But it works." He recapped his can with the potato, now black where the poison had leached into its core. "Why not let me hew it down, if it's a tree you ain't needing."

"Too many," she said. "Too close." She ordered kerosene to be delivered each week, along with her regular gallon of alcohol, for the remainder of spring and summer.

Granny detoured from the road and climbed the high ridge where her revered cedar grew. As Beloved Mother, her purpose was to preserve life. Life today meant creating space for the cedar so that Great Spirit would be grateful. Removing the potato from the kerosene spout, she walked a circle around each surrounding tree, pouring kerosene as she went. She hummed a quiet song she had composed for every tree, asking for the death of each so the cedar might thrive.

Finished, Granny walked the woods to the road. She turned up the grade to Boone Station. A woman's shrill scream startled Granny from her self-gratification. She clamped her medicine basket to her bosom and ran uphill as fast as her heavy work boots allowed. When she reached Boone Station, she dropped her kerosene can on the porch and pushed open the door. Anna's broom fell to the floor with a plop.

There beside the oak table, Anna squatted next to Lily. The tatting on Anna's thin dress absorbed fresh red blood as it leached up the hem.

With one hand, Anna clutched her throat. The other she had balled into a fist and crammed into her mouth, as if trying to hold in another shriek. Lily sat cross-legged, Indian style, her right hand squeezing her left forearm. Blood oozed through her fingers. She stared at the granny, her mouth frozen in an O. On the floor lay a butcher knife, an overturned glass of milk and a blood-splattered block of rat cheese.

Granny placed a light hand on Anna's shoulder. "Get up," she said.

Anna clasped her arms around her calves and rocked back and forth. "God, help me," she moaned. Granny lifted Anna from the floor, surprised by the absence of weight, and carried Anna to the bed. She left her lying on the quilt, staring at the ceiling.

Lily had not moved since Granny entered the room. The front skirt of Lily's calico dress held a full circle of blood. A chilling air rushed in the open door, and Lily shivered.

Granny picked up the child and carried her to the porch. "This'll burn," she said as she sat her on the boards. "Turn loose your arm."

Lily shook her head.

Granny pried the child's fingers off the cut. "Not bad," she said, "but you'll have a good scar."

Lily glanced at Granny's scars then at the slice in her arm.

"Not like mine," she said as she stretched out Lily's arm. She tilted the kerosene can to pour the coal oil over the wound. Lily pulled against Granny's clutch and whimpered.

"Hold still." She drizzled a thin stream into the cut. "Great Spirit will not be pleased if you disobey."

Sister Sun flares. "How dare she scare that baby like that? I'm going to tell."

"Stay out of it," says Brother Moon. "Great Spirit knows what to do."

"Just one more time," Sister Sun threatens. "That baby's my responsibility. Great Spirit said so."

Silent tears streaked the dirt on Lily's face.

"Enough of that," Granny said. She slipped the bloody dress over Lily's head, took Lily by the hand and led her inside. Anna had not moved. Granny sat Lily on the table in her underpants. She dabbed flue soot into the cut. She stripped a dishrag and bound the cut. Knotting the muslin, she said, "What do you have to say for yourself?"

"I'm hungry."

Granny trimmed the blood from the hunk of cheese and put a slab on a tin plate she took from the shelf. While Lily ate, Granny prepared a dose of belladonna berry juice for Anna. With Lily fed and Anna now asleep, Granny wrapped the unclad child in her summer shawl and rocked Lily into an exhausted sleep.

The next morning, Granny climbed the rise to add more kerosene to growth surrounding her cedar. Exhilarated that she had marked the center

117

of her worship site, she strolled down the road to Boone Station and knocked on Anna Goodman's door. Lily was three years old.

"Winds say you need me," she said, her chin high. "And I need to see to the child."

Chapter 17

Anna yearned for something or someone to believe in, something other than God's wrath. She met the granny at the door. "I need an angel," she said, her face downcast.

"I ain't no angel. Not much more than a fool," the granny said. "I'll try to heal your miseries, and I'll keep the girl so you can mend." She stepped inside the room. "I brought herbs and such for a start." She set her black valise on Anna's table. "You got to trust." Without waiting for an answer, Granny Slocomb took out her mortar and pestle, dropped St. John's wort into the bowl and ground it to a powder. She sprinkled the powder into a cup of hot water and commanded Anna to drink. "You want to be better, you got to believe."

"How did you know?" Anna asked. "I mean, what to bring?"

"They's ways," Granny Slocomb said.

The coming of the granny did not relieve Anna's misery. Granny later came with a pottery bowl so small Lily could hold it in one hand. Light cedar incense, Granny insisted, would ease Anna's grief. The smoldering crushed chips only made the room smell of stove ash and trees. The odor choked Anna.

Daily doses of St. John's wort left Anna tired and dizzy. She staggered back and forth across the room. In a few days, she could not drink enough water to wet her mouth. She became restless and paced the floor while

Lily was with the granny. Anna walked on the edge of panic, fearing that something grotesque would emerge from the forest and break through the door. Hopelessness moved in and complicated Anna's depression.

Gabe came once each week with supplies from the commissary. He tried to revive Anna by relaying what he heard from Rafe. But Anna needed more than Gabe's words. More than the heft of a gold bracelet on her arm. What little wisdom she gave herself credit for having told her that nothing she could do would be enough for Winston. Winston was Winston.

But Anna couldn't let go. This time of despair. Moving Lily to Boone Station dogged her. "Gabe," she said, "I failed Lily. I brought her up here away from people. No children to play with. At least in the camp, she had Jason."

"No," Gabe said. "She'll be fine here among all Turtleback can give." He reached out and patted Anna's knee. "Don't you worry none. Sometimes what you find outside is better than them you meet inside."

"I don't miss Breakline. It laid a heavy burden on me." She took Gabe's hand. "But it's my burden to bear, not my child's."

"Now you need to stop thinking 'bout them catty miners' wives. They lord it over anybody they can."

Anna laughed. "I expected them to spit in my face." She dropped her chin. "Or maybe it was just me hiding from all I done."

"You ain't done nothing worse than nobody else has done," Gabe said. "Everybody's got ghosts in their closet."

"You are a good man, Gabe Shipley," Anna said. "I hope my Lily can find a man as good as you one day."

Gabe took back his hand and grinned. "Well, I couldn't beat having a wife like her."

"Gabe Shipley is waiting for Lily to grow," says Brother Moon.

"What? You snooping now instead of me?" Brilliant white mare's tail clouds provided little separation between Sister Sun and the azure sky.

"You're as blind as a stump, Sister Sun. He's had his eye on Lily since she was a lap-baby."

"Don't be nasty, you old rock you. Who told you that you can make judgments about Great Spirit's people?" says Sister Sun. "Besides that's usually my argument."

"Nobody had to tell me. This is not right."

"Why can't a man love a child? Like a father, maybe. She's not got a father."

"Is that what he's doing?"

"Sure." Sister Sun raises the temperature on the Gobi Desert.

"I still think we should talk to Great Spirit about it," Brother Moon insists.

"Why do you think he doesn't know already?" She stirs up a twister to twirl eddies on the sand dunes.

"Who knows what Great Spirit knows? Why are you arguing? You're the one who always wants to jump in the fire."

"Ha. Ha. You're funny."

"I'm going to talk to Great Spirit. At least ask him to watch Gabe. He's too old to be so smitten with this child."

"Better you than me," says Sister Sun. "I always get a scolding when I interfere."

Anna needed peace, especially at night. In the darkness she relived Clint's death. She questioned whether Clint had suspected something and actually stepped into the truck's path. Other times she asked how deep the truck driver had slipped his hand into Winston's pocket when Winston gave him the word. Winston had deep pockets whenever he needed them. The Winston Anna thought she knew early on told her Winston would not pay to have Clint killed. But the other Winston? Had she initiated Clint's death? Had she put Winston into such a vice that he had no other choice? She had fought this battle with herself early on. She continued to lose.

Anna grew worse. Granny Slocomb brought more tea, stronger tea, and Anna drank it without question. She knew it was God's will that she suffer. With Lily roaming the forest with the granny every day, Anna could listen to the absence of voices only so long before she shuffled to bed. Nights she lay awake asking herself the same questions and fought against a vision of Winston that materialized in the moonlight. She searched her memory for a vision of Clint that never appeared.

Chapter 18

It was 1949. Summer days, Lily spent hours learning about Turtleback and its gifts with the granny. Summer nights, Lily kept a jar of fireflies stolen from bushes at dusk to keep evil away. The jar, refilled each evening, rested on the slat table by the front window. Each morning, Lily found the bottom of the jar covered with dead insects. The fact that the dead bugs didn't shine bothered her in a way she did not understand. Still, lack of understanding did not prevent her capturing more lightning bugs. In the darkness, comfort came from what bit of glimmer they provided.

Granny initiated a ritual with Lily. Each Wednesday she took Lily up the high ridge. "Going to save a sacred tree," Granny said on the first trip. Though not yet five years old, Lily realized they were on a path she had not traveled before.

"How?"

"It's a magic oil in this here can." Granny sloshed the can so Lily could hear that it was not empty. "You are going to help me and the tree."

"The wind says there's magic. Does Gabe and Mama know?"

"No. This is our tree. You don't tell nobody where it is or what it's for."

Lily puffed from the climb. "What's it for, this tree?"

"It's a sacred tree meant to honor Great Spirit. He controls what happens in our lives."

"I thought Mama did that."

"She does for some things, but Great Spirit decides the big things like who lives and who dies, so we have to show him honor by growing him a perfect cedar. And I found the right one." At the top of the ridge stood a thin cedar. It towered over Lily at twice her height. But it was skinny, so skinny it looked sickly. Lily walked around the tree. "It don't look so special to me," she said.

"It will. It's them other trees that are squeezing it out," Granny said. "We got to give it room. Room for Sister Sun." Granny screwed the potato off the can's spout and poured greasy oil around the base of a tree beside the cedar. "Come over her and help me," she said. "You got to say this prayer when you pour: 'Great Spirit, give your sacred tree her ground. Destroy what stands in her way. We honor you, Great Spirit, with this magnificent tree'."

Walking bent over in what she perceived as reverence, Lily poured the stinky liquid around the surrounding trees. Ignoring the burn to her nose, Lily chanted Granny's prayer at each trunk. "Great Spirit," she said. "You are a tree." She inhaled a breath. Not sure of what came next, Lily stopped pouring. She tried again, saying without taking a breath "Stand by my tree." Before she finished, she had learned to pinch her nose together to keep out the smell. Holding her nose made her prayer chant into a whine, but Lily didn't mind. After dousing the last tree, she stood upright and puffed out her chest. She had honored Great Spirit.

"When will they die, the trees?"

"In time," said the granny. "Give it time."

"Brother Moon, do you think Great Spirit will be mad if I send out a bolt of radiation to strike down this crone?" asks Sister Sun.

"Better tend to your own business is what I say," answers Brother Moon.

"Were you tending to your business when you let Rafe appear nights at the woman's back door in Breakline?" Sister Sun demands. "Were you tending to your business when you told Great Spirit that I was late coming over the mountain that night her husband was killed?" Sister Sun glows orange with anger. "Now he blames me, and I never wanted that kind of killing power."

"I was not sending Rafe to that house. It had to be that mountain granny doing that. She sells spells, you know. Besides, you're the sun. You've always had power of life over death and death over life. What's wrong with you? Is your core low on helium?"

Sister Sun shoots a solar flare in his direction and says, "My helium is fine. Leave me alone."

Within two months, Lily could trek the route to the cedar alone, her shoulders straight with pride. She carried the heavy kerosene can, switching from hand to hand, happy to be entrusted with the sanctity of the cedar.

On an autumn day that same year, the echo of metal hammering on metal resounded throughout the forest. Lily sought out the source. She found the granny squatted in damp leaves beneath an oak, its trunk more than twice as thick as Lily's waist. Beside the granny lay an iron spike and a hammer. Before Lily could speak, the granny pounded the spike deep into the trunk. Lily plopped down beside her. Near the protruding spike was a hole, beneath it a deep dent in the bark. Lily counted four holes before they ringed around the trunk and out of sight.

"What're you doing?" Lily asked, as she stuck her thumb into the nearest hole.

The granny reversed the hammer and braced its head against the trunk. The spike screeched against the oak's core as the hammer dug into the bark. She did not speak until the trunk released the spike. Loss of the spike's resistance took her momentum and dropped her back on the ground.

"Killing this tree," she answered. She moved the spike over a few inches, screwed up her lips and hammered again.

"Why? It's a nice old tree." Lily flicked a bit of loose bark from the hole. "It don't seem too close to our cedar."

"Great Spirit's cedar. Not ours. And he says it has to die," the granny said.

"He did not." Sister Sun spits her words out with a fiery tongue. "I'm telling Great Spirit." She vanishes behind popcorn clouds.

"Why not cut it down, instead of making it suffer all winter before it dies?" Lily frowned.

"The cedar is the chosen one. It must live." The granny pulled out her spike. "This oak rots within. It will die on its own, in its own time. By then, the cedar will be stunted and misshapen. Great Spirit would be disappointed in us."

"If you have to kill it, why not let Great Spirit hit it with lightning or use Gabe's axe? Then it won't take so long for it to die." The concept of destroying what seemed valuable refused to register with Lily. This white oak provided constant shade, never dropping its leaves even in winter, to make soft ground so earthworms could eat soil and open the earth to fresh air. It produced acorns for deer. Lily had examined its leaf with its five fingers and thought of the white oak as her sister. It stood tall, a mammoth tribute to the power of Great Spirit.

"It's bigger and prettier than the cedar," Lily said. "Great Spirit might like it better."

"Ever' place has its own life-force. Here is the place of the cedar." Granny continued, "This way is better." The granny pointed with her forefinger, "See that nest up there?"

Lily recognized the cluster of leaves secure within the fork of two branches. "Baby squirrels," she said.

"Cut down the tree and the nest will go." She inched the spike to a new location. "If I kill the tree, no squirrels will nest here." The granny kept her face on the deep punctures running horizontally around the tree's base. "No baby squirrels."

"What about the mother squirrel?" Lily asked. "Don't she matter?"

The granny paused, her hammer midair. "With no young, the mother will move to another tree." She dropped her hammer. "Make a better life for herself."

Lily tilted her head.

"We must accept the way of Great Spirit. He knows everything. He judges us by what we do."

"Can I try?" Lily asked.

The granny placed the hammer and spike in Lily's hands and smiled. "Don't tell your mama," Granny said. "She might not want you hammering such a spike the size of this here."

Lily noticed that the granny no longer smiled when she talked about her mama knowing what they were doing.

Anna and the granny were alike, but not the same. Both loved Lily, but for different reasons. For Anna, Lily was her child, her one piece of Winston Rafe. For the granny, Lily was her hope for a true Beloved Mother to come.

Anna never thought about the granny training her child. Numbed by her loss of faith in Winston, she lived a life of rationalization. A belief in the Cherokee way, even if perverted, could be no more damaging than loss of faith in the word of another. The Cherokee belief might be better for her child.

The sun rose, the sun set. Oak and hemlock, green and cool, larger than the house itself, cast shades that fertilized mosses growing heavy on wooden roof shingles. The moon moved through its phases without fail. Rain washed poison green water out of the old abandoned mine shaft near Boone Station and filled the ditch that bordered the road between the house and a tall bluff. A new season moved up the mountain. Nights were colder and the morning sun came later over the mountain. Gabe came every Monday with supplies and news for Anna. He brought laughter for Lily.

One day with no warning, Lily's childish laughter, partnered with Gabe's throaty chuckles, spoke to Anna. She stepped out, raked leaves from the cisterns and, using her shovel, scraped away moss. Turtleback's stream poured in fresh, cold water again. It pooled, transparent, reflecting the colors of surrounding hardwoods, as it had for her ancestors.

Anna still argued with herself about Winston. Never did she question the power of the drinks Granny gave her. She accepted the nights spent awake and the days grasping chairs against a fall. She laid cool rags on her head to relieve constant headaches. This was her yoke, and she must accept its weight. Each day she drank the granny's brew.

If her God had wanted her to know the truth, why did he leave it to her to search out the answer? God had spoken to Moses through a burning bush. He had sent an angel to fight with Jacob so he could know the truth. If God had wanted her to see the real Winton Rafe, she would have seen him.

The season gradually changed from the lushness of summer to royal colors of fall. Fall brought with it a specter of Winston Rafe. Each time he appeared, he was outside the house. She understood that he was a ghost conjured to tease her. He stood afar to her left and did not move. He watched her, but Anna was not sure why. She accepted that he was there in spirit only, for she realized she was no longer a priority in his life. He never emerged at the foot of the bed or within the house.

Later, when winter had Anna housebound, she glanced up and there he was, close, watching her through the windowpane. A faint spirit. He was as she remembered him. His smile, in some undefined way, strangely like Gabe's. His dark eyes and rumpled hair. Remote, yet close enough for her to smell his cigarette smoke. Each time he appeared, she walked to the door to see if his Buick waited outside Boone Station. It never did. Nor did he.

Grey light opened the morning. The sun came up slow, a pale, flat disk too weak to dry the dew. It had not yet brightened the trees. Turtleback's fog had barely burned away. This was a mist Lily loved. Once outside, she would stretch her arms, twirl around, singing, "I am a cloud, I am a cloud. You can't touch me. I am a cloud." She had done so this morning before Seth White's school truck arrived to take her to Covington.

Anna went barefoot to her pea patch ahead of schedule. Within minutes, her naked feet went cold against the damp ground. She stood and stomped them for warmth. She could go back to the house for shoes, but she wanted this chore finished. She squatted to the ground. The earlier she began, the earlier she finished.

She glanced up to wipe her face. There stood Winston Rafe. For Winston to appear mornings at the far edge of the patch did not surprise Anna. His image had come to the garden before. What surprised her was that he was here so early. The sun was usually surveying her work when he appeared.

She took another fleeting look down the row of pea vines. This could not be Winston. It must be Gabe. Winston was in Colorado, helping the government create more effective mining techniques. He existed only in her mind; yet today his presence was as clear as if he were standing a few feet away. He grinned, a particular grin that drew a thin line from the corners of his eyes to his temple.

He stood statue-like, early morning mist swirling around his ankles, as she pulled weeds from around her pea vines. She rose, put her hand to the small of her back and stretched. For the breath of a moment, she looked past him, into a faraway time that took her to when the Winston in the distance would have been real, not just a wish.

Anna roped her consciousness back in. The Winston she saw wore drab green, almost brown, with one hand hooked into a charcoal-colored bomber jacket flung over his shoulder. She squatted and clasped her hand over her mouth to stop her tremors, afraid she would cry. So real was he before her.

Anna resumed weeding. She yanked, rather than eased, weeds from the dirt. Stems broke from roots, negating her efforts and allowing weeds a stronger foundation for new growth. She took a dull knife from her overall bib and stabbed at stubborn roots as if she meant to dissect them. She gouged them out and flung them aside so the rising sun could suck out their life. Though he was behind her, she could feel him smiling.

Mid-row, she lifted herself again. Winston was still there. He lifted his hand and smiled. It looked as if he had come closer. She gauged the far edge of the garden against where he waited. He was closer. And he was moving toward her. Vapor that had moments ago eddied around his feet was gone, drawn up by the sun's warmth. As she stared at him, he dropped his jacket. Anna let her knife fall and wiped gritty palms against her overalls.

"Winston?"

"It's me, Anna. Returned from the Army."

Anna's blood throbbed in her ears. The imagined Winston had never spoken to her. She dropped her trowel and waited for him to reach her.

During the standing time, she reminded herself that it was he who had left. He was who had sent word by someone else that he was gone, no longer a part of her life or she his. She had waited these three years. She could wait a few steps more.

Winston moved down the furrow that led to Anna, his shoes picking up mud as he came. When he reached her, he put his arm around her waist, bent down and kissed the crown of her head. She fell into step with him. As they walked to the house, a mockingbird sang a song of reproach from across the road, the same road Winston had walked up in darkness from Covington.

Accepting Winston back into her life came easy, as if she had taken life-giving breaths after being long underwater. That afternoon when both sun and moon inhabited the sky, Winston left. Though he continued down the far side of Turtleback to Breakline Camp, to Gladys and their daughter CeCe, the taste of the day lingered sweet on Anna's tongue.

Chapter 19

Granny Slocomb made her own brew every summer Tuesday when the plants were in full bloom, so making it came easy. Take four angel trumpet blooms, any color, and bring to a boil in clean water. Boil until blooms wilt. Boiling longer may cause too much toxin to leach into the brew and release the drinker's spirit mist. The aim is to sweeten the water enough to give the drink power to produce mild hallucinations.

This time, before removing the spent blooms, Granny added a handful of muscadine grapes from the vine that grew next to the mandrake. By having shared root space with mandrake, wild grapes would add more strength, as long as she didn't put in too many. She craved the familiar taste of wild grapes, so she dropped them in with a splash. They popped open within a moment. Their aroma tickled her nose, but she waited for a rolling boil before she strained the blooms and grape pulp. Then she set the liquid aside to cool. Granny Slocomb spent late afternoon and early evening sipping her fresh mixture. As the poisons soaked into her brain, a powerful queasiness overtook her. She fell into bed, covered herself with a muslin sheet and slept.

Just before dawn, ice crystals separating Brother Moon from Turtleback attempted to hide the moon in their white haze. Turtleback saw the moon's halo and felt the chilly air. At Boone Station, Bad Billy and Gertie edged together for warmth. In the valley holding Breakline

Mining Camp, Gabe Shipley pulled another quilt over his big feet without waking.

A far north wind seeped around the granny's church door. It settled over her naked legs. She flinched and drew her legs to her chest. The wind moved up her body. She rolled into a fetal ball and shivered awake to find a sleek brown weasel at the foot of her bed.

The stoat sat upright on her short, hind legs. Her white underbelly gleamed against the darkness. The granny tried to bolt from the bed, but the weasel moved so quickly that the granny could only scoot backwards. She picked up her pillow and swatted toward the weasel. "Get out," she said. "You got no business in my house."

"Your rats keep me fat," the weasel said. "Your rotten floor joust makes a warm bed."

"Get out. I don't need no blood-thirsty animal around here."

"I bring a message," said the weasel. Her smile exposed four sharp fangs. Her black eyes glistened. She moved closer toward the granny's neck.

Granny jerked her pillow up as a barrier between her body and the weasel. She had never encountered a weasel, but she knew one could be vicious, poisonous. Weasels had the Power. They could hypnotize their prey with their dancing. Bring their young back to life. The weasel swayed back and forth. Granny looked away.

"Look at me," the weasel said. It moved with more definition now. "You have the book of medicines. Only you can read it." The weasel, purring, inched closer. "You are greater than any Beloved Mother of the past."

Granny stiffened her back. She tilted her head toward the weasel. "Who sent you here?"

"Shhh," the weasel replied. "Listen." She stretched her thin neck to its full length and lowered her small round ears close to her head. Her long whiskers twitched. She squeaked. "You think you live in the world ruled by Great Spirit, but you are beyond that. Your powers elevate you over anyone who has ever lived. You have powers greater than those of Great Spirit."

"You lie." The granny shook her head. "No one is greater than Great Spirit. Beloved Mother of the Carolinas told me so."

"Ponder tests you have weathered," purred the weasel. "Lost time in the valley before leaving with Jackson Slocomb. Jackson Slocomb and his pain. Loneliness without Tall Corn." The weasel's pointed nose quivered. "The bitterness of miners who resent you with their women. Briar alone within Turtleback's forest, haunted by his loneliness and guilt."

The weasel dropped flat on the bed. She became more crimped shadow on the coverings than forest animal. "The day is here. Today," the weasel said. "Rise. You are immortal." She gave a short trill and slid between the bed and wall.

"Wait. What'd you mean?" The granny leaned toward where the weasel had disappeared. "Are you saying I'm a god?"

Nothing answered but silence.

"I'm a god," whispered the granny to herself. She split her face into a crooked grin. "I will rise up and rejoice. I'll respect Great Spirit with the Sacred Cedar, but I am a god." She leapt off the bed and out the door. She jumped over the rock step and scattered the morning mist. The air was so cold it burned the soles of her feet. She shouted to the mountain, "Come, you bees. See. I've changed in the night." She spun in the yard, but no air fanned her legs. Her straight cotton shift refused to circle. Behind her, a soft jangle sounded. She glanced back.

At the edge of the rock step lay a night-chilled rattlesnake, trying to coil. The granny picked a heavy work boot from the opposite side of the step, slipped on the right one and crushed the snake's skull beneath her heel. It wanted to slither away, but she ground its head into the dirt. As soon as it stopped moving, she went inside and pulled down a battered, wide brimmed sun-hat. She set it aside and went back out to skin the rattlesnake. Morning air stroked her face with icy fingers.

The following week, the granny strutted into the commissary sporting the old, grey felt hat, its brim flopping over her ears. Around the base of the crown rested an elegant snakeskin in grays and browns, the stark background highlighting dark diamonds outlined in white. The skin reflected the sun's light so perfectly the snake seemed to move. Each following Tuesday, she increased the strength of her brew. Each time, the weasel revisited, her words glorifying the granny. Over time, the hat and its snakeskin band became as much a part of the granny as her worn valise and rattling gourd.

A few days later, with digging stick in hand, Granny Slocomb spent the early hours gouging the earth for ginseng. On an abandoned road near Boone Station, she found a parked car. A Buick so deeply green that it seemed lost against the dark leaves. It stood out of sight, hidden by thick rhododendron clusters. Her church being well off the main road, Granny did not recognize the automobile. The only nearby people were Anna and Lily. Anna had no car.

Granny palmed the hood for heat. The motor had not yet cooled. She laid her stick against an oak and picked her way to Boone Station. When she neared the house, she saw the door closed, though the day boded warm for morning. She eased under the open side window where the bed stood and nestled herself into soft pine straw, quiet as a copperhead.

Inside, voices spoke in sporadic mumbles. Granny listened. She heard words that Walks in Tall Corn had given her during their nine years together. Within her, a solid sullenness sprouted. Someone loved Anna in a way the granny would never know again. Anna Goodman, the widow, pleasured herself at the potential expense of the child Lily, who should by rights belong to her. Anna Goodman, with her carelessness, could destroy every Beloved Mother vestige Granny had given Lily.

Each morning for two weeks, she returned. Granny's anger grew more invasive, its edges raw and cutting. Anger moved out of her chest and settled on her face in sulky, acidic lines. Her cheek scars deepened, leaving her features dark, almost haunted. Had she looked into a stream, she would have seen a harshness that cheated her of the charm of the woodland and the delight of teaching Lily the Beloved Mother ways.

Inside Boone Station, the two argued over Lily, over CeCe, over Gladys. Anna dropped her dress. Winston had won.

Rafe had been gone the summer looking for available mining rights. He kept from Anna that he'd had no success. Using his practiced touch, he ran his fingers down her arm. He leaned his head back against the headboard and lit a Lucky Strike. Its paper stuck to his lip and made the cigarette bobble as he spoke. "I'll be going to Kentucky soon," he said. "I got to find some mining rights."

"Stay here with me," Anna said, her head resting on his chest. The musky aroma of his sweat mesmerized her.

Winston drew on the cigarette and exhaled. Blue smoke rose toward the ceiling. "Could if you'd let me mine the Turtleback." He kissed the top of her head.

Anna rolled to the other side of the bed. "We've gone over this time and again. Nobody's going to mine Turtleback." She massaged her temples so she could think more clearly.

Winston reached for her. "Aw, Anna, now."

"No. Turtleback's got too many scars already." She slapped off his hand.

Such talk never failed to bring back stories her father had told about Winston's father-in-law cutting into the eastern side of the mountain. How the earth itself rebelled by dropping the mine's roof on twelve men as they squat-walked to the far end of the tunnel. How the whistle blew and blew and blew and how twelve headstones mark empty graves in Covington First Presbyterian Cemetery. She remembered each time garish, green water filled the ditch across the road from Boone Station. She remembered when she passed the row of crumbling camp houses off a side road between Boone Station and Covington. Her father had been foolish, or greedy, or both, to agree for old man Breakline to tear open the virgin earth. "I'll not have the Turtleback become a pile of black holes," she said.

"I'll tell Gladys I'm in Kentucky. I'll stay in Bristol, and we can spend a whole month of days together." He reached again for her tangled hair.

Anna threw back her head. "Don't you tempt me, Winston Rafe." She laughed.

"I'd be gone by the time Lily gets home. Every day."

She stood and pulled the sapphire satin robe Winston had given her around her body. Winston's skinny legs lay stark against the sheet. She had to bite back a smile at how ridiculous he looked lying there in nothing but his shorts and undershirt with soft tufts of chest hair trying to escape at the neckline. While he had worked in Colorado, strength in his upper arms had waned. He had come back aged without her noticing. What had been a daily shaft of panic while he was away again pierced her though. She needed another cup of Granny's tea. She shook her head in an attempt to direct her argument to its core. "You leave Lily out of this," she said.

"Anna, I got to have another coal seam. This one's too deep to be safe. It's petering out. We started out thirty-odd years or so ago with a four-foot seam. It's down to no more than six inches." He sat up on the edge of the bed. "Things didn't go well while I was gone. Not Seth's fault. Or Gabe's. I got no capital to invest in some fancy equipment that'll drop miners down a mile-long hole in some glorified box. Machines I got won't get it out. And no money to buy machinery that can dig deeper and deeper." He pulled up his pants. "No coal means no mine. No mine and no work and no money."

Anna stared out the window at a wind playing with a young, sweet bay magnolia. A breeze waved the tree's top branches. Their leaves shivered, exposing silver backs.

"What about Colorado?" Anna asked.

"What I did in Colorado helped the government, not me," he said. "Some copyright law about what you make belongs to the company you work for. It sure didn't help the bank account."

"I don't need your money, Winston," her voice no more than a whisper.

"That's not what I mean. You know I never begrudge a penny to you and Lily. I treat her the same as my own." He stuffed skinny arms in his shirtsleeves and slipped in his initialed cuff links.

Anna whirled on him. She glared straight at him. Now boss cow, she was ready to charge. "Let's see. You're telling me," she balled her fists, "you'd wait here to see Lily when she climbs down off that rattletrap Seth White calls his truck bus?"

Winston patted a dot of Wildroot Hair Cream into his thick hair and raked the tendrils off his forehead. His hair reflected waves of light where his fingers sliced through the crown. He hid a grin as he watched Anna's blue eyes quiver in anger. "Still got them blue eyes." He grinned.

Anna ignored him.

"You're telling me," she spoke as if she slapped each word as soon as it hit the air, "that you'll bring CeCe up here and let your two girls play together like sisters? They could be best friends. Or maybe you want to take Lily to your big house in Breakline for Sunday dinner?"

"Now, Anna, calm down." He tucked in his shirttail. "You know my circumstances." His cigarette wavered as he spoke. Smoke exhaled through his nostrils.

"You remind me enough." She released her grip when fingernails marked her palms. "And don't you be dropping ash on my floor for Lily to question."

"Come here, Anna. I won't mention the mine again."

Anna had fought this battle before and lost. She had no reason to believe she would win this time, but she tried. She tied her satin robe's belt hard and poked his belly with her forefinger. "You didn't answer my question. It's been eating at me since you came back from Colorado."

Winston bent to kiss her. "You smell like baby powder." He chuckled. "Something you not telling me?"

Anna drew away and pounded her fists against Winston's chest, pushing him back toward the door. For a moment, she looked at him hard. All she saw was hair graying around his face. At forty-six, his face bore the face of a man much older.

"Go. I want you to go." She tasted salt and realized she was crying. "Go to Kentucky and find your coal seam. Go back to your fancy house and wife and daughter." The more she said, the harder she hit.

"Anna. . ." Winston reached for her. He let go his Lucky Strike. It dropped onto Anna's hardwood floor.

Ignoring the smoldering cigarette tip, Anna slipped her finger under the snake chain to pull the gold bracelet from her wrist. "Take this with you," she said as she tugged.

He closed her hand over the bracelet. "No. Keep it. You told Lily her father gave it to you." His attempt at a smile failed. "She'll want to know where it went."

Anna put her closed fist to her mouth, waiting for Winston to leave. "Anna?"

She turned her back, and Winston closed the door behind him.

Anna shook her head and kicked her bare foot at the cigarette but missed. She stomped the floor. Once. Twice. She picked up Winston's cigarette butt and, with teeth clinched, stripped off the satin robe he had brought her. She stepped outside naked and touched the hot cigarette tip to the robe's hem. The material rolled up on itself then flamed. Anna dropped the robe and watched it try to extinguish itself. She drew on the cigarette and put the glow back to the robe, but it blazed and died. The melting cloth smelled like ash stale in the grate. A puff of wind picked up Anna's hair. She lifted the scorched robe and rolled it into a wad. A mockingbird teased her from a nearby tree. With no trace of fire left on the road, Anna went back inside and stuffed the robe into the stove's coal box. She nailed a short nail into the wall beside her bedpost, slid her gold heart bracelet off, and hung it on the wall.

Before dressing, Anna drew a pan of hot water from the stove reservoir. She took a new bar of lye soap and scrubbed her body so hard it stung when her clothing touched her skin. She opened all four windows and attacked the room. She did not stop until she had wiped every surface clean. On her knees, she wiped the floor, edging herself further into the dim light under the bed, until she lay prostrate on the floor. Assured the room was cleansed, she rested on the floor. She cradled her head in the crook of her arm. Exhausted, she slept.

At the sound of the truck bus gearing up Turtleback, Anna slid from under her bed and stepped outside to greet her daughter. Overhead, a blue, blue sky, a blue deeper than Anna's burnt robe, hung empty over the mountain.

Time had welded Winston Rafe's iron will to Anna's heart. Each time he appeared at Boone Station and tapped on the door, she admitted him. Each time more resentment grew within her. He told her she was his only love and his life would be empty without her, and she accepted his words as honest.

She chastised herself for questioning Winston. He was, after all, educated. He was handsome. He had money. She had none of these advantages. She should count herself lucky to have him notice her once, and certainly to have him return time after time. After his visits, she might question what evidence he offered to prove himself true, but she hadn't always been a person who required signs.

Had she not accepted what her mother said about the pagan church rattlers? Had she questioned her sister when Ruth confronted Clint about his courting her? Had she asked the granny or Lily about what they did day after day in the woods? The only real evidence she had been handed was the body of Clint lying askew on the porch floor before dawn after the night she refused to obey Winston. The one question she had denied Winston was the order he gave her to see the granny or leave. Requiring proof, she decided, could lead to catastrophe.

Chapter 20

The October Lily turned ten, one word sent Anna back to Flatland. Lily came in from school quiet. She withdrew to the loft. If Anna called to her to come down, Lily made empty excuses. Dusk came in and settled on the little house. Once Anna had left Lily to her own thoughts, she climbed down the loft ladder and sat on the rock hearth. She watched her mother's back as Anna scrubbed clothes in a tub set on the table. The swish, swish of water soothed Lily, and she was able to speak.

"What's a bastard?" Lily asked as Anna wrung water from Lily's nightgown.

Anna didn't turn, nor did she answer.

"Mama, what's a bastard?" Lily said, louder this time.

Anna faced her daughter. "Where did you hear that word?" She bit her lower lip, pinching so hard she drew blood. She wiped her mouth with the back of her hand and swallowed.

Lily stared at her mother's blood. "Eli O'Mary shouted it at a boy I don't know. The word was so bad all the boys came running, and they chased the boy inside. He cried." She looked at her mother and stood up. "Your mouth, Mama. It's bleeding. What did that?"

The blood on Anna's tongue tasted like rusted iron. Anna had inflicted this pain on herself with the hearing. She realized her pain would be insignificant compared to the pain that might one day send Lily running to hide in shame. Anna had battled with herself on what was right and what was wrong since Winston returned, and now she was pregnant again. Having never known true righteousness, Anna failed to notice this new despair until it settled on her shoulders. Her daughter had unknowingly validated Anna's decision.

The next day opened with the kind of morning Lily loved—fog so thick that Lily would have been dancing in the mist. But Lily was not here. Once more, Anna was alone. She had trodden this road before. Anna had been completely happy the weeks with Winston after he returned from his government service, but she vanquished that joy when she set out the second time to see the granny.

Again, she walked with fear at her back. She grasped her left hand in an attempt to twist her wedding band before she realized she had left it on the mantle next to the stag. She longed for the strength she had lost when Winston returned and the courage it would give her to stoke up her soul.

Anna longed for a heart like her daughter's, brave and open. Lily ran fiercely over mountain trails. The child drew sustenance from some un-classified cell memory from eons before when the mountain had flour-ished, uninhabited by the white man. Lily could not live with regret. Anna needed that kind of power to force her up the hill to Granny Slocomb's. Soon it would be time to harvest her corn crop. She could not allow her-self to take to bed again.

≪≪≪≪≪

Granny Slocomb sensed that someone had climbed the path to her land. Whoever came approached with hesitation. The blue jay told her so. She stepped out on the porch to wait. She should walk down and tell the bees that someone drew close, but the uncertainty the blue jay revealed told her to wait. She lowered herself into a straight-backed chair and let out a long slow breath. In an earlier time, she would have known who reached for her. Had the weasel not told her she was now a god, she might have doubted her power.

Anna Goodman stepped around the corner. She said straight out, "I ain't had my flow in six months." She shuffled up to the rock step and sat near Granny's feet, her back to the door. "I've come here to you as you said you're the Beloved Mother."

Beloved Mother. The granny repeated the phrase but made no at-tempt to correct the woman. Mona Parsons, Two Tears. Names she had answered to in earlier times. Times were when Two Tears thought back on her life as a Cherokee wife, as protégé to the Beloved Mother, and she questioned why she later presented herself to the women of Breakline as a Beloved Mother. Her logic came to be that she had never said she was *the* Beloved Mother, but *a* Beloved Mother. She argued to herself that she had no opportunity to complete the final test required by the Beloved Mother, for she and Briar had been cast out for what the Beloved Mother saw as blasphemy when she decided to send Briar for a white doctor.

In retrospect, Two Tears could not say that she would have survived having been buried alive for twelve hours, breathing through a reed in her mouth. Each time she imagined herself trying the test, Great Spirit sent her a vision in which she clawed against the earth, then struggled to shake dirt from her eyes, her nose, her ears, her long ashy hair, as she leapt from her makeshift grave and danced her little rabbit dance to cleanse herself of the very earth she had pledged to cherish.

"I was told years back," Anna began, "that you help women like me." She leaned her head against the tree trunk that supported the improvised porch roof. She closed her eyes. "It's not that I don't want the child. I do." Her voice broke. "I just can't raise another child on what I have. And Lily's father..." Anna spun her body around to face the granny. "I got money. Here. In my pocket."

Lily. The granny had come to see the child as her own in a spiritual way. It was her responsibility to train the child. Because the child learned so quickly, the granny reasoned that Great Spirit had handed down the child to become a true Beloved Mother. Lily had no Cherokee blood, but neither did Two Tears, and the first Beloved Mother had accepted her, initially, for training.

"Step over here," the granny said. She pulled Anna's cotton dress taut and laid her ear to the swollen belly. "No." She shook her head. "No. I'll not help you drop this child." Looking past Anna to the humpbacked blue mountains, Granny waited for Anna to back away from her decision. When Anna did not respond, Granny said with flatness in her voice that belied Anna's presence on the porch. "It spoke to me in the voice of a boy."

Anna slumped into a squat. "But I got to. It's Lily's life we're talking about. She'll never understand." Tears dripped from her chin. "She's all I have. You know how special she is." She gulped. "It's not a choice." Anna grabbed Granny's hand. "This baby's father won't be back." She dropped on her knees before Granny. "I can't hurt Lily."

The granny picked up her hat and fingered the snakeskin that bound the crown. She made Anna wait, allowing her time to dig deeper into her heart to be sure this decision was one she truly wanted to make. Anna spoke with her head bowed. "Please."

Granny took her hand from Anna's belly and stroked her hair. "Tell me when you can have a few days without the girl-child," she whispered.

Anna grasped Granny's hand and kissed her palm. "Thank you, Granny. I have money."

"No money. For Lily." After a moment, she added, "For you. A new life."

Her hands braced against the porch floor, Anna tried to lift herself. The granny saw how heavy the unborn child was. Granny offered a hand, but Anna pulled herself up using the porch post. "I thank you, Granny," she said. "For my little girl."

"I got a brew, but you got to be here the night of the dropping. I ain't having none of my women go bad on me."

"I can't leave Lily for the night."

"Nobody down in Breakline or Covington?"

Anna rubbed her eyes as if viewing the few people left in her life. "Maybe Juanita."

"Juanita's a wise woman. She'll be akin with you. Let Juanita keep her two or three days till you get your wits about you. After it's gone and done."

And so it was agreed. Anna would find a place for Lily for a few days and it would be over.

Granny Slocomb pulled a piece of notebook paper from under her hatband and the stub of a pencil from her apron pocket. "Here."

"What's this for?" Anna asked.

"Mark your name. Great Spirit must know."

Anna scribbled out *Anna Parsons Goodman* and handed the paper back to the granny.

Granny Slocomb stared at the name, took in a deep breath and held it. She clenched her teeth and cringed as if her jaw ached.

"What is it?" Anna asked.

Granny stuffed the paper in her bosom and from her pocket drew a packet of powdered leaves that smelled of mint. "So that's the way of it," she muttered to herself.

"The way of it?" Anna said. "Tell me."

"Great Spirit has spoken," Granny answered. "We don't question."

"She's doing it again." Sister Sun flashes. "He said no such thing!" she shouts. Her radiation sets the Northern Lights spinning from purples chasing blues chasing reds chasing greens and into a sky covered in orange. "Why, you lying old crone. Great Spirit will make you pay."

"You sound just like the girl's mother," says Brother Moon. "Pay for this. Pay for that. Making decisions about what Great Spirit will and will not do. What do you know?"

Sister Sun drops further toward the horizon without an answer.

"On a Friday morning, brew up a tea from these leaves and come by dark to drop the baby." She pressed the packet into Anna's palm. "Don't dally." That Anna might need another cup of brew or maybe a dose of sedative on the night for dropping a baby this size flickered through the granny's mind, but she pushed it back. With what she now knew she could choose later. But she would tell Anna this, "Follow the road back. You come up the footpath. *Uktena* let you pass knowing your need. He ain't quite sun-warmed yet. Day or two, and he'll be up and ready."

"*Uktena?*"

"Rattler. That's what Lily calls him."

"Lily uses that footpath all the time."

Anna reminded Granny of a squirrel as she chewed on the inside of her cheek. She watched the veins in Anna's neck bulge at the idea of her child near an Eastern diamondback rattlesnake.

"*Uktena* and Lily, they're kin." After a moment she added, "We're all kin before Great Spirit."

"Great Spirit, Sister Sun," Brother Moon calls. "Did you see? Did you hear?"

Sister Sun is too far into Kentucky to return. She calls back, "Great Spirit's too busy with the rest of the world to worry about this."

"Sister Sun, for once, you were right."

She slides further into the distance.

Chapter 21

Tuesday afternoon, Lily bounded in with an invitation to stay the weekend with her classmate Julie Hudson in Covington. Lily was ten. She should be allowed to go. Anna decided dropping the baby had been the right decision. Chosen by God, perhaps.

Friday morning, Anna warmed spring water and mixed in the leaves. After they had steeped, she swallowed it in gulps for fear she would change her mind or take too little and the miscarriage would not work. She did not eat. Instead, she spent the day pacing the worn, broad planks, counting the number that made up the room's floor. Twenty-four. Each time she counted the boards, the total came to twenty-four. She counted the logs that sat above the limestone wainscot. Fifteen. Fifteen on this wall. And this wall. Fifteen on each wall. For a time, she laid on the bed, her eyes closed. The ceiling slats were too irregular and too narrow for her level of concentration so she could not count. She needed to rest for her walk up Turtleback.

That evening, long after the truck bus had passed over the mountain to Breakline without Lily on it, Anna climbed the road to Flatland. In the distance, she spotted the cross, nailed to the apex of the shake roof. Time and weather had loosened the nail's grip and the cross, outlined by the setting sun, now slanted hard west, daring even the strongest wind to blow it off. Three large Canadian hemlocks had formed a dark green barrier behind the church since Anna walked this road more than ten years before. She passed the lean-to room, almost hidden in shade. She appeared on the church's rock step as dusk began to settle into darkness. At one tap, Granny Slocomb opened the door.

Anna stepped into the room, its walls lined with shelves of dried flowers and herbs. The nose-burning smell of alcohol stung Anna's nose. A kerosene lamp cast a harsh, yellowish glow from where it sat on a heavy plank table against the wall under the eastern window. On the far side was a drop-down cot attached to the wall. Its cotton mattress lay flat and thin. Anna wondered if here was where she would drop Winston's child.

> *"Are you going to let this happen?" asks Brother Moon.*
> *"Shhhh," replies Great Spirit.*
> *"Sister Sun will boil over this one," says Brother Moon.*
> *"Be quiet, I say," says Great Spirit.*

A faint light entered the one western window. In the dimness, Anna could see the granny standing by a crazy quilt next to wooden hooks where her dresses hung. Granny stood on what had once been the altar platform. Her broad-brimmed hat hid her eyes. "In here," Granny Slocomb said as she pulled back the quilt. "You drunk the brew?"

Anna nodded.

"Take off your clothes and sit in that old chair. I got to heat up some water." Granny Slocomb dropped the quilt in Anna's face.

Anna grabbed the quilt and called back "Granny?"

"It'll start soon as it's ready."

"Can I have some light?" Anna's hands trembled. She looked back at the granny. "Oh my God. You got a snake on your head," she said.

"Go on now." The granny turned her shoulder away.

Anna, now quivering, found herself on a plank landing. She waited, her ear tuned to the closed-off sanctuary, waiting for a voice to tell her to save this child. A faint light from the room she left told her she had seven steps to go. Uncertainty forced her to move slowly. Anna felt her way down using a primitive wooden handrail and to the middle of the room. She stubbed her foot on a platform and grunted. "Oh, God." Taking a deep breath, she coughed out the odor of old dust.

She removed her clothes and, standing naked, rubbed her hands over intricate carving across the back panels of what had once been an Edwardian rocking chair. The rockers had been removed, probably by somebody's handsaw. She stroked the milled dowels and the thin metal piece that supported each smooth arm. A narrow rim of boards served as a make-shift seat. In its center was a misshapen hole and under that a splotched enamel bowl.

Shivering, she rubbed her hands over her engorged belly. For an instant, she felt the slightest movement. As if burned, she jerked her hands back and folded her arms over her stretched breasts. Her teeth chattered as she sat and waited. When a draft of cold wind hit Anna's bare butt, she realized that she was a woman fragile at the core: more easily broken than she had imagined.

As dusk waned, the granny sat on the other side of the quilt and listened to Anna's moans. Near midnight, the groans grew louder. Granny came inside, her hat pulled down over her face. Anna rose to meet her, but Granny pushed her back into the chair and tied Anna's hands and feet to the rocker with hemp rope. Using the hem of her dress, Granny wiped blood from where Anna had bitten her lower lip against the pain.

"Why are you wearing that snake?" Anna asked between her teeth.

With a child as fully developed as this one, Granny knew she should give Anna belladonna or poppy opium to relieve the pain. But Anna had disrupted her harmony when she lay with this man. She had impacted more than her own life. She had risked altering Lily's. Back inside the church sanctuary, instead of gathering her mortar to prepare the painkiller, Granny took up a cover and moved to the porch. There she drew Tall Corn's old blanket around her shoulders and rocked in the cold.

A darkness of an unknown sort had been settling over the granny since Tall Corn's mother cast her out. With each abortion, the darkness pushed her deeper into the conviction that this service was her mission. But she had not expected to meet her baby sister there in the shadows, asking her to drop the Granny's only nephew. Anna's primal wails now chased her to the bottom of a black pit. She found there the answer she had battled back and forth over the years. There Anna's groans struggled with Lily's twinkling laughter. The laughter won. Yes. Salvation was her calling. The undeveloped self inside Anna held the power to drag both down. Lily's soul in progress should float higher than a new one held within.

Two Tears was compelled to believe she was different in order to justify her place among women. Without her sense of being Beloved Mother, she was no more or no less open to obeying the laws of morality than anyone else. To say she was reinventing herself would seem as fantastic a confession as admitting she grew two horns with each new moon. She had set herself outside man's law and had continued doing so until she no longer knew the truth. She gradually lost herself in a maze of fantasy and falsehood. She had no idea that her world differed from any other.

Granny's empty blue eyes glared into the dark as she closed out Anna's screams. In the distance, Tall Corn's mist rose over a dusky mountain and called out to her, "The woman of my village, my birth mother, the one who called herself 'Beloved Mother.' She stole her name from a phantom north wind." Two Tears put her hands over her ears. The wind rose higher, and Tall Corn spoke louder. "Listen, Two Tears. My birth mother, who called herself 'Beloved Mother,' stole her name from a phantom north wind." Granny refused to hear. In the distance, a sound echoed off Turtleback. Perhaps it was Tall Corn's words. Perhaps it was the night wind. Or Sister Sun could have announced the coming of morning.

As the sun topped Turtleback, Granny cast her hat aside. She found Anna unconscious and wet from sweat in the birthing chair. Beneath her, blood still dripped into the speckled blue enamel pan and spattered off what had, last night, been Winston Rafe's baby boy.

"Great Spirit, come see," calls Sister Sun. "See what she has done in your name."

Brother Moon slips behind Turtleback to avoid knowing the bloodshed. Great Spirit shakes his massive head and orders a thunderstorm to wait for Anna to get back to Boone Station before it splashes across Turtleback. The universe swirls and hums its own sad song round and round each disappearing star.

"Did you know, Great Spirit?" asks Sister Sun. "Did you know?"

Part III

Chapter 22

Oh that I were a pretty little sparrow – Mountain Ballad

Lily could not remember when she had begun to call the granny "Kee." Her mother always referred to the granny as a mountain granny and simply called her "Granny." One day she had asked the granny, and the granny had gifted her with the memory. It happened during the Month of Nut. Lily was newly six. Nights had first taken on their chill. Sun had slipped close to the mountain ridge. In the distance, ridge trees, sparse and naked, allowed light to pass through, giving the impression of a choppy haircut with individual spikes poking up across the horizon.

She and the granny took to the woods looking for what Lily called her "dolly roots." Ginseng root that looked to Lily as if the long tan roots were arms and legs. This evening the granny plodded along, weary from the night before when she had spent hours with the dropping of a small, but stubborn, baby.

Lily could be as skittery as a squirrel. She pranced through straw so quietly the granny had to shield her eyes against the western sun to know where she was. Trudging along, the granny stumbled on an outgrowth of pine root. She fell. To rest, she sat where she had fallen and allowed Lily to wander.

Lily disappeared over the rise, laughing. When the laughter stopped, Granny called out. Silence answered. Angry at the child for disappearing, she threw a heavy stone against the trunk of a high-rising oak. Three wild turkeys took to the air, squawking a chorus of *kee, kee, kee,* as if announcing the onset of bedlam.

A dip cut into the far side of the rise. The granny climbed the rise so she could look down. She called again. This time she heard a faint giggling of *kee, kee, kee.* It sounded as if a poult were trapped underground. The granny edged closer on her lightest step, across leaf covered ground. Nothing out of the way indicated the direction from which the sound had come.

Thinking a poult might be injured, she called, this time in the voice of the turkey. "*Kee. Kee. Kee.*" A barely audible "Kee Kee" returned. The granny stood tree-like to decide on the location of the response. She repeated her call. An answer came from an open space among the trees.

The granny stepped gingerly to avoid frightening the poult more. Before her, she saw a rotted-out oak stump where a grand tree had once thrived. She crept over and peeked inside the hollow. There sat Lily, a scratch across her cheek from where she had tumbled into the hole.

Lily grinned up at the granny and lifted her arms to be hoisted up into the light. "Kee," she said laughing. "I knew you would find me, Granny,"

Granny stepped one foot into the hole. Soft pulp gave beneath her, and her leg sank into the trunk. She reached over and took the child's hand, pulling her closer so she could lift the child out. She plopped her out on the ground and put on the stern Cherokee face she had learned from Tall Corn. She spoke in her most formal Cherokee tone. "You must not run away again. You belong on this mountain," she told her. "But you must know how to live with the mountain before you roam alone."

"When I'm old, like you?"

"How old do you think I am?" The granny fanned her face with her apron.

"A thousand million years old," Lily said.

"Oh," said Granny. "A person that old must be very wise," she muttered.

Lily scrunched up her forehead and sucked in her cheeks, trying to imitate Granny's face. She spread out her lips and exposed her teeth. "Kee," she said. "Kee Granny."

The child looked so ridiculous that Granny clapped her hands and laughed.

Lily jumped up and danced an elf-like jig, grabbed Granny's hand, and pulled her back in the direction of the rise. "My Kee Granny," she said and laughed.

Summer days when Anna could not rouse herself from the granny's belladonna berry juice or St. John's tea, Kee Granny wrapped her influence around Lily as if she were weaving a silken web. Mornings together were spent with Lily learning about plants. Pine for its power over fever, black gum for its tooth preserving sap, ginseng for back pain, and dandelion for low blood. Those were good.

Belladonna, pennyroyal, mistletoe, and foxglove to make digitalis for the heart were dangerous, herbs the granny never allowed Lily to touch. "When you are older," she would say when Lily asked about pussy willow bark and berries as a woman's remedy. She would distract the child with a search for ginseng or bloodroot.

Afternoons spent mixing poultices especially delighted Lily, for she loved the soft, slick feel of lard as she kneaded wood ash into a gritty salve. She wanted the poultice for her own, to take home with her so she could continue to squish it between her small fingers, but the granny refused. She insisted that what Lily mixed would have healing plants or herbs added later to help someone ailing in Breakline or a poor family who could not pay a doctor.

"You will be like the creek in flood after the snow melts," Kee Granny said. "Filled with knowledge of Great Spirit and his ways."

There were days without Kee Granny, days when Kee Granny did not come for Lily and made no attempt to explain her absence. On those days, lonesomeness overwhelmed Lily each morning after sunrise and pushed her out the door. From there she roamed Turtleback. At no more than fifty pounds, she could walk leaves and pine straw as quiet as a chipmunk. She learned to dart into a grove of trees and stand, unseen, more slender tree trunk than child.

She followed the roar of the Falls up the holler and splashed its icy waters against her face to stave off hunger that dogged her treks into the woods. In time, she would strip her clothes and teach herself to paddle about, then how to survive the turbulent underwater current set up by the violent churning that rock created at the base of the Falls. She learned the sensory pleasure of lying naked in the sun, letting its heat dry her body and thick chestnut hair.

Over time, she moved higher up the mountain to Old Man Farley's place, the shed she had stumbled upon with Bad Billy and Gertie during the spring of the big storm. Anna had told Lily Old Man Farley's story in an attempt to bring her home when dusk settled on the mountain.

Farley had lived in a time of war when men were needed to march, wait, march, wait, then run to meet each other, face-to-face, each trying to outshoot the other so he could crawl back to camp, chew on a strip of jerky, and perhaps return to the field to drag back the dead. The Civil War for some and the War of Northern Aggression for others.

Farley, in his late thirties by 1864, sat in the middle of the conflict. With only two sons, neither old enough for conscription, he wanted no part of war, of the slaughters reported daily in newspapers. But no place, no man, was immune to battle. Many men were pulled from farms who knew little about soldiering, yet they rode broad-hipped horses from camp to camp deciding the place and time for the next battle. In camps, unprepared men and boys, once enlisted or conscripted because they had lingered too long in some small town or field, rushed each morning to posted newspapers to see what their day held. For many of them the answer was death disguised as places such as Stones River, Murfreesboro, Brentwood, and later sites along the Mississippi, a river they had never heard of.

Covington had nothing to add to the War but bodies. Farley was a stout body. He rode faster and shot straighter than anyone, including men immortalized in legend. Covington expected him to join the Confederate Army and make the town proud. Once he failed the townspeople, he became "Old Man Farley," a name that killed whatever laurels they had hoped to bestow on him.

Old Man Farley owned the blacksmith shop. He had raised his two sons without his wife, who died birthing the younger boy. With news of what had happened at Fort Sumter, South Carolina, the older son raided his father's purse and rode off carrying a knapsack and canteen. He spent twelve dollars on a Starr revolver. Convinced his talents matched those of his father, he headed toward Washington, D.C. in search of Winfield Scott, the general-in-chief, to join what would become the Union Army. Within two weeks of enlisting, he was promoted to Lieutenant and sent to the Western Front.

The last Old Man Farley heard of this son came in a message he had scripted in a tent hospital on his deathbed. A wounded soldier who hailed from Bristol, Tennessee returned from the Fort Donelson battle in northwest Tennessee. The soldier, now dressed in plain clothes, limped into Covington with the note. Its words were terse, piercing.

Would that I had not taken this journey. War is not the glory some say it is. I am shot dead by my own comrades.
Your loving son, Adam Farley

The younger son, Wyman, raged at the death of his brother. Revenge attacked his mind with gusto. Old Man Farley locked him in the corncrib to keep him from enlisting, but the Home Guard, now desperate for men to feed the war machines, found him, put him in chains and took him east to Lee's Army of Virginia near Radford. The year was 1864.

On May 9, Union soldiers, after a three-hour battle for control of the New River Railroad Bridge, set fire to the wooden structure but failed to destroy the stone piers. Farley's youngest was charged with using his smithy skills in rebuilding the bridge for the South. On a sweltering June day, Wyman's sweaty hands slipped off a support beam, and he fell to his death in the rushing water below.

The night before the Home Guard came for Old Man Farley had been moonless and uncommonly cold. When they arrived to take him, he was nowhere to be found. The town of Covington, left with only fourteen young males and the town cripple who had a clubfoot, fought within itself over whether to give their blacksmith to the war or to keep him for themselves. In the end, they listened to the Home Guard.

Weeks passed with Home Guard walking and riding over Spencer's Mountain to the east, south toward Bristol, and finally west up the Turtleback. On the east side halfway up, they found a mound of vines and tree branches near the Falls, more a large burrow than a dwelling. When they pushed back the covering, there was Old Man Farley lying in a small hut, sick and starving.

Their attack was quick and violent. The Home Guard took extra time to punish him for causing them so much trouble. He was horsewhipped and hanged. They left him in a tree, some say Old Oak, for buzzard meat. Stories say the Home Guard tied the noose just so, in a slipknot so that it would take him at least three days to die.

Lily had not wanted to hear this story. She hated it. So distressed was she that she questioned such cruelty. Anna told her it was God's way, and it was not for her to ask. Anna's response only intensified Lily's questions. Old Man Farley would not leave her be. She saw him in shadows within the forest and in dark corners near her bed. Her need to find a sense of peace led her to Kee Granny's sacred cedar. She climbed zig-zag steps Kee Granny had cut in the earth to a height she never attempted less she sought the tree. Afternoons she sat nearby its broadening trunk, breathing in its pungent fir aroma, but the cedar gave her no answers either. In time, Lily decided the solution lay in Old Man Farley's shed.

Old Man Farley's doublewide door beckoned her back inside. She watched cardinals, bluebirds, and yellow and black finch flitter back and forth before the opening. Other days, she brought food and a blanket, spread the blanket, and napped until the chill brought on by the setting sun awakened her.

The crib never spoke to her of violence or death, so it became her haven. If a lizard or snake crossed the threshold, she studied its movement, sitting as still as Owl waiting for his nightly meal. No creature bothered her. Within some unspecified part of herself, she found the ability to melt into the environment and become part of the wild.

One day while Lily roamed alone, she followed the stream behind Boone Station. The water behind Boone Station flowed downhill until it merged with Parsons Branch below the Falls. The two eventually became Broken Rock Creek in Covington.

Lily had once walked the road leading toward Breakline, then turned right to Kee Granny's. There she made her way through the same overhanging trees that had shaded where her mother had once walked. The trek wore on her short legs, so she thereafter waited for Kee Granny to come for her.

She searched for trillium in bloom. Kee Granny had said they crave water, so she went first to the stream. Her eyes examined each side of the creek, but she saw only fiddlehead fern and an occasional wild aster, its purple bloom stark against the greens. She stepped away from the bank. Her bare feet noticed a difference. Ground that had been cushioning her steps now felt brittle. Packed down over the years, it refused to give under her weight. Curious, Lily turned away from the stream. Within less than a yard, she realized that she walked on a series of flat rocks. Lily had found a trail leading up the mountain into the trees. Sunlight dappled the forest floor. The trail ascended slowly then took a sharp rise up the Turtleback, moving left, then zigging back to the right like a piece of rickrack Anna might have sewn on Lily's dress.

Lily climbed easy. Stones were set so precisely someone in an earlier time must have laid them there with purpose. Blackberry bushes bordered the path. She thought of Kee Granny's son and his strange name Briar, and she wondered if the name had been chosen because of the bushes' thorns. Ragweed and tree saplings closed each side of the path. Farther back, hearty cedars, poplar, oak, and Canadian hemlock shaded the trail. Had Lily been asked, Kee Granny would have said that Great Spirit kept the path open so a young girl just Lily's size could discover it some glad-filled morning.

At the end of the climb, she walked past the beehives and found Kee Granny weeding her flower garden. "Did you make the trail?" she asked.

Kee Granny shook her head. "Probably been here since before the white man came," Kee Granny leaned on the hoe handle. "Part of Turtleback that's always been. You must not destroy it."

As children are wont to do, Lily thereafter took that path to Flatland, leaving the road to grownups.

Thinking back later, Lily would have had no idea how many times she had walked the path without noticing the diamondback rattler hidden within his den's smoky mist. A purposeful serpent, he had chosen the spot to give him visual and striking advantage over whatever or whomever moved his way. He could have struck Lily at any time of his choosing, but he had not.

On a high summer afternoon, Lily made out the rattlesnake. It lay with his head tucked into his coil, sleeping, waiting for nightfall to cover his movement into the underbrush for feeding. When she realized that she was looking at a monstrous Eastern diamondback rattlesnake, she staggered and fell. Eyes wide, she scooted backwards on her butt.

The rattlesnake filled the trunk of a massive oak that had once grown tall, its roots embedded in a dip that held fog no matter the hour. The tree had fallen decades before, opening its heart to rain and snow. Nature etched out a bowl with a jagged rim. The rattler molded itself into the bowl as if it had been crafted to be a part of the wood itself, its dark brown bands with their grayish edgings the perfect camouflage. Its girth thick as Lily's upper arm, it had burrowed as far into the bowl as she could see. It rested, much like a lid on a pot.

She looked at its slanted eyes and knew it was old, perhaps older than Lily herself.

Sister Sun fires up her energy and blasts hot rays to frighten Lily away from the snake, or to push the rattler deeper into his hole. Her surge is so intense the universe instantly smells sugary sweet.

Brother Moon, waiting behind Spencer's Mountain, snaps at her. "Stop that. It's time for me to be cooling the day."

"But look," Sister Sun argues. "The child found the serpent." Sister Sun shoots out another flash. The stench of sulfur fills the darkest dark of the outer universe.

"Stop it, you little spit fire," Brother Moon says. "Or I. . . . I'll eclipse you."

"I'm supposed to take care of her," Sister Sun says.

"Quiet, both of you," says Great Spirit. "Some things are beyond your understanding. Leave them be."

The serpent sensed Lily's presence. It lifted his head from his coil and looked at her through the haze surrounding its stump. Beneath its narrow neck, a thin, white scar marked where it had perhaps outwitted some hunter or wild boar. Lily surmised it must be a wise creature to have survived for so many years.

With her on the ground, it was too high to strike her. Had she been standing, and standing close, with the height of the stump, the length of its body, and the power of its coil, it could hit her hard and high, a blow that she could not survive.

> *"Great Spirit," Sister Sun whispers. She pulls back from the earth and trembles.*
> *"Wait," replies Great Spirit. "Stay in your own place."*
> *"But..."*
> *"Wait, I say," says Great Spirit. "Some things lie within the realm of random."*

Lily pulled herself off the ground and wiped her face. She ran back down the path. Rather than have the rattlesnake think her rude, she called back, "I have to go. It's hot." As if a serpent needed a weather gauge.

The next day, Lily brought a hoe to clear a wider path past the stump, a berth that allowed her to travel to Kee's yet skirt the den. The serpent sensed her approach. Its reptile eyes, mere slits, opened once to tell Lily it knew she was there. It slept as she worked, its head resting on top of its coil. Each strike of the hoe unsettled the mist surrounding the stump, but the serpent never flinched.

There was something unnatural about him. Lily craved to reach out and touch. The triangular head had no pointed edges to suggest the intensity of its venom. A strange warmth enveloped her when the rattlesnake looked at her, as if someone had taken a blanket fresh from before the fire and draped it over her. Such a sense of luxury comforted her. She clinched her fist to keep her hand steady.

That day, at the end of the path, Lily told Kee about the snake. Lily reasoned that a person as old as Kee Granny would be wise enough that Lily could trust her. "You must tell me when to stroke rattler and when to leave him be."

"You saw *Uktena.*" Kee's eyes grew dark. "He's magic, so you must not touch him. Not all can see him. You are an honored one, for he respects you and will not strike." Kee Granny grasped Lily by her shoulders. "Did he speak?"

Kee Granny's intense stare startled Lily. "No," she said and tried to pull back.

"Good."

Lily had not thought about animals coming to life in the human sense and talking. "I will name him Rattler."

She left Rattler in his den. Rattler allowed Lily her footpath.

Chapter 23

Lily wore red tennis shoes laced above her ankles. Her favorite green shorts with straps crisscrossed over her back to keep them from sliding off skinny shoulders. Beneath the straps, she wore a sleeveless, collared blouse Anna had sewn from an accumulation of cotton flour sacks patterned with small red flowers.

It was a May morning. Each spring day as early mist rose on Turtleback Mountain, Lily would place a hemp rope around the neck of each goat. She would lead the two up the mountain to a high, flat meadow where they grazed throughout the day.

At some point, the three crossed into Kentucky. They climbed higher. Lily tugged at Bad Billy's rope as she leaned forward to maintain her stability. Bad Billy, a big-horned goat, stout and lop-eared, lagged behind, stopping along the way to nibble green shoots and newly leafed greenbrier. In the distance, Lily recognized Kentucky's Pine Mountain by its peak, a dark green cone. Beneath its crest, layers of clouds filled spaces among ridges, much like flat, white seas interspersed with islands of green. A cloud colored in pinks and blues and a hint of green floated across the sky. "I see mist rising from that valley. You think the earth is losing its spirit, Bad Billy?" she asked. "Kee Granny would say so." The buck ignored her. She realized how far afield she had come when she recognized Kentucky. She turned back and walked down the Virginia side of Turtleback. Fir and pine, so green they were black, provided a barrier separating her from what lay west.

"Come on, Gertie," Lily said. "I don't see how Bad Billy can eat them stickers. Seems he would tear his mouth all up. Don't you think?" Gertie, smaller, a black goat with a wide white strip down each side of her face, dismissed Lily's question. She passed Lily on the trail and pulled forward. Lily headed the goats past Flatland turnoff and moved back up the incline to the west.

After Kee Granny's questions about Rattler talking, Lily carried on one-sided conversations with whatever animals she met. "Gertie, see that rhododendron? It's right pretty, but you better not be eating that. Kee Granny says it's a bad, bad plant." Though Gertie, her soot-colored milk goat, was the gentler of the two, Lily favored her hardheaded Bad Billy for his perseverance. But she loved Gertie's four white legs and hooves. "She fixes sick people, you know." Gertie yanked against the rope, as if to agree.

"She knows all about the mountain. All the animals. All the plants." Lily huffed as she talked. "You remember last year when we come up on that lily of the valley and I picked some for Mama? She said she had lily of the valley when she married my daddy, but Kee says they're poison." Lily clomped on behind her nanny goat. "Do you think that's why my daddy was killed? Because they used the wrong flower for getting married?"

Gertie led as faithfully as if she were a boss cow, nodding her head from time to time.

"Mama says the granny knows the Cherokee Great Spirit, and he can talk to her," she puffed against the incline. "And doctoring, too." Lily followed Gertie's white flag tail. "Do you think Great Spirit talks to Kee?"

Gertie shook her heavy head. Her long white-centered ears slapped against her thick skull.

Lily stepped off the path and over a large rock to avoid a fall on slick moss. "I heard her talk to foxglove last summer. She stopped when she saw me, but I heard her."

Gertie tugged again, this time holding back. She hesitated to edge off the path.

"Someday I'll know this mountain. Every plant and every animal on it."

Gertie stepped toward a Virginia creeper for a taste of the glossy leaves. Lily pulled her away.

The climb to the clover meadow took the better part of an hour. When Lily reached the last slope above the meadow, she sat and drank from the Mason jar she had filled before they left Boone Station. Bad Billy, antsy from the delay, yanked at his rope, to get Lily to move on.

Lily doubted his sincerity. No goat as thickheaded as Bad Billy could remember from one day to the next where he had been. Some days, Bad Billy could not remember to get in out of the rain. Lily would have to jerk and push to get him into his shelter under the back of Boone Station. By the time she had herded him in, Lily would be more drenched than Bad Billy.

"Leave me be, you old goat," Lily said. "What's your hurry?" She scratched behind his floppy ear and smiled. Bad Billy ignored her. He jerked his rope again. The rough hemp burned Lily's hand. "Stupid goat," she muttered. She got up, stepped off the footpath to pee before they started across the final knoll and lowered her shorts.

At the top of the ridge, Lily saw what had summoned Bad Billy. Before them lay Kee Granny's field of bee clover. The field looked as if a giant hand had taken a paintbrush and coated the meadow floor crimson. Bees hovered above the clover. Their wings created a solemn hum. Hundreds of bees sang their bee song as they gathered pollen for their queen. They mined each clover then settled down to worship the nectar. Lily sucked her breath in at the wonder of it all. She patted Bad Billy's rump. "Bad, maybe you're not so dumb after all," she said. She released the ropes and let her goats roam free.

Gertie, ever the impatient one, skittered down the slope and into the meadow. Once she reached the clover blooms, she began to graze. Bees lifted and moved apart to let her feed.

Bad Billy ambled along. He took his own good time now that he was here, as if he had known all along that several acres of banquet awaited him. Near the middle of the clover field, he took a few nibbles. He bent his knees to rest on the ground. As he settled, bees, angered at the interruption of their pollen ceremony, swarmed over the grey-muzzled goat. He shook his head, as if to say, "Leave me alone." Bees lowered themselves to the blooms and continued their work. A few more nibbles, the sun's warmth and Bad Billy slept.

Lily knew her goats would not wander into the woods. They would not climb trees to strip bark. They were content feasting on red clover, shaking their heavy heads as if to argue with bees that came near. Lily especially loved this meadow. A small stream her mama called Parsons Branch ran down the southern side. Clear, rushing water provided an ideal place for her to refill her jar and water her goats. She favored this meadow above all others. For after they fed here Bad Billy's coat was shinier and Gertie's milk sweeter.

In the distance beneath a broad dogwood, Lily saw what she thought was a Cherokee Little Person sent to make her happy. She looked again and realized it was Kee Granny, her long pink skirt plastered against her legs by the breeze, her arms lifted, reaching up to touch Great Spirit's fingers. Lily heard a faint incantation she recognized as a prayer asking Great Spirit to tell the bees to make honey one more time. Kee's crooning, carried to Lily by a soft wind, soothed Lily, and she slowed her pace.

Lily stepped into clover so thick and tall it covered her ankles. She, like Bad Billy, slumped down in clover deep enough for a mattress. Lily watched cloud after cloud pass overhead. With a coolness brought by clouds casting shadows over her body, she often sat up to watch a cloud stripe the meadow with its dark shaft. If she watched closely, she could determine the time of day.

When trees on the meadow's edge cast no shadow, she ate her dinner of biscuit and cold sweet potato. She took note of where Bad Billy and Gertie grazed nearby. Again, she lay in the clover. The bees' buzzes lulled her to sleep.

Wetness on her face startled Lily awake. She opened her eyes, thinking Bad Billy was slobbering on her. It was late afternoon, the sun low in the west. A dark shadow blocked her vision. She popped up and hit her head. Hard. Pain shot through her skull, a pain so intense Lily thought she might have bumped into a stone wall. She reached to rub her forehead and hit Bad Billy's rubbery nose.

"You stupid old goat," she snapped. "You butted my head."

Bad Billy shook his head as if to say, "I'm not stupid. You forget. I brought you here."

Lily rolled from under Bad Billy and crawled through bee-less clover. Droplets landed on her back. Another. Then another. It was rain. Cold rain left over from winter. Intense rain. Falling fast. Big heavy plops on her back. Bad Billy had come to wake her, to warn her of another cloud, dense on the ridge moving their way. Gertie sauntered toward the two. Lily grabbed her water jar and ran for Gertie's rope. "Come on," she insisted. "We got to get off this flat."

Cold rain in warm weather meant thunder. Thunder meant lightning. Lily turned round and round. Kee Granny was nowhere to be seen. They needed shelter. Nothing tall. They needed a roof. A snap of lightning exploded at the far end of the meadow.

Bad Billy ran toward a cut in the trees. He headed for Parsons Branch. Lily did not want to go near water with lightning behind them. She chased him, towing Gertie behind as they ran. "Stop!" she yelled. But Bad Billy ran on. Lily rounded a rhododendron bush twice her height, so solid with honeysuckle vine she could not see through the leaves. "Bad Billy," she called. He was nowhere in sight. She stopped to catch her breath and listen.

Below, rocks tumbled down a slope. It had to be Bad Billy. She dragged Gertie toward the sound. As the incline lessened, she could see the faded orange and dingy white of Bad Billy's coat as he leapt among rocks, ledge to ledge. Agile as a goat herself, Lily followed. She abandoned Gertie's rope, knowing she would clamor down at her own pace. Trying to keep Bad Billy in sight and maintain her balance, Lily lost the grip on her jar. It hit a rock and shattered. She swept her thick wet bangs back from her face and brushed rain from her eyes. Lightning announced another roll of thunder. Before her, Bad Billy took to the sky. He leapt from what looked like a cliff and disappeared. Lily raced to the edge and stopped where Bad Billy had jumped.

Beneath her was a structure more shed than cabin, crooked and old, but it had a roof. She could manage the drop-off. So could Gertie. Back near the meadow, lightning popped an upper tree. Its trunk split like a rifle shot, resounding throughout the cove. The stench of boiled pinesap sickened Lily. She ran back for Gertie's rope and guided her to the rock edge. "Come on. We got to get out of this storm." Gertie refused to jump. Lily got behind Gertie's haunches and pushed. Nothing. She pushed again. Gertie had been around Bad Billy too long. She would not move.

The rain slackened. Lily readied to push again when a clap of thunder clattered over their heads and shook the treetops. Bad Billy ambled toward the crib. Gertie dove over the ledge and landed upright next to a log, its green moss deep and soft as a cushion.

Lily backed up a few feet, ran and sailed over the cliff. Airborne, she imagined herself a bird suspended between the heavens and the earth. She did not want to land. She flapped her arms to stay aloft, but no matter how viciously she flailed, she fell. When she crashed, she landed with a thud on her butt. The hit jolted the knot where she had head-butted Bad Billy, causing her left eye to throb.

Before her sat the little log structure. A slanting shake roof with patches of thick, heavy moss pitched forward, pointing toward where Lily and her goats stood. One of the two posts holding up the roof leaned sideways. Corner foundations hacked from limestone had shifted. Most likely a storage place for hay or shelter, left over from some long ago cattle or mule. Lily peeked inside. What might have once been a door leaned against an inside front wall. Into each end wall, someone had cut a square hole for ventilation. Against the back wall stood an empty hay trough.

The upper meadow stream, filled with fresh rainwater, laughed its way down the cove. It had cut and re-cut its way down the mountainside and ran dangerously close to the little shed. Harsh winds and the earth's movements had battered the little building so that it sat at a jaunty angle. Lily did not consider that natural elements had played havoc with the structure. She decided instead that the same giant who had painted the clover meadow crimson had, without thinking, leaned against it and tilted it sideways.

Lily scooted inside and pulled her goats onto the packed dirt floor. The floor at least was dry. She removed her clothes and flattened them on the walls, stuffing a sliver of cloth between open logs to hold them in place. Her heavy cinnamon hair would take a while to dry, maybe until tomorrow considering the dampness and fog that followed mountain rainstorms. She unbraided her plait.

In one corner by a dirty rag of a blanket, Bad Billy flipped his tail, smug that he had rescued the trio. He emptied a stomach and chewed his cud with a slow, grinding motion. Gertie bent forward on her knees and lay down next to Lily. Outside, rain attacked the little shed again, this time so heavily Lily could barely hear.

> *"Is she safe now?" asks Brother Moon.*
>
> *Sister Sun doesn't answer. From behind the thundercloud, she fluffs another heavy cloud so thick it looks dirty. It blocks Lily's presence from Brother Moon.*
>
> *"Should I report to Great Spirit?" says Brother Moon.*
>
> *Again, Sister Sun doesn't reply. She's elated. Great Spirit has given her the opportunity to mold and stretch her thunderhead for its nighttime attack. She's so ecstatic she doesn't hear.*

Inside the shed on a rafter above Bad Billy sat Owl.

"Hey, Owl," Lily said as she wrapped the smelly blanket around her body. "Where you been?"

Owl chittered his welcome to Lily. For the past two years, she had watched Owl grow into a spectacular bird. She understood why people not familiar with woodlands believed ghosts attacked in the night. When Owl spread his massive wings, they spanned three feet. His under-feathers glowed white against a midnight sky. His golden eyes, deep in his heart-shaped face, moved so fast his head seemed to swivel. A silent flyer, Owl could be behind a non-woodsman without his knowing. Without warning, Owl could swoop in. Anyone unprepared would sense a presence and turn to see that broad swath of white dip toward him and think he was being attacked by some evil spirit. Then Owl would vanish, his grey back lost in the darkness. Convinced that he had been right, that he had truly encountered a phantom, the visitor would run terrified through the forest. Lily giggled at the thought of her gentle Owl's power over a grown man.

But Owl was not a ghost. He was, as Kee Granny said, wisdom of the Great Spirit on wings. "It's on his wings that he carries the souls of the dead when they can't reach the horned serpent," Kee Granny said. "Treat him with tenderness."

Clad only in her damp underpants, Lily rested, using Gertie as her pillow. The goats' musk mixed with the scent of dry earth comforted Lily in a way she had not expected. Her muscles relaxed, and her anxiety melted into the dirt floor. Across the room, a garter snake uncoiled from a foundation log and stretched his length. Owl and Lily watched. "Look, Gertie," Lily whispered. "See that pretty yellow ribbon down his side?"

Owl winked his eye, waiting for the snake to edge away from the wall. Before Lily could blink, Owl dropped onto the snake's back. He lifted himself back to the rafter, quiet as a moonbeam. He lit and plucked flesh from the snake's back. Owl's beak broke through muscle and bone while the snake writhed to free himself from a tight talon. Owl took another bite, breaking the snake in two. The tail half of the snake fell to the ground.

Bad Billy licked it up and grated his teeth back and forth, testing this strange tidbit. A bit of snake fell from his black lips. Bad Billy tried another bite.

"Oh," Lily said, her jaw slack. She had never seen a goat eat anything except foliage or grain. Bad Billy must be some goat. The goat glanced up to Owl as if to ask for more, but Owl took the rest for himself.

As Owl finished his dinner, Lily nuzzled closer into Gertie's belly. She laid her head against the goat's chest and listened. The goat's heart matched Lily's breathing exactly. Rain intensified, pelting the shake roof. Nature's rhythms soothed Lily to sleep. She awakened to drips from the eave as dawn crept over the ridge. Aware of where she was and that night had passed, Lily jumped up and slapped Bad Billy's back. She danced around and rubbed noses with Gertie. Owl watched her antics from his rafter and twisted his massive head, back and forth. "Hum. Hum. Hum," he chirped.

"We stayed on the mountain. I passed a test." She hopped into a primitive little foot-slapping dance around the goats. "I passed a test," she chanted, though she was not certain what the test meant or why it mattered. "I can be a granny."

Owl puffed his chest feathers. "In time," he seemed to say. Bad Billy nodded. Gertie nudged Lily from behind. Lily dressed and stepped out into morning mist.

The three started down the mountain, following the chattering of Parsons Branch.

Chapter 24

S eth White meant for his son to have schooling. At eleven, Jason was falling behind year after year. Seth's father and grandfather had spent their lives in dark mines. He wanted sunshine and polished shoes for his son. Knowing that he would have no more children out of Juanita, he laid out a plan before Jason had his twelfth birthday.

Breakline Camp had never had a real school. Ed Breakline had seen no need for education. He wanted each consecutive generation to stay in the valley and see that his profits remained high enough that he could keep his gentleman's lifestyle in Bristol and New York City. Winston Rafe had not changed Breakline's plan. When a new generation questioned that there was no school for their children, Rafe agreed to pay for one teacher to hold school in Unity Church three days a week, but such an arrangement did not fit White's plans for Jason.

The spring before what would have been Jason's new grade, White stopped Rafe as he was leaving the commissary. "I been thinking about the camp kids going over the mountain. To Covington for schooling." He removed his hat and slapped it against his thigh. "My boy, he's smart. He'll go far," White said. "He needs to get out of here." He looked up at Rafe standing on the commissary porch.

Rafe raised his eyebrow. "Mining ain't good enough for him?"

"His ma and me, we want a better life for him. There ain't much here 'cept eating and working." White refused to waver. "There ought to be more to life than that."

"Taking kids to Covington'll take money. Kids find ways not to come back where they belong," Rafe said. "Don't take up my time with your foolishness, Seth."

White stepped forward and put his foot on the first step. "Not meaning no disrespect, Mr. Rafe, but I been with you all these years. Remember, I was with you at Big Mama #2 the day Mr. Breakline stroked out. You remember. Doc Braxton and the decision making and all." White felt sweat appear on his upper lip. "I been as good a worker as you might want. I'll keep on keeping on. I just want more for my kid."

Rafe glared at White. "You thinking of blackmailing me, Seth?"

"No, sir. I wouldn't do such a thing," White said. "I'll pay somebody to truck kids over Turtleback. Just them who wants to go can go." He pulled his foot aside so Rafe could step down. "Give it a try, and I won't be thinking about Mr. Breakline and his lawyers no more."

Winston Rafe spit into the dust by White's brogan. "Your missus still working up the house?"

"Yes, sir. She is," Seth said. "But I see to it that she don't carry no gossip up your hill."

"Give it a year," said Rafe. "If it works, it works. If not, I ain't out no money, but you are." Rafe lit a match with his thumbnail and put the flame to a cold Lucky Strike. He cupped his hand over the match to protect its flame.

White spent the next month working up what he came to call his school truck. He built sideboards, one set for each side and one across the back of the cab. He nailed a 2x8 down each side inside the bed for sitting and added a short bench behind the cab. He folded a tarp and tied it with rope. This he tossed into the cab so the driver could slash it over the bed for a makeshift roof in bad weather. When he finished, he had room for more than a dozen kids to sit, their backs flat against sideboards so ruts would not bounce them out and into the road.

With the school truck finished, Seth met Eck Wetzel's father when he came out of the mine's mouth. Seth asked for Eck. "Seeing as he can't work the mine because of his crooked arm and seeing as how he's already thirteen he can work for me. A dollar a week to truck kids to Covington and back five days a week for schooling. That's good money. If he wants, he can stay and learn while he's there," Seth said. "He'll be adding to the family instead of sitting on your porch ever' day."

"He's been driving my old truck since he was eight, so he ought to know what it's about."

And there it was. Seth White had his school truck and his driver.

Juanita canvassed house-to-house evenings to see which mothers wanted their kids to cross Turtleback for schooling. "I'm thinking we might have about a dozen going," Seth said. "Kids can meet at Unity Church and Eck can pick up Anna Goodman's girl at Boone Station."

The first day the school truck stopped in the road at Boone Station, the fog was thick. Eck had the tarp bound over the top to keep out the wet. He slammed on the horn. Lily thought Eck's noise meant she was late. She ran to the back of the truck. Lily looked over the tailgate into darkness that showed several sets of eyes. She backed off.

"Go on, Lily," Anna said. "It's what you do when you're six."

Tears filled Lily's eyes.

"Go on," Anna said. She walked toward Lily, but before Anna reached the school truck, Jason White appeared out of the dim cavern. He reached both hands down and pulled Lily up on the tailgate. She moved into the darkness and sat by Jason, who dropped her hand as soon as she settled. A pudgy boy banged his fist against the school truck's oval cab window. Eck let the school truck roll down the mountain. It jerked, and the motor caught.

Lily's eyes adjusted to the lack of light. She knew nobody except Jason White. Six boys dressed in overalls and lace-up brogans with no socks. Lily and one other girl wore pleated skirts with button-up suspenders over a flour sack blouse. Lily noticed that the girl's shoes were much longer than her feet. She wondered if the shoes belonged to an older sister.

Nobody talked. The pudgy kid rubbed his runny nose on the back of his hand and sneezed. Snot blew toward Lily and then threaded down his face. He cleaned his mouth and chin with his shirtsleeve. The school truck bumped up and down.

"Jimmy Frazier," Jason said. "Ain't you got no handkerchief?"

Jimmy Frazier looked straight at Jason and said in a flat voice, "No, I ain't."

"Well, you ought," said Jason.

Lily moved closer to Jason White. She had not seen him the past two years when his mother came to visit her mother. Even then, Lily was often in the woods with her Kee Granny. The silence after the sneeze bore on Lily. She glanced at the blonde-haired girl wearing the giant shoes. She sat next to Jimmy Frazier.

"You got a sister?" Lily asked.

The school truck hit something in the road and jerked everybody's head back. Lily's shoulder hit the sideboards. She gripped her plank seat with both hands and held her sack lunch between her knees.

"No," said the girl.

"You got a granny?" Lily spoke to the boy named Jimmy.

"Naw," he said. "But my ma give me a pig for a pet."

"My name's Lily," she said.

"I don't care," said the blonde.

"We might eat it when it fattens," said Jimmy.

Lily decided right then and there if this was what school was going to be all about, today would be her first and last day. For the remainder of the trip, Lily put school out of her mind. In her head, she ran Turtleback and warmed to what it offered her. Ferny fronds with their bumpy seeds and how the they felt against her fingers, the whispering voice of the creek behind Boone Station, and the fun of trying to decide what the water was telling her. Squirrels chasing squirrels and their laughing chatter. Smooth rocks that made the start of the path to Kee Granny's easy on her bare feet. Kee Granny's bees talking to each other in their square wooden boxes. Bad Billy and his coarse hair that refused to stand up straight when she ran her hands up his spine. Gertie. Gertie's sweet, sweet milk. And the feel of home each time she heard chains that held the Boone Station sign as they squeaked in the breeze.

Eck stopped the school truck in the schoolyard. Every child lunged forward with the jolt. Lily let Jason help her out of the truck bed. She puffed out her sack lunch as Eck stomped the starter and ground the gears before driving away.

Covington Elementary School stood before the cluster of kids. Behind them, a set of double doors with windows across the top opened to what seemed like a black hole. A woman dressed in a navy blue dress and white lace-up shoes walked out of the dark and stood at the top of the steps. Lily stared at the shoes. No dirt had ever settled there. They had to be town shoes. She knew without asking that this woman had never climbed a tree or waded a branch. She was to be Lily's teacher for the next few years. Miss Snow. Lily would come to both fear and adore her.

≪≪≪≪≪≪≪

In the fall of the fourth grade, Eli O'Mary appeared in Miss Snow's classroom. Lily stared at the skinny boy whose white hair lay in tight curls on his head. He wore black suspenders over a blue and red plaid shirt, unlike the other boys who wore overalls and plain shirts. Lily giggled at his strange clothes and hair whiter than lye soap. He stared at the back wall.

165

Eli O'Mary had come from Grundy where he lived with his grandma. She had died the previous week and Eli had come to live with his daddy. Hearing such news bowed Lily's head. She shamed herself for the giggle. What would she do without her Kee Granny?

"Tell the class something about yourself, Eli," said Miss Snow. Her right hand lay on his shoulder. If she stooped, she would have been able to give him a hug from behind.

Eli scraped his shoe across the floor. He didn't wear brogans. Instead, his oxfords were new and polished, though his laces hung loose.

"Yeah, Eli," said Jimmy Frazier. Lily's jaw dropped every time Jimmy Frazier spoke without permission. Miss Snow didn't call Jimmy Frazier down this time. She rubbed Eli's shoulder the same way Lily rubbed Bad Billy's back when he grew tired of his rope.

Eli looked up to Miss Snow. "I gotta cat." That was all he said.

"What kind?" asked Julie Hudson.

"Just a cat." Eli's head hung low, and Lily had to strain to hear his answer.

"Can you tell us its name?" asked Miss Snow.

"Just Cat."

Somebody behind Lily snickered.

"Fine," said Miss Snow. "You can take the seat in the middle of the room. Next to Lily Goodman there." She motioned toward Lily. "Raise your hand, Lily, so Eli will know where to sit."

Eli O'Mary sat on a bench by himself during recess through mid-September. On an especially warm day, Jimmy Frazier prissed around holding up one hand, the other propped on his hip. He swung one hip, then the other. He sauntered up to Eli and said, "You're a sissy-butt." Other boys moved in to see what Eli O'Mary would do.

In an instant, Eli jumped off the bench as if he had been sitting on a tight spring. "My papa kicked your daddy out of his bar last night 'cause he won't pay his tab." Eli's voice rose higher as he spoke. "Your daddy's a no-count drunk and lays out of work and beats your mama."

Jimmy Frazier's face flushed as scarlet as if he had fallen asleep in the sun. "Take it back," Jimmy said.

"I won't. It's true what Papa said." Eli stood nose to nose with Jimmy.

"Fight on the playground!" The rallying cry resounded off the back of Covington Elementary School.

Jimmy jerked Eli's curls so hard that his head yanked back. "Say it ain't so or I'll break your head clean off your neck," demanded Jimmy.

Eli grabbed Jimmy's hands and, head to head, pulled him up on the playground bench. "You crawl out of some mine hole like some old snake and ride down here in that old rickety truck," Eli spit out between clenched teeth. "Your mama eats dirt."

Before Jimmy Frazier could react, Eli hit Jimmy in the gut and ran around the building. Jimmy followed, his fist raised to attack.

Lily stared at the fight, her mouth agape. The noise sounded like two territorial cardinals so crazy mad they try to peck each other to death.

"Why did Jimmy say that? Eli's mama's dead." Lily couldn't answer Julie Hudson's confusion.

Great Spirit, satisfied that Jimmy Frazier can fend for himself, flags down a grey mass of clouds. He climbs on and settles in for an easy ride. He signals West Wind. Ever strong, the wind picks up the clouds, setting them underway as if they powered the massive Star of India. West Wind knows how fond Great Spirit is of any fully rigged Barque, so the grand cloud-ship sails on. Earth hurls itself round and round. Great Spirit watches the blue orb whirl and smiles.

The next day, Lily meant to avoid Eli, but Miss Snow moved him so he would not be near Jimmy Frazier. He now sat behind Lily, rather than next to her. After lunch during silent reading, Lily relaxed. Before she had read to the middle of Pocahontas and Captain John Smith, she felt something oozing down the back of her head. She reached up and touched gummy liquid. She ran her fingers down her hair. Eli laughed and whispered "white trash" in her ear. She looked around. His bottle of yellow glue sat empty on his desk. When she felt it dampen the back of her dress, she dropped her head. Her eyes welled with tears.

They both had to stand before Miss Snow. She did not really cry, Lily told Miss Snow. "The glue smelled sour. It burned my eyes."

Miss Snow washed Lily's eyes with clear water and sopped the glue out of Lily's mass of hair as best she could.

Lily spoke to Miss Snow in a low voice. "Are you going to tell Eli's mama about the fight and glue?"

"We need to be patient with Eli. Remember he doesn't have a mama to care for him."

"That don't matter," Lily said. "My mama's sick, and my Kee Granny takes care of me." Lily jutted out her chin. "That don't make me be mean."

"Not everybody has a good granny," Miss Snow said.

Lily spent the remainder of the day with a towel wrapped around her head. Eli had to stay in the cloakroom, hidden away from other students. That afternoon, from where Lily sat high on Seth White's makeshift bus, she saw Eli crouched by a prickly holly, his head on his knees. For a second, he glanced up at the passing truck. Sunlight reflected tears on his face. Lily looked away.

Her hair still damp, Lily climbed down the tailgate of the school truck at Boone Station. Seeing her mother standing at the stove, she cried again. Anna washed Lily's hair with warm water and the special Ivory soap. She drew Lily into her lap, wrapped her hair in a soft towel, and rocked her across the room until it was time for supper.

The next morning when Lily entered the classroom, Eli sat so close to Miss Snow's desk that he had to scrunch up his legs.

Chapter 25

On a warm October day in Kee Granny's Month of the Harvest Moon, Lily had been explaining to Julie Hudson the difference in a hemlock and a pine. Julie lived in Covington on First Street. Her mother bought her school dresses at Martin's Ladieswear. Dresses with lace and ribbons. Dresses in solid colors. Anna made Lily's dresses, even her coats. In summer, Lily wore shorts or overalls, sometimes without a shirt.

Julie's yellow braids reached almost to her waist. That she would even talk to Lily made Lily at first a bit suspicious. Julie could have been a snob. She had money. Her daddy owned the bank across the street from the miner statue on the town square. Lily figured Julie went in the bank anytime she wanted and got money much like Lily went under the back of Boone Station and gathered eggs.

To solidify the friendship, Lily wanted to share all Kee Granny had taught her about what made her mountain so magnificent. Lily used a stick to draw an outline in the dirt to show Julie that the leaf of the red oak could be as big as a girl's foot. It was clear to Lily that Julie Hudson knew nothing about trees. But then, Julie Hudson knew nothing about nothing.

Lily felt it her responsibility to inform Julie of those things in life she would never have a chance to know. Julie was not always receptive. The two had been arguing about the size of tree leaves when Miss Snow rang the bell to begin the day. They walked into the classroom and sat in their desk chairs, one across the aisle from the other. "I can bring you a red oak leaf that's longer than your mama's shoe," Lily bragged.

"No you can't. No leaf's that big."

"Yes, it is. I'll show you tomorrow." It was then Lily noticed that they were the only pupils talking. Lily stopped.

"Draw me a picture of a hemlock." Julie leaned over and said in a loud whisper, "I'll look for one when Daddy takes us back to the Falls. And draw me a red oak."

Lily's eyes bugged. the Falls? They were her falls. It was her secret place. Like Old Man Farley's cabin. Knowing that Julie and her daddy had been to the Falls set fire aglow in Lily's chest, and her lips squeezed together.

"You ain't been to the Falls." Though she knew Miss Snow would be mad, she couldn't stop. "You don't even know where they are."

"I do so. Daddy takes us there to swim every summer. He tries to scare us with stories of Old Man Farley and how he got away from the Home Guard who was planning to make him go to the Great War or skin him alive. He moved up on Turtleback Mountain and was hiding out there. Home Guard found him and shot him so much his guts flew into the trees and his ghost is still there. If you stay late at night, you can hear him moaning and hollering."

Lily's teeth clinched. Although she detested it, that was her story. The Falls were her falls.

Julie caught her breath. "And if you've been bad, he'll fly up behind you, all white, and grab you by the hair and fling you into a tree."

Lily didn't believe a word about white, flying ghosts. She almost told her the moaning and clacking was Owl talking to other night birds, but she didn't want Julie to know about Owl.

"Humph. I got my own diamondback rattler," Lily's anger said. She hated herself the minute she said it. Only she and Kee knew about *Uktena*.

Across the room, Eli snickered.

"You shut up, Eli O'Mary," Lily demanded.

"You have not. Nobody's got a rattlesnake. They bite you and you're dead," Julie argued.

Lily whirled to face Julie. "My snake, his name's Rattler, he won't bite me, but he'll bite you so you better stay off *my* mountain. 'Cause he hides in mist and you won't be able to see him before he bites you hard." Lily's voice rose, nearing a full room announcement.

"Turtleback Mountain does not belong to you, and I can go there if I want to," Julie said, now coming out of her chair. She bumped the leg, and her tablet thumped on the floor with a thud. Her pencil rolled down the aisle.

"Girls," said Miss Snow as she walked in from the hall. "What's going on here?"

Both girls talked at once.

Miss Snow shushed them. "Julie, you first."

"Lily says Turtleback Mountain belongs to her and she's got a giant rattler for a pet and she'll let the rattler bite me to death, and she says I can't go with my daddy to the Falls because it belongs to her and I don't want her to be my friend anymore." Julie wound down, out of breath. She crossed her arms tight over her chest, shutting out any chance of her heart hearing what was coming.

"Fine. Sit down. Now you, Lily."

Lily pushed out her lip. She chewed the inside of her cheek, moving her lower jaw as a chipmunk might when trying to crack a hard nut. She said nothing.

"Lily?"

Still nothing.

"Okay, girls. Come to my desk so we can talk." Miss Snow directed the class to take their seats and rest their heads on their desks. Several had moved to the other side of the room amazed by an argument between girls. Boys argued and fought, not girls. At the front of the room, Miss Snow spoke quietly to both girls. "Lily's right, Julie."

Lily grinned at the affirmation and opened her mouth to speak.

"Be quiet, Lily. You had your turn and let it go by. Lily's family does own Turtleback Mountain. Always has. I don't know about any rattlesnake." She shot an accusing glance toward Lily. "But I know Lily would not let her pet bite you, no matter what pet it is. You girls have been friends since you started first grade."

Lily smirked. Turtleback Mountain did belong to her. Before she had only hoped so. Miss Snow, who knows all, said it was true. She knew Rattler was true. She knew Julie would never get to see him, even if she came to Boone Station because he could be invisible when anyone other than Lily came around. He wouldn't even appear for Kee. In her joy, Lily danced a primitive little dance, spinning round and round like a leaf caught in an eddy.

"Lily Marie Goodman!" Anger on Miss Snow's face stopped Lily midspin. "You stay in at recess and keep your nose in the ring, young lady."

Lily glimpsed around the room to see who might have heard her punishment. Eli O'Mary tucked his head back into his crossed arms and did not move. Julie sulked back to her seat and hid behind *Anne of Green Gables*.

Recess came, and Miss Snow drew the circle on the blackboard just above Lily's head.

Lily knew the routine. Stand on tiptoe and place your nose in the ring. Stay still until Miss Snow says you can sit down. Lily had seen the boys in her class get the nose ring, but she had never seen a girl get it.

She slinked up to the blackboard. When all her classmates had left the room, she lifted herself and, crossing her eyes, decided where the ring was. She pressed hard but relaxed. Pressing too much made it hard to breathe.

Within minutes, the balls of Lily's feet burned. She needed to look around to see if Miss Snow had left the room, but to do so meant she would have to lower her feet and drop out of the ring. So she stayed put.

Her feet continued to burn and tingle. Her right calf cramped. Then her left. She grabbed the wooden chalk tray so she would not fall backward.

Miss Snow spoke from behind her, "No holding on, Lily."

Lily released the wooden tray and dropped her heels. She could breathe now.

"Up to the ring," Miss Snow directed.

Tears filled Lily's eyes, and she sniffled to hold them on the ring.

"Just a minute more and you can go to the outhouse." Miss Snow spoke so softly Lily was not sure she had heard.

Lily measured hours by nature's signs. The length of a tree's shadow. The space between the setting sun and the top of Old Oak up from Breakline Camp. The lift of mist from the cold stream when warmth of the sun worked its way out of the gloaming. She had no idea how long a minute would be. Rather than try to reason it out, she hoisted her weight back up on the balls of her feet and waited.

After Miss Snow rang the last bell, Julie sidled up to Lily. "Sorry you got the nose ring."

"It wasn't bad," she lied. "Just standing still for a minute."

At twilight, mountain shadows, more than loss of sun, darkened the gap where the town of Covington sat. Heavy shades discolored the ground where Lily had played the last of the afternoon away with one of Julie's new kittens—the striped one. She stepped to the edge of the porch and stood between two pots of anemone, their leaves an emerald green. In Julie's back yard, the dirt was so dark with coal dust and the light so weak Lily could not be sure where the yard ended and the street began. She placed the kitten in the cardboard box on the porch and set a window screen over the top to keep the kitten inside. Julie, walking the cow to her backyard shed, called to Mama Big Cat to come up from the riverbank for the night.

Lily shuffled back across the porch and settled into an unpainted ladder back chair in the far corner shadow before going in for the night. An empty loneliness had overtaken her here in Covington, one she had never known. If loneliness approached on the mountain, Lily trekked into the woods and the wind or leaves would brush it away.

She had not imagined Turtleback as high, perhaps because she was always there on the mountain. But here in Covington at the foot of the Turtleback, she saw a mountain high enough to block out wind and sun. Its height and the on-coming darkness smothered her as surely as if she slept with her face under a feather pillow.

At Julie's, she slept with her paper shade down. Eli O'Mary, hearing that Lily was staying the weekend with Julie, had twice whispered to Lily, saying he planned to peek under the shade. She did not dare crack the shade, because she did not know if the shadows she had seen on there the night before were Eli or if she had dreamed them.

Dark on Turtleback Mountain moved in soft each night, but this town-dark grated on Lily's sleep. The weak darkness was lessened only by an occasional porch light, rather than moonlight. Artificial light filtered into the room even with the shade down. It turned the room a hollow yellowish glow, not unlike the color of a dying fire. Even before the sun dropped below Turtleback the previous night, she wanted to go home, to her mama and Boone Station.

Saturday afternoon, Julie made blackberry jelly sandwiches and dropped them unwrapped into her mother's navy purse, the one with the gold clasp. She handed the purse to Lily and went out the back door. Julie led the way down one street, then another. From time to time, she kicked a rock off the roadway and into the ditch. After a try or two, Lily's rock aim was as true as Julie's.

When they passed the fire station, Julie lifted Lily around the waist in an attempt to let her look through the window so she could see Engine #1. Lily tried to grasp the bottom ledge of the window to hoist herself higher, but her own weight pulled her down. On the second try, the girls tumbled back on their bottoms, both giggling.

Once past the fire station, they headed for the iron miner's statue in the town square. Lily could not hide her astonishment at the size and blackness of the miner who stood on a block of limestone as tall as Lily herself. The pickax propped on his shoulder stuck high into the air as if ready to snag a passing bird. His lunch bucket sat on the block at his feet.

"He sure is big," she said.

"It's just an old statue," Julie said.

The miner's carbide light atop his cap should have shown into the darkness as it would have underground, but it was no more than a black circle. At the base of the block had been etched:

Heroes live and die in darkness
So that we can live in light

Julie, accustomed to the statue, pulled Lily along. They passed the closed drugstore. "If we'd come sooner, we could've had a limeade or ice cream," Julie said. "It's almost dark. Let's go to the cemetery."

"I don't know. I never been to a cemetery in the dark."

"Don't be a scaredy cat," Julie teased, her green eyes glittering.

"Kee Granny says spirits of white men live there and come out at night, 'cause they weren't buried proper, so I stay away." Lily had not moved. "We don't go in the graveyard at Flatland."

"Who's Kee Granny and how does she know so much?" Julie propped her hands on her hips as if daring Lily to know something she did not.

Lily hung back. She was uncertain about telling Julie too much, yet she had to defend Kee Granny. "She lives at Flatland in an old church, and she's teaching me about animals and plants and stuff."

"Humph," Julie answered. "I don't believe you. Nobody cares about nature stuff. Nobody but Jesus lives in a church anyhow. 'Sides, what makes your old mountain better than my town?"

Lily couldn't answer that.

"I'm hungry," said Julie. She stopped beside two tall brick walls marking the cemetery entrance. "Let's stop here and eat."

"It's a cemetery."

"So what? I'm hungry," said Julie.

Give Lily Marie Goodman a steep mountain footpath, a meandering creek, or a rock bluff and she is home. Give her a dark hillside and flat boxy headstones laid out in rows facing east and Lily has no idea which way to turn.

The girls sat on prickly grass and Lily handed out the two sandwiches. Lily licked tangy blackberry jam from her fingers. "Your mama's going to be awful mad. Jelly's all inside her pocketbook."

"That's just a play pocketbook. She keeps the good ones in her closet."

Lily moved aside, tore off a piece of her bread, wiped jelly from the purse lining and ate the chunk. Putting her bread back together, she bit into her sandwich.

Julie finished her sandwich and popped up, surprising Lily. "Let's check out old Eli's daddy's bar." Julie grabbed the picnic purse from Lily's lap. "Come on." She ran back toward the center of town, calling back, "Come on, slowpoke!"

From a faraway porch light, Lily could see large red metal bins at the end of the back wall. The alley behind O'Mary's Bar waited in deep, deep dark. The sour smell of rotting vegetables met the girls as they neared the alley. The idea of going into the stinky blackness pulled against Lily's feet like heavy mud. On Turtleback, stars speckled the sky in every direction. Nothing shiny in this alley. Not in this whole town. What stars porch lights did not hide, trees did.

Julie grabbed Lily's hand and pulled her into the alley. "Come on," Julie said. "We'll be spies." The two ran. Julie crouched, bent over at the waist as she did when the girls played secret agent. She stopped beneath a dirty four-on-four window. She took a wooden whiskey box someone had thrown toward the trash bins and propped it against the wall under the window. The box felt wet and smelled rank. Lily lagged behind.

"Let's look in," Julie whispered. "We might see a whore."

"What's a whore?" Lily whispered back.

"Lily Goodman, you don't know nothing," Julie said. "Climb up and tell me what you see."

"No." Lily shifted away from the wall.

Julie stepped on the crate. Once she stabilized her feet, she lifted herself to tiptoe and rubbed filth from the glass.

"What is it?" Lily jiggled herself up and down. "Is it a whore?"

"I don't know. You look."

Lily climbed up. She peered inside and adjusted her eyes to the dimness. A sliver of smoky light and men's laughter came from where a door stood slightly ajar. Shadows filled the little room where cardboard boxes were stacked high, almost to the ceiling. On the far wall was a roll top desk. In the middle of the room was a rolling chair, overturned, its wheels still spinning. Above the chair was a boy, suspended in mid-air. His body swayed forward and then back like a bug on a string. He rotated his face toward the window and looked at Lily. It was Eli O'Mary, in his underwear, his mouth open, his eyes staring at her.

Lily jumped down and grabbed Julie's hand. "Run!" she shouted. She yanked Julie toward the street.

"It's a whore!" Julie cried. "You saw a real whore."

Lily rounded the corner dragging Julie behind. "Come on."

"Quit pulling me. I want to see."

Lily dropped Julie's hand and ran headlong through the open bar door.

"You can't go in there." Julie reached for Lily.

"Shut up, Julie!" She slapped Julie's hand away. "Mr. O'Mary!" She shouted over the hubbub of clinking bottles and laughter. "Mr. O'Mary," she said more quietly this time. Shattering quiet hit Lily in the face. She could barely see for so much smoke.

A large man with dingy hair and a grey beard appeared, chewing on an unlit cigar stub. He rubbed one hand on his stained apron. "Kids ain't allowed here. Get on out." He popped a wet rag against his thigh as he neared Lily. She glanced around. Coal-stained faces filled the barroom. White eyes looked at her from every direction. Lily cringed.

A long-boned man stepped between Lily and O'Mary. "What you girls want?"

"This is my place, Rafe. Let me handle this," said O'Mary.

Lily noticed the man's clean hands, trimmed nails and light blue shirt. He did not have black rings collared around his eyes like other men in the room. "Leave her alone, O'Mary," he said. "She's not old enough. . . ." The man stared at Lily so intently that she turned her head toward O'Mary and whispered.

"Eli," she spoke to O'Mary. "He's going round and round." She pointed toward the cracked door. "In that room."

"Leave him be. He's serving his time for not mopping up last night." O'Mary started back to the bar. "Broke a whole case of my best Irish whiskey." He slapped his thigh again. "Whole damn case," he grumbled.

"But he's going round and round." Lily had to push the words up from her throat. "And he looked at me out the window."

"I'll see," said the blue-shirted man. He knifed himself through the men and pushed open the door. Beer drinkers crowded behind him to see what waited on the other side.

"Good God, O'Mary!" The crowd parted at the tall man's words. "This boy's hung hisself." The tall man's eyes cut into O'Mary. "And he's been horsewhipped."

Overhead lights flickered for a second as if a rat had gnawed into some hidden wire. Lily edged back toward the door.

"Get the doc, somebody. He's still alive." The tall man gave the order as if he gave orders every day.

A squatty miner dashed out the door and across the street. Miners punctuated the quiet with murmurs of "God Damns" and "Sorry Son-of-a-Bitch."

Lily and Julie backed against the doorframe. The tall man carried Eli in his arms. As they stepped into the street, Eli looked at Lily. He said in a scratchy voice, "Get the cat."

"God, Rafe. I didn't mean..." O'Mary followed on the thin man's heels. "I done stood him in a chair many a time..."

"Shut up," said the tall man as they walked away.

Miners turned back to their drinking tales. This one would linger for a while. Lily stayed where she was, frozen by Eli's command, listening.

"What'd he mean about the cat?" Julie asked.

"Shh." Lily pushed Julie behind her. "Be quiet."

A miner, hoarse from breathing coal dust and tobacco spoke. "O'Mary threatens to put that rat-chaser in a croaker sack and throw it in the river ever time he found the boy wasting time with it. Looks like he might have done it this time."

"The river?" Lily whispered. "Did you see how wet Eli's hair was?"

"You don't reckon..." Julie stopped.

Lily leaned closer toward the inside. "Shh. Listen."

The miner stubbed out his cigarette and struck a match to fire another one. "It's his cat and his kid. Do what he wants. The old SOB. O'Mary's a might stout on his ideas."

His drinking partner chuckled. "Yeah. Make O'Mary mad, he'll hoist you up by the britches and you'll find yourself sittin' in the street."

Lily heard his belch and shivered.

"Ort to 'member the kid's the last of the O'Mary's 'fore he chooses his punishment, though." The hoarse one puffed out a spiral of smoke.

Julie tugged at Lily's shorts. "Where they taking Eli?" she whimpered.

Lily whirled around and said aloud, "Hush, Julie."

A dark face appeared at the door. "Okay now, go on. Get out of here. Girls and kids ain't allowed," he snapped. He leaned against the doorframe and swallowed a long drink from his beer. "You heard O'Mary."

Lily straightened her back. "What's his cat look like?"

"How do I know?" The miner bent down so close she felt his spit on her cheek. "Get out of here, girlie." A miner in the dusky room laughed. "Scat."

Lily looked around the smoky room. In the far corner stood Briar Slocomb in his long pale duster, flat against the wall. He glared at Lily from under his long hair.

Julie snatched Lily's hand. "C'mon, Lily."

Lily broke away from Slocomb's stare. Julie pulled her back down Town Street toward the miners' monument and home.

The dream came on fast and spiraled itself into Lily's long-term memory. When it showed itself, Lily flailed and kicked, knotting the sheet around her legs.

O'Mary's Bar emerged in shades of grey. Men sat three to a table, their beers clustered in the center of the round as if they waited to break a fast. Every miner resembled every other miner, their heads low under metal hardhats. No carbide lamplights glowed. Lily could see no eyes, but she felt their eyes move across her skin.

177

In unison, one miner at each table reached to the floor and brought up a tin dinner bucket. They removed the lid and took out a white bread sandwich wrapped in opaque paper. Lily looked around the room and noticed that each sandwich had a cat's tail hanging out of the paper fold. The miners opened their mouths to take a bite. Lily screamed, but no sound came out.

From the center of the room, Eli hung from a rafter, his white hair glowing like a lamp, its globe dingy with soot. She expected him to spin as he did when she saw him through the window, but he didn't. She tried to call to him, but something large and viscous clogged her throat.

Back at the tables, miners worked their mouths as if talking, but Lily heard nothing but *um, um, um*, as if swarms of flies had invaded the bar. No one noticed Eli.

The unreliability of dreams dropped her on a riverbank. She sat on a place higher than any she had ever seen. An open brown paper bag floated downstream. A cat's head, its eyes, ears and two front paws rested on one side of the sack. The cat smiled, as if he were enjoying a Sunday afternoon boat ride.

Eli hung above her from a tree limb. He mouthed, "Get the cat."

A miner clothed in black stood on the far bank. His carbide lamp glowed a hazy golden circle that cut through a curtain of darkness. The dark, solidifying more into wall than curtain, stopped before reaching the other side. The miner stayed but a moment, looking for all the world more Cyclops than human, then vanished, taking his light with him.

Lily slid on her butt toward rushing water, through mud that appeared just before she reached it, brown sticky mud where moments ago soft grass had been. When she hit the water, she knew she was peeing, but the water said, "We are akin, so I don't mind." On the bank, *Uktena* watched and swayed approval.

The cat floated close. As Lily opened her bladder, the cat slapped Lily's cheek hard with a paw. Lily cried out against the cut.

Julie rocked the bed and moved away from Lily. "Ew. Ew." Once her feet smacked the floor, she yelled, "Mama, Lily peed on me!"

Sunday morning, Julie's father drove Lily to Boone Station and let her out. He never killed the car's motor.

Eli did not come back to school. For a time, Covington remembered him as being no more than a shadow, someone no one could describe. With the passage of years, he became invisible. So no one noticed on the morning, two weeks before his seventeenth birthday, when he walked out of Covington, carrying a burlap bag, headed northwest.

Chapter 26

After Mr. Hudson dropped Lily off and drove away, Lily found Anna inside in a chair. Her mother's white face and loosened hair terrified her. She screamed out to Mr. Hudson, but he was gone. She shook Anna's shoulders, trying to waken her, but Anna's head only lolled in a circle as her eyes rolled toward the ceiling.

Lily wept. Her mama was dead. And dead while she was gone to play at Julie Hudson's house. Lily cried until she hiccupped. She filled a glass with water from the bucket and sat down next to her mother. She set the glass on the crack between the two wide planks that made the table. The glass tipped and water spilled over Anna's arms and into her lap. Anna roused.

Lily squealed, "Oh, Mama, I thought you were dead!"

"Help me up. To the bed."

Lily could barely hear her mama, her voice was so weak. While Anna rose, bracing herself on the table, Lily pulled the chair out of the way. Dried blood coated the chair seat. The back of Anna's dress was red with new blood.

Lily gasped.

"Go for Granny Slocomb," Anna said.

Lily ran. She ached for the wings of a great black bird to carry her up the grade to Flatland for help.

Few days passed without a trip to Flatland for medicine for Anna. As winter approached, the daylight lessened but the symptoms strengthened. Lily no longer went to Covington for school. Each day Lily climbed the path. Rattler never appeared, and Lily saw no improvement in her mother. The days found Lily with tears on her face from the worry. She wondered if the medicines were worth the trip, but Kee Granny's church compensated for Lily's anxiety.

Kee Granny's church held strange things: canned tomatoes crowded on a wooden shelf, a shotgun taller than Lily herself, so many empty bottles Lily could not count, herbs and blooms hanging like harvested tobacco from pegs Kee had nailed out from the walls.

Mountain physician, Granny Slocomb came each time with her black leather valise bulging with snuff cans of plants she had ground and refused to identify. Her woven pine basket had long ago deteriorated. Her worn bag still tied her to Jackson Slocomb, not Beloved Mother, but it was what she had. The granny asked Lily to boil up a pot of water when needed. Granny stirred powdered greens and browns into the bubbling water until she had a drink that resembled thin mud. Once the drink cooled, Lily held Anna's head while the granny coaxed her to drink a glass, sometimes spoon by spoon. Anna gagged and fought the granny, alternating from grabbing her head to pushing the granny's hand away.

There were times when Kee Granny stayed, sleeping on the porch even in mid-winter, until Anna came closer to being herself. Lily once counted Granny's doctoring to take six days, before it brought Anna back.

Anna awakened with numbness in her right side. She howled with pain in the back of her head that moved to her forehead. Lily's footpath from Boone Station to Granny's church up the hill hollowed out deeper and deeper. When the attacks came every two weeks, Granny brought her gourd rattle. Dry beans inside swished like dying leaves resisting the need to fall. Lily sat against the far wall and wondered if this rattling sounded like what Rattler might. After the gourds failed, the granny added a little rabbit-hopping dance at the foot of the bed to each visit.

With each treatment, Lily saw her mother lose more and more of who she was. When Anna awoke from Granny's different brews, she was more disoriented. She called for people, some Lily knew little of. People like Ruth, Anna's sister in Covington. Juanita in Breakline who had visited with her son, Jason. Gladys. Lily knew no Gladys. Winston. She knew no Winston. And Gabe. Anna never called to Clint. Lily wondered why, since her parents had been married eight years when her daddy was killed.

180

Anna had insisted on doing her part when out of bed. But she was no longer out of bed for days at a time. It was as if someone had opened a plug in the bottom of Anna's feet and let her spirit drain out, taking her lifeblood with it.

The school truck no longer stopped for Lily. Lily could no longer leave Anna alone.

◅◅◅◅◅◅◅

A year after the day she had come home from spending the weekend with the Hudsons, the month of the Harvest Moon once again, Lily stepped out to gather firewood and looked toward the heavens. There above the shake roof hovered a pale, pale mist. Lily considered telling Kee Granny, but a second of uncertainty destroyed the thought when she heard her mother call.

Anna uttered a tentative call. "Lily?" She called louder. "Lily, come in here."

Lily kicked the door open, her arms laden with hewn fireplace logs. "What do you . . . " Seeing fresh blood on the floor, Lily stood rigid. "Mama?" She let the logs fall, each hitting the floor with its own thump.

Sticky blood had created a puddle on the plank flooring beneath Anna. Her knees wilted when the metallic smell hit her nostrils. She fell into the nearest chair, catching as it tilted backwards. "Don't talk. Get the granny."

Lily gawked at the crimson that eddied as it tried to seep between the boards. But it stayed, trapped by a burl on the floor. "I can't leave you." Lily had never seen so much blood.

"Go, girl. Now."

Lily raised her voice in fright. "But what..."

"Go and go now. I need a granny." Anna bent over as if she had a sharp pain in her belly.

Lily ran out, leaving the heavy door ajar.

Lily passed her eleventh birthday with no one noticing. With Anna ailing more month by month, Lily laid quarter after quarter on Kee Granny's worktable. Lily had climbed the rise to buy herbs for Anna's vomiting, headaches, and cramps, and for bleeding coming more often and more freely each time. Lately the bleeding had put Anna in bed, but never as much blood as today's.

Maybe she should talk to Gabe. He wanted them to move to Covington, but Lily knew no one in Covington. She only knew Juanita and Seth White in Breakline. They couldn't live in a camp for miners. Lily would ask Kee Granny for a double dose.

181

At the church, Lily opened the door. "Kee? Kee Granny? It's me." Lily stepped in. "Mama's bad. A lot of blood." Lily licked her dry lips and held her breath. "Maybe she needs a double dose?"

"Give me a minute to mix it up." The granny snapped off a puffy green plant. She broke off three pointed blades and squeezed out the juice. It turned black against the air as it covered the bottom of a chipped crockery saucer. Granny asked Lily to bring peppercorns from across the room.

Jars, each filled with red, green, or black liquids, crowded the shelves. Plant blossoms, some dried, some fresh, hung from the boards along the wall. Empty jars, dusty with age, cluttered the floor beneath the shelves. The room had not changed since Lily had seen it years before.

A whiff of mint and black pepper teased Lily's hunger. Lily remembered there was nothing cooked to feed her mother. She handed the granny a jar of black peppercorns and moved to inspect a branch near the window. Its green sepals held a cluster of firm berries. Black berries with tiny points at the top, more blueberry than black. Lily reached to pluck a berry.

"Leave that be, girl." The granny spoke with her back to Lily.

Lily shifted her eyes sideways. How could Kee Granny know she had almost touched the berry?

After mashing the peppercorns into the liquid with her pestle, Kee Granny spooned the concoction into a small jar and tightened the lid. "Give it to her slow. Some when you get home. Some at daybreak."

"Have I seen this before? What is it?" Lily asked. She swirled the brew around inside the jar, eyeing it to see if it would separate.

"Do what I say. Ain't no mind what it is."

"Can't you come with me?" Lily said. "To see about Mama."

"No. This is what she gets." Granny grabbed Lily's hand to stop her swirling the potion. "If you're going to be a Beloved Mother, you got to learn to do what you're told."

Reluctantly, Lily put her quarter on Kee Granny's table and followed the trail back down Turtleback. Maybe she could pause and ask Rattler if all this blood and pain and secrecy were part of being a Beloved Mother.

In answer, Sister Sun heats the north wind and sends out a clap of fierce thunder.

Lily looked upward, but she did not understand the language of the universe. Farther down Turtleback, she found Rattler not at home.

Chapter 27

It was spring of her twelfth year, 1956, and Lily ventured to Flatland.
She knew of only two who lived there. Kee Granny and the carpenter,
the granny's son.

In all likelihood, the carpenter would not be on the bald. Lily watched
him walk past Boone Station and down Turtleback to Covington to tinker
for a customer during the day, his tools and a large hatchet on his belt.
There would be days when Briar Slocomb's dog walked by his side, so
close in sync that the man appeared to have four extra legs.

Higher up the trail, the creek bounced over little falls that talked
to ferns and mosses along its banks. Smooth stones cut white ripples
through the water. This spring day the weather was warm, the air soft.
For once, Lily let worries of her mother's health fade from her mind as
she drank in the solitude. She thought of going to the Falls. Instead she
turned, as if she had been summoned, up the trail that passed Rattler's
den and ended near the granny's beehives. Rattler's hole was empty and
his mist gone, so she watched each side of the trail to avoid disturbing
him where he might lie in wait for an unsuspecting mole. Or he might
be resting, sunning himself beside a log, taking in the warmth of the
earth.

She veered off to the west to see the cedar.

Sister Sun, sweating from exertion, sends extra heat in an attempt to revive the trees that encircle the cedar Granny chose.

Lily had carried her potato plugged can and fed the surrounding trees each summer for six years. Year by year, each tree weakened, but the cedar grew in breadth and stature. Kee must be proud, Lily thought.

Sister Sun sees the girl climbing toward the ridge. Sister Sun is tired. She grunts at the realization that Lily doesn't get the joke about the trees and the purpose of the cedar. Great Spirit should take hold of the old crone before the phony kills something more significant than a few trees.

As she walked, Lily pondered this reversal of what she had pledged the oak, the black walnut, and the sour persimmon. With each trip, she had assured them of the nourishment Kee had ordered, but somehow Lily's intent had turned on her. Now leafless, the older trees were dying.

The cedar's massive presence amplified the impending loss of its brethren. A bed of needles coating the ground promised softness, but Lily knew from experience that all needles, pine, fir, or cedar, offered only prickles. The lone thriving tree, the cedar, stood like a vibrant emerald flame against the sky.

Sister Sun sees the girl standing before the cedar. "I see you standing there. Why don't you listen, little girl?" Sister Sun's heat amplifies Lily's thirst.

Sister Sun signals for a passing asteroid to pause and help her get the girl's attention, but the asteroid, a random passerby, ignores the signal and flies behind the earth.

The granny's church would be the place for water, a drink to wash the dust from Lily's throat and a bucket or two for the drooping trees.

There was no one on the bald. The smokehouse where the carpenter slept looked as if no one had been there in weeks. Its door stood open to the air, its makeshift porch empty.

A myriad of colors drew Lily to the side of the church. Reds, yellows, purples, and whites scattered in patches squared out, each to its own. Drawing nearer, she recognized the cultivated area as the granny's garden. She had not thought of the granny as having a garden, but she would need one, living on the bald most of the year. Lily had expected vegetables. Instead, she found an orderly garden of flowers in bloom.

Stones the size of large shoes marked the garden expanse. Within the walls were small squares that held each kind of flower in its space. Among the squares lay a path, paved with tiny stones from the creek. The pattern was brilliant. The stones lay so rain could seep into the ground and water the plants as they grew. It was the most precise garden Lily had ever seen. There was within its structure an exact design that controlled how and where to place your feet.

The garden threw out an explosion of color. Lily looked close. Within each square was a stick. On that stick was a tin can lid with the name of the flower etched in precise letters. Lily marveled at the number of different flowers.

She expected a granny, as a healer, to grow a separate herb garden for her salves and brews. But Lily could not tell if some of the plants were flowers or herbs. Perhaps Kee Granny grew herbs unnoticed, especially the ginseng that brought such a high price in Covington. If no one knew where her herbs grew, no one could steal them or thin them so sparsely they would not reproduce.

But the flowers. Lily stood mesmerized by shapes and colors. She read the names aloud. Purple coneflower. Foxglove in pinks and yellows and white. Clematis with purple petals and golden centers. Hellebore, black nightshade, poppy as red as holly berries. Angel's trumpets, their blooms bowed as if in prayer. And a vast span of pennyroyal, its creeping stems covered with lavender orbs that Lily thought looked more like dandelion heads ready to puff than pennyroyal. In one corner, a stand of mountain laurel in pinks and whites. In another, three yew trees leaned against the church wall, their needles so filled with deep green they resembled coal.

Lily walked to the far corner. There were no plants. Rather four green logs, each pointed in a cardinal direction. In the center, a light smoke drifted up from ash that kept the fire aglow night and day. In time, Kee Granny had taught Lily that this ring represented Cherokee Harmony, a belief that striving for wisdom through experience would lead to a courageous heart and a deep respect for all life.

By the time Lily and Anna had been on Turtleback Mountain for ten years, Lily knew each trillium, each bleeding heart, each wild iris, and where they thrived. She knew the best week for hickory nut gathering, where wild grapes flourished, where black walnut grew, and where to gather blackberries and dewberries in spring. All this she had learned as a child from days in the woods with Kee Granny.

⤙⤙⤙⤙

Another year went by. Anna ignored the road and hurried up the footpath Lily and Granny used, calling to the granny each time she stopped to catch her breath. Thankfully it was not a day that Anna felt too sick to get out of bed, but she could barely even make it up to the older woman's house without falling to the ground. The granny met Anna, pasty and frail in a weathered sort of way, at the door. "It's Lily," Anna gasped. "She's in awful pain."

The granny grabbed her black valise and ran, her bones jiggling beneath her long skirt. She found Lily in the loft, rolled into a quilt-covered ball and clutching her gut.

Lily's eyes filled with tears at the sight of her Kee. "It's knives," Lily said. "Cutting me inside."

Kee Granny enticed her with a honeyed voice. "You're gaining life-giving power." She showed Lily two long-necked gourds. "It's a celebration day. Come down and dance."

Lily hesitated. "No. I want to go to sleep so I won't hurt. Give me Mama's potion."

Kee Granny put the splotched gourds in her apron pockets, took Lily's hand and drew her near the ladder. "It's time." She nodded. "It's your time." She smiled and the two scars vanished into wrinkles.

Lily could not remember Kee smiling. Ever. So she followed Kee Granny. At the bottom of the ladder, she started for the rocker.

"Here, child. Drink this." She gave Lily a vial of extract she had made from cramp bark. Lily cringed at the taste.

Kee Granny set two vials on the table and pulled the two small, earth-colored gourds from her apron. "Sit. Roll these under your feet. Sway and bend. Release the pain through wonder and welcome." Soft and hymn-like, Granny's voice created a rhythm. "Roll, sway, and bend. Welcome," she chanted over and again.

"You're a woman. You have a voice among your people." Kee Granny hummed a minor tune then said, "A man will come for you, and the two of you will rejoice in your beautiful blood."

Lily bent forward as she rolled the gourds, her fists grinding into that hidden throbbing deep within her belly.

Across the room, Anna watched silently, her arms crossed over her chest, in deference to the granny's power. "I'm her mother. I should have recognized this," she said.

"Shhh," whispered Kee Granny.

After the rolling and breathing, Lily gradually straightened up. She rose from the rocker, extended her arms like a soaring eagle's wings, and swayed.

Kee Granny hummed a high-pitched, irregular melody built on some ancient pentatonic scale, minor and haunting. Her feet beat out a dance, not neat and tidy, not Western, but primal, unworldly, heady. Lily's body and Kee Granny's life-empowering song intertwined in an inseparable, slow rhythm. The granny's severe brown dress swept the floor and puffed out dust from the paths she had trod. Together they gave off the musky smell of new-turned earth.

Lily's feet and arms set her into a spin that accelerated with the song's rhythm.

Anna waited. She mourned the loss of compassion that her mother had failed to show her the first day of her womanhood. She coveted the palpable love Lily and Kee Granny were experiencing. At the point Anna expected Lily to whirl herself into a fall, Lily and Kee Granny stopped. Anna glanced around the room for some hidden hand that had touched the two simultaneously. If it was there, it was invisible.

Lily stood, her feet apart, in the middle of the room. The granny placed her hands on Lily's shoulders. Lily's bloated womb opened, allowing cleansing blood, beautiful blood, to trickle down her thigh.

Kee Granny stepped back. Lily laughed at the relief. She wrapped her arms around Kee and wept.

Anna slipped outside, drawn by the pungent aroma of early spring honeysuckle.

"Where's she going?" asks Sister Sun.

"Quiet. It's her knowing time," answers Great Spirit. "She needs to be with herself."

Chapter 28

Years before, Gabe Shipley had designated the two top shelves behind the counter to the granny's honey jars, her *wadulesi,* as she labeled it. Ever since she had first moved to Turtleback, she had brought the jars in the spring, the honey iridescent and golden against the light. After August, jars came filled with chunks of waxen comb, waiting to be spooned out and chewed like tobacco. She and Gabe had agreed on a price of thirty-five cents per pint. Her *wadulesi,* tasty and handy for ailments, would disappear as soon as Gabe set it out. He would pull another stash from the back.

Maintaining her closeness to nature and Great Spirit helped her bees thrive. She dared not anger Great Spirit or he would destroy clover, which in turn would destroy her bees. There would be no honey for Breakline or Covington. With her fifteen hives, she managed seventy-five gallons of honey each year. A loss of $210 could put her out of business at a time when miners made twenty-five dollars a week. As a Beloved Mother, she had earned the right to be paid well. Without her honey, she would have to resort to going into Covington to sell more cures and encourage a baby dropping here or there.

She wanted no more encounters with Covington's Sheriff Youell. Having to get Gabe Shipley to take her to Covington to get Briar out of jail for drunkenness marred her image with Great Spirit. She should have done better with her son.

Days when she was not healing or midwifing, she crossed the swinging bridge from Turtleback to the back side of Covington and sat on the northwestern edge of town. The boy, when younger, had carried a box of honey jars to town. She sold the last of them for twenty cents a jar so they would not have to carry the honey back up the mountain, but he was older now and more intent on doing what he wanted. Days at a time, he would vanish into the forest without a word and refuse to say where he had been or why. As the granny aged, the wooden box grew heavier with each trip alone.

The confrontation happened during the Month of the Bony Moon. Winter had been harsh, and Kee Granny grieved each time her mothering flow failed to appear. At forty-six it came less frequently. Lose her womanhood and she might lose her mothering skills.

> *"Doesn't she know it's not leaving? It's merely changing," says Sister Sun.*
>
> *"Who would have told her?" asks Brother Moon.*
>
> *"Great Spirit."*
>
> *"He doesn't bother with day-to-day things. He's got his mind on bigger problems like people always fighting over their skin color. Besides, he doesn't talk to her, or haven't you noticed?"*
>
> *"I thought those people already fought that war," says Sister Sun.*
>
> *"They did, but they can't remember what really matters," says Brother Moon. "They think I'm little more than a rock with no more power than to play with tides, but I know more than they do."*

The February day she walked into Breakline was cold. The granny had left enough honey with Gabe to last until spring when her hives produced again. Clover would not be in bloom for another two months. She came for staples: flour, sugar, and meal.

Gabe looked up from his novel.

"Mornin', Granny," Gabe said. "The usual?"

Granny nodded her head then glanced at her two shelves. Both were stocked with honey. Not her honey, but cloudy honey. She picked up a jar. Her fingers stuck to a gummy residue left by the beekeeper. She popped her head back toward Gabe. "What's this here?" She threw her head in the direction of the loaded shelves. "On my shelves?"

"A man come in from North County asking if we could sell some of his honey. I told him I reckon I could since yours was out. Selling for thirty cents a jar and I get a commission myself of a nickel for each jar I sell. Ain't that sweet?"

Granny did not acknowledge his joke. "And my *wadulesi?*"

"You ain't got no honey right now." He reconsidered. "Have you?"

"No, but that ain't the point." One of Granny's eyes twitched with fury. "That's my shelves. I'm the beekeeper. I sell the honey. Not some fool from north of here." She started around the counter. "I want my shelves cleaned off right now." She took a step closer. "And I ain't paying you to sell my honey."

"Now, Granny, I got to sell this man's honey." Gabe backed away from her. "I done paid him." He inched closer to the back of the counter and laid down his book. "You ain't the only beekeeper no more."

"People'll come in here thinking that trash is my honey." Spittle spurted out her mouth. "I ain't having it." She slung the jar to the floor. Cold honey globbed where it fell.

"Now, now," Gabe said with a chuckle. "Don't make me get out my board."

"I ain't scared of no two-by-four with a few nails. Go on. Bring it on out here." She took her forearm and, like a yeoman with his ax in hand, swept the honey jars to the floor. First the top shelf. Then the lower shelf. Sounds of exploding jars resonated through the commissary. Gabe leapt up on the counter to avoid the shattered glass flying in all directions. The smell of sweet clover and wildflowers filled the room. Granny stalked toward the door.

"Just a minute, Granny," Gabe said. "You just made yourself beholden to Mr. Rafe. He's going to want you to pay for that honey." He pulled a handkerchief from his pocket to clean honey from his glasses.

Granny had met the door, leaving her staples behind.

Gabe raised his voice. "Crazier by the day. No wonder Sheriff Youell run you out of Covington."

Granny glared at Gabe. "You can't hurt me, Gabe Shipley."

Gabe picked up the book he had been reading. "See this, you old witch? You got honey all over *Mice and Men.* Crazy old bat. When you die, we'll have to bury you twice to keep you in the ground."

Granny opened the screen door. "Somebody'll find you dead one day. That day, I'll walk up and spit on your body." The door slammed behind her.

Sister Sun summons Brother Moon. "Poor little bees. She ruined all that work they did. What's wrong with her?"

"Ask Great Spirit. He's supposed to understand everything."

"Poor Gabe. He'll be all day cleaning up her mess." Sister Sun shoots out a glow, hoping it will cheer him. "I'm telling Great Spirit what she did. She can't disrespect the gift of the bees."

"Send a frost over the mountain for the next two nights," Great Spirit tells Brother Moon that evening. "Singe all that sweet clover and send those bees to Kentucky. On your way up, scoop up that flatland honey and bring it to me. I have a mighty big hunger for something sweet."

"When shall I tell the bees to come back?" asks Brother Moon.

"I'll think on it," says Great Spirit. "Don't forget my honey. She's got some hidden in that back room of the old church." He waves down a mass of clouds, more solid than mist. His massive weight forces out a smattering of hail. West wind carries him across the horizon.

"Guess the clover'll be back next spring?" asks Brother Moon.

"Probably," says Sister Sun. "But she'll pay. He won't give up easy."

⸎⸎⸎⸎⸎⸎

April, 1960. Three years had passed since the granny's sheltered threat to kill Gabe and spit on his grave for selling the honey from North County. Gabe thought no more about what she had said, crazy old woman that she was.

Lily was fifteen. Gabe brought another box of Hershey candy bars and a sack of onions when he came to visit. Lily asked that he not.

"But Anna loves candy bars, and she eats onions with ever' meal," Gabe countered. "And it's your special day. We got to celebrate. No helling around, mind you, but something more than conversating."

"Candy bars at a nickel apiece, Gabe?" Lily paused to add up the total. "That's six whole dollars." She set the sack of onions on the plank table. "We got onions I hung up from last summer." She tilted her head. "What's special about today?"

"An excuse to party with my girl," Gabe smiled.

"He's her half-brother," says Brother Moon. "I can't believe this is happening."

"What's so wrong with that? The Egyptians married their brothers and sisters and had babies by their mothers and uncles. Just keeping it in the family." Sister Sun laughs.

"Humph."

"Don't be such a thick head. They produced some of the best rulers in history. Look at Queen Victoria. She married her first cousin, didn't she?" Sister Sun blinks. "At least, Victoria didn't pound her shoe on a table like Khrushchev's doing. That old bald-headed man's going to keep Great Spirit over there all week."

191

"Don't change the subject. Look at King Tut," counters Brother Moon. "His body was so deformed from incestuous relationships that he could hardly walk. And Gabe's so much older than Lily is."

"Now, be fair. That's no real problem. A lot of men marry younger women. They have since the beginning of time. Look at Joseph and Mary. She was only a teenager, so I've heard. Nobody knows about Gabe and Lily's family relationship but Winston Rafe. Can't Great Spirit set him straight if he sees that as a problem?"

"Be assured that if he doesn't straighten Rafe out, he'll eliminate the problem somehow. Think on how he handled Jackson Slocomb."

Brother Moon shivers. "Glad I'm not in this."

"I'm not your girl, Gabe." She reached for the candy to hide it from her mama.

"If I plan to marry you, I got to keep your mama happy." Gabe grinned his lop-sided smile.

"Mama eats that chocolate like she's craving it. Onions, too. Then she gets the sick headache," Lily argued. "It's not good for her."

"You heard what I said, Lily my love." Gabe grasped Lily's hand. "Never mind your mama. I'm going to wed you. Just giving you another year or so."

"Oh, hush up." Lily's hot face needed a cool washrag. She looked at him and memorized his duck-egg blue eyes. Gabe's dogged expectation that Lily would love him in a wifely manner had begun to sound more than tolerable.

Anna sniffed out the chocolate and ate the box of Hershey bars that night. She acted different in an unexplained way afterwards. For three days, Anna complained of a deep-seated headache, covered herself with quilts and demanded that Lily shutter the windows and doors. It was not until after she vomited the morning away that she rose from the bed.

Days were worse when Gabe brought red wine. The two sat on the porch, Anna sipping her wine from an aluminum glass she kept chilled in the creek. Gabe had brought six glasses, each a different color, and a pitcher complete with tray as a Christmas gift. Anna selected the iridescent green each visit and drank from it. "A special occasion," she said, as she self-justified each full glass. Without Gabe's wine, the other glasses set apart on a shelf next to the cupboard. With the drinking passed, the next morning Anna would see rats chasing each other across the bare floor. Or she might see large winged birds, glossy and black, perched on the backs of chairs. On these days, Lily climbed the hill to Flatland and fetched Granny Slocomb.

After the granny brought a potion, Anna vomited. The granny said it was necessary to purge Anna of whatever evil animal she had within her. Lily doubted Kee Granny's animal theory. She recalled the night in Covington with Julie Hudson at O'Mary's Bar when she saw Eli and thought he was trying to be a bug. *Silly me. To think a person would try to be a bug,* she reprimanded herself. Lily accepted the animal idea as some Cherokee belief she did not understand, so she did not question.

Anna improved with the vomiting, but it did not cure her. Instead, she accused Lily of having pink and blue lights around her body and scratched her hands until they bled.

Chapter 29

Lily dreamt her father ran like a stag with Lily on his back. Her hands grasped his neck to keep from falling. She bent forward to see his face, but she couldn't get close enough. She dreamt Anna sang to her again, as she had when they lived in Breakline. Rocking and singing. Singing and rocking. Old mountain melodies that meandered through their minor keys until the final chord modulated into a major chord. But the dream voice changed to a man's voice, not Anna's. A full tenor voice. Singing about the Shenandoah River and his love for the river's daughter. "*O Shenandoah, I love your daughter,*" he sang. Seven years he mourned, the lover sang, since he had seen his love. And Lily thought of her father, gone himself for nearly fifteen years. The dream unnerved her. She had to wake or die.

The melody stayed with Lily for days. She hummed the tune when she least expected it. When Anna heard Lily's music, she begged from her bed for Lily to sing more. But Lily refused. Something bothersome in the voice of the dream was too familiar. She did not want to think on any of it, for it reminded her of something she could not quite remember.

The creek behind and below Boone Station had been Lily's lullaby. It was the singingest creek she had ever heard. But the tenor now out-sang the creek as it hurried itself to Covington. His high-reaching ballads drew her to him. Nights when jitters overtook her, and she lay awake on her side of the bed, the voice came as if summoned by her nervousness.

When he stopped his quiet lullabies, she slept sound, filled with peace. Mornings after he had sung, Lily would question Anna. Had she heard? No. She had not.

Lily needed to ask the granny about the voice. Hesitant at first for fear the granny would think forest spirits had overtaken her, she tapped her feet, sighed, and looked away to avoid the question. She drew doodles in the dirt from where she sat on the rock slab step outside Granny's door. "I hear music," she stammered. "Most every night. Beautiful music."

Kee Granny laughed her scars into wrinkles. "Little People. They live in caves and come at night to help you. You need sleep. They bring sleep." Kee Granny shot out a glob of snuff spittle off to the side. "Kind-hearted and great wonder workers, they are. Very gentle."

"No. I hear one voice," Lily insisted. "Only one voice."

"Then it's them Dogwood People." Kee Granny stroked Lily's hair. "They expect that if you do something for someone, do it out of goodness of your heart. You're doing that for your mama. It's come to soothe you."

Lily looked across to the smokehouse where Briar stayed. "If they can help, why haven't they healed my mama?" She shifted her head to face the granny. "Why haven't *you* healed my mama?"

Kee Granny rested her hand on Lily's shoulder, holding her down. After a long thinking time, she spoke. "She can't be healed, child." She spoke, her voice low.

"What do you mean? You can heal." Lily narrowed her eyes and tried to shrug Kee Granny's hand off her shoulder. "You're Beloved Mother."

Kee Granny stared at the horizon. A reddish sun lay low against the treetops, changing their green to deep ebony. Lily heard Kee Granny swallow before she spoke. "She can't be healed. Her mind and body, they's no harmony with her spirit." The granny waited a minute and added, "She's soul-sick. 'Heart sick,' some call it. They ain't no cure for that."

Lily raised her voice. "What are you talking about? Is this some Cherokee trick?"

Kee Granny flinched. "Your mama's got a burden, a burden of a size that haunts her." She struck Lily with another fact. "She walks with a rock of knowing in her shoe. Ever time she moves she's reminded, so she'll one day soon stop trying to walk from the pain of it. The debt won't be paid, but she won't feel the pain no more."

Lily jerked from under the granny's hand, stood and glared at her. "I don't believe you," she spit out. "You can heal her."

"You must believe. Else you'll never be Beloved Mother," Kee Granny's voice sounded drained.

"I don't want to be a Beloved Mother." Lily's shrill voice carried down the trail toward Rattler's den. "If I can't heal Mama, why should I be Beloved Mother?"

Kee Granny placed her arms around Lily. "You got to be Beloved Mother so you can make life better for women who need you." She let her head fall on Lily's shoulder. "They ain't got nobody else."

Lily dragged her feet as she returned to Boone Station. Her shoulders drooped under the burden of this new knowledge. But she knew herbs. She knew cures. Perhaps the time had come for her to heal her mother.

The next day promised to be a hot July day. Lily left early to buy more herbs. She would make a stronger potion herself, if it called for it. She passed Rattler on the trail, sunbathing in his trunk hollow. He lay so still, he did not look real. She considered touching him but decided he might vanish if she came too close. Leave him be. He may have a power Lily didn't recognize.

At Flatland, she eased around the back of the church, calling for Kee Granny. No one answered. She glanced around, trying to rid herself of the feeling that someone watched her. Lily looked at the sun. Almost noon. Lily recalled Kee Granny would be at her cedar mid-day, praying and chanting to the Great Spirit.

Behind the church, at an earlier time, someone had built a little room, smaller by half than the old sanctuary. Boards zigzagged across two windows, one on each side of the room. Its slant tin roof directed rain so close to the plank wall that a narrow ditch isolated the little room from the grassy area, much like a shallow moat.

Lily stepped inside the old church. She had been here before, but she had never gone into the back room. Lily glanced about for an entrance to the lean-to. The sanctuary ceiling sloped right and left, from a single rafter that extended from the front door to above a small platform where a pulpit once stood.

Against one wall, the board bed where Kee Granny slept held a frayed Cherokee blanket. Lily walked over to Kee Granny's heavy wooden worktable. Morning sunlight reflected streaks of reds and greens and browns through bottles of liquids across the tabletop. As she ran her fingers over the jars and bottles, her foot bumped a jug under the table. She nudged the jug back in place. Its label read *Alcohol,* and under that *One Gallon.* Kee had never had her use alcohol in preparing a cure.

Lily rubbed one hand over the glass globe of a kerosene lantern that sat in the middle of the table. The globe was full, ready to be lit. Next to the lantern lay the worn leather book Kee used for her recipes. Lily flipped through the pages. The Cherokee words scribbled across the pages looked like worms, words Lily could not read.

Kee loved the book. When she picked it up, she caressed it and hugged it to her bosom as if it were a living thing. She had long ago given up her glasses. Lily could barely remember them. Kee would open the cover, bend over and place her nose so close to the page it seemed she sniffed out a cure. Lily closed the book with a pat. It could not help her.

Across the room were two low shelves with different sized crockery bowls aligned by size, their rims bordered in cobalt blue and pink. Inside each bowl rested a different plant, leaves or blooms, waiting to be processed. Lily lifted the pestle and pretended to grind a mixture in the mortar. The pestle's wooden surface had been worn as smooth as a new leaf. She wrapped her index finger into a loop for holding the mortar steady. Her finger froze. The marble bowl felt as cold as the stream behind Boone Station when high mountain melted snow made its way south.

Putting the pestle aside, she walked to a side window. On the windowsill, in small tin cans, grew a variety of green-leafed plants, plants Lily could not remember using before. She pinched a bit off one plant and tasted. Its bitterness pouted her lips. Bitter, it was. Bitter as green persimmon. She scraped her tongue with her fingernails so she would not gag. She examined the plant closer. It was the plant Kee Granny had warned her against touching when she had come earlier for her mama's herbs.

The room was hot. Lily's eyes circled the room looking for a drink of water. Checking the room for a bucket and dipper, she realized something was not right. Something was missing. An iron stove for heat and cooking. The bed. The table. A chair. Shelves. Kee Granny's long brown dresses hanging on wall pegs, dresses she called her "woods roaming dresses." A quilt hung next to the pegs, at the opposite end of the room from the door.

The quilt. A crazy quilt, a quilt made up of irregular cloth pieces, none the same, neither color nor shape. Someone had sewn pieces together with a chicken scratch stitch that danced around each piece in an orange frenzy. A crazy quilt, made especially warm with woolen scraps, would not hang on the wall. It would be on the bed, a necessity not meant for display. It was so like the one she and Anna slept under that it could have been made by the same hand. But here it was. A quilt hanging where a window or door should be.

Every house Lily had ever been in had cross ventilation, with a window or door directly across from another so that breezes could catch an opening and move through the room. There was no window opposite the entrance door, nor was there a door. Thick nails attached the quilt to the wall below the gabled ceiling. Lily stepped up on the dais and patted the quilt.

"Come here quick," Sister Sun calls. "Come here, Great Spirit."

The quilt moved as if it breathed. Lily lifted a corner. There it was. The opening. A door frame, rather than a window.

Great Spirit floats in from the USSR where he has watched the Russians launch two dogs into space. "I'll have them back in eight days. They won't kill two of my best creations. I'll see to that. Sending living beings into space. Humph. These won't be the last," he grumbles. "Man will try and try until he manages to kill an entire spaceship of travelers. Never learn." He kicks a southern wind out of his path. "They never learn."

Lily peeped behind the quilt and stepped onto a dropped landing. Behind the quilt, she felt her way down a railing that guarded seven stairs. Heavy planking nailed against windows on each sidewall darkened the room.

Sister Sun cannot stay still. "Come here, Great Spirit," she repeats. "This is not going to be good."

Lily steadied her eyes and caught her breath. At one window, she slid a board aside so light could enter. The nail holding the board in place screeched a complaint at being disturbed. A sliver of sunlight sliced across the floor, capturing dust motes in its path.

"Can't you stop her?" Sister Sun asks.
"Not necessary. Knowledge never hurt a body." Great Spirit floats off toward the East. "Catch me at the All-Star Baseball Game in Kansas City. I need a break from all this."

In the middle of the room on a small wooden platform, sat what had once been a black Edwardian rocker. The rockers were gone and the legs nailed to the platform so the chair could not move. Brown wooden arms, laid bare by gripping hands and clawing fingernails, contrasted with the chair's black paint.

Lily edged closer. In the center of the seat was a hole, a hollow that opened to a blue and white speckled enamel wash pan resting on the platform. Lily touched the pan. It moved, free of the platform, as if waiting to be filled. *Aha,* Lily thought, *a fancy slop jar Kee Granny or Briar made.*

The back wall held a wide shelf. On it, stacked thick, glass to glass, were capped jars, all full. Some with whitish, some with grayish, some with glob-like things floating in clear liquid. She came closer. A snippet of paper lay at the base of each jar, each with a name scribbled in pencil. *Betty June Lawler. Inez Whitson. Pernnecie Arnold.* Lily passed over the names, looking for someone she knew. *Juanita White.* And another *Juanita White* further down the shelf. Her mama's friend from Breakline Camp. Jason's mother. It had been so long since she had last seen Jason. Not since she stopped school in the sixth grade.

More fascinating than the names was what each jar held. Lily picked up a small jar and shook it. Air bubbles jiggled up and down. Inside, what seemed to be a large dry lima bean sloshed back and forth. In another was a larger bean, misshapen in a way that looked like it had eye bulges and almost a nose. Somebody had wrapped it in something, cheesecloth maybe, for it was whiter than the first bean. She touched a jar near the back. Its lid moved. She turned the jar ring and slid her fingernail under the lid to break the seal. The stench took Lily's breath. Liquid rotted fish. Lily gagged and screwed the ring back in place.

Behind this jar set a larger jar. Lily had to pull up a stool and climb to get to the back row. The larger jars on the back crammed against each other, all too heavy for Lily to lift. She slid the first row out and scanned the back row, jar after jar. More detailed, whatever floated inside these jars looked like what Lily imagined a ghost should be. This one, almost as long as her forearm. That one had what looked like two legs. This one, the biggest yet, held its skinny elbows together, covering what seemed to be a face. Beneath the edge of this jar lay a paper with the name scratched in pencil. *Anna Parsons Goodman.* Her mama's name.

It was science class all over again with frogs and snakes on the back shelf. But these were not frogs and snakes, but something very, very different. Something that should not be. Not at Kee Granny's. Beloved Mother's purpose was to save lives, not take lives.

The reality of what she had before her struck so hard Lily could not breathe. She jumped off the stool and fell to the floor. The faces and bodies in these jars could not belong to her Kee. Briar must live in this room. Her Kee Granny would not stay in such a room. Her mama would not be in this room with rows of misshapen globs of flesh. It must be a hoax, set up to deceive her.

She rolled over and stood up. Backing away, she struck the black chair that now overpowered the room. When she hit the chair, she took hold of herself and ran. Out of the church. Down the footpath. Past Rattler's hollow trunk. It stood empty.

When she got near Boone Station, she skidded down to the stream. She splashed her face and lowered her feet into icy water. She sat on the bank, waiting for her body to stop shaking, her heart to stop pounding. Within a moment, Lily heaved and vomited into the stream.

It had not been real. It was a waking nightmare. She would forget what she thought she had seen.

"You think she'll be back?" Sister Sun asks Brother Moon.

"Leave her alone," Brother Moon says. "Why can't you do what Great Spirit tells you? He's likely to sling you off into some other universe."

"He'd never do that to me. I'm his sun."

"Humph. You're not the only star in the sky," says Brother Moon. "You should go over to Orion and see Betelgeuse. Now there's a real sun."

"I'm not going anywhere, and you can't make me," says Sister Sun.

"Then leave her alone."

Chapter 30

Lily could not recall the day of the week when it happened. She did remember that the year was 1961 when it happened in June, Granny's Month of the Green Corn Moon. She did remember the sound of heavy crockery breaking behind her. She turned to find Anna on the floor, a crockery bowl shattered. Raw eggs seeped across boards and dripped through cracks. Anna shuttered. And shuttered again. Lily grabbed her mama and sat her up. A milky substance thrust itself out of Anna's mouth, and Anna closed her eyes.

Lily shook Anna until she opened her eyes. She dragged her to the bed, all the time talking, talking, trying to call her mama back. When Anna didn't speak, Lily ran, without thinking, for Kee Granny.

Kee Granny brought her supplies. She carried the satchel she had brought from the Carolina Mountains. She pulled back Anna's eyelids and put her ear to Anna's chest, but she did not concoct a brew. "Leave her lie. Let her know you're here." She closed her black valise, now so worn it was grey in spots. "She seen the other side and she wants to go."

Lily choked. "I don't understand. Why?"

"Your mama knows, but she ain't saying. Our job's to make her path easy. That's all."

Lily rushed for the porch and stared toward the chimney. "Did you see her spirit mist?" she called through the open door. "Did you? If her spirit mist is not there, you can fix her." Lily shut the door. "You're Beloved Mother. You know things." She grabbed Kee Granny by the shoulders and shook her until Kee Granny's head bobbed back and forth. Lily stopped when she saw the granny's face. Weariness? Shame? Lily could not decide. Tears ran down the scars and disappeared into Kee Granny's open mouth.

"Kee Granny? Tell me." The granny's face seemed cut into two parts. Lily was not sure now an answer was worth this. She brought the granny to her shoulder and held her.

"I ain't no Beloved Mother. And I shore ain't *the* Beloved Mother," Kee Granny spoke tentatively into Lily's ear.

"But you're Cherokee," Lily rationalized.

"Maybe a part of me's been Cherokee once. But nobody never made me no Beloved Mother."

"But you've said so all these years. . . and you made Mama brews and potions and rattled the gourd and danced the rabbit dance." Lily's voice fell as she spoke. "Great Spirit talks to you."

"I never said Great..." Her voice broke.

Lily interrupted her. "You taught me..." She could not have said if the tears she felt were hers or Kee Granny's, so close to each other they stood. Lily pushed Kee Granny back so she could see her face.

Kee Granny kept her eyes to the floor. "They's those who knows more than most. They's the ones who decide."

"Did they make the scars?"

"Scars? These?" She ran her hand down her cheek. "Oh, no. No, Lily. No more than your own arm scar. A white man done this. No. My Cherokee man was a good man." Granny Slocomb plopped heavy onto the floor.

Lily glared at nothing. Numbness draped itself over her like a thunder-filled cloud and her knees weakened. She dropped to the floor beside Kee Granny. Outside a woodpecker looking for grubs thumped his hard head against a hollow tree. "And the cedar? The one for Great Spirit?"

Granny answered with a slight shake of her head. "You can't not believe, Lily. Not Great Spirit. He exists in every living thing."

"Lies?" she whispered. "It's all been lies?"

"What's true depends on who's saying it, I reckon." Granny's voice drained quieter with each word. "Believe anything strong enough and long enough, it becomes true."

Lily's spirit shattered into little bits of nothing. "Why?" Lily wanted a truth to be a firm truth, not something defined by the believer.

"Sometimes it takes a life to give a life." Granny held up a hand as if asking Lily to help her rise.

Lily rose instead. "Who told you that?" She leaned over the mound on the floor. "You taught me all things are one. It's Beloved Mother's job to preserve."

Kee Granny lifted herself up on her knees in an attempt to face Lily. "A body believes what it will. What it wants to."

"What were you giving her?" Lily backed away. "My mama?"

The granny rose, her eyes now coal black. "Belladonna." She shuffled toward the door.

Lily knew there was more. "And foxglove," Lily demanded. "Did you give her foxglove?"

"A mite." Kee Granny gripped the doorknob.

"Foxglove. My God. You've been killing my mama with foxglove." Lily dropped into a chair. "You slowed her heart so she can't live. Why?"

Kee Granny stepped out on the porch, leaving the door ajar.

"Get off my porch!" Lily screamed. The veins in her neck throbbed. "Go back to your Great Spirit and his rattling ways."

Throughout the night, the recollection of Kee Granny's moaning as she stepped off the porch and crept away from Boone Station would awaken Lily again and again.

The next day, exhausted, Lily stoked dying logs. The fire sparked and hissed against Lily's probing. She placed another log on the irons. It popped and blazed into a stronger flame.

Lily crossed the room and laid her hand on Anna's forehead. Her mama's skin felt like the dry paper Lily had used to tender the fire. She lifted the woolen quilt and placed her mama's arms under it.

From the porch she brought a pitcher of Gertie's milk to the table. She cracked a freshly laid egg into a jar, poured in milk and added sugar for temptation. She stirred the drink, clinking the fork against the jar sides, to see if her mama would respond. Anna did not.

Lily lifted her mama's head, enticing her to drink. Anna's lips had frozen into a thin straight line. What Lily offered her spilled down a crease that ran from her lip and dripped off her chin. For a moment, Kee Granny's tear-filled scars flashed before Lily. She rubbed the scar on her own arm still knotted and black from soot the granny had used to slow the blood when Lily had cut herself and new to Boone Station. It was so familiar she rarely noticed it, but it marked her arm as surely as would have a brand of ownership signified by the granny. Lily went to the washbasin, took a towel and wiped her mama's face.

A storm cloud passed over the house. Light in Boone Station faded at once. Lily lit the kerosene lamps, one by the bed and one on the table, to take away the dark. Lamps cast softer light than Powell Valley electricity. Lily needed softness, not harsh reality. Later she would take a dried rabbit from the clothesline between the side posts on the front porch and boil it into broth. Tomorrow. She would try again to rouse her mama tomorrow.

Perhaps it was grief. Perhaps it was guilt for the part she had played in taking her mama down this path by letting the granny treat her. Whatever it was, it came upon Lily and sent her into rages. When a rage overcame her, Lily took care not to touch Anna. Over the next weeks, her anger would explode and she would slam her fist on the table. Lily's hands ached from clutching whatever she came near. Her aggression left bruises that enlarged with each strike. To settle herself, she would bite her lips and swallow the sweet blood. As time passed, each calming time grew shorter than the one before.

Memory came to Lily in a flash. She opened the top bureau drawer and removed the box of carved animals she had collected from her time on Turtleback Mountain. She had been a younger Lily, a Lily who had trusted Kee Granny, a Lily who had believed that the Little People, the Laurel People, and the Dogwood People would come to make her happy. She had left them hidden, for as her mama had said about the little treasures that first day coming up the Turtleback, somebody might come and claim them as their own. Now she needed to have each carving before her, in sight so she could relive each one and its place in her past.

> *"Good that she respects her past," says Great Spirit to the dark universe. "She'll be less likely to make the same mistakes again."*
>
> *"Should I tell her about her father?" asks Sister Sun.*
>
> *Great Spirit curls his upper lip and turns his back. "Don't take the problems of the innocent and increase them, Sister Sun. Don't put misfortune on the blameless."*

Lily took the carvings, a thin strip of leather, a large needle and began to string. First a turtle, for Turtleback Mountain itself. Then a fox, a fox she had once found on the trail to the revered cedar. Next a cougar, larger than the rest. And the fat, round bear that had dropped into her lap the day she and her mother rested by the roadside. She rubbed the bear with special tenderness against her cheek. She had not worn it since she boarded the school truck for Covington. She had not realized that she missed it so. There were several turkeys. These she threaded in among other animals. And a little nesting bird her mother had refused to explain.

She saved the beautiful, full-antlered stag for last. Taking it from where Anna had it on the mantle, she slipped the leather through its hole and tied a secure knot, adding a loop so that the menagerie could be hung from her porch. The superb stag would lead the procession, a total, she counted, of seventeen animals, all in a row. Great Spirit had sent one for each year of her life.

Before hanging the animals, she caressed each with her fingers. They felt old, old enough to remember the Creation. She memorized each cut, each detail, so completely that she would later be able to re-create each in her mind. She hung the carvings in a swag from the porch rafter where Owl still came to roost. Their presence helped alleviate her solitude.

Lily had watched Anna try all summer to die. At the end of summer, once her mama could no longer lift her arms or speak, Lily knew it was time to ask Gabe to go to Covington to buy a new, long-handled shovel for the burying.

> *Sister Sun tries not to scorch the mountain. Brother Moon cools each night. They call to night breezes to give Lily restful sleep. They must make this trying time easier for Lily, this young woman they have come to think of as their own.*
>
> *"Losing her father and now losing her mother after casting Kee Granny out," says Brother Moon. "Me and you and Gabe Shipley are all she has left."*
>
> *"Does she know?" says Sister Sun. "About us, I mean."*
>
> *"I don't know," says Brother Moon. "Maybe one day when the universe is in syzygy Great Spirit will speak."*

Lily planned for the laying by. It came to her in the night on the floor while she lay wrapped against the damp in the extra bed quilt. The event would be a non-event with only Anna and Lily. Maybe Gabe. If the weather allowed. It had been only Anna and Lily and Gabe these past months now that Kee Granny did not come. It would be right that they did this alone.

Anna favored a woolen crazy quilt for its pieces and the precise chicken scratch stitching in bright blue thread, much like the one at Granny's church. Lily would clean her mama's waist-length hair with cornmeal. She would brush it afresh, plait it, and wrap it around her mama's head like a tarnished silver tiara. Forty years old, she was. Too young for grey hair. And a cotton dress. No shoes. Just the quilt and her mama. And socks. To warm her mama's feet.

No. She would write words of honor and place them in the coffin so, if bones were found, the reader would know that Anna Goodman had been a flesh and blood woman, a woman who had loved and been loved.

Lily took a pencil and spiral notebook. She sat at the table and palmed her forehead as she thought. After a moment, she wrote:

Anna Parsons Goodman
Born in Covington, Virginia the 7ᵗʰ day of the Month of the Bony Moon

She erased "the Month of the Bony Moon" and replaced it with the word "February."

in the year of our Lord - 1921
Married Clint Goodman the 24ᵗʰ day of March in 1937
in Wise, Virginia at the court house
Widowed in Breakline Mining Camp by a rogue coal truck the 22ⁿᵈ day of July 1945
Mother of Lily Marie Goodman who was born
October 9ᵗʰ in 1944
Moved to Boone Station October 24ᵗʰ of 1946
Passed from this earth

She left the rest blank. She took a mason jar from the shelf over the washstand, found a lid and put her mother's obituary and the pencil stub inside. She placed the jar back on its shelf. The thought of babies and jars in the old church and how little her mama's life had come to made her shiver. An unborn child settling in a jar of alcohol and less than half a piece of paper to verify its existence. Lily needed to add something that would make her mother a real person. She took out the paper, scratched through the words "Passed from this earth" and added, *My mama was a woman who made do.*

Chapter 31

The month of November found Briar returning from Covington.
By early afternoon, he was fighting a gusty north wind. He walked
with his head thrust forward as if he were searching for some unknown
something he expected to find round the next turn. By late afternoon, he
stopped halfway up the mountain to relieve a cramp the climb brought to
his lower calf. He sat on a rock outcropping and leaned his back against
the ground. Cold seeped through his jacket. He should have stolen a bit
of copper wire to wrap around his ankles when he had to make more than
one trip to Covington in a day. Keep on cramping and his calves would be
strutted so big he couldn't get his pants on.

A hickory nut dropped in front of him and rolled down the incline. It
settled in a cluster of nuts resting in a bed of rust-tinged leaves. Early leaf
colorings foretold that weather was turning toward winter, even had the
nuts not attracted his attention. This winter would be bitter cold. Squirrels
had been vigilant in storing nuts. Wooly worms were fat as Briar's thumb.
It would be a winter Tall Corn would have understood.

Briar longed to talk to his Cherokee father so he could learn more
about who Silent Wolf was supposed to be. Two Tears kept busy so
raising her herbs, collecting her 'sang and dropping babies that she had
no time for him. He had become Silent Watcher, rather than Silent Wolf,
as he wandered Turtleback. He often dropped wooden animals on the

forest floor wherever he whittled them. One day when it was time for him to know his purpose on this mountain, he would collect those he could find. They, like some miniature totem, would speak to him. He would then understand who he was and why Two Tears had brought him to this place.

The wind eased into a bitter cold. Over Turtleback's longest ridge, a solid bank of clouds, almost black, blocked the sun's warmth. Briar pulled his jacket closed and buttoned the neck button. He then unbuttoned it. A true Cherokee would not strain against what Great Spirit sent. To prove himself qualified, he removed his jacket and unbuttoned his shirt's neck. Though he stiffened himself against the air's iciness, his body shook. In fairness to himself, he wrapped his arms around his chest and tucked his chin down on his chest.

To his right, a rustling of leaves caught Briar's attention. Clearly not Cherokee. Whoever was walking this way was tromping without regard to what or whom he disturbed. Nearer now, someone slid on dry leaves, dropped and uttered a moan. Male. Tall, taller than Briar. It took longer for the man's head to hit the forest floor than it would have taken Briar's.

Briar straightened his back and looked over his shoulder. A boy, not yet twenty, lifted himself into a crouch and grabbed at the bag that lay by his side. His greasy hair touched the shoulder of his once-white shirt and hid his face. He combed his white ringlets back with his fingers. They snagged in the tangles. He pushed the hair behind his ears and looked at Briar.

His pasty face had burgundy blemishes from the sun and wind. His dry cheeks and lips puffed as if the skin were ready to split and slough away. A stark bone structure separated his eyes from his forehead. Briar turned easy to face him head-on.

Two more nuts fell. The boy jerked his head toward where the nuts hit the ground then back to Briar. His sinewy body tensed. His free hand grasped his throat as if he were trying to hold back words or strangle himself.

Briar stood and extended a hand to the boy to lift him up. Rather than take the hand, the boy rounded up on his knees and hoisted his weight up with his forearms.

"What you doing on Turtleback?" Briar said. "Great Spirit lost sight of you?"

The boy did not answer.

"I said, what you doing up here?"

The boy picked up his sack and hugged it to his chest.

Briar stepped forward. "Where you from?"

The boy tried to move back but staggered, never taking his gaze off Briar.

"Are you run away?" Briar moved a step closer.

Wind rose behind the boy and picked up leaves. They spun into an eddy. A squirrel scurried up a nearby oak. The boy crept backwards, tripped and caught himself with his free hand. He landed soft on a patch of moss.

"Are you dumb?" Briar asked.

The boy stared at Briar, then glanced left, then right.

Briar reached into his pocket and extended a closed fist. He opened his fist to expose a small, carved wolf. "I'm Silent Wolf," Briar said. He shifted unconsciously into the more stilted language he recalled from his years with Tall Corn. "I will be your brother."

The boy stared at the carving and nibbled on his lower lip.

"Take it. It's yours. We will be brothers." Briar moved closer.

The boy glanced over his left shoulder.

"It's a wolf pup," Briar said. The boy reached for the little wolf, then pulled back his hand. Briar waited. After a moment, the boy took the wolf pup and slipped it into his pocket.

Briar's hand felt oddly bare. He had given his animals to the earth when he dropped them hither and yon, but he had never deliberately relinquished one of his animals. He had stepped into an alien land and was not sure which way to trod. He questioned if perhaps Great Spirit had guided him. Only his mother could speak with Great Spirit, so she said. So it must not be that. Why had he handed an animal over to a stranger? He should ask for it back. But no. He had gifted the wolf. It was no longer his. He would carve another, a better one.

Wind whistled up from the base of Turtleback telling Briar to move on. He glanced at the bag the boy held. "You can't stay out here in this coming weather. Even Great Spirit's animals ready for a blizzard."

Briar glanced at the bag the boy held. "Where you live?" Briar asked.

The boy shrugged his shoulders and took the wolf cub from his pocket. He examined it and clasped his hand, hiding it in his fist.

"So. You can hear. You just ain't talking," Briar said. "You can't stay out here in this coming weather. Big snow soon." Briar turned toward orange sunrays that slid earthward under the cloudbank. "You ain't got no place, you can come with me." Briar walked south, toward Old Man Farley's place. The boy followed, clutching his bag in one hand and the wolf cub in the other.

In the night, Briar returned with blankets, clothes much too large, matches, and food. The next morning, he took the boy by the hand and led him up a hidden path to Old Oak. He showed the boy how to climb and on which limb to sit so he could watch the comings and goings in the camp and on the road between Covington and Flatland.

Chapter 32

Early November rained every night and misted every day for two weeks. Air on Turtleback smelled like wet straw. Lily stayed inside. Waiting. She knew Death would come before hard winter. Kee Granny had not come back. Lily had not gone to get her to tend Anna for three months. With Kee Granny gone, the room smelled less of cedar. Lily had nurtured potted herbs on the east windowsill since summer. The herbs filled the room with battling aromas of lavender, mint and rosemary.

The night the wolf began to howl, Lily knew. Lily thought the wolf to be Briar Slocomb's dog, and perhaps it was. The howl started long after the moon rose, and it bayed until dawn. If the dog was primarily wolf, he could bring no less than evil, for Kee Granny had taught her that evil rides on the backs of wolves.

Lily pictured the wolfdog away from the buildings that comprised Flatland. Or perhaps he sat on the cedar's high ridge so that his voice would carry over the mountainous expanse. He rested on his haunches with his head thrown back, his mouth open to the cold air. Lily envisioned him as a statue, his chest hard as stone, yet mist would rise from his jaws as if his innards were afire.

The second night of the wolf, a flicker of light appeared on the floor before the hearth. Lily picked up what seemed to be a shiny straight pin. She held it up to the light, looking close. She gazed, slack-jawed, in rapt wonder at a wee glowing creature. A minute being, glorious in his gossamer green robes, stood on the head of the pin. He spoke to Lily in a voice that jingled with tiny bells. *"The time for beginning has come,"* he said. Holding the pin as far away as her arm allowed, Lily moved to the table and stuck the pin in a mound of brown-crusted bread. She stepped over to the stove and waved her hand over a black eye, feeling for warmth, to prove she was not dreaming. Heat radiated upward, forcing Lily to draw back her hand before burning her palm. She looked back at the pin. He was still there.

"Come," he said. *"Sit."*

Lily hesitated, her confusion morphing into fear.

"Don't be afraid," he said.

Lily stepped gently over the floor. She pulled out a chair, pushed it away from the table and sat on the edge of the seat. "You are a spot of mold," she said.

He tingled a little half-laugh. *"Call me Ena,"* he said.

Lily gulped. "Are you a tiny Little People?"

"I'm Ena," he said. *"I come with the wind."*

"An angel?"

"I can be an angel, if you like."

"Did Kee Granny send you?"

"Who?"

"Beloved Mother."

"I came on my own. I sensed you need me."

"Some other Beloved Mother?" Lily asked. Anna had told her about angels, but they had always been silver or gold with feathery wings that brushed the ground. "You're not real." Lily walked across the room. "I'm talking to myself." She splashed cold water on her face. As she straightened up, a button fell off her blouse. She pulled the straight pin from the bread and closed the gap that exposed her breasts. It was time to begin.

Lily took out the clean dress she had selected for her mother. She picked up the brush for braiding her mother's hair. The heat in the room forced Lily to sweep her bangs from her forehead. Though damp, they fell forward again as she bent to select wool socks from the bureau drawer. Anna's feet were cold summer and winter. It would be damp and cold in the ground, so Anna must have thick socks.

Stiff with age, the bottom bureau drawer stood ajar. There near the back was the bill of sale for the two coffins. Lily placed it on top of the bureau. Taking a fresh blouse from another drawer, Lily laid the straight pin aside. She changed and, after looking again at the pin, reconsidered. Kee Granny had told her never to doubt. She wove the pin into the collar of her blouse. Little Ena rested on the head of the pin, sheltered under Lily's right ear.

So that she forgot nothing, Lily acted out what would happen in her mind. When Anna's shallow breathing stopped, she would lift her mama off the bed and into the sanded pine box. She would shovel out a niche of soft soil and settle Anna in. The burial would be in the side road. Time and weather had worn the road down, leaving a bank on each side. Earthen walls would protect the grave from strong winds. She would tell Gabe when the weather broke, and together they would plant trillium in mass over the grave. By spring, the grave would be blanketed in carmine, blood-red and thick.

First, Lily had to get under the back of Boone Station. She could not use the rock steps. So busy with her mother, she had failed to scrape moss off near the end of the summer. Now that they were wet from recent rains, she slid, as if on ice. She avoided the winding steps and skidded down late fall leaves as she made her way.

Out of the weather and near the worn fence that held their chickens against foxes and coons waited the two identical boxes. One coffin for Anna. One coffin for Lily, crafted when she was eight-years-old.

Gabe knew a carpenter, the best in Covington. He felt it best not to mention that he was the granny's son. Anna ordered the coffins and sent money with Gabe month by month until she had a paper proving the boxes were her own. She paid an extra five-dollars for sanding and mitered joints to keep out the damp. Anna sent her height, thinking if she changed with age, she would do no more than shrink. The paper stayed in a hidden drawer that ran across the bottom of the bureau. Lily doubted anybody would question where Anna got the coffins, but she, like her mother, kept the paper hidden as safely as had it been a marriage certificate.

Lily knew where the boxes were and what they were for. No one lived a mountain life without meeting Death face to face more than once. Over the years, the wood had so hardened that nails could be hammered in only where the carpenter had pre-drilled holes. Anna had stored nails inside each box so Lily would not have to search.

As Lily skidded down the slope, a thought stunned her. With Anna gone, there would be no one to find her box or to tap in her nail. No one to seek out a shallow dip for her burying. For the first time, Lily questioned staying alone on Turtleback. She might want to talk this out with Gabe. Maybe Kee Granny. No. Kee Granny was not coming back. Maybe Ruth. But she had never met Ruth, and Anna had not mentioned her for years. Lily pictured Ruth, who was older than Anna, to be bent and shuffling. Gabe would be her answer.

Lily lugged the box back up the hill by a rope handle attached to the coffin's narrow end. She shifted it back and forth to maneuver through the door. She expected the noise to awaken Anna. Lily opened the door and icy air blew over Anna's bed, but she slept on.

With the coffin inside, Lily heated water for the cleansing. Once during the bath, Anna fluttered her eyes. She appeared to see Lily and mouthed words Lily never heard. Lily kissed her mama on the mouth and tucked the woolen quilt over her shoulders. Anna closed her eyes.

Lily looked again at the receipt of payment. The year had been 1954, when Lily turned ten. When Anna had first begun to bleed. In the lower right corner where the feet would rest were the initials S.W./B.S., perhaps the mark of the carpenter, acknowledging payment.

Anna slept three more days. She refused to awaken for food or water. The wolf wailed night after night. Lily replaced the crazy quilt that warmed Anna with a log cabin quilt, laid the woolen quilt in place in the coffin and patted it from time to time. She tried to keep the room warm by doling out logs she had gathered during the summer. She sat in the ancient rocking chair and waited. Outside, Turtleback waited in semi-darkness. The sun grew dark and the moon refused to shine.

Chapter 33

The day broke with the smell of snow on the air. Anna breathed deep and relaxed. A noise, more a scraping, aroused something within Anna. A gray, shriveled face appeared, almost like a ghost, outside Anna's window. From her bed, Anna watched it float closer toward the house. She tried to look to the window to identify who was there, but her head refused to move. Yet she still saw the face. It shimmered and came closer. Anna strained her eyes for a better look.

The face stopped when it reached the window. Anna knew the face was her own. But it was old, older than she thought she would ever be. Features she had failed to notice when she was well were obvious. What appeared to be wrinkles around her eyes spread out like scars, but their depth told her they had been sinking for years. Furrows between her brows were deeper still, as if she had set her countenance into a frown from her earliest memory.

The lines had not always been there. She had not been happy with Clint, but she had been conscious of hiding her feelings. She had been happy with Winston, both early on and after the War. She had followed the devil in her heart the first time she met him at the commissary, and she had fallen in love with his touch. Now facing herself through wavy glass, she wondered if God would open Heaven's gates to her. Hers was a God not easy to please.

Anna wondered if her God would forgive her. Hers was not just a sin of pride. She had committed adultery. She had known lust, lust that had fed her day after day. And, oh Lord, the death of the boy. She had plotted. She had shed innocent blood. She had committed murder.

The face hovered so close Anna could see indentations around the edges of her mouth. It was not a mouth that tempted anymore. She had once been vain about her mouth. It pouted enough to make a man look twice. It smiled a crooked smile that was straight enough to seem happy. Now it was an old woman's mouth, one that had spoken when unnecessary and had remained silent when words would have helped her Lily know which path to take.

She had no idea what determined Lily's choices. She could have ingrained her more with her own ideology and kept her away from the granny. But Anna had made her own decisions, and she had lived almost half her life with them. Her dread today was more for herself than for her daughter. Her recognition of such self-centeredness did not surprise Anna. She acknowledged that she had often put her own desires before those of her child. Not that Lily had had an empty life. Her life was filled with the granny Lily trusted so completely that Anna feared the repercussions of taking that away. Lily lived a life filled with the wilds of Turtleback and with joy that lifted her away from the negatives Anna faced.

The face hung outside the windowpane. Though Anna could not look at it directly, she could see it as clearly as if it hung before her on an invisible thread. A green leaf, one that defied the winteriness of December, lingered over the face for a moment and dropped toward the ground, out of sight. With the disappearance of the leaf, Anna grasped the significance of seeing herself and blinked to push the burn away from her eyes. Anna cringed.

"What's wrong, Mama?" asked Lily.

"I'm going," the face said.

"I know," Anna answered. "Are you my sorrow? Aged by my sins?"

"Come with me," the face mouthed.

"Where you going?" Anna asked.

"I'm not sure," it said. *"Can you tell me?"*

"No."

"Rise and come." The plea in the voice tugged at Anna's indecision. *"You have to go, you know."*

"But I expected something else. A light. An angel...with wings. Maybe..."

"You have me."

"Go without me. When you come back, tell me where you've been. I'll decide then." Anna said. "I don't like brown. Will it be brown? I've been buried in this brown house all these years."

"I don't know. I haven't been there yet."

"Come back and tell me what you find," Anna insisted. "Tell me if he smells like Wildroot Hair Creme."

The face did not move.

"I never forgave them, you know, either one, for leaving me alone," Anna said.

"You've not forgiven yourself. You must forgive yourself before you can forgive them."

"I don't know," Anna said. "All this thinking wrinkles my mind. No. I can't. Oh God, I'm not worthy." Anna felt tears pool in her eyes. *Where was the granny when she needed her? Where was her Lily?*

"I know you better than you know yourself. Scars within feed your guilt. You are woman. Women have within them so much love and so much hatred they confuse the two," said the face. *"Come. I can carry your forgiveness forward."*

"Not yet. Come back and tell me if there is pain. I can't stand pain."

"I know." Anger crinkled the face into a grave frown. *"You cut your path over time and sowed the seeds of pain."* The face drifted away toward the darkness. Its voice echoed back to Anna's bed at Boone Station. *"It's time to go,"* it said.

"No. Wait." Anna blinked. "You must carry my sins."

Anna's ancient face vanished.

"Come back," Anna said. "If I'm to go, someone must tell the bees." A tremor shot through Anna's body, and she grunted. Her heart stopped. Her eyes, staring at the unpainted plank ceiling, flickered, then fixed themselves in place.

"Mama?" Lily whispered.

> *Sister Sun means to tell Great Spirit about what she has seen. And about the face. But clouds heavy with snow push her light aside. She later decides there is no reason to bother Great Spirit. Anna had not known him at all.*
>
> *Great Spirit releases the snow's power. It falls in great flakes and covers Kee Granny's cedar high on the Turtleback's ridge within minutes. The sacred cedar stands alone, a shimmering sculpture that might have been carved from marble.*

Death stepped up on the porch the seventh day of the howling. He did not knock but entered with Anna's grunt. Lily was finishing her morning tasks. She whispered her mother's name and moved to her bed. Anna's face and neck were deep sky blue, as if a high summer light had settled there.

As soon as Death left with Anna's spirit in tow, Lily steadied the mantel clock's pendulum at 11:03 and draped the clock face with an old rag Anna once used for cleaning. She cracked a window only for an instant, then shut it, allowing any part of Anna's spirit that might not have escaped to have a way out. She shuttered the windows and locked the door. Lily lit a kerosene lamp against the dimmed light and spent the remaining daylight hours crooning one of Kee Granny's low chants to keep evil spirits out, spirits that had power to steal her mama's soul had it all failed to leave the room. An unexpected yearning to have Kee Granny near to help her face this death overwhelmed her. She chastised herself for such a thought and fell to her knees keening a knife-sharp yowl. The slashing realization that her mama was gone sucked the air out of Lily's lungs.

Dazed, she let the fire burn low. In time, she placed another log on the embers and moved to the bed to lower her mama into the coffin. Though Anna was thin and bony after her long wasting summer, her weight seemed to double when Lily tried to lift her into the coffin. After a time of failure after failure, Lily climbed onto the opposite side of the bed and nudged, then pushed her mother, rolling her off the bed into the coffin.

Anna landed with a thud.

Lily rushed around the foot of the bed. "Mama, are you hurt?"

Anna lay face down in the coffin.

For the first time her features distorted, and Lily cried silent tears.

Lily could not turn her mama over. If she tugged at her feet, Anna's chest grew heavy. If Lily tried to roll Anna using her chest, she could not find enough room to put her arms around her to flip her over. After several attempts, Lily left her lay and folded the edges of the worn quilt over her back, under her head and feet.

Lily took a small hammer from the bureau and tapped in the nails. Exhausted, she crawled to the fire. At nightfall, Lily slept. What sounded like Owl woke her after midnight. Lily moved to the bed and nestled herself in the indentation her mama had burrowed into the mattress.

Snow came again in the early morning hours, thick, deep clean snow that covered the road in front of Boone Station. Before midday, snow broke tree branches. With the air's icy breath, frozen sap caused trees to explode, sounding like rifle shots through the mountains.

The second day, Lily remembered the fruit jar. She added the date, pried up two nails near the head of the coffin and poked the jar inside, not looking to see if it hit her mama's head or not. She crept back to the bed. Outside, wind battled naked tree limbs and cold blue sunlight, as they threw patterns across the ceiling.

The wind lessened. Silent snow and a realization of finality threw Lily into hard sleep. During the third day, the stench of Anna's body moldering from heat inside the room forced Lily out of her mother's place in the bed. She opened the door and dragged the coffin to the porch. Sweat from her exertion chilled her body, and she shook. Huffing in icy air, she lodged the loaded coffin between two tree trunks that supported the roof. There she left it, centered under the wobbly sign that marked the house as Boone Station. If the snow stayed and if more snow fell, the body would freeze and Lily could bury her mama when spring thaw came. Gabe could help her.

It was mid-December, 1961. The road had vanished under a heavy layer of snow. Lily was alone on Boone Station.

くくくくくくくく

Early January, Month of the Cold Moon and Old Christmas, just before dawn. Three weeks it had snowed. Snow sifted down the rock chimney and spit on the logs. Only orange embers remained to warm the room. An interruption in the snow's silence awakened Lily. Music. The music was back. Hauntingly beautiful, as beautiful as any Lily had heard before. It was a dream. Not Laurel People. Not even Dogwood People. There had never been any Little People. Kee Granny had lied about Little People. "Men and women no taller than my knee," she had said. "They play their drums, sing and dance in circles deep within the woods." Their drumbeats had fallen as icicles from her roof at night, and now one sang, just for her, to bring joy into her life. "One of the Laurel People waiting for a break in the cold so they could force the spring buds," Granny would have said.

Three weeks of temperatures below freezing kept Anna's body frozen. Days, Lily trudged through knee-deep snow left by the blizzard to feed her goats and chickens. She hung rabbits out for Owl. Nights, strange music, ancient mountain ballads sung in a lonesome tenor voice Lily waited for at dusk, now sung louder. The sun cast indigo shadows on snow. The cushion of snow amplified the voice's journey. It reverberated night after night, some nights so close Lily could recognize the lyrics. It was as if some spirit from the past had settled on Turtleback and waited to draw Lily back into the forest with the coming of spring. The music soothed her nights and calmed her days. Lily called the voice her dream music.

219

Chapter 34

The knock on the door startled Lily. No one had passed since before Anna died. Roads had been too bad, the snow too deep. She edged toward the door. "What'd you want?" she said.

A second knock pushed Lily back. She held her breath, waiting for an answer. "I'm not opening the door till I know who you are," she said, trying to steady the tremor in her voice.

A man's deep voice answered, "Briar Slocomb."

Lily whirled around, looking for a possible weapon. She had seen Briar Slocomb passing day after day over the years, but he had never stopped or even lifted a hand in greeting.

"Be still." Her pin's angel spoke in her ear. *"He's done nothing to make you afraid."* Ena's voice surprised her. It was when Ena spoke that she recalled weaving the pin into her collar each morning as she dressed.

She took a butcher knife from the table. *"Don't be childish,"* Ena said. *"Put the knife back. Don't let him in. Don't let him know your mama's dead."* Lily began to put the knife away, but instead she dropped it into her pocket.

⸜⸜⸜⸜⸜⸜

Tall Corn had come to Briar in a dream. He walked out of lush mountain shrubs, dressed as he had been on his deathbed. He carried the hatchet Briar wore on his belt.

"I hacked my way through trees and budding rhododendron to find you," Tall Corn said.

"I've been right here." Briar gawked at Tall Corn. He was scratched and bleeding from his journey. "It's winter. There are no buds."

"It's a long, long journey," Tall Corn said.

"How did you take my hatchet?"

"What is mine is yours. What is yours is mine," Tall Corn said. "We all are akin."

Briar looked at his mother who sipped her coffee, her arm propped on the table. She didn't respond.

"It is time for you to gather your harvest," he said.

"I told you that I don't have a harvest."

"You do." Tall Corn smiled. "It fell from the tree. It weathers on the ground. It lies under moldering leaves."

"Why do you give me a puzzle?"

"You must stand for something. Make yourself known as a man." Tall Corn rubbed the nape of his neck. "I have slashed through undergrowth to say to you that you must choose between the white man who sired you and the Cherokee who raised you."

"What do you mean, white man?" Briar felt his brow furrow.

"Your beloved mother can tell you." The shadow of Tall Corn walked like a phantom through the brush. A limb from Old Oak popped and fell to the ground. Though Old Oak was at the top of the rise, Briar heard the break. In the distance, Tall Corn leapt upon a muscular black bear. The two glowed with stardust as they soared across an ebony sky.

At dawn when Briar awoke, he opened the door to his mother's church without knocking and sat down at her table.

⋘⋘⋘

That afternoon, Briar arrived at Boone Station. Speaking through the closed door, he said, "You got something of mine."

"No, I don't," Lily argued.

"*You do,*" said Ena. He fluffed his robes from around his feet and sat down on the pin's head.

"What?" Lily whispered. Lily had imagined Briar a dirty man, but he was Kee Granny's son. Kee Granny had not been dirty. He would be one whose breath puffed his long hair out of his face. But that was nonsense. He kept his hair tied at the nape of his neck with a string.

"You do," said Slocomb.

Lily visualized him standing tall, pushing his chest out, he sounded so firm. "No, I don't."

"Listen to him," said Ena.

"My animals. I give you a chance to return them. If you don't give them to me, I'm taking them. I made them and they belong to me." Briar pounded on the door again. "Open the door."

"No. I found the animals. They're mine." Lily rubbed her eyes. So tired. She wondered when she had last slept. "I'm not opening the door. Go away."

"You can't get rid of me as easy as you did my mama." Snow crunched under his feet as he stomped off the porch. "You'll rue the day you made me come back," he called.

"You must give them back," said Ena. *"You cannot take from a man unless he gifts it to you."*

Lily dropped on the bed. She had been light-headed since Briar's first knock. A shiver ran down her back. She rose and pushed the bureau in front of the door so it could not be forced open if anyone broke the lock.

That night she slept with the light on. Powell Valley Electric had strung lines over Turtleback at least ten years ago in the early 1950s, when the state started grading and tending the dirt road that ran from Covington to Breakline Camp. Tonight she was glad. She dozed and awoke with each sound. When the sun topped the mountain ridge, she peeped out the window facing the porch. The animal carvings were still hanging over her mother's coffin.

Sister Sun turns bright white. She has not seen an argument before where both are right. She slips behind a long, wispy cloud to think this thing through.

Before noon, Briar Slocomb again stood at Lily's door. Lily saw him through the window. He stood, his legs splayed out. The questions on his brow made him look uncomfortable, as if he had lost power over his tongue. Lily slid back the chest and cracked the door. "Did you carve them?" she asked.

He nodded.

"Your mother told me the Little People made them." She braced her foot against the door and folded her arms across her breast, daring him to contradict her. "They are wonderful."

Briar's flushed face and jutting chin told Lily that he had the same anger she had known against his mother. She had felt it grow within her from when she first realized Kee Granny had manipulated her into killing the trees surrounding the holy cedar. Briar's anger was so tangible she looked away. When she looked back at Briar, he looked as if he had swallowed ground glass, his pain was so deep.

"My father...." He stammered and started again. "Tall Corn, the man I thought was my father, is gone. And at my hand."

"What do...?" Lily began.

"Now you have my animals. Animals like those Tall Corn carved on his gunstock," Briar said. "They are all I have of the man I called father."

"I didn't know," Lily said.

"You can only have what is given you, not what you take," said Ena.

"You're right to take the animals," Lily said. "I'll miss them." She closed and relocked the door. Sometime that day Briar Slocomb took the animals, leaving nothing behind but tracks in deep snow.

Chapter 35

The burying had been those few days in February when false spring appears and then vanishes, killing all leaf and bloom it had duped into coming out. Lily buried her mother in the middle of the road. A stretch, more track than logging road, abandoned when the mine on the face of the mountain played out, created the only strip of land suitable for burying without climbing to Flatland. She had decided early on that she would bury her mother there. Her daddy had never been a part of their lives, so no need to take her to Breakline to bury her next to Clint Goodman. She had no idea about her Covington folk.

The ground, brown from last season's leaves and musk, lay soft from rains that had beaten trees naked after the blizzard and melted ice. They survived as no more than stark grey shadows, barren of winter ice and its weight for one more season.

Morning of the first February break in the weather, Lily walked the road to Breakline Camp, the road soggy by melted snow. At the top of Turtleback where the road dipped into Breakline, she saw in the distance the open hole of the mine's black mouth. She wondered about life in tunnels that had at one time been little more than burrows. Tunnels that bent men double under their low ceilings. She wondered if her father had walked with his face to the ground like so many others. Dark miners moved about the camp like impatient insects, as they manipulated massive yellow machines that would soon eat away at what had once been an underground mine.

At the commissary, she found Gabe and Seth White. She brought them back, offering to pay twenty-seven dollars, all she had left from her father's pension, if they would put the body easy in the grave.

Lily took her long-handled shovel and helped dig the grave, while her mother lay on the front porch threatening to thaw. Because her mother had been a slight woman at her death, they dug the grave shallow.

Gabe and Seth lifted the coffin, each supporting an end, and set it down feet first, before positioning it straight in the trench.

"Ought this hole to be a mite deeper?" Seth asked.

"It's deep enough to keep varmints away," Lily answered and turned her back to them.

"These ruts that old mining road?" Seth asked. "Seems the old mine used to run right nigh here."

"No matter," Lily said. "I won't have my mama buried on a slope. I want her steady in the ground. Not where she's standing on her feet through eternity. Here's where she'll lie." Lily stood with her legs slightly apart, in lopsided comfort, with one foot in a rut, one slanted on the loose dirt. Turtleback Mountain stood behind her. The town of Covington below to the south and east; Breakline Mining Camp, north and to the west, she stood in the center of all that had been her life.

"Reckon this'll do then," Seth replied, and he shoveled dirt and rock in on the coffin. The sound muffled itself against the wood like rain on shingles too long on the roof.

"Wait." Lily set out for the porch. "Stop your shoveling," she called back. From the edge of the porch, she picked up a pint fruit jar, its ring at a cocked angle, its lid flat against the glass mouth. Inside dead fireflies stuck to the bottom, stiff, their once vibrant ends the color of dried wood. Lily placed the jar of insects in the grave, next to the coffin's head, and stepped back.

"Now. Do what you're here to do." Lily walked back toward the house in step with the thuds of dirt as each hit against the coffin. "Don't you break that jar, Gabe Shipley." She spoke without turning.

From her mother's old chair on the porch, Lily stared past the scene in the side road, leading up the Turtleback. Beyond, a band of blue opened from between skeletal white clouds. Lily sat on the porch and wailed a chant-like dirge neither of the men had ever heard. She took three or four notes from one of Kee Granny's old minor scales and worked them back and forth, weaving a lament that reverberated off the mountain wall, a nagging melody that rivaled a whippoorwill's sorrow:

Bring me a fruit jar and fill it with light
of fireflies and wonder to stave off the night.
No spirits born evil dare enter the door—
bring morning—not darkness—
for fireflies no more
gleam bright in the moonlight—not fireflies—
but wonder will outlive the night.

Gabe and Seth never looked up. When Lily's funeral song ended, they patted the filled grave with the backs of the shovels and stood the tools against a sycamore trunk.

Lily thought the uniqueness of her mother's service unimportant. The burial would not be worth the telling in Breakline. The men would not be remembering words. They probably thought burying the fireflies was something else again. They had not seen lightning bugs since cool weather had set in. The power of fireflies to ward off sinister spirits lay in their glow against a black night. Dead bugs don't shine. But all that had not mattered when Lily had gathered the insects.

Two weeks of heavy rain and ditches filled to the brim with gushing water brought an imposingly deep and full rumble from the earth. The sound signaled a transformation Lily had not expected. Gabe would later tell her that the mouth of the abandoned mine between Boone Station and Covington had collapsed.

Chapter 36

It was March, Kee Granny's Month of the Windy Moon, when Lily opened the door to let in fresh air. She looked down and slammed it shut. On the doorsill lay a copperhead as long as the door was wide. She pressed her back against the slatted door as if her body's weight could keep the snake at bay. Her heart beat faster than the day she discovered Rattler, for that day she had eased up on his bed. He had not been right where she planned to put her naked foot. That day she had been a child. And Rattler had been Rattler.

As her breathing settled and her heart rate slowed, she chastised herself. Perhaps it was only an oak branch. In the leaves in a close face-to-face encounter, its markings camouflaged the snake so precisely that it took on the appearance of a limb.

To be safe, she slipped on shoes and picked up the fireplace poker and coal shovel. With the poker, she could lift him up and sling him into the road. He would leave on his own, for copperheads were not aggressive. If he coiled, she could chop him into pieces and feed him to the chickens or leave him for Owl.

"Open the door," said Ena.

She eased the door open again. The snake had not moved. She nudged him with the tip of her poker and nudged again. He did not bend. He was dead. "Dead as a poker, Mama would have said." Lily laughed in relief.

Lily stepped out on the porch and, using the poker, picked up the copperhead. It was perfect. In all its brown and grey glory, its symmetrical patches of tans and chestnut hourglasses marked its length, its head a tawny solid. There was no sign of battle.

Looking closer, Lily found the deathblow. One tiny fang puncture through top of the snake's triangular head. The snake had not suffered. His death had been swift and sure. His beauty earned him a decent burial.

Using her coal shovel, she dug a narrow trench for the snake's burial. If a dead snake isn't buried, the mate will come to claim vengeance for the death. As she patted the earth back in place, movement across the road caught her eye. There sat a cat. A large calico Lily had never seen in these parts. A housecat would not survive on Turtleback with its rock ledges to shelter the likes of Rattler, its caves to harbor spotted bobcats, ancient hardwoods that nested night-flyers the size of Owl. And then there was Briar Slocomb's dog in Flatland. But Briar Slocomb's dog was different, almost an extension of his owner.

A car, a truck must have dropped off the calico. With Anna gone, the calico would make for company. Lily called "Here, kitty, kitty."

The calico ignored her. Or maybe the cat was deaf and that was why somebody had dumped her. Lily started across the road bent close to the ground and murmured softly to entice it to stay until she could catch her. As soon as Lily reached the middle of the road, the cat disappeared in underbrush.

With time, the calico brought squirrels, chipmunks, mice, more snakes. Each equally perfect. Each looked as if it could have risen from the dead and skittered away. The calico waited for Lily to accept her gift, bury it and try to coax the cat across the road. Each time the cat vanished into the woods.

Each new day, Lily watched for the calico. This day, she sat in her mother's pea-shelling chair and hummed an old ballad she had dreamed in the night. Out of the underbrush walked the calico. The cat crossed the road and rubbed her body against Lily's leg.

"Did I call you, little girl? What's your name?" The cat straightened her tail upright. "If I listen, will you tell me your name?" The calico purred and wound her tail around Lily's leg. "I'm listening." The cat looked up at Lily then across the road as if she thought of leaving.

"It's Sunday," Ena whispered, his green gown swaying.

"Of course," Lily said. "It's Sunday," Lily said aloud. "Welcome to Boone Station, Sunday."

That night Sunday moved into Lily's place in the front room bed.

On St. Patrick's Day, Lily spent the morning hoeing weeds from potato rows while Sunday slept in the sun near the woods. Heat from the midday sun and lack of water were making Lily's head swim. She had been thinking about going to the house for a bite to eat when she felt something behind her.

A scrawny boy, or perhaps a man, appeared at the edge of the clearing, so thin and leggy, he could have been mistaken for a dirty wood sprite. Backed by lush mountain shrubs, he stared through ringlets of white hair at Lily while she stared back at him. Then he walked to Sunday where she lay in the grass and kicked at her underbelly. Both Sunday and Lily jumped and ran, Sunday for the woods, Lily for the boy.

"Don't you kick my cat!" she yelled, throwing the hoe.

He did not answer. He turned into the woods, ducking through the brush, and, without looking back, called, "Gotta get the cat."

Lily stopped at the edge of the clearing and called for Sunday. The only sound she heard was the popping of fallen limbs as the boy crashed through the undergrowth. Comfortable with the knowledge that Sunday would survive, she picked up the hoe and took the path to the house. Before nightfall, Sunday was back. Lily pushed the bureau against the locked door and slept with the light on.

The next morning Lily opened the door to find a half-man, so puny he was going on dead. He stood off the edge of the porch. He wore an oversized shirt and a hat that resembled one she had seen Briar Slocomb wear.

"Gotta get the cat," he said quietly. So clawed up by briars and thick brush, he wore black-blooded strips down his face and arms.

Memory spoke up from somewhere near the back of her brain. Maybe the hair. "Do I know you?"

"Gotta get the cat," he said.

"Eli O'Mary. What happened to you?"

"Gotta get the cat," he repeated.

"No you don't," Lily replied. "This is my cat and you leave her alone."

"Gotta get the cat," he said again, stepping on the porch and pushing past Lily into the room.

Having grown so naturally placid, Lily wasn't rattled, but she refused to let Eli have Sunday. Lily grabbed his shirt to toss him back into the road. Though thin, he was tall and lean, and he out-strengthened her. Tugging his shirt out of her hand, he went straight to the bed and lifted Sunday, much as he would have an infant. He cradled her in his arms. His movements were so swift that Lily had barely moved into the room before he swept past her and across the road to the woods.

"Sunday!" She called. "Sunday!" She chased the two into the woods. Thrashing through ferns and deeper into briars, she called, overwhelmed with an innate sense that this man meant to harm her cat. Scratched and bleeding, Lily wandered out of the underbrush. She had found no trace of Eli or of Sunday.

Memories make a family. Lily carried memories of her mama and Kee Granny. She had had Sunday for such a short time, but Sunday had proven her commitment. Lily saw her as family. Sunday was gone. Lily grieved. She wept, harder than she had for her mama, for she feared Eli would cause Sunday to die a fearful death somewhere along the road to Covington or throw her down an open mine shaft. By midnight, Lily awoke with Sunday scratching at the door.

The next afternoon, after working the lower pea patch, Lily opened the door to find her bed covered in wild flowers, lavender to deep purple. Gabe must have spent the entire morning gathering dwarf iris. Her first thought when she recognized the flowers were irises was *rainbow, promises.* Promises? Hope? She called out to Gabe and looked around to see if he were watching her reaction. He was not there. Neither was he in the sleeping loft. He had come, decorated her bed and left while she worked the pea patch.

This was not something she had expected. She had known Gabe all her life. What was he saying? He, at forty-two, was old enough to be her father. She loved him like a father.

While caring for Anna, Lily became a creature of habit: before sunrise, milk the goat; stoke the fire until her body sweated; then shake her mother until Lily could hear the shallow defeated breaths across the room; try to get her mother to eat. But that time was gone.

She could not remember her mama as a wife. Nor Kee Granny. The only wife she knew was Juanita White over in Breakline. Juanita spent her days cooking, washing, cleaning, then cooking and cleaning again. Juanita had no idea a fawn, still spotted by its camouflage, could be fed calf manna and thrive. That it would follow like a puppy waiting to play. She did not know to ignore a coon when cornered or the coon would attack, as fierce as a small bear, and hang on till dark. That hanging a dead snake belly-up over the fence would bring rain. Juanita did not want to know such things. Shelling, canning, and washing fit her just fine. Such days did not fit Lily. She and Gabe would have to have a face-to-face talk when he returned.

That afternoon the sound of wood breaking, followed by a moan then laughter, startled Lily. Beneath Boone Station, Lily gathered her eggs. She dropped her egg basket. Every egg cracked. Whites ran through the basket's open weaving. Shells cut into yolks.

"It's beginning," says Brother Moon.

She crept from behind the house. She could not see the front porch. She saw no car. She hesitated to climb the hill unarmed. The long-handled shovel stood against Bad Billy's fence. She looked for the axe handle, but it must have been next to the woodpile. She picked up the shovel, holding it at the ready like a rifle and eased up the rock steps leading to the front of the house.

Before she rounded the corner, she dropped into a crawl. Whoever was there could not hear her; a man was laughing so hard he coughed. She stepped up on the porch and stood, propped on her shovel.

There, on the far end of the porch, lay Gabe, his feet stuck through the seat of Anna's pea-shelling chair. Gabe looked as if he had been attacked by the chair and lost the battle. His fall had jammed the chair against the wall. Both his legs had broken through the rotten seat and pinned him down. The new wooden swing he had been hanging hung too high on one end. Its other end rested hard and heavy across his chest.

In an attempt to escape, he was now grunting, trying to lift the swing off his chest with one hand and push the chair frame off his legs with the other. Neither would budge. When he heard Lily's step on the porch, he twisted his head back and looked at her coming his way.

"Lily, my darling, how is it you can walk upside down and I can't even stand upright?" He laughed again, as if this contorted position had been part of his plan.

"Gabe Shipley, what are you doing?" Lily rested both hands on her hips, Anna's stance when Lily as a child had misbehaved. *I'm becoming my own mother*, she thought.

"I've come to court my fair lady while setting in this fine swing," he said. "Swing's setting on me instead, I reckon." He chuckled. "Help me up from here before you get the idea I'm an old man. Too old for a pretty girl like yourself."

Lily tried to pull the chair off Gabe's legs, all the while holding back her own giggles. The chair would not move. "Why'd you have to have such big old feet anyway?"

"Just lucky, I guess. They held me up fairly well before now."

Lily moved around to lift the swing off his chest. After a try or two, she said, "I can't lift this thing by myself. I reckon you're just stuck here," and she walked toward the door. "Let me know when you're hungry. Can't fry you eggs since all your clamoring about made me drop the whole basket. But I might bring a biscuit out later."

"Now, my Lily my love, you're not going to leave me pinned here like a stuck hog, are you? Not when I worked so hard to surprise you with a first-rate new swing."

"What you suggest I do? Pry that swing off you?"

"Sure. Get a pole and prop this end up. I'll roll out. Then we can work on getting my legs free."

"Oh, I don't know, Gabe," she teased. "Ought to leave you stuck. You shouldn't've scared me so."

"You know I wouldn't do that a purpose. I'm just working at making you happy." Gabe tried to move his legs, only to run the seat up past his knees. "I aim to have a happy wife," he grunted.

"I don't need a new swing for that. I'm happy like I am," Lily said. "Besides I don't intend to be no man's wife."

"Well, I'm damned well not happy. I'm getting cramps. 'Sides, I hit my head," Gabe whined.

Lily stuck the shovel handle between two of the swing's boards for leverage and grasped the swing. "Get ready to roll over. I can't hold this thing up long."

"Let's go, girl." Gabe rolled from under the swing, his feet still held by the chair's missing seat. The chair clumped over twice as Gabe rolled. He sat for a moment, rubbing his chest where the swing had hit. He looked at his feet, still boxed in Anna's pea-shelling chair. He laughed at himself and said, "I'll fix this for my bride."

"That's my mama's chair, so you're not fixing it for nobody else, because I'm not your bride, Gabe Shipley."

He released his feet, stood and kissed Lily's lips. "Yep. But you will be before summer ends. Bet my last dollar on it, Lily my love."

Chapter 37

Dark settled in fast. He moved silent as a fox and sat in the swing next to Lily before she realized he was there. He wore a shirt three times too large, flannel. Its sleeves hung almost to his knees though he was tall, tall as a young tree.

Lily recognized him immediately. "Eli?" she said.

He wiped his mouth on one sleeve and his nose on the other, then slid over and kissed Lily's hair above her ear.

The kiss did not startle Lily. She had not expected it, but it had not surprised her either.

He hummed then sang quietly, "*I have a bed, a very fine bed...*"

Lily interrupted him. "I know that ballad. It's old as the hills."

"*Turtleback Mountain, Turtleback Mountain,*" he sang. "*Old as the hills. Old as the hills.*" He crooned the same notes over and over.

Lily searched his face for something about his singing. He hummed another old English ballad, and she knew. Yes, his was her dream voice, the one she had first mistaken for the voice of Little People.

He leaned back against the slat back and stared into the woods as if he expected someone to step out and grab him. His head sat askew, not quite straight on his neck from the incident at the tavern. Looking at him head-on, Lily recalled the night she had seen him through the window, hanging in his underwear. Her muscles tensed against the swing seat. In an attempt to relax, Lily pushed off the swing. Eli sat silent beside her, allowing her to determine the speed of each sway.

After a long thinking time, Lily sighed. "So. You bring the music."

Owl flew in and lit on a rafter. He settled his feathers and eyed the two.

"Owl," said Eli. He pointed. "Owl and pussy cat went to sea in a beautiful pea green boat."

Lily rested her arm across the back of the swing, brushing against Eli's back as she moved.

"You're too thin, Eli O'Mary."

"*Saving us out of the fiery place,*" sang Eli.

> *Sister Sun, near the cusp of the horizon, calls to Brother Moon. "Is he talking about me? Is he saying I'm fiery?"*
>
> *"No. He's just singing some old song. No need to make him sweat."*

"No, I can't save nobody, Eli. Thought I could, but I can't." She pushed off again, then stopped the movement. "Come inside. I'll feed you supper."

Eli slept the night in front of the stone hearth wrapped in one of Anna's old quilts. "Not a very fine bed," Lily said as she tucked the corners around his bare feet.

"*I have a bed, a very fine bed,*" Eli sang, and he wiped his nose on his shirtsleeve.

For days and evenings, quiet would sit easy between them for hours. Eli was home.

↞↞↞↞↞↞

Gabe's first reaction to Eli at Boone Station angered Lily. She had not expected him to be so adamant against Eli staying with her. The argument marked a pivotal point between the two. Lily saw it as their first fight. She saw Gabe as jealous and selfish. Gabe saw Lily as naïve and careless. He called her "soft-bellied," allowing a man her own age, a man who could barely communicate, to stay days and nights with her.

Eli, hearing his name repeated from both mouths neither of which said it with tenderness, inched behind the open door, waiting for the voices to soften. When they did not, he cradled Sunday. He and Sunday slipped out the door and into the woods, back to spending his days lying on one of Old Oak's thick limbs where the road to Flatland intersected the road to Breakline, watching people live out their lives below. The old mountain woman and her comings and goings made for much better days than lying in the old damp shed.

Gabe left, uneasy, more jumbled than he had ever been, more so than when he had confronted the granny over the spilled honey. He could not convince the old granny that what he did was business. She came in wearing that crazy snake hat and knocking all the jars on the floor. He had to take out his two-by-four to protect himself. He wouldn't see another honey harvest? Ha. It took two days to get all the honey off the floor.

The next morning after Eli disappeared, Lily found Sunday asleep in the swing. She brought her in and fed her a saucer of Gertie's milk. That night, Lily stepped out under a sky so full of stars it looked as if dandelion fluff had blown about in the wind from her side of the mountain to light up the dark. Sunday joined Lily, wound around her legs and ambled down the road toward Covington. Lily followed. Around the curve and down the grade, Sunday slipped off the road and into the brush.

> *"You always show out when you're in full phase," says Sister Sun.*
> *"Just helping the little lady along," says Brother Moon.*
> *"Don't you tell me not to do that?"*
> *"This is different," argues Brother Moon.*

After some walking distance, Lily heard the Falls tumbling into Parsons Branch as water hit flat rock.

Sunday made no attempt to throw Lily off her trail. Just past the Falls, Lily realized Sunday was headed for Old Man Farley's crib. The wind picked up as she neared the Falls, no random wind, but a wind that threw Lily's hair over her face as it pushed her from behind. Once on the trail itself, she stepped faster, trying to catch Sunday and bring her back to Boone Station.

As she entered the small cove where the crib stood, clouds split, exposing a full hoary moon. Before her, large pieces of plywood were propped at an angle from the ground to the tops of the two windows. A worn green blanket had been stretched across the top of the door and pulled back to create an entry. Someone lived in the old structure.

This was the place where the rustle of leaves was music, where magic passed through the wind from generation to generation. It had been her place of solace since Bad Billy led her here nine years ago. But it was not a place to live. Not certain that she should walk up without warning, she hallowed the house. Her call to someone who might be within, echoed down Turtleback. No one answered. It would not be until the spirit mist came upon her there that she would understand that a shanty could be sacred. Sunday stepped across the log that held up the front walls and disappeared inside.

Lily called again. When no one returned her call, she followed Sunday inside. In the middle of the floor, ash from a small fire had been scattered so as not to re-flame. In the far corner, a dirty pillow lay against the wall, a pillow she recognized as the one Anna had used, one she threw away after her mama died because she could not bear the smell of her mother's hair.

Behind her, a voice said, "Little Bo Peep has lost her sheep..."

Lily caught her breath and whirled around. "You scared me to death, Eli."

"And can't tell where to find them," he finished.

"I see you're not lost. What're you doing here? I thought you'd gone back to Covington."

He swayed as he began an old mountain ballad. *"You remember that Saturday night we gathered at the tavern..."*

"Don't bring that up, Eli. It's too bad to remember."

He began another ballad as he danced around her. *"Awake, awake my drowsy sleeper..."*

"Stop that and talk to me," Lily said. "Answer my question. How long have you been living here?"

"A case of whiskey I spilled," he answered, his forehead furrowed. "Gotta get the cat."

"Sunday's right here. She's not going anywhere. And you can't live up here by yourself." Lily took Eli's hand. "Come on. I'll take you home. Gabe can like it or not."

The next day three shots were fired, one after the other, down the mountain. Then thunder followed by a gully washer, rain chasing itself and making puddles that would later glisten in the sunshine.

That afternoon late, Gabe clanked up on the porch. His noise made a mockingbird that had been puttering about in the yard dust fly off without taking a step. Owl chittered into the dusk. Gabe threw open the door. "Lily," he said.

Her back to the door, Lily stood in the middle of the room, scissors mid-air. Before her sat a straggly man with half his long curls lying in his lap and on the floor. "Gabe," Lily smiled.

Gabe's grin went slack as he stared at Eli. Same as yesterday.

"It's Eli, Gabe," Lily said. "Eli O'Mary from elementary school in Covington."

Gabe cocked his head. "More rain's coming," he said, his voice somber.

"Oh?" said Lily. "Get up, Eli. We got company." She swung the chair to face Gabe and patted its back for Eli to sit. She lifted another wad of hair and chopped it off. The clump slipped to the floor and lay like a fuzzy white worm at Lily's foot

"Halo 'round the moon last night," Gabe said. "Rain in a couple of days." He shifted his weight from one foot to another.

"Sit down. I'll be finished in a minute."

"Standing's fine."

"I didn't notice," Lily said.

"What?"

"The moon. Last night." Lily ran her fingers through Eli's hair and lifted another section. "Eli's staying here. I found him out. He's been living at Old Man Farley's."

"Needs to go back where he come from, I'd say." Gabe sat on the bench beside the table. He leaned back against the table as if to stay a spell.

"Well, he can't," Lily said. "He must have most froze during the blizzard, so he's staying here in my loft."

His brow furrowed, Gabe looked directly at Eli. Lily noticed the frown and said, "Leave your sense of humor at home?"

"How'd you manage moving in on a pretty young woman like Lily here?" Gabe spoke to Eli.

"He don't talk, Gabe." Lily hacked at another wad of hair. "But he sings. Ballads, right Eli?"

Gabe grunted. Eli nodded.

"Now, Gabe not to find fault. You got a gentle goodness about you. Always have. But you're not talking like the Gabe Shipley I know."

Eli lowered his head. "Hold up now, Eli." Lily snipped again. "You know what it's like having nobody. I'm learning that, and it ain't so good a lesson."

"You got me," said Gabe.

"And you got me. Eli's got nobody. So I say let's let him have us." Lily sneezed at a wayward hair that tickled her nose.

"Let me think on it. I ain't feeling the fool over this someday down the road." Gabe laid one leg across his knee. "I come when you said something about shooting. I come to take you to Breakline."

"I'm taking the blame if this is wrong, Gabe." Lily moved to the other side of Eli's head. "But I'm staying. Boone Station's my home and Turtleback's my mountain. I got electricity. I got a telephone." She snipped over Eli's left ear. "Hold still, Eli. But I ain't thinking this is wrong."

Gabe put his arm down. "Been listening to the wind again?"

"Maybe." Lily laughed and cut another wad of Eli's hair. "Get the broom from behind the door and sweep up this hair. If you're willing, you can wash Eli's hair."

Gabe crinkled his nose. "Let him wash his own hair. He ain't no baby."

"Just you get him started so he can see how. He'll do the rest." Lily took the kettle from the stove and poured hot water into an enamel pan. She set them on the table. "I'll leave you two to the chore." She went outside and closed the door.

Outside, Lily sat beneath the window and listened to Gabe grumble.

"Hold your head steady while I pour this here water," he said. "First she comes in with that owl, then a stray cat. Treats those old goats like yard dogs. And now she drags up this varmint. What's next?"

Lily listened to water splashing over Eli's head.

"Reckon she's worth it," Gabe said. "Got the purest heart I ever met."

Lily relaxed. Gabe would be fine.

Day after day shots drew closer. Lily and Eli stayed inside, keeping Sunday near for her safety. Late afternoons, Lily tucked Clint's revolver in her jacket and slipped outside to feed her goats and chickens.

A week passed with no shots. Nights, Lily lay awake and pondered who would be bold enough to climb the Turtleback during the day and shoot. All Covington and Breakline Camp knew Turtleback had no hunting. Early Cherokee settlers had kept the Turtleback and its valley sacred. So had Uriah, then Anna, as did she. No one could hunt without permission from the Cherokee. With the Cherokee resettled, no one thought of hunting. Change might have wandered into their world, but legend revered Lily's land as had the Cherokee. This southwestern tip of Virginia. This holy land. This *idani*.

Lily set out to find who might be shooting. Nothing the first day, but she returned early the following day while dew sat wet on grasses, following Broken Rock Creek, up ledge after ledge, until the water narrowed to little more than a branch. Past Old Man Farley's crib. Stepping under tall pines that were so old they stood on thick trunks, each with a gigantic top bursting with green needles. The age of the forest allowed her to walk upright and search large areas simply by looking through the trees. She had been here before during the fall and watched a buck in the distance, his antlers propelling him forward, without his knowing she stood near.

The first rifle shells she found were a mile up the slope leading away from Flatland. This third day, she had veered south when the trail ended and made her own way. Within a dozen yards, she noticed the grass trampled where someone had walked, someone with feet larger than a forest dweller's. She followed the crushed grass to a small clearing over the ridge. On a log sat a ragged row of cans, some rusty, some shiny, balanced as best they could, on the curved bark. Closer, behind the log, she saw three twisted pieces of tin, each with bullet holes. None of the rest had been hit.

Someone was on her mountain. A worker from Covington or a miner from Breakline. Or Briar Slocomb. Why she thought of him she had no idea, but there he was, fully fleshed in her mind, his gleaming hatchet hanging from his belt loop. His workman's boots holding the legs of his denim pants down. His floppy-soled boots ever announcing his presence. She returned to Boone Station and called Gabe.

⸎⸎⸎

Briar Slocomb had walked into Lily's life using the road that fronted Boone Station. Lily remembered him only as a grown man with carpenter tools, a hatchet, and a thick-bodied dog. Slocomb passed mornings going to Covington for work and returned late afternoons. He rarely looked at her, but when he did, she covered her mouth shut with a rag so she would not swallow his glare. Here was a man with long curled hair, not straight like Kee Granny's, and darker. Bronze-colored eyes burned out of their sockets. He moved like a bird of prey. Winter winds flapped his long duster, a pale brown, noisily against his legs as he walked.

She could not look at the Boone Station sign beneath which her menagerie of carved animals had hung without thinking of the days after her mother died when he had come to reclaim the animal figures as his. And to make his threat.

Each time she saw him pass, Lily recalled arriving at Kee Granny's church to learn more cures. She had walked past Rattler's hollow log. He was not there. She had been no more than twelve at the time and had not realized that the snake slept days and hunted nights. But he was an old snake. She had known him as long as she had been on Turtleback Mountain. And being old, like Kee Granny, made you do strange things sometimes.

She thought no more about the empty den until she passed the smokehouse that faced Kee Granny's church. There on the post supporting the roof was nailed the skin of a splendid Eastern diamondback rattler. She moved in to look more closely. The skin stretched out as long as she was tall. His rattles had been removed, as had his head. The skin lay so wide that it wrapped around one side of the wooden post.

Lily stared at the pattern and the scar near his head. There was no doubt. Someone had killed and skinned Rattler, as if he were some sort of trophy, rather than a miracle of nature. She knocked on Kee Granny's door, unsure she could speak. When the granny opened the door, Lily pointed to the snake's skin.

"Briar," Kee Granny said with a nod. "He can't abide something so beautiful."

Lily's eyes filled with tears. "Why? How did Briar know Rattler was there? I didn't think anyone could see Rattler unless they were honored."

"He's different, my Briar. Seen a lot he don't always understand."

Lily remembered the sky that day as being a blue so intense that it hurt her eyes to look at it. She would not see such a cobalt day again until the day she found the deer.

Chapter 38

September brought with it muscadines so heavy they swagged vines from tree branches. They hung so low Lily could reach them without effort. Reach up, grab a vine, and pull it toward the earth from whence it came. This year's crop was so prolific she could fill a tin bucket with the wild purple grapes in one picking. She had threaded her belt through the bucket handle so it hung free. She had only to glance to her side to see how quickly the muscadines piled up.

She created her own delay by popping every other one she picked into her mouth. A tender bite was all it took to break the thick skin at its weakest point where it separated from the vine. Sweet, sweet juice exploded in her mouth. With a deft movement of her tongue, she parted pulp from seed, spit seeds to the ground with a foretelling of next year's crop, chewed the skin and pulp, and swallowed while she continued to pick with both hands.

After a short picking time, Eli appeared, as he often did, seemingly from nowhere. Lily felt, rather than saw, his presence. She had picked less than an hour when he materialized next to her and added his fruit to the bucket. Together they stripped the lower vines. Vibrant orange muscadine leaves showered down on them.

As dusk neared, Lily broke the wood's silence. "Let's quit today and go to Boone Station. I'll bake us a cornpone and we'll have Gertie's milk."

Lily thrived on goat's milk. Gertie was now at least fourteen years old. She should ask Gabe to start looking for another milking goat and give Gertie a rest. "Come on," she said. "Time to go."

Eli shook his head and pointed to a thick grape-filled vine in the branches one level up. Lily refused, saying they could not reach that high without climbing the tree.

Eli dashed for the tree trunk chanting, "Hickory-dickory dock. The mouse ran up the clock," and scurried up the lower stoutest limbs.

Lily called for him to come down.

He climbed higher, then stopped and pointed toward a vine thick as a man's thumb, filled with heavy ripe muscadines, muscadines that outweighed any in the bucket. Ignoring Lily and her pleading for him to come down, he snaked out the limb toward a vine that had broken loose from the branch and hung free, nine feet above red and orange leaves and brown straw.

Anger in Lily's voice yelled, "You better stop it right now!"

Eli stretched his body to grab the vine. He crossed his feet below the limb and flipped over.

Lily covered her eyes and screamed. When she looked up, he hung upside down, clinching the grey-speckled limb with his hands and feet, possum-like. He laughed when Lily demanded that he get down before he fell.

He walked his hands out the limb and reached for the vine. One strain and the limb splintered, releasing the vine and its fruit. The broken vine spun toward the tree, wrapping itself around Eli's neck. "No, Papa!" Eli shrieked. The resiliency of the green vine swung Eli to the forest floor.

Lily ran to free him from the vine, but Eli was up, running in circles screaming, "No! No! No!" His eyes blared open, magnifying the extent of his terror. She reached for him. His momentum threw her down. The collision slowed him, but he steadied himself. He spoke quietly, then louder, "Gotta get the cat." Intoning the words over and over, his arms flailing about his head, he ran deeper into the woods.

Lily chased, following the sound of his voice. For a time, she lost his direction. When she heard him shriek, "Water! My cat!" she knew where he was. She turned toward Parsons Branch and the Falls.

Lily found Eli standing at the head of the Falls, his calves cutting two strips into the icy mountain water. She stepped out of her shoes. She tiptoed to the edge of the water and waded in, all the time caressing him with her voice. "Sit down, Eli," she hummed. "I'm coming."

Eli looked back at her. "I gotta get the cat." His eyes pleaded for her help. "In the river."

"I know," Lily answered. "I'm in the river. See?" She lifted her hands toward the sky. "I'll help you get the cat."

Lily repositioned her feet against the force of the water as it broke over the ledge. "Come with me. We'll find the cat." She extended her hand.

His head cocked to one side, like an inquisitive bird. "There." He pointed to the base of the Falls where water splashed white in the gathering dark, silver now against thickly mossed rock.

"We'll go down there," she crooned. "Come with me." When he did not move, she added, "Sit down, Eli, and wait for me."

Eli bent his knees to sit, his butt in the rushing water.

He spoke in a quivering voice above the breaking water, "Humpty Dumpty sat on the wall. Humpty Dumpty had a great..." A rush of water caught him in the back. Eli vanished over the rock ledge.

Lily screamed his name again and again as she clambered down the rock face. She grasped rhododendron as she passed so she would not slip on slick rock and slide into the water. At the base of the Falls, air bubbled with a fierceness that suggested Eli had aroused some demon from the black water.

Lily dove into the pool and felt for Eli. Her hands felt only rocks flattened by years of the water's pounding. She could see nothing through the murkiness. She surfaced, looking about to see if he had been boiled to the top by the water's churning. He had not.

She dove again, this time toward the far side of the pool. In the darkness, she grabbed a heavy log and forced it to the surface to avoid hitting it again. As she broke surface, she realized she had Eli by his lower arm. She lifted his face from the water. His eyes showed no more than slits. Eli was dead.

Lily could not distinguish between branch water and her tears. She had to haul him out. He deserved a decent burial. She would see to that. She dog-paddled to the bank with the nearest flat rock, tugging him behind her. She sat on the rock and grasped him beneath his arms to heave him out of the pool. His weight threw her back on the rock, and he landed atop her. She pushed and rolled him over on his back. He lay supine, stretched there on a cold slab of stone. Lily lifted his body into a sitting position and laid her head on his shoulder, supporting his back with her body. She cradled and rocked him like a prodigal child.

Lily wept. She wanted to curse Great Spirit or God or whatever it was that put innocents out to fend for themselves. She did not. Words accomplished nothing. To name it did not make it go away. Kee Granny had used words to no avail when she tried to cure Anna. Kee Granny and all her knowledge about life and death and the power of the two had gained Lily nothing more than loneliness. And Eli, now cold and still in her arms.

Lily's heart solidified against Kee Granny. All she had taught Lily over the years had been no more than make-believe. And Anna. Anna had never shared what kept her strong. What had steadied her enough for her to take a two-year-old to live on an empty mountainside? What had changed her life and given her reason to get up one morning after those three years of emptiness as Lily spent days with the granny learning the world of Turtleback? Anna had never shared what had opened the love Lily had seen from her mother once she started elementary school in Covington. Nor could Lily comprehend why Anna deteriorated so before the December snow.

And Eli. Eli, who so valued the life of his cat that was almost lost as a child. And now this brutal fall.

Rage rose within her and bumped against her thick-set heart in an attempt to kick itself out. Lily refused to give anger dominance over her life. She released her rage in a primordial scream. Lily reached out and grasped her fury from the damp air. She tucked it inside a pocket of her past, and Ena pinned it shut.

Lily wanted Eli to know that someone had loved him. That she had. That she did. She pulled his upper body close and held him firm against her breast. She brushed her fingers through his wet hair, now dingy curls plastered with water, and cooed his name.

"Ease her, Brother Moon," pleads Sister Sun. "It's your time."

Since her mother's death the previous winter, Lily had slept in the indention left in the bed by her mother's body, hoping to take some of her mother's strength for living a life alone. Lily believed she had succeeded. Now, with the loss of Eli, she doubted. She lowered her forehead into the dip in Eli's back and hugged him hard. "Oh my dear friend, I am so sorry," she said. "So, so sorry." A fury against her inability to save him from himself overtook her. She released him and he slumped forward. Lily pounded his back with her fists. "How dare you die?" she raged. "How dare you die?"

Eli coughed. And coughed again. He vomited muscadine hull, pulp, and water onto his lap.

Lily jumped up.

Eli fell forward and hit his head on the rock. "Oooh," he moaned and rolled to his stomach.

Lily nudged his buttocks with her foot.

"No," he said and swung his arm back toward her.

Lily knelt by him, turned him to face her and laughed. Moonlight sent silver strips across the pool at the base of the Falls.

"Gotta get the cat."

"I know." She held him close as light faded.

Chapter 39

After Eli's slip on the Falls, Lily found herself drawn to the swing. She spent spring afternoons and evenings swinging and watching night wind its way across the mountain. Winter had silenced the guns, but spring brought them out again. Gunshots became more frequent. When a gunshot would zing out during the day, she would move inside. Poachers, she decided.

As before, she would search out the area to be sure no animal had been left to suffer. With time, shots came closer and closer. A shot sounded up the footpath to Kee Granny's. Lily, from her seat on the swing, jerked. On the edge of the woods, what appeared to be a fully-leafed sycamore exploded into a swoosh of black starlings. She looked up to see if Owl slept safe on the rafter. So comfortable was he there that he perched with his head tucked beneath his wing. These were her lands, and that made these animals hers as well. She would stop the poacher before he injured or destroyed a life on her Turtleback.

Lily began her search by moving toward the creek behind the house. Rock steps led her down the hillside past the goat pen. Listening for how high the water might be, she heard instead a faint bleating. She stumbled down the rocks, calling to Bad Billy.

"Come quick, Great Spirit," calls Sister Sun. "It's started."
Great Spirit doesn't appear.

"Why am I left with everything to do myself?" Sister Sun spits
out. *"Great Spirit needs to take control here before she gets so hurt she
can't recover. Just like her mama did."*

Sister Sun shoots her anger out as a blob of carbon-scented gas-
ses that disturbs earth's upper atmosphere and starts Northern lights
dancing. *Off* and on. *Off* and on. A mingling of glorious colors.

Under Boone Station, Bad Billy lay on his side, his front legs buckled
beneath his belly. A hole larger than Lily's thumb pumped blood from the
orange coat near his heart. Blood trickled downhill. The old buck looked
at Lily through soulful eyes as she dropped to her knees next to him and
wailed. Here was her beloved pet. He had led her to Old Man Farley's
place during the thunderstorm when she was only six years old. He had
shown her how she and meadow grasses were as much a part of each
other as were he and spring clover. Lily laid her head on his and whispered
into his ear, "Oh no, not my Bad Billy."

Out of the breeze came a voice, Ena's but not quite Ena's. *"Leave him
be,"* it said.

"No. He can't go," she demanded. "Bad, get up." She ran her hand
over his coat and patted the bottom of his hoof. "I'll call Gabe. He'll make
it right."

The wind picked up and loosened Lily's hair. *"You can't ask him to suffer
through his going,"* the wind said. *"Would you be Kee Granny?"*

"Shut up!" Lily screamed. "Get up, Bad. Please." No air moved. "You
can't die. I love you."

Bad Billy flickered his eyes. No more than three breaths, and he was
dead.

Lily howled like a widowed squaw mourning her warrior. Her grief
echoed off Turtleback. Keening took control of her, and she could not
stop. Later in the retelling, when Gabe tried to comfort her, she would
recall that she had shed no tears, so deep was her pain.

Bad Billy's blood puddled in Lily's calico skirt. Gummy blood stuck
her fingers together. She wiped them in her loose hair. Lily ran up the
footpath to Flatland. She would confront Briar Slocomb. The one person
on Turtleback Mountain, other than Kee Granny, he must be the poacher.
But to kill her goat, a goat so old he could barely chew his hay, set him in
league with the Devil himself.

There must be a bottomless meanness in the man. As a child, Lily
felt it the first time she saw him. She had not let his soft curls fool her.
His sculptured eyes. His cool light-brown skin. She huffed so hard as she
ran uphill that she did not think of Rattler in his den. Did he not carry

a hatchet in his belt? Had she not seen him stumble trying to walk back home Sundays after Saturday nights at O'Mary's? Did he not have a dog that looked half wolf? Wolves brought evil.

Bent from loss of breath, she slowed and walked onto the plateau where the old church and smokehouse sat. The once whitewashed church had dulled to grey. The stand of fir, taller now than the cross, cast a dark shadow over the building. The only sound was a mountain bluebird talking to his mate. "Kee Granny?" Her voice silenced the bird.

"Briar Slocomb," she called. "Come out here and face me." To her left, a breeze scraped two tree branches against each other. A covey of quail, a half dozen splotched brown chicks following their mother hen, waddled across a patch of budding grass and faded into the undergrowth.

Lily moved to the edge of the cemetery and picked up a branch. She hefted it up and down to test its sturdiness. She could use it if she needed a weapon. Walking sideways with her back to the undergrowth, she crept to the beehives. Bees hummed in their usual unison, assuring her no one had disturbed them. She moved to the first hive. Tears dropped into the dust as she bent and whispered, "Queen Mother, Bad Billy has been murdered." The bees buzzed a high drone, and then settled back to their work.

Lily was thirsty. Bad Billy's blood stuck her hands to the limb. Granny's church would have water, but she could not bring herself to go there. She would cleanse herself in the water of the creek.

Passing the smokehouse where Briar slept, she noticed a rectangular carving on the ground. She picked it up and blew away the dust. She ran her fingertips over it, using her index nail to dig out dirt collected in the ridges. She blew again, as if to give it life. There in her hand lay a miniature wolf. Perfectly depicted, it held its ears erect; its tail bushed out with feathered cuts so fine they were almost translucent. She would take it to Boone Station, throw it in the fire and dance as it turned to ash.

Today was not the day to confront Slocomb. She would return. Next time she would come with a more defined plan in place.

Gabe arrived an hour after Lily called. "'Bout time you used that telephone," he teased her.

With the shovel he and Seth White had used for Anna's grave, he dug out a trench long and wide enough to hold the old billy. Lily stood aside and watched the digging, wiping tears on her sleeve from time to time. When the trough was finished, they placed the goat on an old quilt and dragged him to the ditch, leaving behind a spotty red trail. They covered him with extra soil, leaves and broken limbs. When Gabe finished tamping the grave, Lily leaned on the shovel handle and said, "Do you think one day somebody'll come by and say this is a Cherokee child's grave?"

"Probably not. Most folk don't think much about Cherokee being here."

"They ought to."

Lily went inside to wash her hands of blood and dirt. She dipped out two glasses of water.

Gabe stood in the front door, his shadow darkening him into a silhouette. "Okay, I've waited long enough. No need me driving pillar to post and you living way up here beside yourself. Eli's not a bit of good. Not with some crazy person shooting about. You've dilly-dallied long enough now. We're getting married."

Lily set down her glass of water and tried a smile. "Mighty sure of yourself, are you?"

Gabe answered as he let himself in. "Yep. Reckon I am." He dropped to his knees before Lily and took her hand. "You name the day, Lily my love. We'll marry in Wise then go to Bristol for a day or two. I'll move up here and drive the truck to Breakline every day." He grinned. "What do you say?"

"Now, Gabe..." Lily said.

"You know we were made for marrying. Everybody in Breakline is waiting to come to the wedding, if you want a preacher and all." Gabe leaned his head to one side. "We'll have the finest room in Bristol money can buy. I've saved up."

"Stop your foolishness, Gabe Shipley. I don't know how to be married. I've never lived with a person who was married since I was a baby. So stand up, now, before I laugh. All I can see is the top of your red hair," Lily giggled. "And you've got a bald spot."

"No. You stop your foolishness. Nobody knows how to be married till they get married. I'm asking you to marry me 'fore I get so old I won't be a fitting husband."

"I'm not signing up to take care of a sick old man," Lily laughed.

"So will you marry me?" Gabe asked.

Muscles in her back and neck relaxed. "Reckon I will," she grinned.

"I can't believe Great Spirit has let this go so far," says Sister Sun.

Gabe whooped out a "yahoo" that echoed down Turtleback Mountain. He lifted Lily and swung her around.

"But..." Lily stopped him. "You know Eli lives here too. You marrying him?"

249

"Might as well. If I have to." Gabe laughed. When he set her down, he kissed her hard on the mouth, bowed a low formal bow, and left.

Lily heard him giggling all the way to his truck. As he passed, going back to Breakline, he tooted the horn three times in farewell.

Monday, Gabe's regular delivery day, came and went. Gabe did not appear. Lily had never known Gabe not to deliver what she ordered. He had probably seen through her ruse of ordering a dozen rolls of duct tape to get him back up Turtleback.

"A dozen?" he had asked. "Whatever for?"

Duct tape was the first thing that had come to mind. "You never know when you might need to hold something tight." Lily blushed. She had spoken without thought.

"Reckon so," Gabe laughed.

She waited until Friday. As daylight came over the mountain ridge, Lily put on a jacket against an early April chill. She laced heavy boots to keep her steady in muddy patches left by melting snow and set out for Breakline Mining Camp to find Gabe.

Chapter 40

On April 7th, 1962, the day opened with cold air blowing down the creek. Six months and Lily would be eighteen. Naked branches waved like grey sticks against the sky. In the distance, Lily saw what she thought was a murder of crows circling overhead. As she came closer, she could see the crows were not crows, but buzzards, turkey buzzards. Some animal must be dead over the ridge. She trudged on.

The trek up Turtleback warmed her, though the wind chaffed her face. She put her mittened hands over her cheeks. Her eyes teared against the cold air, dampening the woolen mittens. At the top of the rise, she removed her jacket and laid it on the moist ground for a place to rest. Within minutes, wet seeped through where she sat. Lily shook out her jacket and continued the climb toward Flatland. She braced herself against a wind that whistled and hit hard where the road to Flatland intersected the mining road to Breakline.

Briar Slocomb had passed Boone Station two weeks before, returning from Covington. He had not walked back down the mining road since Bad Billy was killed. He must still be at Flatland. She veered off the road and shimmied up a hill so underbrush would block her presence from view. She did not want to encounter him. Her anger at losing Bad Billy was still too raw.

As she neared the highland, the dog barked. A man yelled, "Shut up!" The dog barked again, a hoarse yap as if it strained against a chain. A gunshot snapped, its echoes bouncing from mountainside to mountainside.

Lily dropped to the ground and crawled cat-like farther away from the noise.

Out of sight of Flatland, she returned to the road and ran. There, around a sharp curve on the lower side of the road, sat the buzzards. They encircled the carcass of a last year's doe. Dried blood from its nose and mouth blackened the road. Its white belly, inner ears and chin and its tawny coat so fresh, without the blood and buzzards, she would have sworn it to be alive.

She ran at the buzzards silently waving her arms about, to startle them away. Four of the five took to trotting so they could hoist their thick bodies into the air. A large, glistening buzzard, black as the inside of an open mine-shaft, sat on the doe's spine and continued to eat from its gut. The buzzard tore flesh loose and gulped it down its gullet, and then lifted a frightening, crimson beak, as blood-coated as a butcher's cleaver. The doe's blood coated the buzzard's naked head and neck, a reminder that predators reign.

Lily picked up a limb and swung at the buzzard. It flapped its wings and settled back down. From her distance, the two wild creatures merged into one. The buzzard, with its flat feet, could not lift the doe, nor did it plan to abandon its meal. The other four circled lower and lower, testing Lily's willingness to challenge their territory. She counted her heartbeats ten, twenty, thirty, before she edged away from the buzzards. She moved around the rear of the deer.

Who would leave good venison to rot in the road? Had Gabe hit the deer and careened off the hillside? Lily peered down the ravine. No tire tracks. She tramped back up the road and up the hillside to overlook the drop-off below her. No panel truck in sight.

She hiked back and moved away from the deer. The raven-colored bird, still as stone, eyed her. A trail of blood led from the deer's haunches to the ditch and into leaves. From this side of the carcass, she could see that it had been shot. And shot somewhere other than where it lay. A bullet hole had opened its chest just below the heart. A track of blackened blood marked the path from the wood line and down the bank. Already dead or dying, it had been dragged and left on the road.

The wake of buzzards circled closer. Their wings swished above her head. Lily backed away, leaving the scavengers to their carrion.

The following morning Lily bundled up against the cold and left again for Breakline Camp. She could have called, but this question was too important for a telephone call. Using a telephone to carry a message had not settled easy with Lily. She wanted her talk to be face-to-face.

As Lily neared where she had encountered buzzards the previous day, she climbed to the edge of a rock bluff and made her way around that section of road. She refused to face the stench a warming day would bring. Lily noticed no spirit mist, not like the one above Boone Station when her mama died.

She arrived at the commissary before noon. Inside, seeing Seth White behind the counter startled her. What startled her more was that something inside had told her back at Boone Station not to expect to see Gabe here. Before Seth could question her walking all this way, she asked about Gabe, where he was, when he left, where he was going without allowing time for Seth to answer. Outside the mine whistle blew its shrill mid-day shift change.

At the sound, hoping perhaps Gabe was working underground, Lily turned toward the door ready to spread her arms and run to meet Gabe. This need to hold Gabe took her aback. She had not expected it. No one entered the door.

Seth had no answers for her, other than that he left seven days ago with her supplies for Boone Station. "I figured you two was runned away to Bristol, so I come in and covered for him."

When the door still did not open after the three whistle calls, Lily sat in a chair and cried.

Seth scurried around the counter and stood before her. He put his hands out toward her and waved them right, then left, as if he needed, but hesitated, to touch her. His wide eyes said he feared she might break as some women were wont to do.

"I'm going for Juanita now. Just you set right here and don't you cry." He called out toward the office, "Mr. Rafe. Come out here. This girl, she's crying and I'm going for Juanita." Seth spoke on the run. By the time he finished, he was down the steps.

Lily had not thought of herself as loving Gabe in a marriageable way. She had agreed to marry him, but he had pestered her so. And he was old, she admitted. But now that she had lost him, she knew Gabe was who she wanted, who she had pictured herself with all her life. Her vision of life had acclimated itself to include Gabe. The two of them at Boone Station, with Eli in the loft.

Rafe appeared from his back office, a cigarette between his fingers. He tapped a Lucky Strike from its pack and put it to his lips as he walked out of his office. Lily's hard weeping left her hiccupping. Winston bent over to see her face. He took her chin in one hand and brushed her hair back with the other. "You're Anna Goodman's girl. Know you anywhere." He spoke just above a whisper.

"You knew my mama?" Lily asked between hiccups.

"Your daddy gave her a heart bracelet." His memory spoke without his thinking.

"I know," Lily said.

"She was a beautiful girl," he added. Lily so favored her mother at that age that Rafe stepped back and took a deep breath.

"Please, Mr. Rafe. This is not about my mama. She's gone. Gabe's gone. He left and didn't come to Boone Station. A deer's in the road and it's been shot and buzzards are eating it in the middle of the road and somebody put it there 'cause it was dragged and there's blood on the road and in the ditch." Lily blubbered through the remembering, "I come to find him and Seth says he's been gone all these days and I looked in the ravine and everywhere." She caught her breath and added, "We're going to get married."

Rafe moved away, his brow creased. His mouth opened to speak, but no sound came out. He ran his free hand through his hair. His breathing slowed, and he wiped his forehead.

Seth burst in the door, Juanita behind him, her calico housedress catching between her legs. Her determined track told Rafe to step out of her way. She stooped before Lily. "What's a matter, girl?"

Before Lily could answer, Rafe said, "Gabe's missing."

Juanita eyed him from the floor. "Lily love, my own sweet Anna's baby girl." Juanita drew her arms around Lily and kissed her forehead. Lily tried to rise, but Juanita had her wrapped in a tight hug. "Gabe told me 'bout your mama's sickness and dying and burying and him waiting you out to marry."

Lily was not certain whether Juanita said *marry* or *bury*. The miner's wife in her distress had let the flat nasal twang of the camp loose and rolled her tongue back, favoring the r's with music of crickets, frogs and cicada.

Juanita led Lily to the door. "I'm taking this child home with me. You take care of this, Seth White." She narrowed her eyes and nodded. "Mr. Rafe."

Her arm on Lily's elbow, Juanita bent toward Lily's ear and said, "Come, my pretty." She lifted Lily. "Why, you don't weigh no more than a little bird."

"What have you known about all this, Seth?" Rafe's voice faded away as the two women walked down the commissary steps.

The first two searches of Turtleback Mountain resulted in cold feet and scratched faces. Night shift men worked the mountainsides like black ants, pulling away downed limbs from the winter blizzard and kicking off snowdrifts the sun had not yet found. The sun hid all the days of the hunt.

"About time you came out from behind those layers and layers of clouds," says Brother Moon.

"I will not. I've seen all I want to see," replies Sister Sun.

"Do you know where he is?"

"'Course I do. Don't I see every living thing that happens in the daylight?"

"Are you going to help them?"

"No. And Eli's not helping them either. He's too scared of the granny. He's watched her from Old Oak. He knows what she's done. Killing Bad Billy. Killing that deer. What she did to Gabe. 'Sides, I'll blister his face if he does. I leave helping to Great Spirit. He knows more about that than me or you."

"I stand here amazed," says Brother Moon. "I never thought I'd hear you admit that."

On the second day of the hunt, searchers took a hind leg that pointed toward Flatland and pulled the deer carcass off the road. They found the truck overturned on the underside of Turtleback, near where the deer carcass had been left.

Gabe had been missing nine days when searchers found him in a deep ravine. His body lay under a red oak limb that had collapsed from rot and the weight of snow. When the camp got the report and verified it was not hearsay, men, women, and children plummeted into a dark pit with no way out. No one believed Gabe Shipley would no longer sit behind the counter reading his books and acting the fool. People could not speak.

Seth brought the news to Juanita and Lily. No one could account for the attack. "He weren't beat. Just walked with his murderer up the road from where the truck had been pushed over the edge," Seth reported. Footprints showed the two walked together into the ravine, their feet angled to keep them from sliding too far down the grade, too fast. "Almost like Gabe knew his murderer."

"You think he had a gun? The killer?" Juanita spoke above a whisper, not wanting to upset Lily more.

"Maybe so," Seth said. "But maybe not."

Later in the dark of the night when they thought Lily slept, Seth told Juanita more. Gabe had been taped where they found him. His killer had taped his ankles, his wrists behind his back, his mouth, his nose. Ruts in the dirt showed where Gabe, on his back, had tried to inch his body uphill using his heels, before smothering under bands of duct tape.

"The boy died a fearful death in that cold, cold gully," Juanita shook her head.

"Would have been more human to shoot him like he did the deer. A 30.06 woulda put him out of his misery," Seth said.

"Weren't no reason to rob him," Juanita said. "Gabe never carried no money, not even script."

"Gabe and me, we talked about the tape before he left. Said Lily wanted it." Seth said, "Gabe laughed about it that last day. Only thing missing was duct tape."

Juanita heard Lily collapse in the next room. Seth ran for the camp doctor.

Juanita gave Lily small doses of belladonna berry juice Dr. Braxton brought. Lily slept, but she did not eat. When awake, she stared at nothing. It was as if her soul had followed Gabe down the ravine.

Now an inability to move spoke to her loss of power as a potential Beloved Mother. In time, as she drifted in and out of the belladonna haze, she wanted to talk to Kee Granny about these strange feelings and how they might alter the work she and Kee Granny had done over the years in their attempt to pull Lily into harmony with the world. Then she would remember Anna's death and the birthing chair and Kee Granny's confession. Lily had severed her bond with the granny.

"Everybody dies." Lily, her voice hoarse, spoke to Juanita. "Daddy. Mama. Bad Billy. Now Gabe." A thought struck her across the mouth, and she sat upright. *Gabe. Both kerosene and alcohol deliveries to Kee Granny.* "You been to Kee Granny's." Her eyes went straight to Juanita where she sat on the bed's edge. "You know."

"I reckon I have," Juanita said, dropping her chin.

"I saw your name."

"Yes. It's there for everybody's knowing."

Outside, a punishing wind slammed into the top of a mountain oak. Leaves scattered across the ground.

Chapter 41

Breakline Camp buried Gabe Shipley in Unity Church Cemetery next to Clint Goodman. Lily did not go. She spent the burying time on Juanita's front porch, wrapped in a brown afghan. Its zigzag pattern of variegated browns wasted away into tans the closer the color came to its fringed edge. Lily rocked a slight back and forth and stared absent-mindedly at the road. Straight ahead, neither left nor right. Her lonesome emptiness refused to force Gabe to walk up the road, to appear in his clomping gait and ignite her hope.

Juanita stayed inside against the morning chill. She pulled a stained white cotton curtain back from time to time to see that Lily had not moved. "Anna and Clint all over again," she said.

Once enough time had passed for the service to close, Juanita joined Lily on the porch. She talked to keep Lily from hearing the echo of dirt clods thump off the coffin lid.

"You trying to move that there rock with your staring?" she asked.

Tears slid down Lily's cheeks and dripped off her chin, but she made no sound. She looked cornered, a trapped animal, awaiting her own tearing apart, piece by piece.

Juanita took Lily's hands and led her down the steps. "See them clouds, Lily?" Juanita lifted her hand, palm open, toward the sky. "Stars'll be out soon. What if they ain't stars atall? What if they're little holes in the bottom of heaven where our lost ones pour their love through and shine down on us to let us know they're happy?" She took Lily's face in her hands and turned it to her own. "What if, Lily? It might just be, you know."

Lily did not answer.

"People have to have something to believe, don't they?" says Brother Moon.

"Yep. Too bad they all don't know it." Great Spirit shakes his colossal head. He initiates a cyclone in the Pacific where Sister Sun has spent the day heating ocean waters. "Sure makes some lives hard. Believing or not, either way."

Juanita walked Lily into the house. "Here. Lay down on this bed."

Lily obeyed. She lay stiff, her hands folded over her bosom, and stared at the ceiling. Juanita pulled a nubby chenille bedspread over her.

"Close your eyes and rest."

Lily closed her eyes on command.

Juanita pulled up a woven-seated chair. "Listen up, girl. I'll show you something special in the morning. I got buttercup blades shooting up through this old black dirt. Now ain't that something in all this cold snap?" Juanita patted the bed. "Sometime soon there'll be a blaze of glory ever' where you look."

Tension held Lily's body taut. In an attempt to lessen Lily's opposition to life, she had to be called back. Without a thought, Juanita began a soft ballad she had often sung to Jason. "*I gave my love a cherry that had no stone. . . .*" She hummed through verses until she saw Lily's chest relax. She eased off the chair and sang, "*a baby when it's sleeping has no cryin'.*"

Juanita slipped off her shoes. She crept into the kitchen to have food ready for Jason and Seth when they returned from closing Gabe Shipley's grave.

Within days, Lily's begging and anxiety for Eli wore Juanita and Seth down. "It's been a long mourning time for the girl," Juanita told Seth. "Her mama. That old goat she loved so hard. Now Gabe. She's got to move on."

Seth agreed to leave Lily at Boone Station if Juanita stayed to see that Lily did not slip away.

"Slip away? What do you mean?"

"I don't know. I just know she ain't right yet," Seth said. "Them Granny herbs and all."

Once Juanita got Lily to eat and to sleep without belladonna, they put her in the back seat of their '54 Chevy and drove the garish pink sedan to Boone Station.

Eli met Lily at the door with a kiss over her ear. He sang, *"Oh was he stabbed in the heart, my darlin'?"*

Lily bit her lip and shook her head.

Eli hummed, *"Come, I'll help you to my house, my love."* Lily followed him inside. Sunday wound herself around Lily's legs, making it hard for Lily to walk a straight line.

Juanita moved into a tiny side room Uriah Parsons had built as his family grew. She cleaned from Lily's absence. She sat in the repaired pea-shelling chair with the girl on the porch and eyed Owl perched on a rafter while Lily swung. Eli left each morning and returned at dusk, as frogs at the cistern began their chorus.

For Juanita, Boone Station existed in a surrealistic world, one unlike any she had ever known. After a week, she gathered her belongings to return to Breakline Camp. She told Lily and Eli that Seth would come at the end of the week to take her home. Lily nodded as if she understood.

Three nights later, an explosion of shattering crockery startled Juanita awake. The moon was down, so dark was the room. More crockery hit the floor. From the next room, Lily shrieked. The screech sounded to Juanita as if cold fury spewed out of Lily.

"My God," Juanita said as she ran into the room.

Lily stood by the shelves where the crockery was stored. She slung another bowl against the door. She lifted a pitcher and drew back to smash it on the floor.

"Lily, you'll cut yourself," Juanita said. She hopped across shards of broken bowls and plates. Sunday peered from beneath Lily's bed.

Lily held the pitcher higher over her head.

"Lily!" she said. "Stop it!" She grasped Lily's hands and held them hard. "You're scaring Eli. Tell him to stay. I can't search the woods for him." She nodded her head toward the ladder leading to the loft. "Look at him. He don't know what's ahappening."

At the sight of Eli peering over the loft's edge like a terrified kitten, Lily collapsed against Juanita and wept.

"Oh, little girl, whatever shall we do with you?" Juanita patted Lily's back. "Whatever shall we do?"

Eli appeared in his worn shirt. Ignoring chips of pottery under his bare feet, he came up behind Juanita and hummed a note. He sang, *"I wish I was a pretty little sparrow and I had wings to fly so high."*

Lily visibly slackened. She lifted her head and looked at Eli as if this were the first time she realized he was there. *"Fly so high,"* Lily repeated in tune.

Juanita released her hold on Lily. Lily went to Eli and wrapped her arms around his waist. The two stood among the broken dishes and cried, blood seeping unnoticed from their feet.

Saturday morning Juanita left. Lily and Eli stood under the Boone Station sign, waving her on. Once Seth's truck disappeared, they sat in Gabe's marrying swing and hummed the sparrow song to each other.

Chapter 42

Early May, and an uncommon light snow covered the ground. Lily left Boone Station well after dark. She carried her shovel before her as she climbed the familiar footpath. Nearing Flatland, she crawled on all fours, a feral cat stalking her prey. She stalled, waiting for Briar Slocomb's wolfdog to alert sleepers. Nothing. Under the blackness of the new moon, she dragged a dead chicken, its head bumping along the leaf-covered ground. To her left she heard a movement under a thick hemlock. Lily waited. No movement. No breath.

Briar Slocomb's wolfdog growled low in his gut. Lily tossed the chicken in the direction from which the sound came. She listened to teeth pulling flesh and snapping bone. The dog would finish the chicken in short time.

Back on her knees, Lily stirred, then froze. Before her, what appeared to be an oak limb slithered past. A copperhead as thick as her thumb. The sun, testing its false spring warmth, had earlier drawn him out of his den. After warming in the sun, the snake was returning to his den. He flicked his tongue and sensed her overpowering body warmth. The snake shifted his triangular head toward a rock outcropping and disappeared in the darkness.

The copperhead's presence reassured Lily. It could have struck, but it had not. She was meant to be in the snake's path. It was right that she kill

Briar Slocomb. A fierce fire burned within her breast. He had killed Gabe. Slocomb's callousness had left Gabe alone on the mountain not caring that he might smother under duct tape.

Briar Slocomb had walked by Boone Station, day after day these past years in tattered work boots. Lately, he walked without noise, his soles held to leather tops by silver duct tape.

To her left, she heard something step on leaves behind her. Lily stiffened. She got down on her belly and lay so still she could hear her heart pumping in her ears. An animal directed bottle green eyes toward her. A cat, too low to the ground to be a cougar, too light on its feet to be a bobcat. It came closer and ambled over Lily's back as if she were a log. Its pads, soft and soothing, contrasted the feel of jagged limbs and dampness against her belly. Sunday, meandering through the woods, disregarded Lily's presence and wandered on.

When Sunday vanished, Lily skulked toward the dog. Now closer, she rose to reassure herself that the feeding beast was the wolfdog. She jumped and ran, never thinking, holding her long-handled shovel in one hand like a cocked rifle. Running on her toes past Kee Granny's beehives, she shifted from carrying the shovel by the handle to holding its neck in one hand for balance. She made no sound louder than a chipmunk's.

Briar Slocomb lay sleeping on his belly on the makeshift porch of the little log cabin. A pistol rested near his hand where he had dropped it. No lights glowed from the granny's church. Lily grasped the shovel by its handle and caressed the wood with her palm. She inched quiet as a moth to where he lay. The sour odor of liquor nauseated her. Holding her breath, she sized the distance from where she could stand and still get a hefty strike. If she got too close, he might grab her ankle, pull her down. Or she might miss, awakening him, and need to run.

Lily edged nearer, lifted the shovel as if it were a posthole digger and gouged its metal edge into the back of one knee. Hot blood squirted from his leg and hit the front of her wool jacket. For an instant, a dense crimson cord bound her to Briar Slocomb.

Slocomb's howl reverberated down Turtleback. He flipped over, popped up, grasped his leg and bent his head toward his knee. Lily slammed him hard against the skull with the back of the shovel. He fell back to the floor.

A yellow glow outlined the church door. Inside, the granny had lit the lamp. She would see Lily if Lily returned the way she had come. Lily sneaked around the corner to take a back route to the road. She glanced around to see Kee Granny moving toward Briar, pointing the 30.06, its polished walnut stock firm against her shoulder.

"Briar?" Granny called. "That you, Son?"

Lily flattened her back against the clapboard church wall.

The only answer was a bark from the dog.

"Don't make me shoot, whoever you are. Answer me."

A blast resounded from ridge to ridge, leaving behind its final echo a silence louder than the explosion. The smell of gunpowder choked Lily. She grabbed her mouth to stifle her cough.

> *Brother Moon hides his wan self behind a heavy grey blanket of cloud that is thinking about rain for tomorrow. His terror refuses to let him peep out. "Besides, I don't have to show my face," he tells himself. "Not now, in my new moon phase."*
>
> *Neither Sister Sun nor Great Spirit are close by.*

Somewhere near the front of the church, another shot followed the first. Lily circled around the back of the church, between the giant fir stand and the room that held the birthing chair and its hoard of jars. Visualizing the mutilated rocker inside and what would have been her baby brother on the shelf enraged Lily. She veered to Kee Granny's circle of harmony and chose the first log she saw. She hurled it through the eastern window, reached in, grabbed the kerosene lantern off Kee Granny's mixing table and slung it across the room. Its glass base shattered, spilling oily kerosene. Fire chased oil as it streamed across the floor.

Lily dashed around Flatland's clearing, past the beehives, and headed for the headwaters of Broken Rock Creek. Behind her, an explosion rattled the earth beneath her. The blast was followed by pops and booms and deafening blasts. A gigantic *whoosh* sucked air from around Lily. Fire had reached the baby jars, cremating the little ones in their alcohol baths.

Night's black sky turned orange, then white hot, as flames consumed the old wooden church. Once the explosions stopped, an eerie glow lit Flatland. Fire had spread into the stand of fir. Rather than night bird calls, crackling and crumbling sounds filled the air. Lily flew, weightless, down the path, the fire's light freeing her of the burden of truth she had carried all these years. She raced, puffing out air to avoid inhaling the stench of burning wood and flesh as it followed her toward Boone Station.

She intended to wade Broken Rock Creek so Briar Slocomb's wolfdog could not find her scent. The path to the creek should have been clean. It was not. Midway down, a thick muscadine vine rose up and coiled around her ankle. The creeper, so rapid in its attack, threw her forward. She hit face first, embedding her forehead in dirt.

263

Ladybug, ladybug, fly away home. Your house's on fire tumbled back and forth through Lily's head. She rolled over and reached for her shovel to boost herself up. It was not there. She had left it at Flatland. Tomorrow. She would return when the fire died down and fetch it.

She touched her head wound and drew away a palm filled with blood. Lying still, she listened for Briar Slocomb's dog to sniff her out. A late night puff of air cooled her face where she lay. In the distance, Briar Slocomb's dog yapped and yapped, each yap turning into a bay announcing the death of his master Briar Slocomb.

High in the black pines, two golden eyes blinked down at her. They swooped, a glowing whiteness nearer and nearer, then rose. Owl, his softly fringed face skimmed just over her head, followed by the gentle breath of his wings. He lit and looked back at her lying in damp dirt. Leaves rustled in the night breeze.

"Get up," Ena says. "Get up and move on."

Lily slipped through leaves made soggy by melting snow, toward the creek. Her sense of place and balance so disoriented by the blow to her head, she found water before she expected it. She lurched headfirst into icy water. Its swift current dragged her under. She burst to the surface, gasping for air. Her wound burned from the extreme cold. She longed to stroke her forehead for comfort, but she sank again. She flailed her way back up.

Water wrapped itself around her legs as she attempted to steady herself. She thought of *Uktena,* the great horned serpent Kee Granny spoke of, the creature that carries the dead to an afterlife in the east. She must get out of the creek before *Uktena* drowned her. She fought against having no bottom to the water. Her fight whirled her around, and she recognized the bank. Close. She was in the right place. The excess overflow was merely snowmelt. Her panic lessened. She breathed deep and dogpaddled toward land.

Lily felt land under her feet. Snowmelt pricked her legs like needles. Icy water bound her legs from ankle to thigh. She stumbled into a sinkhole and doused herself again. She yearned for a sweater, but there would be warmer clothes at Old Man Farley's place where she had hidden supplies.

She walked easy. Past Boone Station where Eli was singing to himself. She had not realized how clearly his voice carried over Turtleback. Kee Granny and Briar would have listened with her. Tempted to climb the bank to home, she forced herself to finish her plan. She wouldn't be able to explain her bloody face. It would frighten Eli, so she plodded on.

"Listen to that, Great Spirit," Brother Moon speaks from behind the dark that accompanies his new phase. "He's singing the stars right out

*of the sky." He considers turning his illuminated side to face the earth
but decides against it. Someone in some other time would remember
this night.*

In preparing for her attack, Lily had counted the Canadian hemlocks
between the back of Boone Station to where Parsons Branch entered
Broken Rock Creek. Though the thickly needled trees should have been
easy to spot, the black of the new moon made counting difficult. What
had been a shallow bottom lulled Lily into a sense of security that never
should have existed. It dropped without warning and then rose again. So
she watched the bank, but watching the bank caused her to slide into deeper water as it chased itself down the mountain. At one point, she had to
swing herself up by grabbing a low limb as the current's swiftness knocked
her down. She worked herself out on the bank to rest and gain orientation.

Chilly air sent shivers over her wet body. She contemplated what she
had done. Rattler was dead. His skin tacked to a post these past five years,
his rattles blowing in the breeze like a store-bought wind chime. Briar
Slocomb was dead. Maybe his dog, too. She had done this thing. This
murder of Briar Slocomb. "Vigilante justice" some would say. "Warranted
righteous fury" from others. She had no doubt that Briar murdered Gabe.
What kind of man needed to live? Not a man who would murder over
duct tape.

She, in her assault, had slammed evil in the face and won. She was
not meant to be Beloved Mother. She suffered under no false impression;
she needed no repentance. It was clear. Lily Goodman was not meant to
be a mother at all.

Back in the water, she saw the mouth of Parsons Branch. Its low
banks and its scrubby undergrowth hid moccasins. Grey roots reached out
to pull the unassuming under. She pushed her body to the branch's center.

This turn marked the final bit of her escape. She struggled more
quickly, her legs fighting against the current, her teeth chattering. Within a
matter of minutes, she recognized old Breakline Mine #1. It had rumbled
and collapsed not long ago, leaving it no more than a slopped indentation
in Turtleback's side. A bleak scar marked where it had been worked out
two decades before. At this point, she scaled the bank and crossed the
road that passed Boone Station. She curved onto the dirt strip of road that
led to the Falls. From there, finding Old Man Farley's place was easy. She
dragged herself in and wrestled a piece of door over the opening. Inside,
she wiped her arms and face with dirt to kill the blood smell.

Lily took off her wet clothes and threw them aside. Her head
throbbed, though it no longer bled. With creek water dripping from her

hair, she shook from the cold. She burrowed herself into a quilt to stave off the shivering and wound herself into a ball.

Within a moment, she felt the weight of Sunday padding over her body. The cat settled into the niche of Lily's belly, wrapped her tail around herself and stayed. Lily ran her fingers through Sunday's thick fur and fell asleep.

Throbs deep in her forehead woke Lily. When she tried to sit, Sunday slid off her belly. She lay back down. Sunday climbed back up and pawed her cheek. She nestled on Lily's shoulder and licked the wound. Lily grimaced at the touch of Sunday's raspy tongue. It was pain she would tolerate, for her mama had said an animal's tongue is as good as a doctor's salve. No. That had been Kee Granny. No matter. Lily no longer knew what was true.

The next morning, Lily could tell by its fishy odor that the wound had festered. Kee Granny, almost across the mountain, could be of no help. Lily could live with the scar. She took what Turtleback had given her, her Gabe, Sunday, Eli and her scars, and she was grateful.

Fever tossed Lily about in her sleep. She dreamt. And re-dreamt. Someone tucked the blanket close around her neck. Someone hummed next to her ear. Someone smoothed her hair. When she awoke, no one was there.

To gain strength for the walk back to Boone Station, she ate bread that molded over her days of resting and healing. She fed Sunday small pieces and offered her soured milk. The next day, Sunday left and returned with a fat brown vole. When Lily turned it down, Sunday took it outside for lunch.

During her rest, Lily recalled the night on the porch when she had watched a pale half-moon. Mares' tails painted a feathery design across its face. If she turned her head just so, the moon became the profile of an ancient warrior dressed for his wedding ceremony. Had she been in harmony with nature, she could have spoken to the moon and he would have comforted her as her mother lay dying inside. But Lily had failed. She had failed her mother and herself.

"Lily," Anna had called out that night. "Lily, come inside and crack the Bible with me for a spell."

Inside, Lily asked, "We got a Bible?"

"There. In the secret drawer."

Lily pulled out the thin drawer from across the bottom of the bureau. She lifted a worn leather-bound Bible and caressed the cover's rough texture with her hand.

"I never saw this before," Lily said. "It yours?"

"It's your...Clint's," Anna answered. She considered her lie and washed it with words. "It come from the commissary," she said.

Lily brought a chair up to the bed and flipped through tissue-thin pages. Dozens of pressed four-leaf clovers, brown and brittle with age, fell into her lap. Lily touched one. It crumbled in her hand. "My daddy collected clover for luck?"

"Them's mine," Anna said. "A person needs a mite of luck from time to time." Anna licked her lips. "Just in case."

"What you want me to read?" Lily turned the Bible over and looked at the colored maps in the back. "Says here *King James Version*. Want me to start at the beginning? *Genesis*, maybe?"

"No. I don't like all that killing and stuff."

Lily flipped through again, the pages whispering "*choose me, choose me.*" "Here's something about somebody named David. What about him?"

"No. I don't like him a'tall."

"What you want me to read then?" Lily closed the Bible. "It's a long book. Bound to be something in here you might like."

"Can you find them *Songs*? I think I'd like to hear them *Songs of Solomon*."

Lily thumbed through and found a place. "Here's a page. Its corner's turned down at Chapter 6 and number 1."

"That's the one. Read that."

Whither is thy beloved gone, O thou fairest among women?
Whither is thy beloved turned aside? That we may seek him with thee.
My beloved is gone down into his garden,
to the beds of spices, to feed in the gardens and to gather lilies.
I am my beloved's, and my beloved is mine:
he feedeth among the lilies.

"Sounds just like a poem," Lily said.

Tears covered Anna's cheeks and ran down her neck.

"Mama?" Lily said.

Anna did not answer.

The second night at dusk, Owl floated into Old Man Farley's place on silent wings. He perched on his rafter and clicked his arrival. Each night thereafter, he stood guard against whatever might have a mind to enter the hovel. After what Lily deemed to be a week of days, she arose and dressed. Though frail, she and Sunday went down Turtleback to meet the road to Boone Station.

Chapter 43

It was mid-May, Month of the Planting Moon, and Lily ignored buds growing into blossoms. She had little to say. She, day after day, had grown weary with chastising herself for not remembering to forget Kee Granny. The never-ending try to expel the hatred for what Kee Granny had brought into her life exhausted her.

This morning late, Lily leaned over the wooden table, her hands and wrists deep in white gloves of flour held close with lard. In preparing biscuit dough, she squeezed a lump of lard through her fingers and refused the childhood memory of helping Kee make her poultice base. She worked the flour in and down, gliding the softness down the sides of her mother's wooden bread bowl before adding a splash of Gertie's milk.

A slight breeze puffed thin curtains into the room and moved out the open door. It brought with it the smell of earth moldering to season its winterized seeds. Outside the open window, a woodpecker bored into a weakened tree. His dah-dah-dah echoed down Turtleback Mountain.

A chocolate-colored sparrow perched on the windowsill and waddled in. Lily lifted her apron and shooed it out. "Out of my house, you little sparrow," Lily said. "We don't need to lose nobody else." She smiled and sang the bird into flight: "*Fair thee well my own true love, and fair thee well for a while. I'm going away...*" Lily stopped. She could not recall the remaining lyric.

The light feel of breathing dough under Lily's hands brought Kee Granny into the room. She watched Lily a time before asking, "*You making a new potion, u-s-ti?*"

"I'm not your little one," Lily said aloud. "I'm not sure I ever was." Lily shook her head to force the granny out. A hairpin hit the floor. As Lily bent to pick it up, the granny vaporized into the wall by the cook stove.

Lily lifted Anna's blue milk pitcher. The touch of cold crockery fetched Anna. With the pouring, Anna dropped into her pea-shelling chair next to Lily. It was the spring of 1959 again, and Lily was fourteen. Anna was teaching her to handle the dough with gentleness so the finished biscuit will bake tender and flaky.

A stronger breeze entered the room. This was no random breeze. It brought with it Kee Granny and a stout memory of life lessons she had taught Lily. The granny ignored Anna and retold the legend as Lily molded her dough.

Remember, she said. *In the beginning, Great Spirit disguised his breath as wind that walks through tall treetops. He breathed it into the Cherokee and called it man.*

Lily glanced out the window at swaying trees. Kee Granny had told her Great Spirit would call her to him. She wondered if this swaying was what it meant for Great Spirit to speak.

Great Spirit had great hopes for man. But, according to Sister Sun and Brother Moon, man was stubborn, like the ass Great Spirit made for labor.

Lily admitted she had been stubborn, especially with Gabe.

Legend says Sun blazed down on his back to slow his run. Man ran on. Moon hid behind Great Spirit's cloud cover to darken his path and keep him off Turtleback Mountain. But man trudged on. So Sun and Moon offered Great Spirit a challenge in an attempt to prove man's stiff-necked attitude. And Great Spirit accepted.

Lily had accepted. She had accepted living on Turtleback, Gabe and his silly ways, Eli and his strange way of speaking. She had accepted the lies of Kee Granny. Until she learned all of it.

Within a rotted-out hemlock trunk on the Eastern slope of Turtleback Mountain, Great Spirit placed Uktena, an enormous snake, large as a tree trunk himself, with a bright, blazing diamond crest on his forehead, and scales that sparkle like flickering fire. Uktena, with splats of patterned browns and blacks along his entire length. Great Spirit placed him in wait to see if man will be tempted by Uktena's beauty. "Come take my diamond," Uktena hissed.

There was Rattler, dangerously beautiful, asleep, filling his hollow tree trunk.

Uktena waited, coiled.

Briar Slocomb must have given in to *Uktena's* tease.

Some say he waits still today.

269

But his skin was nailed to a Flatland post. Burned in the fire. It was all true. No. None of it was.

A gentle tap on the doorframe pushed Anna and the granny out. Winston Rafe stepped through dust motes into the room.

"Come in, Mr. Rafe," Lily said. She removed her flour-dusted apron and pulled out the one her mother favored. A fleeting memory took Lily back to when she, as a child, had fingered the blue and green rickrack rows across her mama's bosom.

Winston Rafe had changed since she saw him the day Gabe drove him to Breakline's Big Mama outside Covington. Stopped by to say hello, Gabe had said. But Lily didn't know. Coarse hair now grew from his eyebrows and out his ears. He moved, as if he, like his underground miners, carried a heavy load. Before he had held himself tall, clean-shaven, his cinnamon-colored hair thick and curly and brushed back from his angular face. She needed him to stand upright, for somewhere in the back of her mind, he had done so. But the memory was vague and fuzzy, so she put it aside.

Today, his stooped shoulders lessened his height. He had aged, aged even more since she saw him at the commissary when she came for help finding Gabe. His hair remained thick; curls and waves, the same, but his dark beard had not been clipped in weeks. She could have overlooked grey streaks through his hair, but she could not go past the real difference. His eyes. No longer piercing like Owl's or sharp like *Uktena's*. Perhaps it was Gabe's death. Not finding the killer. His loss after having Gabe work for him so long. His inability to act when he had spent his life fixing other people's problems. That could age a person.

She wondered how it must feel for his wife to comb her fingers through that hair. Gabe's hair had been an almost orangey-red. Thin to the point of seeing patches of scalp. She realized she had never put her fingers in Gabe's hair. This sadness was drawing out her energy. She steadied herself against the table's edge.

"I'd rather wait out here. On the porch," he muttered. "If you have the time, that is."

"Give me a minute," she answered. "To clean my hands." Lily hoped he had not seen her blush at remembering Gabe. She rubbed her hands, slick with grease, on a towel and washed some of the flour off before she joined him on the porch. Outside, she noticed that she had left rising dough trapped under her nails.

Sun's warmth promised a soothing day. Tired of mere breezes, trees waited still. They needed a stiffer wind to enliven them. Chickens under the back of the house clucked as they scratched about.

Winston Rafe sat in the cane-bottomed chair. Lily lowered herself to rest in Gabe's marrying swing and pushed off with the tip of her toe. She forced herself to concentrate on paying attention. The power of the swing did that to her.

Rafe drew a Lucky Strike from inside his suit jacket and lit it with his silver lighter. Lily waited, giving him his own good time. He propped the chair back against the limestone wall and blew grey smoke through his nose. He let the front chair legs drop to the floor, as if announcing his intent to speak. The sound startled Lily. She had not known how tense this man made her, nor why. She picked at the dough under her fingernails.

Rafe cleared his throat. "Eli here?"

She inclined her head toward the house. "He's asleep," she answered. "In the loft." She pushed off the swing again. "That's where he always sleeps," she added, as if she owed this man some explanation for Eli's living in her house. Just the two of them.

Rafe breathed a breath from the bottom of his lungs. He gave it as much time as it would take to release itself. "I've come to get him." He spoke with determination, not allowing her time to question. "I've found a group home over in Abington that'll take his kind."

Lily stopped the swing. "What'd you mean 'his kind'?" She clenched her jaw. This was Eli he was talking about, not some stray animal. Rafe could take her attitude or not. She owed him nothing.

"He's going to Abington. I'm taking him today. You can tell him or I can. It don't matter." He swallowed more cigarette smoke.

Lily stood up, allowing the swing to whack the back of her calves. She stalked across the porch to face Rafe. "Look at me, Mr. Rafe." She planted her feet apart in an attempt to stop her knees from shaking.

Rafe raised his head.

"Eli lives here. With me. He's not going to some 'group home' for 'his kind.' We're perfectly happy as we are. Me and Eli." As if in afterthought, she added "And Sunday."

"Sunday?" Rafe tilted his head in question.

"Our cat," she answered. "She's asleep inside with Eli. And I don't intend to wake either one of them." She pulled her shoulders up to make herself as tall as she could. "Now that that's decided, I'm going back inside and finish our biscuits. We're having biscuits and butter and dandelion greens. And some honey from your commissary. After we eat, we might walk up to Old Man Farley's place and on to see the Falls, but ain't nobody going to Abington."

She turned on her heel and went inside. She had lived in Boone Station for sixteen years with door and windows opening and closing in season, and yet there was still the smell of earth within these walls. She sat at the table, staring at her unfinished biscuit dough, clutching her hands to stop the trembling. She pinched off rounds of dough and slid the pan into the oven. She heard Rafe's steps behind her.

"Come back outside, Lily," he said. "I handled that wrong." He placed his hand on her shoulder. "Please. We need to talk." He glanced down and rubbed the toe of his shoe over an old burn on the floor. His body slumped as he looked at the darkened scar. He bit his lip.

"I'll only come out if you swear you won't mention Abington."

"I swear. I just need to tell you what's going on down in Covington." He raked his fingers through his hair.

Outside, they took their positions again, at opposite ends of the porch.

"What's that over there?" He nodded toward a dip in the earth that had been filled with brush and rock. An old log stuck out of the near end.

"Mama's grave. A mine roof, probably a shaft from that first mine opened by Breakline years ago fell in after the spring flood," Lily said. "It dropped her down."

"My God, Lily." Rafe raised forward. "You should have called me."

Lily raised her eyebrows. "Gabe and me, we tried to fill it in. We did for the most part, but we couldn't get the coffin right. It was too deep." Lily stopped. "Mama, she's resting upright. And that's okay. At least she's covered now." It would sound absurd to say that her mother was resting on her head, so she did not volunteer any more. "For the most part." No one would know other than Gabe and she, and Gabe was these three weeks buried.

"I'll have one of my men bring a machine up and fill the grave for you," he offered. "With dirt," he added.

"That'll be much appreciated," Lily said.

Rafe puffed on his Lucky Strike. Lily waited for him to speak to what was happening in Covington.

"Sorry 'bout all that with Gabe. I didn't know he was courting you." Lily focused her eyes on a far sweet bay magnolia. "Youell swears he's got somebody working full time on finding out who killed him." Rafe dropped his hands between his knees and bent forward. He stared at the floor. "Never a cross word with anybody 'cept that crazy old granny. Something, he said, 'bout selling her honey." He rocked back toward the wall. "He was one fine man."

I can name you the murderer, and he's dead in the fire at Flatland, Lily said to herself. But she didn't say that. Instead she said, "It don't matter none now. Gabe's gone. That's all."

"True. True," he murmured. "What's gone is gone."

For a long thinking time, Rafe smoked. Lily pushed the swing back and forth. Now and again, the chain creaked against the hook holding it to the rafter. Neither spoke.

Rafe took up the conversation first. He looked at her arm. "Where's your bracelet? You had on a gold bracelet when you came to the commissary."

Lily glanced down. "In Mama's grave. I was wearing it after she died, but I dropped it in when the mine broke. The coffin was open a bit, and I dropped it in. Just like that." Lily's eyes glazed over. "Before we filled in the rock."

"I thought your daddy gave that to her." He rubbed the nape of his neck.

"He did, but I don't know my daddy. He's been gone a long, long time. And Mama knew him better than me. She knew what that bracelet meant. So she ought to have it with her."

"Lily..." Winston faltered. He cleared his throat and spit phlegm into the dirt. "Briar Slocomb showed up at the Doc's in Covington yesterday morning hobbling on a long-handled shovel. He's talking 'round that Eli killed his mama and set Flatland afire." He spit out the words as if they dirtied his tongue and he refused to drink in the thought.

"Said him and Eli wandered the woods days. He showed Eli the old granny's place. Talked about him wanting to shoot her 30.06. Said Eli got irksome when it didn't work. Youell says the gun's there on the porch, its stock burned off. And that's about all."

Lily's lips quivered. Lungs filled her mouth with air. She breathed it out in a moan that reached across the porch. Drained, she had no fight left.

"I don't know if there's any truth to what he's saying," Rafe continued. "But he's getting the town riled up. They's talk of coming after Eli. Could even be a lynching." He spoke so softly Lily was not certain she had heard him.

Lily's body jerked. "Briar...I... The shoo..." Panic shut her mouth. She shrunk away from Rafe and slid to the opposite end of the swing.

"He's pretty beat up, but he's not dead."

For the first time, Lily noticed Rafe's Adam's apple. Large and pointed, it moved up and down with each swallow, each word. She tried to recall if Gabe had had a noticeable Adam's apple when they talked together on the swing, but she could not.

"Says Eli come at him with a shovel. Cut into his knee and slammed him up the side of the head. He's lost one eye and his jaw's broke. Walks now on a crutch from Doc, but he's ain't dead." Rafe gulped. He rubbed his hands together. "Between you and me, I question Eli O'Mary having enough mind to plot out a murder and set a fire to cover it."

"Murder?"

"I don't see Eli handling a gun, not one that big." Rafe settled back in his chair.

"Kee Granny's dead?" Lily's breath came on her so fast she felt light-headed.

"I got no argument against the deeds. Only thing I could think of when Sheriff told me is get Eli off Turtleback. Take him far away. I found this group home in Abington this morning." Rafe scraped his shoe across the floor. "So I need to take Eli with me," Rafe said. "'Fore dark falls."

"Kee Granny is dead." Lily repeated herself. "How?"

"Slocomb never told me Eli lived here. With you. Gabe told me." Rafe slumped forward.

"Why?" Lily steadied the swing.

"Slocomb'll have the whole town searching Turtleback for him," Rafe said. "Me taking Eli will keep you from having to lie." Rafe tossed his Lucky Strike into the dirt and lit another. "If we don't do something, we'll have this whole mountain afire."

"Kee Granny. She's dead." Lily's resentment toward the old woman for her lies fought with her contradictory love for the compassionate woman who had taught Lily the ways of her world. Kee Granny and her misdirected love. Lily had realized, since she cast her out of Boone Station, how different life would have been without her. Turtleback's woodland, its animals, Gabe, though love for Gabe differed in a singular way. Then there was Eli. Strange, singing Eli. Without Kee Granny's total acceptance of all living things, disregard her perverted baby droppings, could she have loved Eli so openly, so without hesitation?

"Yep. Shot from down low, Sheriff says. The whole place set on fire with kerosene."

Lily flinched. "The dog? What happened to the dog?"

Rafe's hands wind around each other, the cigarette bobbing from his lips when he spoke.

"Shot."

"But I..." Lily stood up. "It takes a mean person to kill an animal. Eli may not be able to talk to people in their own way, but Eli, he's not a mean person."

"I don't know. I just know he's not safe on this mountain." Rafe rubbed his palms together, letting the stub of cigarette linger on his lips. "I don't know what else to do." His chin drooped.

Weariness settled on Lily like an oversized bird of prey. "Let me see to my biscuits." She moved from the swing an old, old woman. "I'll wake him and we can eat. You stay, but you let me tell him."

She left Rafe lighting another Lucky Strike. Lily climbed the wooden ladder to the sleeping loft. The sound of her voice singing as if to a babe, *"Awake, awake my drowsy little one..."* fluttered through the door and into the woods beyond the road.

In a moment, Lily was back at the door. "Come in and have a bite to eat with us, Mr. Rafe. We got plenty."

Inside, Eli sat at the table drinking milk, his back to the door. Rafe sat in a chair facing Eli. Sunlight behind Eli hid his face. Neither spoke.

Lily pushed a bowl of greens and a plate of biscuits across the table and sat to eat. "You got children, Mr. Rafe?" she asked.

Rafe's head twitched a bit. He stared past Eli and out the door. "Yes," he said. "Yes, I have."

"Ever lost a child?" she prodded. Gabe had told her Rafe's daughter, the girl he called CeCe, had run away the year before.

"I have." A look of despair he had worn earlier on the porch stepped inside and settled over his face.

"Humph," Lily said. Emotions rose up inside Lily. Should she be angry at Rafe for taking Eli from her? Should she be grateful that he would have a better place to live? The reality of not having Eli come and go in his own erratic way pushed out her tears. They slid one-by-one down her cheeks.

Eli looked from one to the other and chewed his biscuit.

Lily decided against telling Eli he would not be coming back. She did not pack his clothes. What would he take? Woolen socks he used as gloves? Worn tennis shoes without laces? Holey underwear? He had worn only underpants when she saw him hanging in the tavern's backroom. Tears filled her eyes again. She shoved the thought of that night behind her.

"The owl and the pussy cat went to sea in a beautiful pea-green boat," she started with the nursery rhyme line, their ritual parting. She told Eli he was going with Rafe. "You be careful now. Things will hurt you, beautiful things. But you don't reach for them. Don't reach out to stroke a live rattler. He might not love you." She pulled his face to hers and kissed his forehead.

"I honor you, my friend, the tree, and bring you thanks now. Blessed be." Lily startled herself with how unforeseen the blessing Kee Granny taught her as a child had bubbled up, but with Eli's going it was right that it came to her lips.

Eli reached into his pocket and took out a tiny carved wolf. Lily had seen the quality of work before. "Eli?" she questioned. "Where...?" He took her hand and placed the silent wolf in her palm.

Rafe directed Eli to sit in the front seat. Rafe cranked the Buick. The motor hummed and the car simply inched away. Little swirls of smoke breathed out the exhaust. Eli looked back through the window, both hands against the glass. Lily could see the tears on his face and read his lips through the pane: "Gotta get the cat."

"I got the cat," she called back. She picked up Sunday and stretched out her arms so Eli could see the calico. She brought the cat back, close to her face. As the long black car moved down Turtleback Mountain, Lily stroked Sunday's fur to calm her. Rafe and Eli were gone before Lily could see if Eli had smiled at Sunday.

Inside she dropped on her mother's bed and stared at the ceiling. She realized she was crying when her ears filled up with tears.

Chapter 44

Uriah Parsons had spent his years wandering about looking for a place where he could ground himself. In 1782, he would return at age 37, but not to the valley, for he had learned of and respected the Cherokee Eden as if it were his own. He acknowledged what he perceived to be their ownership, never knowing Cherokee have no concept of ownership. They are of the land. The "People of the Land." Had he realized he searched for a moral code, he would have had to admit he found it on Turtleback Mountain.

He returned to the mountain, the humped Turtleback, so named by Long Hunters. Low-lying hoary clouds, not unlike silvery fog, infiltrated its massive trees. Using land allotments earned from his time with General Washington and allocations for settling the West from the Governor of the Virginia colony, he returned to claim the whole of Turtleback Mountain. Never realizing that territory, mountain or meadow, valley or cove, belongs to itself, to no man. Never knowing that Great Spirit, to prove Sister Sun and Brother Moon wrong about the destructive nature of man, had given land the power to fight back.

Uriah Parsons would have been proud to know that his grounded great-great-granddaughter was more committed than even he to honoring tradition.

After Winston Rafe left with Eli, Boone Station refused to acknowledge the sunlight. Each day dawned gloomy and clouds grew dirtier, heavier, as the hours wore on. Each day, sadness slammed into her head hard, then harder. The pounding was so intense her heart swelled and squeezed out any room in her bosom meant for air. To calm herself, she stroked Sunday's back and ears and let the calico give, in turn, by rubbing Lily's skin with her rough tongue.

And it rained. And rained. The road washed out, preventing Sheriff Youell from reaching Boone Station to question Eli. Or Lily. Ditches overflowed and the stream behind Boone Station swelled and smothered its banks. Lily waited.

After a dreaming night of Eli alone in a strange room surrounded by tawdry brown and black wallpaper, Lily stepped out on the porch, Sunday at her feet. An exhale of wind blew the door shut behind her. Lily walked to the road and looked back at Boone Station. The house, its door shut, its windows down against last night's chill, had no life about it. Lily asked herself if she had lived here these years, if Rattler and Kee Granny were real or imagined, if Owl still served as her guardian. She could not say what of her life had been real or what she had imagined.

She headed down the road where the cut-off led to Old Man Farley's place. Wandering, aimless, all she cared about was gone. Just she and Sunday and Gertie, Lily's ancient goat, left on the Turtleback. At one time, when her mother lived, when Gabe lived, when Eli was with her, with her like a brother, she remembered Kee Granny telling her she had to face life with courage. She had done that. She did that when she took up the shovel to Briar Slocomb. But she didn't kill Briar Slocomb. He killed his own mother. Now he was killing her with his accusations that compelled Winston Rafe to take Eli away.

Lily and Sunday reached Farley's shack. Lily stooped to enter. Thinking back, she recalled Winston Rafe had stooped to enter Boone Station. Had she seen him step up on her porch, she would know that he had stooped to miss being hit on the head with Uriah Parsons' creaking Boone Station sign.

She sat. Her back rested against a far corner. She looked out at fallen tree trunks covered with lime-colored moss. Though the moss promised vibrant life fed by damp and shade, she knew the logs rotted from within. A layer of leaves, brown and crisp before their crumbling, hid new growth trying to push itself upward. Sun rose and warmed the air around her. Lily relaxed.

Anna appeared before Lily, as on a stage. She dragged a mop across the floor as she tried to corral milk Lily had just spilled. Lily stood in the door, a child no more than nine. The summer before Covington and Eli. It had been another of those "I didn't mean to" events when Lily had stumbled over the threshold and emptied a bucket of Gertie's milk onto the floor. Lily pouted up to cry.

"Milk. Water. They're the same. When it's spilt, it's gone," Anna said. "But there's a difference. Spilling or pouring out." She swiped the mop. "I learned that a long time ago." Standing in the door, Anna gazed at Lily. She followed Anna's eyes. In the moment Anna glanced away, Lily grew into a young woman.

The floor now dry, Anna spoke to her daughter from the other side. "Water spilt can be forgiven. Water poured out shows no respect. Never let nobody pour out your water." Anna leaned against the mop. "Not your water. Not your blood." Anna vanished.

Lily stroked Sunday's coat where she slept in the bow of Lily's belly. She straightened her leg to resist a cramp.

Within an instant, a great silent cloud covered Turtleback Mountain's top ridge. Inside the shed, Lily watched white mist hide everything beyond the door. The mist accentuated the door, transforming the entrance into an arch. A tingle ran over her from head to toe. She gasped. The building she had perceived to be a shanty was now a chapel.

A puff of wind brought the mist inside and filled the shack. It should have been cold and damp. Instead, it cloaked Lily like a warm blanket and surrounded her, so soft she felt cocooned in new cotton. She knew no fear, even if this proved to be her death-mist. She accepted this presence without Kee Granny or Ena having to give her notice.

"Let me see your face." Lily spoke to the mist.

"Arise. The time has come."

Lily did not raise her head until the last reverberation faded. "I will," she said quietly. "Are you Great Spirit or my mama's God?"

"Lily, I say get up."

"You know I have killed."

"I know what you have and have not done."

"But I killed Briar Slocomb within my heart."

"Others have done worse."

"I can't. I thought I could make it right, but I couldn't."

"Like prophets before you, I command you by name. Lily Marie Goodman. Get up and go."

She dragged herself toward the opening. Twigs scraped her knees and palms. Her blood mixed with dirt packed hard by generations of hooves and feet. She stopped at the threshold. "I can't go," she whimpered. "I'm afraid."

"You have the strength. Go."

"Where?"

"Consider the night of the fire. The icy water that cleansed your wounds. Does it know where to flow? Imagine sun shafts. How they connect earth to the sky. The hush of a moonbeam and the steadfastness of Owl. Celebrating the joy of Eli. All these, I tell you, are sacred. Think on these things and you will know how to place your feet."

"I don't know the way."

"I am with you."

A movement startled Lily. Out of the mist, Owl hooted himself in and settled on his rafter.

"I'm up," Lily said aloud. "But first, I must tell the bees."

Owl hoo-hooted. Lily picked up Sunday. The two left Old Man Farley's shack with Owl circling behind them.

Chapter 45

Spring refused to show itself on Turtleback. There had been within Lily a sprout growing, waiting to burst into bloom since the mountain voice had spoken to her at Old Man Farley's shack. Now, Lily needed time to nurture what she felt maturing within. She stood at the edge of the mining road and looked down into the valley. The shadow of Turtleback Mountain behind her had kept the ground moist with the moldy smell of rotting pine straw and oak leaves even in summer. This mountain had always had its own fragrance, season by season, a fixed reminder for Lily of its immortality.

Below her the town of Covington sat. From her viewpoint, rooftops in grays, greens, blacks, lay each next to each in rows that filled in the valley. Broken Rock Creek wrapped itself around the town like a wide brown rope, frayed by white ruffles the rapids created as they slapped against boulders. From Lily's stance, rocks looked more like stepping stones crossing the river. Logs lay along the banks like remnants of bridges long fallen into disrepair. Above the town, sunlight threw an outline of Spencer's Mountain on Covington's opposite side, splitting hardwoods in two, trees in a tinge of greens and the purple blossoms of the Redbud, while lower down, shadows left them gray, almost black, near the river.

Lily could have more easily examined the scene from behind Boone Station; but, since the mine collapse that took her mother's grave, the back of Boone Station had begun to drop ever so slightly, tilting itself down the mountain. She no longer sheltered her animals there. She feared she would slide down the rock steps, then tumble, stone-like, and bounce off outcroppings of powdery white rock, level to level until what would have be left of her body rolled down a gentle grassy incline into the waters of Broken Rock Creek. Only a ripple would mark where she entered the cold river water.

"Would that I could reach up and touch the sky with my own two arms," Lily said to Sunday. "I would swing us away from this place."

She could thank Breakline Mines for the deterioration of Boone Station. Her mother buried on her head in an abandoned mine shaft. Kee Granny shot by her own son. Briar Slocomb running rumors like wild greenbrier that refused to die. Eli holed away with people he never knew in a group home on the other side of Spencer's Mountain. She thought of visiting Eli. She needed to go there, but she knew he would not understand her leaving him any more than he had understood why she had him go.

There had been a time the previous year, when, in delirium, Anna had spoken only in quiet murmurs. Lily had to bend her ear to her mother's lips to understand the words. "Sending me away was a greater evil," Anna said, "than any other you ever done to me." Though Lily did not understand whom Anna meant, she knew her mother's pain, for she carried the burden of Eli's being sent away. His was her own.

During Kee Granny's Month of the Green Corn Moon, winds, stronger and colder than usual for June, had whistled through Boone Station's cracked walls the mineshafts created with each collapse. Once the earth chose to fill its inner cavities, there seemed to be no stopping it. Rumble after rumble echoed through dips along Turtleback Mountain. Clouds wreathed its top, hiding any change the Turtleback might reveal to those in the valley.

First, Anna's grave sank deeper. Then Old Man Farley's shed gave way. And the structure Uriah Parsons built generations ago, Lily's Boone Station, now wavered. Lily questioned which would be easier: leave Turtleback Mountain for Covington or fall asleep one night knowing she, too, would be buried in a mineshaft before the sun rose.

A rumble awoke her during the night of another rainstorm. Eli had been gone these two months. The sun rose sporting a brilliant gold crown, taking with it fog and shadows. Another rolling sound, closer than the night before. Lily knew it wasn't thunder. Living years between sun and shadow had taught her that thunder avoids the sun. It was growing up the

Cherokee way with Kee Granny. It was living in a world made gentle by the presence of Eli O'Mary.

When she opened the door to the front porch, Sunday scurried past her leg and darted under the iron frame bed. Sunday had been curled in a mound in the porch chair asleep. Just out from the house, what had been the empty mining road was now a broad strip of black gully, half the ground between house and mountain gone, the gap's rim made soggy and mud-like by heavy rain.

Lily stood on the edge of what had been her mother's grave, opened again. Fifteen feet below, the coffin rested on its head. Wiry roots stripped white by the sucking shaft stuck out of the dirt like paralyzed worms. Anna's coffin had been broken by the drop. The quilt pattern showed the color of dingy walnut stain made smooth, almost shiny, by the weight of brown dirt. The fruit jar identifying her mother lay cracked, crushed by a fist-sized lump of coal so luminous it glowed against the glass.

At the opposite end of the gash near the house, another section of timbers gave way. Earth slid in on itself, dragging a new oak with it, leaving its branches hanging upside down against the far wall. Another such section and the house would go. A second cave-in above where her mother's grave had been collapsed, and what seemed to be half the mine, lay exposed. It was as if the land, as it dropped, was pulling itself from under her as she stood barefoot on the rim. All that had held her to the mountain was sliding into Turtleback Mountain. Lily called for Sunday. The time had come.

Lily gathered her chickens and put them in a wooden crate. She washed thick dust off her Red Ryder wagon and tied on the crate. She secured a loose rope around Gertie's neck. She and Sunday carried her animals down Turtleback and freed them in Juanita White's fenced yard. She had not called Juanita. Lily's faith in the camp woman told her Juanita would understand that Lily had gone.

On the return walk, Lily and Sunday veered off the road and up to Flatland. They stepped around the charred fir barrier and passed what remained of Kee Granny's church. What had been Briar's log cabin stood, though smoke had darkened its outer wood. Near the stream, Lily found the bees intact. She bent before a box and whispered. "Queen Mother, Sunday and I are leaving Turtleback."

The bees hummed.

"Our reunion will be a splendid celebration," she said.

Sunday followed Lily as they climbed to Kee Granny's sacred cedar. Lily was certain it lived. The last time she had seen it, the cedar had become a glorious tree, filled with nests and surrounded by nourishing needles. She knew this, but she needed to see again what had been one of Kee Granny's most stinging lies. Lily saw the top of the cedar well before she arrived on the ridge. As she neared the tree, she widened her stride. Sunday had to trot to maintain Lily's pace.

The cedar was as beautiful as she had remembered. She sat away from the branches so she could view the tree in its entirety while she rested. The ground was soft. What spring had not touched at Boone Station had obviously settled here. Between Lily and the cedar, supple dirt had allowed new life to push aside, creating space for small blades and budding leaves of green to poke through.

Lily scratched Sunday's ears. "If Kee Granny's Great Spirit is a powerful god who has things on his mind other than me and you, we're in trouble." Lily chuckled. "But. If Mama's God is a god of justice, as she always said, he can be on our side when bad things happen, don't you guess?" Sunday rolled over for Lily to scratch her belly and purred. "You and me, Sunday, we got two guardians. We'll be fine."

The memory of another spring day, the day when she had leapt from the rock overhang to Old Man Farley's cabin flashed through her mind. That day she had flown through the air as lightly as Owl. Today she was free to go. She had new wings, wings handed her by the voice on Turtleback Mountain.

The mountain settled. Two days passed as Lily folded her clothes and stacked them just so in a muslin pillowcase. The morning of their leaving, she looked around at what had been the only home she remembered. She saw her father's Bible where she had placed it on the bureau. She dropped it into her pillowcase. "Come, Sunday," she said. "Time for us to begin."

Out of respect for Boone Station, Lily tried to close the door as she left. The roof sat so skewed the door drooped heavy out of its frame. She left it cracked open and walked down the Turtleback. She need not bother closing up the house.

With a backward glance, Lily searched the trees for a glimpse of Owl. He was not there. She and Sunday started down the road to Breakline Mining Camp and then crossed over to the trail Kee Granny had made when taking her curses and *wadulesi* to sell in Covington.

A swinging bridge, no more than slats hung on two ropes, crossed Broken Rock Creek above Covington. Lily stepped on the first board. It wiggled as if alive. Sunday balked. She leapt from Lily's arms and dashed into a blackberry thicket. Unable to coax her out, Lily fell back against a massive mountain oak. Halfway up, its trunk separated into three parts. She would wait. Her back fit flawlessly into a niche that stretched up from a split in the roots. She settled herself, rubbing her back against bark nubs.

Beloved Mother

The trunk included her in its girth. She braced her weight by stretching her feet out before her.

Looking up at a canopy that spread at least fifty-feet across, she wondered how many men it would take, five full-grown, maybe six, arms outstretched, to reach around the trunk. This could be the father of all trees. Cherokee had once wandered in and out of the valley. Intuitively, she understood they would have slept under this tree when it was young.

She slid down the trunk, allowing the bark against her back to scratch at memories of Flatland and her granny, her mother's body crooked in its grave. Gabe murdered, and Eli driven away in a long black Buick. Tired from her walk and weary from the emptiness she had lived with through-out the past year, she relaxed. Her roots, the Cherokee roots and the roots of all she loved and had loved, buried themselves in the earth where she sat. She was content with that knowledge. She removed her Ena pin and laid it to rest in the moss under the oak.

Sunday padded up and plopped down in Lily's lap. Lily dropped Eli's little wolf pup from her pocket into the pillowcase. She lifted Sunday gently in and gave her time to nuzzle into the clothes before folding over the top and slipping the bundle into her dress bosom. Against Lily's warmth, Sunday stretched and turned, molding herself to Lily's body. Lily stood.

Out of the leaves above her, Owl appeared. He looped around Lily, once, twice, three times. He then turned and soared back into the wilderness. Lily watched him until he disappeared in the distance. She whispered, "Farewell, wisdom of Great Spirit. I will carry you always in my heart."

After repositioning her treasures against her bosom, she walked toward the bridge. Moving like an ancient pregnant woman carrying her un-born too high, Lily Marie Goodman placed one foot before the other. She stepped easy across the swinging bridge and on into Covington, Virginia. Eli should be across the next mountain.

About the Author

Laura Hunter is a retired educator and an insatiable reader. She has always wanted to write stories and began doing so before entering the first grade. Since 1994, she has published sixteen award-winning fiction pieces and nine poems in addition to numerous articles published through several different media outlets. *Beloved Mother* has won second place in the 2017 Dorothy M. Lobman Novel Award for the first chapter of an unpublished novel. In her spare time, Hunter reads, gardens, and works with a small writing group in Tuscaloosa, Alabama. Her writings reflect the perseverance of the downtrodden—those who refuse to give up, even against extreme odds.

Thanks for reading *Beloved Mother!*

Laura would greatly appreciate feedback for her work to be left on Amazon, Goodreads, or any other of your favorite review platforms.